Praise for *Sycamore Row*:

Sycamore Row bristles with all the old authority . . . It's good to see the troubled attorney back. – *The Independent*

A solid courtroom thriller with plenty to say about the long half-life of prejudice in the Deep South . . . The much-trailed conclusion is powerful. – *Guardian*

A gripping read. – *Literary Review*

Indebted to William Faulkner and Victorian legacy novels, it is Deep South storytelling at its most leisurely, delighting in multiplying subplots and minor characters. – *The Sunday Times*

John Grisham

Sycamore Row

HODDER

First published in Great Britain in 2013 by
Hodder & Stoughton
An Hachette UK company

First published in paperback in 2014

1

A CIP catalogue record for this title is available from the British Library

A format ISBN: 978 1 444 77954 7
B format ISBN: 978 1 444 76560 1

Printed and bound by Clays Ltd, St Ives plc

Hodder & Stoughton policy is to use papers that are natural, renewable
and recyclable products and made from wood grown in sustainable
forests. The logging and manufacturing processes are expected to
conform to the environmental regulations of the country of origin.

Hodder & Stoughton Ltd
338 Euston Road
London NW1 3BH

www.hodder.co.uk

To Renée

Sycamore
Row

I

They found Seth Hubbard in the general area where he had promised to be, though not exactly in the condition expected. He was at the end of a rope, six feet off the ground and twisting slightly in the wind. A front was moving through and Seth was soaked when they found him, not that it mattered. Someone would point out that there was no mud on his shoes and no tracks below him, so therefore he was probably hanging and dead when the rain began. Why was that important? Ultimately, it was not.

The logistics of hanging oneself from a tree are not that simple. Evidently, Seth thought of everything. The rope was three-quarter-inch braided natural Manila, of some age and easily strong enough to handle Seth, who weighed 160 pounds a month earlier at the doctor's office. Later, an employee in one of Seth's factories would report that he had seen his boss cut the fifty-foot length from a spool a week before using it in such dramatic fashion. One end was tied firmly to a lower branch of the same tree and secured with a slapdash mix of knots and lashings. But, they held. The other end was looped over a higher branch, two feet in girth and exactly twenty-one feet from the ground. From there it fell about nine feet, culminating in a perfect hangman's knot, one that Seth had undoubtedly worked on for some time. The noose was straight from the textbook with thirteen coils designed to collapse the loop under pressure. A true hangman's knot snaps the neck, making death quicker and less painful, and apparently Seth had done his homework. Other than what was obvious, there was no sign of a struggle or suffering.

A six-foot stepladder had been kicked aside and was lying benignly nearby. Seth had picked his tree, flung his rope, tied it off, climbed the ladder, adjusted the noose, and, when everything was just right, kicked the ladder and fell. His hands were free and dangling near his pockets.

Had there been an instant of doubt, of second-guessing? When his feet left the safety of the ladder, but with his hands still free, had Seth instinctively grabbed the rope above his head and fought desperately until he surrendered? No one would ever know, but it looked doubtful. Later evidence would reveal that Seth had been a man on a mission.

For the occasion, he had selected his finest suit, a thick wool blend, dark gray and usually reserved for funerals in cooler weather. He owned only three. A proper hanging has the effect of stretching the body, so Seth's trouser cuffs stopped at his ankles and his jacket stopped at his waist. His black wing tips were polished and spotless. His blue necktie was perfectly knotted. His white shirt, though, was stained with blood that had oozed from under the rope. Within hours, it would be known that Seth Hubbard had attended the 11:00 a.m. worship service at a nearby church. He had spoken to acquaintances, joked with a deacon, placed an offering in the plate, and seemed in reasonably good spirits. Most folks knew Seth was battling lung cancer, though virtually no one knew the doctors had given him a short time to live. Seth was on several prayer lists at the church. However, he carried the stigma of two divorces and would always be tainted as a true Christian.

His suicide would not help matters.

The tree was an ancient sycamore Seth and his family had owned for many years. The land around it was thick with hardwoods, valuable timber Seth had mortgaged repeatedly and parlayed into wealth. His father had acquired the land by dubious means back in the 1930s. Both of Seth's ex-wives had tried valiantly to take the land in the divorce wars, but he held on. They got virtually everything else.

First on the scene was Calvin Boggs, a handyman and farm laborer Seth had employed for several years. Early Sunday morning, Calvin had received a call from his boss. "Meet me at the bridge at 2:00 p.m.," Seth said. He didn't explain anything and Calvin was not one to ask questions. If Mr. Hubbard said to meet him somewhere at a certain time, then he would be there. At the last minute, Calvin's ten-year-old boy begged to tag along, and, against his instincts, Calvin said yes. They followed a gravel road that zigzagged for miles through the Hubbard property. As Calvin drove, he was certainly curious about the meeting. He could not remember another occasion when he met his boss anywhere on a Sunday afternoon. He knew his boss was ill and there were rumors he was dying, but, like everything else, Mr. Hubbard kept it quiet.

The bridge was nothing more than a wooden platform spanning a nameless, narrow creek choked with kudzu and crawling with cottonmouths. For months, Mr. Hubbard had been planning to replace it with a large concrete culvert, but his bad health had sidetracked him. It was near a clearing where two dilapidated shacks rotted in the brush and overgrowth and offered the only hint that there was once a small settlement there.

Parked near the bridge was Mr. Hubbard's late-model Cadillac, its driver's door open, along with the trunk. Calvin rolled to a stop behind the car and stared at the open trunk and door and felt the first hint that something might be out of place. The rain was steady now and the wind had picked up, and there was no good reason for Mr. Hubbard to leave his door and trunk open. Calvin told his boy to stay in the truck, then slowly walked around the car without touching it. There was no sign of his boss. Calvin took a deep breath, wiped moisture from his face, and looked at the landscape. Beyond the clearing, maybe a hundred yards away, he saw a body hanging from a tree. He returned to his truck, again told the boy to stay inside and keep the doors locked, but it was too late. The boy was staring at the sycamore in the distance.

"Stay here now," Calvin said sternly. "And don't get out of the truck."

"Yes sir."

Calvin began walking. He took his time as his boots slipped in the mud and his mind tried to stay calm. What was the hurry?

The closer he got the clearer things became. The man in the dark suit at the end of the rope was quite dead. Calvin finally recognized him, and he saw the stepladder, and he quickly put the scene and the events in order. Touching nothing, he backed away and returned to his truck.

It was October of 1988, and car phones had finally arrived in rural Mississippi. At Mr. Hubbard's insistence, Calvin had one installed in his truck. He called the Ford County sheriff's office, gave a brief report, and began waiting. Warmed by the heater and soothed by Merle Haggard on the radio, Calvin gazed through the windshield, ignored the boy, tapped his fingers along with the wipers, and realized he was crying. The boy was afraid to speak.

Two deputies arrived in the same car half an hour later, and as they were putting on rain slickers an ambulance arrived with a crew of three. From the gravel road, they all strained to see the old sycamore, but after a few seconds of focusing it was apparent there was a man hanging from it. Calvin told them everything he knew. The deputies decided it was best to proceed as if a crime had been committed, and they prohibited the ambulance crew from approaching the scene. Another deputy arrived, then another. They searched the car and found nothing helpful. They photographed and videoed Seth hanging with his eyes closed and his head twisted grotesquely to his right. They studied the tracks around the sycamore and found no evidence of anyone else being present. One deputy took Calvin to Mr. Hubbard's home a few miles away—the boy rode in the backseat, still mute. The doors were unlocked, and on the kitchen table they found a note on a yellow legal pad. Seth had printed neatly: "To Calvin. Please inform the authorities I've taken my own life, with no help from anyone. On the attached sheet of paper I have left specific instructions for my funeral and burial. No autopsy! S.H." It was dated that day, Sunday, October 2, 1988.

Calvin was finally released by the deputies. He hustled the boy home, where he collapsed in his mother's arms and said nothing the rest of the day.

*   *   *

Ozzie Walls was one of two black sheriffs in Mississippi. The other had just recently been elected from a county in the Delta that was 70 percent black. Ford County was 74 percent white, but Ozzie had won his election and reelection by wide margins. The blacks adored him because he was one of their own. The whites respected him because he was a tough cop and a former football star at Clanton High. In some aspects of life in the Deep South, football was slowly transcending race.

Ozzie was leaving church with his wife and four kids when he got the call. He arrived at the bridge in a suit, no gun or badge, but he did have a pair of old boots in the trunk. Escorted by two of his deputies, he made the walk down to the sycamore in the mud and under an umbrella. Seth's body was by now soaked and water dripped from the tips of his shoes, his chin, ears, fingertips, and the cuffs of his pants. Ozzie stopped not far from the shoes, raised his umbrella, and looked at the pallid, pathetic face of a man he'd met only twice.

There was a history. In 1983, when Ozzie first ran for sheriff, he had three white opponents and no money. He received a call from Seth Hubbard, a stranger to him, and, as Ozzie would learn, a man who kept a low profile. Seth lived in the northeast corner of Ford County, almost on the line with Tyler County. He said he was in the lumber and timber business, owned some sawmills in Alabama, a factory here and there, and gave the appearance of a man who was successful. He offered to bankroll Ozzie's campaign, but only if he would accept cash. Twenty-five thousand dollars in cash. In his office, behind a locked door, Seth Hubbard opened a box and showed Ozzie the money. Ozzie explained that campaign contributions must be reported and so on. Seth explained that he did not want his particular contribution to be reported. He wanted a cash deal, or no deal.

"What do you want in return?" Ozzie had asked.

"I want you to be elected. Nothing more," Seth had replied.

"I'm not so sure about this."

"Do you think your opponents are taking cash under the table?"

"Probably."

"Of course they are. Don't be foolish."

Ozzie took the money. He ramped up his campaign, squeaked into the runoff, then stomped his opponent in the general election. Later, he had stopped by Seth's office on two occasions to say hello and thanks, but Mr. Hubbard was never there. Mr. Hubbard did not return phone calls. Ozzie quietly quizzed others for information about Mr. Hubbard but little was known. He was rumored to have made money in furniture, but no one knew for sure. He owned two hundred acres of land near his home. He did not use local banks or law firms or insurance agencies. He went to church occasionally.

Four years later Ozzie faced light opposition, but Seth wanted to meet anyway. Twenty-five thousand dollars changed hands again, and again Seth disappeared from view. Now he was dead, killed by his own noose and dripping with rainwater.

Finn Plunkett, the county coroner, finally arrived. The death could now be made official.

"Let's get him down," Ozzie said. The knots were untied, and with slack in the rope Seth's body made its descent. They placed him on a stretcher and covered him with a thermal sheet. Four men labored under the strain as they made their way to the ambulance. Ozzie followed the little procession, as confused as anyone.

He was well into his fifth year on the job and he had seen so many dead bodies. Accidents, car wrecks, a few murders, some suicides. He wasn't callous and he wasn't jaded. He had made the late-night phone calls to parents and spouses, and he always feared the next one.

Good old Seth. Who, exactly, was Ozzie supposed to call now? He knew Seth was divorced but did not know if he had remarried. He knew nothing about his family. Seth was about seventy. If he had adult children, where were they?

Oh well, Ozzie would find out soon enough. Driving toward Clanton, with the ambulance behind him, he began calling people who might know something about Seth Hubbard.

2

Jake Brigance stared at the bright red numbers of his digital alarm clock. At 5:29 he reached over, pushed a button, and gently swung his feet out of bed. Carla flipped from one side to the other and burrowed deeper under the covers. Jake patted her rear end and said good morning. There was no response. It was Monday, a workday, and she would sleep for another hour before scurrying from bed and hustling off to school with Hanna. In the summer, Carla would sleep even later and her days were filled with girl stuff and whatever Hanna wanted to do. Jake, though, had a schedule that rarely varied. Up at 5:30; at the Coffee Shop by 6:00; at the office before 7:00. Few people attacked the morning like Jake Brigance, though, now that he had reached the mature age of thirty-five, he asked himself more often why, exactly, did he awaken so early? And why did he insist on arriving at his office before all other lawyers in Clanton? The answers, once so clear, were becoming more obscure. His dream since law school of being a great trial lawyer was not diminished at all; indeed, he was as ambitious as ever. Reality was bugging him. Ten years in the trenches and his office was still filled with wills and deeds and two-bit contract disputes, not one decent criminal case and no promising car wrecks.

His most glorious moment had come and gone. The acquittal of Carl Lee Hailey was three years ago, and Jake sometimes feared he was now beyond his pinnacle. As always, though, he brushed those doubts aside and reminded himself that he was only thirty-five. He was a gladiator with many great courtroom victories before him.

There was no dog to turn out because they'd lost their dog. Max died in the fire that destroyed their beautiful and beloved and heavily mortgaged Victorian home on Adams Street, three years ago. The Klan had torched the house in the heat of the Hailey trial, July 1985. First they burned a cross in the front yard, then they tried to blow up the house. Jake sent Carla and Hanna away and it was a wise thing to do. After the Klan tried to kill him for a month, they finally burned down his house. He had given his closing argument in a borrowed suit.

The topic of a new dog was too uncomfortable to fully address. They had danced around it a few times, then moved on. Hanna wanted one and probably needed one because she was an only child and often claimed to be bored playing alone. But Jake, and especially Carla, knew who would assume the responsibility of housebreaking and cleaning up after a puppy. Besides, they were living in a rental home with their lives far from settled. Perhaps a dog could bring about some normalcy; perhaps not. Jake often pondered this issue in the early minutes of the day. The truth was he really missed a dog.

After a quick shower, Jake dressed in a small, spare bedroom he and Carla used as a closet to store their clothes. All rooms were small in this flimsy house owned by someone else. Everything was temporary. The furniture was a sad ensemble of giveaways and flea market leftovers, all of which would be tossed one day if things went as planned, though, Jake hated to admit, almost nothing was going his way. Their lawsuit against the insurance company was bogged down in pretrial maneuvering that seemed hopeless. He had filed it six months after the Hailey verdict, when he was on top of the world and bristling with confidence. How dare an insurance company try and screw him? Show him another jury in Ford County and he'd deliver another great verdict. But the swagger and bluster faded as Jake and Carla slowly realized they had been seriously underinsured. Four blocks away, their vacant and scarred lot was just sitting there, gathering leaves. From next door, Mrs. Pickle kept an eye on it, but there was little to watch. The neighbors were waiting for a fine new home to rise up and for the Brigances to return.

Jake tiptoed into Hanna's room, kissed her on the cheek and pulled the sheets up a bit higher. She was seven now, their only child, and there would be no others. She was in the second grade at Clanton Elementary, in a classroom around the corner from where her mother taught kindergartners.

In the narrow kitchen, Jake pushed a button on the coffee brewer and watched the machine until it began making noises. He opened his briefcase, touched the 9-millimeter semiautomatic pistol holstered inside, and stuffed in some files. He had grown accustomed to carrying a gun and this saddened him. How could he live a normal life with a weapon nearby at all times? Normal or not, the gun was a necessity. They burn your house after they try to bomb it; they threaten your wife on the phone; they torch a cross in your front yard; they beat your secretary's husband senseless and he later dies; they use a sniper to take a shot, but he misses you and hits a guard; they wage terror during the trial and keep up their threats long after it's over.

Four of the terrorists were now serving prison sentences— three federal, one at Parchman. Only four, Jake reminded himself constantly. There should have been a dozen convictions by now, a feeling shared by Ozzie and other black leaders in the county. Out of habit and out of a sense of frustration, Jake called the FBI at least once a week for updates on their investigation. After three years, his calls were often not returned. He wrote letters. His file filled an entire cabinet in his office.

Only four. He knew the names of many others, all suspects still, in Jake's mind anyway. Some had moved and some had stayed, but they were out there, going about their lives as if nothing had happened. So he carried a gun, one with all the proper permits and such. There was one in his briefcase. One in his car. A couple around the office, and several others. His hunting rifles had gone up in the fire, but Jake was slowly rebuilding his collection.

He stepped outside, onto the small brick porch, and filled his lungs with the cool air. On the street, directly in front of the

house, there was a Ford County sheriff's patrol car, and behind
the wheel sat one Louis Tuck, a full-time deputy who worked
the graveyard shift and whose primary responsibility was to be
seen in the neighborhood throughout the night and, specifically,
to be parked near the mailbox at precisely 5:45 each morning,
Monday through Saturday, when Mr. Brigance stepped onto
the porch and waved hello. Tuck waved back. The Brigances
had survived another night.

As long as Ozzie Walls was sheriff of Ford County, which
would be at least three more years and probably much longer,
he and his office would do whatever possible to protect Jake and
his family. Jake had taken Carl Lee Hailey's case, worked like a
dog for peanuts, dodged bullets, ignored real threats, and lost
almost everything before delivering a not-guilty verdict that still
resonated in Ford County. Protecting him was Ozzie's highest
priority.

Tuck eased away. He would circle the block and return in a
few minutes after Jake left. He would watch the house until he
saw lights in the kitchen and knew Carla was up and moving
around.

Jake drove one of two Saabs in Ford County, a red one with
190,000 miles on it. He needed an upgrade but couldn't afford
one. Such an exotic car in a small town had once been a cool
idea, but now the repair costs were brutal. The nearest dealer
was in Memphis, an hour away, so every trip to the shop killed
half a day and cost a thousand bucks. Jake was ready for an
American model, and he thought about this every morning
when he turned the ignition key and held his breath as the
engine rolled over and came to life. The engine had never failed
to start, but in the past few weeks Jake had noticed a delay, an
extra turn or two that evoked an ominous warning that something bad was about to happen. Paranoid, he was noticing other
noises and rattles, and he was checking the tires every other day
as the treads grew thinner. He backed onto Culbert Street,
which, though only four blocks from Adams Street and their
vacant lot, was clearly in a lesser part of town. The house next

door was also a rental. Adams was lined with homes much older and statelier and with more character. Culbert was a hodge-podge of suburban-style boxes thrown up before the city got serious about zoning.

Though she said little, Jake knew Carla was ready to move on, to somewhere.

They had actually talked of moving away, of leaving Clanton altogether. The three years since the Hailey trial had been far less prosperous than they had hoped and expected. If Jake was destined to slog through a long career as a struggling lawyer, then why not struggle somewhere else? Carla could teach school anywhere. Surely they could find a good life that did not include weapons and constant vigilance. Jake may have been revered by the blacks in Ford County, but he was still resented by many of the whites. And the crazies were still out there. On the other hand, there was a certain safety living in the midst of so many friends. Their neighbors watched the traffic and a strange car or truck was noted. Every cop in town and every deputy in the county knew the safety of the little Brigance family was of the highest importance.

Jake and Carla would never leave, though it was sometimes amusing to play the old game of where-would-you-like-to-live? It was only a game because Jake knew the brutal truth that he would never fit in a big firm in a big city, nor would he ever find a small town in any state that was not already brimming with hungry lawyers. He was looking clearly at his future, and he was okay with it. He just needed to make a buck.

He drove past the empty lot on Adams, mumbled vile words in condemnation of the cowards who torched his home and managed a few choice ones for the insurance company as well, then sped away. From Adams he turned onto Jefferson, then Washington, which ran east and west along the north side of the Clanton square. His office was on Washington, across from the stately courthouse, and he parked in the same spot each morning at 6:00 a.m. because at that hour there were plenty to choose from. The square would be quiet for two more hours, until the courthouse and the shops and offices around it opened for business.

The Coffee Shop, though, was bustling with blue collars, farmers, and deputies when Jake strolled in and began saying good morning. As always, he was the only one wearing a coat and tie. The white collars gathered an hour later across the square at the Tea Shoppe and discussed interest rates and world politics. At the Coffee Shop they talked football, local politics, and bass fishing. Jake was one of the very few professionals tolerated inside the Coffee Shop. There were several reasons for this: he was well liked, thick-skinned, and good-natured; and, he was always available for a quick legal tip at no charge when one of the mechanics or truck drivers was in a bind. He hung his jacket on the wall and found a seat at a table with Marshall Prather, a deputy. Two days earlier, Ole Miss had lost to Georgia by three touchdowns and this was the hot topic. A gum-smacking, sassy gal named Dell poured his coffee while managing to bump him with her ample ass—the same routine six mornings a week. Within minutes she delivered food he never ordered— wheat toast, grits, and strawberry jelly, the usual. As Jake was shaking Tabasco sauce on the grits, Prather asked, "Say, Jake, did you know Seth Hubbard?"

"Never met him," Jake said, catching a few glances. "I've heard his name once or twice. Had a place up near Palmyra, didn't he?"

"That's it." Prather chewed on a sausage as Jake sipped his coffee.

Jake waited, then said, "I guess it's safe to assume something bad happened to Seth Hubbard because you put him in the past tense."

"I did what?" Prather asked. The deputy had an annoying habit of dropping a loud, loaded question over breakfast and following it up with silence. He knew the details and the dirt, and he was always fishing to see if anyone else had something to add.

"The past tense. You asked 'Did I know him?' not 'Do I know him?'—which would of course indicate he's still alive. Right?"

"I suppose."

"So what happened?"

Andy Furr, a mechanic at the Chevrolet place, said loudly, "Killed himself yesterday. Found him hangin' from a tree."

"Left a note and everything," added Dell as she swooped by with a coffeepot. The café had been open for an hour, so there was little doubt Dell knew as much about Seth Hubbard's passing as anyone.

"Okay, what did the note say?" Jake asked calmly.

"Can't tell you, sweetic," she chirped. "That's between me and Seth."

"You didn't know Seth," Prather said.

Dell was an old tart with the quickest tongue in town. She said, "I loved Seth once, or maybe it was twice. Can't always remember."

"There have been so many," Prather said.

"Yeah, but you'll never get close old boy," she said.

"You really don't remember, do you?" Prather shot back and got a few laughs.

"Where was the note?" Jake asked, trying to reverse the conversation.

Prather stuffed a load of pancakes in his mouth, chewed for a while, then replied, "On the kitchen table. Ozzie's got it now, still investigatin' but not much to it. Looks like Hubbard went to church, seemed fine, then drove back onto his property, took a stepladder and a rope and did the deed. One of his workers found him around two yesterday afternoon, swingin' in the rain. All dressed up in his Sunday best."

Interesting, bizarre, tragic, but Jake found it difficult to have any concern for a man he'd never met. Andy Furr asked, "Did he have anything?"

"Don't know," Prather said. "I think Ozzie knew him but he's not sayin' much."

Dell refilled their cups and stopped to talk. With a hand on one hip she said, "No, I never knew him. But my cousin knows his first wife, he had at least two, and accordin' to the first one

Seth had some land and money. She said he laid low, kept secrets, and didn't trust anybody. Also said he was a nasty sonofabitch, but then they always say that after the divorce."

"You oughtta know," Prather added.

"I do know, old boy. I know so much more than you."

"Is there a last will and testament?" Jake asked. Probate work was not his favorite, but a sizable estate usually meant a decent fee for someone in town. It was all paper shuffling with a couple of court appearances, nothing difficult and not too tedious. Jake knew that by 9:00 a.m. the lawyers in town would be slinking around trying to find out who wrote Seth Hubbard's last will.

"Don't know yet," Prather said.

"Wills ain't public record, are they Jake?" asked Bill West, an electrician at the shoe factory north of town.

"Not until you die. You can change your will at the last minute, so it would be useless to record it. Plus, you might not want the world to know what's in your will until you're dead. Once that happens, and once the will is probated, then it's filed in court and becomes public." Jake looked around as he spoke and counted at least three men he had prepared wills for. He made them short, quick, and cheap, and this was well known in town. It kept the traffic moving.

"When does probate start?" Bill West asked.

"There's no time limit. Usually the surviving spouse or children of the deceased will find the will, take it to a lawyer, and a month or so after the funeral they'll go to court and start the process."

"What if there's no will?"

"That's a lawyer's dream," Jake said with a laugh. "It's a mess. If Mr. Hubbard died with no will, and left behind a couple of ex-wives, maybe some adult children, maybe some grandchildren, who knows, then they'd probably spend the next five years fighting over his property, assuming of course he does have assets."

"Oh, he's got 'em," Dell said from across the café, her radar as always on high alert. If you coughed she quizzed you about your health. If you sneezed she hustled over with a tissue. If you were uncharacteristically quiet she might pry into your home life, or your job. If you tried to whisper she would be standing at your table, refilling cups of coffee regardless of how full they happened to be. She missed nothing, remembered everything, and never failed to remind her boys of something they'd said to the contrary three years earlier.

Marshall Prather rolled his eyes at Jake, as if to say, "She's nuts." But he wisely said nothing. Instead, he finished off his pancakes and had to leave.

Jake was not far behind. He paid his check at 6:40 and left the Coffee Shop, hugging Dell on the way out and choking on the fumes of her cheap perfume. The sky was orange in the east as dawn unfolded. Yesterday's rain was gone and the air was clear and cool. As always, Jake headed east, away from his office, and at a brisk pace as if he were late for an important meeting. The truth was that he had no important meetings that day, just a couple of routine office visits with people in trouble.

Jake took his morning stroll around the Clanton square, passing banks and insurance agencies and realty offices, shops and cafés, all tucked neatly together, all closed at this early hour. With a few exceptions, the buildings were two-story redbrick with wrought-iron laced terraces overhanging the sidewalks that ran in a perfect square around the courthouse and its lawn. Clanton wasn't exactly prospering, but it wasn't dying either like so many small towns in the rural South. The 1980 census put the population at just over eight thousand, four times that much for the entire county, and the numbers were expected to increase slightly after the next head count. There were no empty storefronts, nothing boarded up, no "For Lease" signs hanging sadly in the windows. He was from Karaway, a small town of twenty-five hundred eighteen miles west of Clanton, and Main Street there was decaying as merchants retired, cafés closed, and the lawyers gradually packed their books and moved to the county seat. There were now twenty-six around the Clanton square, and the number was growing, the competition steadily choking itself. How many more can we stand? Jake often asked himself.

He relished walking past the other law offices and gazing at their locked doors and dark reception rooms. It was a victory lap of sorts. In his smugness he was ready to tackle the day while his competition was still asleep. He walked past the office of Harry Rex Vonner, perhaps his closest friend in the bar, and a warrior who rarely arrived before 9:00, often with a reception filled with edgy divorce clients. Harry Rex had been through several wives and knew a chaotic home life, and for this reason he preferred to work late into the night. Jake walked past the hated Sullivan firm, home of the largest collection of lawyers in the county. Nine at last count, nine complete assholes Jake tried to avoid, but this was partly out of envy. Sullivan had the banks and insurance companies and its lawyers earned more than all the rest. He walked past the troubled and padlocked office of an old pal named Mack Stafford, unseen and unheard from now for eight months after apparently fleeing in the middle of the night with money belonging to his clients. His wife and two daughters were still waiting, as was an indictment. Secretly, Jake hoped Mack was on a beach somewhere, sipping rum drinks and never coming back. He'd been an unhappy man in an unhappy marriage. "Keep running, Mack," Jake said each morning as he touched the padlock without breaking stride.

He passed the offices of *The Ford County Times*, the Tea Shoppe, which was only now coming to life, a haberdashery where he bought his suits on sale, a black-owned café called Claude's where he ate every Friday with the other white liberals in town, an antiques store owned by a crook Jake had sued twice, a bank still holding the second mortgage on his home and tied up in the same lawsuit, and a county office building where the new district attorney worked when he was in town. The old one, Rufus Buckley, was gone, banished last year by the voters and permanently retired from elective office, or at least Jake and many others hoped so. He and Buckley had almost choked each other during the Hailey trial, and the hatred was still intense.

Now the ex-DA was back in his hometown of Smithfield, in Polk County, where he was licking his wounds and scrambling to make a living on a Main Street crammed with other law offices.

The loop was over, and Jake unlocked the front door to his own office, which was generally considered to be the finest in town. The building, along with many others on the square, had been built by the Wilbanks family a hundred years earlier, and for almost that long a Wilbanks had practiced law there. The streak ended when Lucien, the last remaining Wilbanks and no doubt the craziest, had been disbarred. He had just hired Jake, fresh out of law school and full of ideals. Lucien wanted to corrupt him, but before he had the chance the State Bar Association yanked his license for the last time. With Lucien gone and no other Wilbanks around, Jake inherited a magnificent suite of offices. He used only five of the ten rooms available. There was a large reception area downstairs where the current secretary did her work and greeted clients. Above it, in a splendid room thirty feet by thirty, Jake spent his days behind a massive oak desk that had been used by Lucien, his father, and grandfather. When he was bored, a common occurrence, he walked to the double French doors, opened them and stepped onto the terrace, where he had a fine view of the courthouse and the square.

At 7:00 a.m., on schedule, he sat behind his desk and took a sip of coffee. He looked at his calendar for the day and admitted to himself that it did not look promising or profitable.

3

The current secretary was a thirty-one-year-old mother of four who'd been hired by Jake only because he could find no one more suitable. When she began five months earlier he had been desperate, and she had been available. She went by Roxy, and on the plus side Roxy showed up for work each morning around 8:30, or a few minutes thereafter, and did a somewhat passable job of answering the phone, greeting the clients, chasing away the riffraff, typing, filing, and keeping her turf somewhat organized. On the negative, and heavier, side of the ledger, Roxy had little interest in the job, viewed it as only temporary until something better came along, smoked on the back porch and smelled like it, nagged about the low salary, made vague but loaded comments as to how she thought all lawyers were rich, and in general was an unpleasant person to be around. She was from Indiana, had been dragged south in an Army marriage, and like many from the North had little patience with the culture around her. She'd had a superior upbringing and was now living in a backward place. Though Jake did not inquire, he strongly suspected her marriage was less than fulfilling. Her husband had lost his job due to dereliction. She wanted Jake to sue on his behalf but Jake declined, and this was still festering. Plus, there was about $50 missing from petty cash, and Jake suspected the worst.

He would have to fire her, something he hated to think about. Each morning during his quiet time, he said his daily prayer and asked God to give him the patience to coexist with this latest woman in his life.

There had been so many. He had hired young ones because they were more plentiful and worked cheaper. The better of those got married and pregnant and wanted six months off. The bad ones flirted, wore tight miniskirts, and made suggestive comments. One threatened a bogus action for sexual harassment when Jake fired her, but she was arrested for bad checks and went away.

He had hired more mature women to negate any physical temptation, but, as a rule, they had been bossy, maternal, menopausal, and they had more doctors' appointments, as well as aches and pains to talk about and funerals to attend.

For decades the place had been ruled by Ethel Twitty, a legendary presence who ran the Wilbanks firm in its heyday. For over forty years Ethel had kept the lawyers in line, terrified the other secretaries, and fought with the younger associates, none of whom lasted more than a year or two. But Ethel was now retired, forced out by Jake during the Hailey circus. Her husband had been beaten by thugs, probably Klansmen, though the case was unsolved and its investigation going nowhere. Jake had been thrilled when she left; now, though, he almost missed her.

At precisely 8:30 he was downstairs in the kitchen, pouring more coffee, then puttering around a storage room as if searching for an old file. When Roxy eased through the rear door at 8:39, Jake was standing by her desk, flipping through the pages of a document, waiting, establishing the fact that she was, once again, late for work. That she had four young children, an unemployed and unhappy husband, a job she didn't like with a salary she deemed meager, and a host of other problems—all this mattered little to Jake. If he liked her he could find some sympathy. But, as the weeks passed, he liked her less and less. He was building a file, handing out silent demerits, piling on the points so that when he sat her down for the dreaded talk he would have his facts. Jake despised being in the position of plotting to unload an undesirable secretary.

"Good morning, Roxy," he said, glancing at his wristwatch.

"Hello, sorry I'm late, had to take the kids to school." He was sick of the lying too, however small it was. Her unemployed husband hauled the kids to school and back. Carla had verified this.

"Uh-huh," Jake mumbled as he picked up a stack of envelopes she had just placed on her desk. He grabbed the mail before she could open it and shuffled through it in search of something interesting. It was the usual pile of junk mail and lawyerly crap—letters from other firms, one from a judge's office, thick envelopes with copies of briefs, motions, pleadings, and so on. He did not open these—that job belonged to the secretary.

"Looking for something?" she asked as she dropped her purse and bag and began settling in.

"No."

Typically, she looked pretty rough—no makeup and a mess of hair. She hurried off to the restroom to put on her face and improve her looks, a project that often took fifteen minutes. More silent demerits.

At the bottom of the stack, on the very last regular-sized envelope of the day, Jake glanced at his name written in blue ink, cursive. The return address stunned him, and he almost dropped everything. He tossed the other mail into the middle of her desk, then hurried up the stairs to his office. He locked his door. He sat down at a rolltop in one corner, under a portrait of William Faulkner that had been purchased by Mr. John Wilbanks, Lucien's father, and inspected the envelope. Generic, plain, white, letter-sized, cheap paper, probably purchased in a box of a hundred for five bucks, adorned with a twenty-five-cent stamp honoring an astronaut, and thick enough to contain several sheets of paper. It was addressed to him: "The Hon. Jake Brigance, Attorney at Law, 146 Washington Street, Clanton, Mississippi." No zip code.

The return address was "Seth Hubbard, P.O. Box 277, Palmyra, Mississippi, 38664."

The envelope had been stamped with a postmark on October 1, 1988, the previous Saturday, at the Clanton post office. Jake took a deep breath and deliberately considered the scenario. If the Coffee Shop gossip could be believed, and Jake had no reason to doubt it, not at that moment anyway, Seth Hubbard had hung himself less than twenty-four hours earlier, on Sunday afternoon. It was now 8:45 Monday morning. For the letter to be postmarked in Clanton last Saturday, Seth Hubbard, or someone acting on his behalf, dropped the letter into the Local Delivery slot inside the Clanton post office either late Friday or Saturday before noon when the facility closed. Only local mail was postmarked in Clanton; all other was trucked to a regional center in Tupelo, sorted, marked, then dispersed.

Jake found a pair of scissors and meticulously cut a thin ribbon of paper from one end of the envelope, the end opposite the return address, close to the stamp but far enough away to preserve everything. There was the possibility he was holding evidence. He would copy everything later. He squeezed the envelope slightly and shook it until the folded papers fell out. He was aware of an increased heart rate as he carefully unfolded the sheets. Three of them, all plain white, nothing fancy, no letterhead. He pressed the creases and laid the papers flat on the desk, then he picked up the top one. In blue ink, and in a neat, cursive hand impressive for a man, the author wrote:

Dear Mr. Brigance:

To my knowledge we have never met, nor will we. By the time you read this I will be dead and that awful town you live in will be buzzing with its usual gossip. I have taken my own life but only because my death by lung cancer is imminent. The doctors have given me only weeks to live and I'm tired of the pain. I'm tired of a lot of things. If you smoke cigarettes, take the advice of a dead man and stop immediately.

I chose you because you have the reputation of being honest and I admired your courage during the trial of Carl Lee Hailey. I strongly suspect you are a man of tolerance, something sadly missing in this part of the world.

I despise lawyers, especially those in Clanton. I will not name names at this point in my life but I will die with a tremendous amount of unresolved ill will aimed at various members of your profession. Vultures. Bloodsuckers.

Enclosed herein you will find my last will and testament, every word written by me and signed and dated by me. I've checked the law of Mississippi and am satisfied that it is a proper holographic will, thus entitled to full enforcement under the law. No one witnessed me signing this will because, as you know, witnesses are not required for holographic wills. A year ago I signed a thicker version in the offices of the Rush law firm in Tupelo, but I have renounced that document.

This one is likely to start some trouble and that's why I want you as the attorney for my estate. I want this will defended at all costs and I know you can do it. I specifically cut out my two adult children, their children, and my two ex-wives. These are not nice people and they will fight, so get ready. My estate is substantial—they have no idea of its size—and when this is made known they will attack. Fight them, Mr. Brigance, to the bitter end. We must prevail.

With my suicide note I left instructions for my funeral and burial. Do not mention my last will and testament until after the funeral. I want my family to be forced to go through all the rituals of mourning before they realize they get nothing. Watch them fake it—they're very good at it. They have no love for me.

I thank you in advance for your zealous representation. It will not be easy. I am comforted in knowing I will not be there to suffer through such an agonizing ordeal.

Sincerely, Seth Hubbard   *October 1, 1988*

Jake was too nervous to read the will. He took a deep breath, stood, walked around the office, opened the French doors to the terrace and had the morning's first good look at the courthouse and the square, then returned to the rolltop. He read the letter again. It would be used as evidence to establish Seth Hubbard's testamentary capacity, and for a moment Jake was paralyzed with indecision. He wiped his hands on his pants. Should he leave the letter, the envelope, and the other sheets of paper exactly where they were, and run fetch Ozzie? Should he call a judge?

No. The letter was mailed to him, in confidence, and he had every right to examine its contents. Still, he felt as though he was handling a ticking bomb. Slowly, he moved the letter aside and stared at the next sheet of paper. With a laboring heart and trembling hands, he looked at the blue ink and knew full well that these words would consume the next year of his life, or maybe two.

It read:

LAST WILL AND TESTAMENT OF HENRY SETH HUBBARD

I, Seth Hubbard, being 71 years old and of good mind but decaying body, do hereby make this my last will and testament:

1. I am a resident of the State of Mississippi. My legal address is 4498 Simpson Road, Palmyra, Ford County, Mississippi.

2. I renounce all previous wills signed by me, specifically one dated September 7, 1987, and prepared by Mr. Lewis McGwyre of the Rush law firm in Tupelo, Mississippi. And that will specifically renounced one I signed in March of 1985.

3. This is intended to be a holographic will, with every word written by me, in my handwriting, with no help from anyone. It is signed and dated by me. I prepared it alone, in my office, on this day, October 1, 1988.

4. I am of clear mind and have full testamentary capacity. No one is exerting or attempting to exert influence over me.

5. I appoint as executor of my estate Russell Amburgh of 762 Ember Street, Temple, Mississippi. Mr. Amburgh was vice president of my holding company and has a working knowledge of my assets and liabilities. I direct Mr. Amburgh to retain the services of Mr. Jake Brigance, Attorney At Law, in Clanton, Mississippi, to provide all necessary representation. It is my directive that no other lawyer in Ford County touch my estate or earn a penny from its probate.

6. I have two children—Herschel Hubbard and Ramona Hubbard Dafoe—and they have children, though I don't know how many because I haven't seen them in some time. I specifically exclude both of my children and all of my grand-children from any inheritance under my estate. They get nothing. I do not know the precise legal language necessary to "cut out" a person from an inheritance, but my intention here is to completely prohibit them—my children and grand-children—from getting anything from me. If they contest this will and lose, it is my desire that they pay all attorneys' fees and court costs incurred as a result of their greed.

7. I have two ex-wives who I will not name. Since they got virtually everything in the divorces, they get nothing more here. I specifically exclude them. May they perish in pain, like me.

8. I give, devise, transfer, leave behind (whatever the hell it takes) 90% of my estate to my friend, Lettie Lang, as thanks for her dedicated service and friendship to me during these past few years. Her full name is Letetia Delores Tayber Lang, and her address is 1488 Montrose Road, Box Hill, Mississippi.

9. I give, devise, etc., 5% of my estate to my brother, Ancil F. Hubbard, if he's still alive. I have not heard from Ancil in many years, though I have thought of him often. He was a lost boy who deserved better. As children, he and I witnessed something no human should ever see, and Ancil was forever traumatized. If he's dead by now, his 5% share remains in my estate.

10. I give, devise, etc., 5% of my estate to the Irish Road Christian Church.

11. I direct my executor to sell my house, land, real property, personal property, and lumber yard near Palmyra, for market value, as soon as practical, and place the proceeds into my estate.

Seth Hubbard   *October 1, 1988*

The signature was small and neat and quite legible. Jake wiped his hands again on his pants and reread the will. It covered two pages, and the handwriting was in near perfect lines, as though Seth had meticulously used a straightedge of some variety.

A dozen questions clamored for attention, with the most obvious being—Who in the world is Lettie Lang? A close second was—What, exactly, did she do to deserve 90 percent? Then— How big is the estate? If it is indeed sizable, how much will be eaten up in death taxes? This question was quickly followed with—How much might the attorney's fees run?

But before he got greedy, Jake took another walk around the office, his head spinning and his adrenaline rising. What a wondrous legal brawl. With money on the line, there was little doubt Seth's family would lawyer up and attack the last will with a fury. Though Jake had never handled a full-blown will contest, he knew such cases were tried in Chancery Court and often before juries. It was rare for a dead person in Ford County to leave much behind, but occasionally someone with a measure of wealth would pass on without proper estate planning, or with a suspicious will. These occasions were a bonanza to the local bar as the lawyers raged in and out of court and the assets evaporated in legal fees.

He gently placed the envelope and the three sheets of paper into a file, and carried it downstairs to Roxy's desk. By now her looks had improved, somewhat, and she was opening the mail. "Read this," he said. "And slowly."

She did as he instructed, and when she finished she said, "Wow. Great way to start the week."

"Not so for old Seth," Jake said. "Please note that this arrived in the mail this morning, October 3."

"So noted. Why?"

"The timing could be crucial one day in court. Saturday, Sunday, Monday."

"I'm going to be a witness?"

"Maybe, maybe not, but we're just taking precautions, okay?"

"You're the lawyer."

Jake ran four copies of the envelope, the letter, and the will. He gave Roxy a copy to enter into the firm's newest case file, and he tucked two away in a locked drawer in his desk. He waited until 9:00 a.m. and left the office with the original and one copy. He told Roxy he was headed for the courthouse. He walked next door to Security Bank, where he placed the original in his firm's lockbox.

Ozzie Walls's office was at the county jail, two blocks off the square in a low-slung concrete bunker built on the cheap a decade earlier. A tumorlike appendage had been added later to house the sheriff and his staff and deputies, and the place was crammed with cheap desks, folding chairs, and stained carpet fraying at the baseboards. Monday mornings were usually hectic as the weekend's fun and games were tidied up. Angry wives arrived to bail their hungover husbands out of jail. Other wives stormed in to sign papers to get their husbands thrown into jail. Frightened parents waited for details of the drug bust that caught their kids. The phones rang more than usual and often went unanswered. Deputies milled about choking down doughnuts and sipping strong coffee. Add to the usual frenzy the bizarre suicide of a mysterious man, and the cluttered outer office was especially busy that Monday morning.

In the rear of the appendage, down a short hallway, there was a thick door covered in white hand-painted lettering that read: OZZIE WALLS, HIGH SHERIFF, FORD COUNTY. The door was closed; the sheriff was in early on Monday, and on the phone. The caller was an emotional woman from Memphis whose child had been caught driving a pickup truck that was hauling, among other things, a sizable quantity of marijuana. This had happened the previous Saturday night near Lake Chatulla, in an area of a state park where illicit behavior was known to be common. The child was innocent, of course, and the mother was eager to drive down and retrieve him from Ozzie's jail.

Not so fast, Ozzie cautioned. There was a knock at his door. He covered the receiver and said, "Yes!"

The door opened a few inches and Jake Brigance stuck his head through the crack. Ozzie smiled immediately and waved him in. Jake closed the door behind himself and eased into a chair. Ozzie was explaining that even though the kid was seventeen, he had been caught with three pounds of pot; thus, he could not be released on bond until a judge said so. As the mother railed, Ozzie frowned and moved the receiver a few inches from his ear. He shook his head, smiled again. Same old crap. Jake had heard it too, many times.

Ozzie listened some more, promised to do what he could, which was obviously not much, and finally got off the phone. He half stood, shook Jake's hand, said, "Good mornin', Counselor."

"Mornin' to you, Ozzie."

They chatted about this and that and finally got around to football. Ozzie had played briefly for the Rams before blowing out a knee, and he still followed the team religiously. Jake was a Saints fan, like the majority of Mississippians, so there was little to talk about. The entire wall behind Ozzie was covered with football memorabilia—photos, awards, plaques, trophies. He'd been an all-American at Alcorn State in the mid-1970s and, evidently, had been meticulous about preserving his memories.

On another day, another time, preferably with more of an audience, say around the courtroom in a recess when other lawyers were listening, Ozzie might be tempted to tell the story of the night he broke Jake's leg. Jake had been a skinny sophomore quarterback playing for Karaway, a much smaller school that for some reason kept the tradition of getting stomped each year in the season finale against Clanton. Billed as a backyard brawl, the game was never close. Ozzie, the star tackle, had terrorized the Karaway offense for three quarters, and late in the fourth he rushed hard third and long. The fullback, already wounded and frightened, ignored Ozzie, who crushed Jake as he desperately tried to scramble. Ozzie had always claimed he heard the fibula snap. In Jake's version, he heard nothing but Ozzie's growling and snarling as he pounced for the kill. Regardless of the version, the story managed to get retold at least once a year.

It was Monday morning, though, and the phones were ringing and both men were busy. It was obvious Jake was there for a reason. "I think I've been hired by Mr. Seth Hubbard," he said.

Ozzie narrowed his eyes and studied his friend. "His hiring days are over. They got him down at Magargel's, on the slab."

"Did you cut him down?"

"Let's say we lowered him to the ground." Ozzie reached for a file, opened it, and took out three eight-by-ten color photos. He slid them across his desk and Jake picked them up. Front, back, right side—all the same image of Seth, sad and dead, hanging in the rain. Jake was shocked for a second but didn't show it. He studied the grotesque face and tried to place him. "I never met the man," he mumbled. "Who found him?"

"One of his workers. Looks like Mr. Hubbard planned it all."

"Oh yes." Jake reached into a coat pocket, pulled out the copies and slid them over to Ozzie. "This arrived in the morning's mail. Hot off the press. The first page is a letter to me. The second and third pages purport to be his last will and testament."

Ozzie lifted the letter and read it slowly. Showing no expression, he read the will. When he finished, he dropped it on the desk and rubbed his eyes. "Wow," he managed to say. "Is this thing legal, Jake?"

"On its face, yes, but I'm sure the family will attack it."

"Attack it how?"

"They'll make all sorts of claims: the old guy was out of his mind; this woman exerted undue influence over him and convinced him to change his will. Believe me, if money's at stake, they'll unload both barrels."

"This woman," Ozzie repeated, then smiled and began to slowly shake his head.

"You know her?"

"Oh yeah."

"Black or white?"

"Black."

Jake suspected this and was not at all surprised, nor disappointed; rather, at that moment, he began to feel the early rumblings of excitement. A white man and his money, a last-minute will leaving it all to a black woman he was obviously quite fond of. A bitter will dispute played out before a jury, with Jake in the middle of it all.

"How well do you know her?" Jake asked. It was well known that Ozzie knew every black person in Ford County: those registered to vote and those still lagging; those who owned land and those who were on welfare; those who had jobs and those who avoided work; those who saved money and those who broke into houses; those who went to church every Sunday and those who lived in honky-tonks.

"I know her," he said, careful as always. "She lives out from Box Hill in an area called Little Delta."

Jake nodded, said, "I've driven through it."

"In the boondocks, all black. She's married to a man named Simeon Lang, pretty much of a deadbeat who comes and goes, off and on the wagon."

"I've never met any Langs."

"You don't want to meet this one. When he's sober, I think he drives a truck and runs a bulldozer. I know he worked offshore once or twice. Unstable. Four or five kids, one boy in prison, I think there's a girl in the Army. Lettie's about forty-five, I'd guess. She's a Tayber, and there aren't many of them around. He's a Lang, and the woods are full of Langs, unfortunately. I did not know she was workin' for Seth Hubbard."

"Did you know Hubbard?"

"Somewhat. He gave me $25,000 under the table, cash, for both of my campaigns; wanted nothin' in return; in fact, he almost avoided me my first four years. I saw him last summer when I was up for reelection and he gave me another envelope."

"You took the cash?"

"I don't like your tone, Jake," Ozzie said with a smile. "Yes, I took the cash because I wanted to win. Plus, my opponents were takin' cash. Politics is a tough business around here."

"Fine with me. How much money did the old man have?"

"Well, he says it's substantial. Personally, I don't know. It's always been a mystery. The rumor has been that he lost everything in a bad divorce—Harry Rex cleaned him out—and because of that he's kept his business buried under a rock."

"Smart man."

"He owns some land and has always dabbled in timber. Beyond that, I don't know."

"What about his two adult children?"

"I talked to Herschel Hubbard around five yesterday afternoon, broke the bad news. He lives in Memphis, but I didn't get much information. He said he would call his sister, Ramona, and they would hustle on over. Seth left a sheet of paper with some instructions on how he wanted to be handled. Funeral tomorrow at 4:00 p.m., at church, then a burial." Ozzie paused and reread the letter. "Seems kinda cruel, doesn't it, Jake? Seth wants his family to suffer through a proper mourning before they know he's screwed 'em in his will."

Jake chuckled and said, "Oh, I think it's beautiful. You wanna go to the funeral?"

"Only if you'll go."

"You're on."

They sat in silence for a moment, listening to the voices outside, to the ringing of the phones, and they both knew they had things to do. But there were so many questions, so much high drama just around the corner.

"I wonder what those boys saw," Jake said. "Seth and his brother."

Ozzie shook his head, no clue. He glanced at the will and said, "Ancil F. Hubbard. I can try and find him if you want; run his name through the network; see if he's got a record anywhere."

"Do that. Thanks."

After another heavy pause, Ozzie said, "Jake, I have a lot on my plate this mornin'."

Jake jumped to his feet and said, "Me too. Thanks. I'll call later."

4

The drive from central Memphis to Ford County was only an hour, but for Herschel Hubbard it was always a lone-some journey that seemed to kill a day. It was an unwelcome excursion into his past, and for many reasons he made it only when necessary, which wasn't very often. He'd left home at eighteen, kicking the dirt off his shoes and vowing to avoid the place whenever possible. He had been an innocent casualty in a war between his parents, and when they finally split he sided with his mother and fled the county, and his father. Twenty-eight years later, he found it difficult to believe the old man was finally dead.

There had been efforts at reconciliation, usually at Herschel's urging, and Seth, to his credit, had hung on for a while and tried to tolerate his son, and his grandkids. But a second wife and a second bad marriage had intervened and complicated matters. For the past decade, Seth had cared for nothing but his work. He called on most birthdays and sent a Christmas card once every five years, but that was the extent of his efforts at father-hood. The more he worked the more he looked down on his son's career, and this was a major cause of their tension.

Herschel owned a college bar near the campus of Memphis State. As bars go, it was popular and busy. He paid his bills and hid some cash. Like father like son, he was still grappling with the aftershocks of his own nasty divorce, one won decidedly by his ex, who got the two kids and virtually all the money. For four years now, Herschel had been forced to live with his mother in an old, declining house in central Memphis, along with a bunch of cats and the occasional freeloading bum his mother took in.

She, too, had been scarred by an unpleasant life with Seth, and was, as they say, off her rocker.

He crossed the Ford County line and his mood grew even darker. He was driving a sports car, a little Datsun he'd bought secondhand primarily because his late father hated Japanese cars, hated all things Japanese, really. Seth had lost a cousin in World War II, at the hands of his Japanese captors, and relished wallowing in his well-earned bigotry.

Herschel found a country station out of Clanton and shook his head at the DJ's twangy and sophomoric comments. He had entered another world, one he left long ago and hoped to forget forever. He pitied all those friends who still lived in Ford County and would never leave. Two-thirds of his senior class at Clanton High were still in the area, working in factories and driving trucks and cutting pulpwood. His ten-year reunion had so saddened him he skipped the twenty-year.

After the first divorce, Herschel's mother fled the place and resettled in Memphis. After the second, Herschel's stepmother fled the place and settled in Jackson. Seth hung on to the home, along with the land around it. For this reason, Herschel was forced to revisit the nightmare of his childhood when he went to see Seth, something he had done only once a year until the cancer arrived. The house was a one-story, ranch-style, redbrick structure set back from the county road and heavily shaded with thick oaks and elms. There was a long, open front lawn where Herschel had played as a child, but never with his father. They had never tossed a baseball or a football, never even set up a kids' soccer goal, or played tackle football. As he turned in to the driveway, he looked at the wide lawn and was once again surprised at how small it now seemed. He parked behind another car, one he did not recognize, one with Ford County license plates, and for a moment stared at the house.

He had always assumed he would not be bothered by his father's death, though he had male friends who had warned him otherwise. You grow into an adult; you're trained to control your emotions; you don't hug your father because he is not the hugging type; you don't send gifts or letters; and when he's dead you know you can easily survive without him. A little sadness at the funeral, maybe a tear or two, but within days the ordeal is over and you're back to your life, undamaged. And those male friends had kind things to say about their fathers. They had watched the old guys age and face death with little concern for the aftermath, and every one of them had been blindsided by grief.

Herschel felt nothing; no sense of loss, no sadness at the closing of a chapter; no pity for a man so troubled he took his own life. He sat in his car and looked at the house and admitted to himself that he felt nothing for his father. Perhaps there was a trace of relief in that he was gone and his death meant one less complicating factor in Herschel's life. Perhaps.

He walked to the front door, which was opening as he approached. Lettie Lang was standing in the doorway, touching her eyes with a tissue. "Hello, Mr. Hubbard," she said in a voice straining with emotion.

"Hello Lettie," he said, stopping on the rubber doormat lying on the concrete porch. Had he known her better he might have stepped forward for a quick hug or some gesture of shared sympathy, but he couldn't force himself to do it. He had met her only three or four times, and never properly. She was a housekeeper, and a black one, and as such was expected to stay in the shadows when the family was around.

"I'm so sorry," she said, backing away.

"So am I," Herschel said. He followed her inside, through the den, to the kitchen where she pointed to a coffeepot and said, "I just made this."

"Is that your car out there?" he asked.

"Yes sir."

"Why did you park in the driveway? I thought you were supposed to park to the side over there, next to Dad's pickup."

"I'm sorry, I just wasn't thinkin'. I'll go move it."

"No, forget it. Pour me some coffee, two sugars."

"Yes sir."

"Where is Dad's car, the Cadillac?"

Lettie carefully poured the coffee into a cup. "The sheriff took it in. Supposed to bring it back today."

"Why'd they take the car?"

"You'll have to ask them."

Herschel pulled a chair from under the table, sat down, and cradled his cup. He took a sip, frowned, said, "How'd you find out about Dad?"

Lettie leaned against a counter and folded her arms across her chest. He quickly scanned her from head to toe. She was wearing the same white cotton dress she always wore, knee-length, a bit tight around the waist where she carried a few pounds, and very tight across her ample chest.

She did not miss the look; she never missed them. At forty-seven years of age and after five childbirths, Lettie Lang still managed to get some looks, but never from white men. She said, "Calvin called me last night, told me what happened, asked me to open up the house this mornin' and wait for you all."

"Do you have a key?"

"No sir. Ain't never had a key. The house was unlocked."

"Who's Calvin?"

"White man who works here on the property. Said Mr. Seth called him yesterday mornin', told him to meet him down to the bridge at two o'clock. Sure enough, there he was." She stopped her narrative long enough to dab her eyes with the tissue.

Herschel took another sip. "The sheriff said Dad left a note and some instructions."

"I ain't seen nothin' like that, but Calvin saw it. Said Mr. Seth wrote he was takin' his own life." She began crying.

Herschel listened for a while, and when she was quiet he asked, "How long have you worked here, Lettie?"

She took a deep breath and wiped her cheeks. "I don't know, 'bout three years. I started two days a week cleanin', Monday and Wednesday, a few hours a day, didn't take much because Mr. Seth lived alone, you know, and he was pretty neat, for a man. Then he asked me to cook for him, and I was happy to do it. More hours. I'd cook a buncha stuff and leave it on the stove or in the refrigerator. Then when he got sick he asked me to come in every mornin' and take care of him. When the chemo was real bad, he'd stay in bed pretty much all day and night."

"I thought he was paying a nurse."

Lettie knew how little Mr. Herschel and Mrs. Dafoe had seen of their father during his illness. Lettie knew everything; they knew almost nothing. However, she would be respectful, as always.

"Yes sir, he did for a while, then he got to where he didn't like them. They were always changin' nurses and you didn't know who might show up."

"So, you've been working here full-time for how long?"

"About a year."

"How much did Dad pay you?"

"Five dollars an hour."

"Five! That seems kinda high for domestic help, doesn't it? I mean, well, I live in Memphis, a big city, and my mother pays her housekeeper four and a half an hour."

Lettie just nodded because she had no response. She could have added that Mr. Seth paid her in cash, and often added a little extra, and had loaned her $5,000 when her son got in trouble and went to prison. That loan had been forgiven only four days earlier. There was nothing in writing.

Herschel sipped his coffee in disapproval. Lettie stared at the floor.

Out in the driveway, two car doors slammed.

Ramona Hubbard Dafoe was crying before she cleared the front door. She embraced her older brother on the porch, and he, to his credit, managed to seem sufficiently moved: eyes tightly closed, lips pooched, forehead furrowed. A man in real misery. Ramona wailed in what seemed to be authentic pain, though Herschel had his doubts.

Ramona moved on and was soon hugging Lettie, as if the two were the natural-born children of the same kind and loving father. Herschel, meanwhile, was still on the porch and greeting Ramona's husband, a man he loathed and the loathing was mutual. Ian Dafoe was a preppy from a family of bankers down in Jackson, the capital, the largest city, home to at least half the assholes in Mississippi. The banks were long gone (belly-up) but Ian would forever cling to the airs of a privileged boy, even though he had married lower, and even though he was now hustling to make a buck like everyone else.

As they shook hands politely, Herschel glanced over his shoulder to check out their vehicle. No surprise. A shiny, seemingly new white Mercedes sedan, the latest in a line of same. Thanks to Ramona's drinking and loose tongue, Herschel knew that dear Ian leased his cars for thirty-six months and turned them in early. The payments caused a bind on their finances, but that didn't matter. It was far more important for Mr. and Mrs. Dafoe to be seen around north Jackson in a proper vehicle.

They eventually gathered in the den and found seats. Lettie served them coffee and colas, then dutifully slipped into the shadows, into the open door of a bedroom just down the hall, a spot she often occupied when she listened to Mr. Seth on the phone in the den. From there, she could hear everything. Ramona cried some more and went on about how unbelievable everything was. The men just listened, agreeing, occasionally uttering a syllable or two. They were soon interrupted by the ringing of the doorbell. Two ladies from the church arrived with a cake and a casserole, and they were not to be denied. Lettie hustled around and took the food to the kitchen, and the ladies, without the benefit of an invitation, plopped down in the den and commenced trolling for gossip. They had seen their brother Seth just yesterday at church, and he had looked so good. They knew about the lung cancer and all, but, heavens, he seemed to have conquered it.

Herschel and the Dafoes offered nothing. Lettie listened from the shadows.

The church ladies were about to burst with all manner of inquiries: "How'd he do it?" and "Did he leave a note?" and "Who gets the money?" and "Any chance of foul play?" But, it was painfully clear such nosiness would not be well received.

After twenty minutes of near silence, they lost interest and began their good-byes.

Five minutes after they left, the doorbell rang again. The driveway was being watched. The three cars were attracting attention.

"Get that, Lettie," Herschel yelled from the den. "We're hiding in the kitchen."

It was the neighbor across the road with a lemon cake. Lettie thanked her and explained that Mr. Seth's children were indeed there but "not taking company." The neighbor loitered for a while on the porch, desperate to get inside and stick her nose into the family's drama, but Lettie politely blocked the door. After she finally left, Lettie took the cake to the kitchen where it sat untouched on the counter.

At the kitchen table, it didn't take long to get down to business. "Have you seen the will?" Ramona asked, her eyes remarkably clear now and glowing with intrigue and suspicion.

"No," Herschel said. "Have you?"

"No. I was here a couple of months ago—"

"It was July," Ian interrupted.

"Okay, July, and I tried to talk to Daddy about his will. He said some lawyers in Tupelo had written it and that we would be properly taken care of, but that was all. Did you ever talk to him about it?"

"No," Herschel admitted. "It just didn't feel right, you know? The old guy was dying of cancer and I'm asking about his will? I couldn't do it."

Lettie was lurking in the hallway, in the shadows, catching every word.

"What about his assets?" Ian asked, in cold blood. He had good reason to be curious since most of his own assets were so heavily mortgaged. His company built low-end shopping centers and strip malls, every deal loaded with debt. He worked frantically to stay one step ahead of his lenders, but they were always howling.

Herschel glared at his brother-in-law, the leech, but kept his cool. All three suspected trouble with Seth's estate, so there was no sense in rushing things. They would be at war soon enough. Herschel shrugged and said, "Don't know. He was very secretive, as you've seen. This house, the two hundred acres around it, the lumber yard up the road, but I don't know about his loans and such. We never talked business."

"You never talked about anything," Ramona shot across the table, then immediately took it back. "I'm sorry, Herschel. Please."

But such a cheap shot from a sibling can never be left alone. Herschel sneered and said, "Didn't realize you and the old man were so close."

Ian quickly changed the subject with, "Does he have an office here, or a place he kept his personal papers? Come on. Why can't we look around here? There's bound to be bank statements and land deeds and contracts, hell, I'll bet there's even a copy of the will, right here in the house."

"Lettie should know," Ramona said.

"Let's not involve her," Herschel said. "Did you know he was paying her five bucks an hour, full-time?"

"Five bucks?" Ian repeated. "What are we paying Berneice?"

"Three fifty," Ramona said. "For twenty hours."

"We're paying four and a half in Memphis," Herschel reported proudly, as if he and not his mother wrote the checks.

"Why would an old tightwad like Seth pay so much for a housekeeper?" Ramona mused, knowing there was no answer.

"She'd better enjoy it," Herschel said. "Her days are numbered."

"So we're firing her?" Ramona asked.

"Immediately. We have no choice. You wanna keep forking over that kinda money? Look, Sis, here's the plan. We get through the funeral, tell Lettie to get things in order, then cut her loose and lock up the house. We'll put it on the market next week and hope for the best. There's no reason for her to hang around, at five bucks an hour."

In the shadows, Lettie dropped her head.

"Maybe not so fast," Ian said politely. "At some point, and

soon, we'll see the will. In it we'll find out who'll serve as the executor of the estate, probably one of you. It's usually the surviving spouse or one of the kids. The executor will run the estate according to the terms of the will."

"I know all that," Herschel said, though he really didn't. Because Ian dealt with lawyers daily, he often acted like the legal expert in the family. One of many reasons Herschel despised him.

"I just can't believe he's dead," Ramona said, finding a tear to wipe.

Herschel glared at her and was tempted to lunge across the table for a backhand. To his knowledge, she made the trip to Ford County once a year, usually alone because Ian couldn't stand the place and Seth couldn't stand Ian. She would leave Jackson around 9:00 a.m., insist on meeting Seth for lunch at the same roadside barbecue hut ten miles north of Clanton, then follow him home where she was usually bored by 2:00 p.m. and back on the road by 4:00. Her two children, both in middle school (private), had not seen their grandfather in years. For sure, Herschel could claim nothing closer, but then he wasn't sitting there crying fake tears and pretending to miss the old man.

A loud knock at the kitchen door startled them. Two uniformed deputies had arrived. Herschel opened the door, invited them in. Awkward introductions were made at the refrigerator. The deputies removed their hats and shook hands. Marshall Prather said, "Sorry to interrupt you all, but me and Deputy Pirtle here were sent by Sheriff Walls, who, by the way, sends his deepest condolences. We brought back Mr. Hubbard's car." He handed the keys to Herschel, who said, "Thanks."

Deputy Pirtle pulled an envelope out of a pocket and said, "This here is what Mr. Hubbard left right there on the kitchen table. We found it yesterday after we found him. Sheriff Walls made copies but thinks the family needs to keep the originals." He handed the envelope to Ramona, who was sniffling again.

Everyone said thanks, and after another awkward round of nodding and handshaking, the deputies left. Ramona opened the envelope and pulled out two sheets of paper. The first was the note to Calvin in which Seth confirmed his death as a proper suicide. The second was addressed not to his children, but To Whom It May Concern. It read:

Funeral Instructions:
I want a simple service at the Irish Road Christian Church on Tuesday, October 4, at 4 p.m. with Rev. Don McElwain presiding. I'd like for Mrs. Nora Baines to sing The Old Rugged Cross. I do not want anyone to attempt a eulogy. Can't imagine anyone wanting to. Other than that, Rev. McElwain can say whatever he wants. Thirty minutes max.
If any black people wish to attend my funeral, then they are to be admitted. If they are not admitted, then forget the whole service and put me in the ground.
My pallbearers are: Harvey Moss, Duane Thomas, Steve Holland, Billy Bowles, Mike Mills, and Walter Robinson.
Burial Instructions:
I just bought a plot in the Irish Road Cemetery behind the church. I've spoken with Mr. Magargel at the funeral home and he's been paid for the casket. No vault. Immediately after the church service, I want a quick interment—five minutes max— then lower the casket.
So long. See you on the other side.
Seth Hubbard

After they passed it around the kitchen table and observed a moment of silence, they poured more coffee. Herschel cut a thick slice of the lemon cake and declared it delicious. The Dafoes declined.

"Looks like your father planned it all rather well," Ian observed as he read the instructions again. "Quick and simple."

Ramona blurted, "We have to talk about foul play, don't we? It hasn't been mentioned yet, has it? Can we at least have the discussion? What if it wasn't a suicide? What if someone else did it and tried to cover it up? Do you really believe Daddy would kill himself?"

Herschel and Ian gawked at her as if she'd just sprouted horns. They were both tempted to rebuke her, to taunt her stupidity, but nothing was said during a long, heavy pause. Herschel slowly took another bite of cake. Ian gently lifted the two sheets of paper and said, "Dear, how can anyone possibly fake this? You can recognize Seth's handwriting from ten yards away."

She was crying, wiping tears. Herschel added, "I asked the sheriff about that, Mona, and he's certain it was a suicide."

"I know, I know," she mumbled between sobs.

Ian said, "Your father was dying of cancer, in a lot of pain and such, and he took matters into his own hands. Looks like he was pretty thorough."

"I can't believe it," she said. "Why couldn't he talk to us?"

Because you people never talked to each other, Lettie said to herself in the shadows.

Ian, the expert, said, "This is not unusual in a suicide. They never talk to anyone and they can go to great lengths to plan things. My uncle shot himself two years ago and—"

"Your uncle was a drunk," Ramona said as she dried up.

"Yes he was, and he was drunk when he shot himself, but he still managed to plan it all."

"Let's talk about something else, can we?" Herschel said. "No, Mona, there was no foul play. Seth did it himself and left notes behind. I say we go through the house and look for papers, bank statements, maybe the will, anything that we might need to find. We're the family and we're in charge now. Nothing wrong with that, right?"

Ian and Ramona were nodding, yes.

Lettie was actually smiling. Mr. Seth had taken all his papers to his office and locked them in a file cabinet. Over the last month, he had meticulously cleaned out his desk and drawers and taken away everything of interest. And, he'd said to her, "Lettie, if something happens to me, all the good stuff is in my office, locked up tight. The lawyers will deal with it, not my kids."

He'd also said, "And I'm leaving a little something for you."

5

By noon Monday the entire bar association of Ford County was buzzing with the news of the suicide and, much more important, with the curiosity of which firm might be chosen to handle the probate. Most deaths caused similar ripples; a fatal car wreck, more so for obvious reasons. However, a garden-variety murder did not. Most murderers were of the lower classes and thus unable to fork over meaningful fees. When the day began, Jake had nothing—no murders, no car wrecks, and no promising wills to probate. By lunch, though, he was mentally spending some money.

He could always find something to do across the street in the courthouse. The land records were on the second floor, in a long wide room with lined shelves of thick plat books dating back two hundred years. In his younger days, when totally bored or hiding from Lucien, he spent hours poring over old deeds and grants as if some big deal was in the works. Now, though, at the age of thirty-five and with ten years under his belt, he avoided the room when possible. He fancied himself a trial lawyer, not a title checker; a courtroom brawler, not some timid little lawyer content to live in the archives and push papers around a desk. Even so, and regardless of his dreams, there were times each year when Jake, along with every other lawyer in town, found it necessary to get lost for an hour or so in the county's records.

The room was crowded. The more prosperous firms used paralegals to do the research, and there were several there, lugging the books back and forth and frowning at the pages. Jake spoke to a couple of lawyers who were doing the same— football talk mainly because no one wanted to get caught snooping for the dirt on Seth Hubbard. To kill time, he looked through the Index of Wills to see if any Hubbard of note had handed down land or assets to Seth, but found nothing in the past twenty years. He walked down the hall to the Chancery Clerk's office with the thought of perusing old divorce files but other lawyers were sniffing around.

He left the courthouse in search of a better source.

It was no surprise that Seth Hubbard hated the lawyers in Clanton. Most litigants, divorce or otherwise, who ran afoul of Harry Rex Vonner were miserable for the rest of their lives and loathed everything about the legal profession. Seth wasn't the first to commit suicide.

Harry Rex extracted blood, along with money and land and everything else in sight. Divorce was his specialty, and the uglier the better. He relished the dirt, the gutter fighting, the hand-to-hand combat, the thrill of the secret phone recording or the surprise eight-by-ten snapshot of the girlfriend in her new convertible. His trials were trench warfare. His alimony settlements set records. For fun he blew up uncontested divorces and turned them into two-year death marches. He loved to sue ex-lovers for alienation of affection. If none of the dirty tricks in his bag worked, he invented more. With a near monopoly on the market, he controlled the docket and bullied the court clerks. Young lawyers ran from him, and old lawyers, already burned, kept their distance. He had few friends and those who remained loyal often struggled to do so.

Among lawyers, Harry Rex trusted only Jake, and the trust was mutual. During the Hailey trial, when Jake was losing sleep and weight and focus and dodging bullets and death threats and certain he was about to blow the biggest case of his career, Harry Rex quietly stepped into Jake's office. He stayed in the background, spending hours on the case without looking for a dime. He unloaded volumes of free advice and kept Jake sane.

As always, on Mondays, Harry Rex was at his desk eating a hoagie for lunch. For divorce lawyers like him, Mondays were the worst days as marriages cracked over the weekends and spouses already at war ramped up their attacks. Jake entered the building through a rear door to avoid (1) the notoriously prickly secretaries and (2) the smoke-laden waiting room filled with stressed-out clients. Harry Rex's office door was closed. Jake listened for a moment, heard no voices, then shoved it open.

"What do you want?" Harry Rex growled as he chomped on a mouthful. The hoagie was spread before him on wax paper, with a small mountain of barbecue potato chips piled around it. He was washing it all down with a bottle of Bud Light.

"Well, good afternoon, Harry Rex. Sorry to barge in on your lunch."

He wiped his mouth with the back of a beefy hand and said, "You're not bothering my lunch. What's up?"

"Drinking already?" Jake said as he backed into a massive leather chair.

"If you had my clients you'd start at breakfast."

"I thought you did."

"Never on Mondays. How's Miss Carla?"

"Fine, thanks, and how's Miss, uh, what's her name?"

"Jane, smart-ass. Jane Ellen Vonner, and she's not only surviving life with me but seems to be having a ball and thankful to be so lucky. Finally found a woman who understands me." He scooped up a pile of bright red chips and crammed them in his mouth.

"Congratulations. When do I meet her?"

"We've been married for two years."

"I know, but I prefer to wait five. No sense rushing in when these gals have such a short shelf life."

"You come here to insult me?"

"Of course not." And Jake was being honest. Swapping insults with Harry Rex was a fool's game. He weighed over three hundred pounds and lumbered around town like an old bear, but his tongue was stunningly quick and vicious.

Jake said, "Tell me about Seth Hubbard."

Harry Rex laughed and sent debris flying over his desk. "Couldn't have happened to a bigger asshole. Why do you ask me?"

"Ozzie said you handled one of his divorces."

"I did, his second, maybe ten years ago, about the time you showed up here in town and started calling yourself a lawyer. Why should Seth concern you?"

"Well, before he killed himself, he wrote me a letter, and he also wrote a two-page will. Both arrived in the mail this morning."

Harry Rex took a sip of beer, narrowed his eyes, and thought about this. "You ever meet him?"

"Never."

"Lucky. You didn't miss a damned thing."

"Don't talk about my client like that."

"What'd the will say?"

"Can't tell you, and I can't probate until after the funeral."

"Who gets everything?"

"I can't say. I'll tell you on Wednesday."

"A two-page handwritten will prepared the day before the suicide. Sounds like a five-year lawsuit bonanza to me."

"I sure hope so."

"That'll keep you busy for a while."

"I need the work. What's the ol' boy got?"

Harry Rex shook his head while reaching for the hoagie. "Don't know," he said, then took a bite. The clear majority of Jake's friends and acquaintances preferred not to speak with a mouthful of food, but such social graces had never slowed down Harry Rex. "As I recall, and again it's been ten years, he owned a house up there on Simpson Road, with some acreage around it. The biggest asset was a sawmill and a lumber yard on Highway 21, near Palmyra. My client was, uh, Sybil, Sybil Hubbard, wife number two, and I think it was her second or third marriage."

After twenty years and countless cases, Harry Rex could still floor people with his recall. The juicier the details, the longer he remembered them.

A quick chug of beer, then he continued: "She was nice enough, not a bad-looking gal, and smart as hell. She worked in the lumber yard, ran the damned thing, really, and it was making good money when Seth decided to expand. He wanted to buy a lumber yard in Alabama and he started spending time over there. Turns out there was a secretary in the front office who had his attention. Everything blew up. Seth got caught with his pants down and Sybil hired me to scorch his ass. Scorch I did. I convinced the court to order the sale of the sawmill and lumber yard near Palmyra. The other one never made money. Got $200,000 for the sale, all of which went to my client. They also had a nice little condo on the Gulf near Destin. Sybil got that too. That's the skinny version of what happened, but the file is a foot thick. You can go through it if you want."

"Maybe later. No idea of what his current balance sheet looks like?"

"Nope. I lost track of the guy. He laid low after the divorce. The last time I talked to Sybil she was living on the beach and having fun with another husband, a much younger man, she claimed. She said there were rumors that Seth was back in the timber and lumber business, but she didn't know much." He swallowed hard and washed it all down. He burped loudly, without the slightest trace of hesitation or embarrassment, and continued, "You talked to his kids?"

"Not yet. You know them?"

"I did, at the time. They'll make your life interesting. Herschel is a real loser. His sister, what's her name?"

"Ramona Hubbard Dafoe."

"That's the one. She's a few years younger than Herschel and part of that north Jackson crowd. Neither one got along well with Seth, and I always got the impression he wasn't much of a father. They really liked Sybil, their second mom, and once it became apparent Sybil would win the divorce and make off with the money, they fell into her camp. Lemme guess—the old man left them nothing?"

Jake nodded but didn't say a word.

"Then they'll freak out and lawyer up. You got a good one brewin', Jake. Sorry I can't wedge in and get some of the fee."

"If you only knew."

A final bite of the hoagie, then the last of the chips. Harry Rex crushed the wrapper, the bag, the napkins, and tossed them somewhere under his desk, along with the empty beer bottle. He opened a drawer, withdrew a long black cigar and jammed it into the side of his mouth, unlit. He'd stopped smoking them but still went through ten a day, chewing and spitting. "I heard he hung himself. That true?"

"It is. He did a good job of planning things."

"Any idea why?"

"You've heard the rumors. He was dying of cancer. That's all we know. Who was his lawyer during the divorce?"

"He used Stanley Wade, a mistake."

"Wade? Since when does he do divorces?"

"Not anymore," Harry Rex said with a laugh. He smacked his lips and grew serious. "Look, Jake, hate to tell you this, but what happened ten years ago is of no significance whatsoever in this matter. I took all of Seth Hubbard's money, kept enough for myself, of course, gave the rest to my client, and closed the file. Whatever Seth did after divorce number two is none of my business." He waved his hand across the landfill on his desk and said, "This, however, is what my Monday is all about. If you wanna get a drink later, fine, but right now I'm swamped."

A drink later with Harry Rex usually meant something after 9:00 p.m. "Sure, we'll catch up," Jake said as he headed for the door, stepping over files.

"Say, Jake, is it safe to assume Hubbard renounced a previous will?"

"Yes."

"And was that previous will prepared by a firm somewhat larger than yours?"

"Yes."

"Then, if I were you I'd race to the courthouse and file the first petition to probate."

"My client wants me to wait until after the funeral."

"When's that?"

"Tomorrow at four."

"The courthouse closes at five. I'd be there. First is always better."

"Thanks Harry Rex."

"Don't mention it." He burped again and picked up a file.

Traffic was steady throughout the afternoon as the neighbors and church members and other friends made the solemn trek to Seth's home to deliver food, to commiserate, but mainly to nail down the gossip that was raging through the northeastern edge of Ford County. Most were politely turned away by Lettie who manned the front door, took the casseroles and cakes, accepted condolences, and said time and again that the family "was thankful but not taking company." Some, though, managed to step inside, into the den where they gawked at the furnishings and tried to absorb a piece of the life of their dear departed friend. They had never been there before, and Lettie had never heard of these people. Yet, they grieved. Such a tragic way to go. Did he really hang himself?

The family was hiding on the rear patio, where they regrouped around a picnic table and kept themselves away from the traffic. Their search of Seth's desk and drawers revealed nothing of benefit. When quizzed, Lettie claimed to know nothing, though they were doubtful. She answered their questions with soft, slow, thoughtful responses, and this made them even more suspicious. She served them lunch on the patio at 2:00 p.m., during a break in the visitation. They insisted on having a cloth on the picnic table, and linens and silver, though Seth's collection had been badly neglected for many years. Unspoken were their feelings that, at $5 an hour, the least Lettie could do was act like a real servant.

As she buzzed about, she overheard them discussing who would attend the funeral and who would not. Ian, for example, was in the middle of rescuing an enormous deal that could, quite possibly, affect the financial future of the entire state. Important meetings were on tap tomorrow and missing them might cause problems.

Herschel and Ramona grudgingly accepted the reality that they could not avoid the service, though at times Lettie thought they were jockeying for a way out. Ramona's health was fading by the hour, and she wasn't sure she could bear much more. Herschel's ex-wife would definitely not be there. He didn't want her there. She had never liked Seth and he had despised her. Herschel had two daughters, one in college in Texas and the other in high school in Memphis. The coed could not miss any more classes, and Herschel admitted she really wasn't that close to her grandfather. No kidding, thought Lettie as she removed some more dishes. The younger daughter was doubtful too.

Seth had one brother, their Uncle Ancil, a man they had never met and knew nothing about. According to what scarce family lore existed, Ancil had lied about his age and joined the Navy at sixteen or seventeen. He'd been wounded in the Pacific, survived, then drifted around the world at various jobs in the shipping business. Seth lost contact with his younger brother decades earlier and never mentioned him. There was no way to contact Ancil and clearly no reason to do so. He was probably as dead as Seth.

They talked about some old family relatives, none of whom they'd seen in years, none of whom they wanted to see now. What a sad, curious family, Lettie thought as she served them a selection of cakes. It was shaping up to be a small and quick funeral service.

"Let's get her outta here," Herschel said when Lettie returned to the kitchen. "We're getting ripped off at five bucks an hour."

"We? Since when are we paying her?" Ramona asked.

"Oh, she's on our clock now, one way or the other. Everything's coming out of the estate."

"I'm not cleaning the house, Herschel, are you?"

"Of course not."

Ian spoke up: "Let's play it cool, get through the funeral and all, tell her to clean the house, then we'll lock it up when we leave on Wednesday."

"Who tells her she's out of a job?" Ramona asked.

"I'll do it," Herschel said. "No big deal. She's just a maid."

"There's something fishy about her," Ian said. "Can't put my finger on it, but she acts like she knows something we don't, something important. Ya'll feel that way?"

"Definitely something in the air," Herschel said, pleased to reach a rare agreement with his brother-in-law.

But Ramona disagreed: "No, it's just the shock and the sadness. She's one of the few people Seth could tolerate, or could tolerate him, and she's sad he's gone. That, and she's about to lose her job."

"You think she knows she's about to be fired?" Herschel asked.

"I'm sure she's worried."

"She's just a housekeeper."

Lettie arrived home with a cake, one graciously given to her by Ramona. It was a flat, one-layer sheet cake coated with store-bought vanilla icing and laden with slices of toasted pineapple, without a doubt the least appealing of the half dozen arranged on Mr. Hubbard's kitchen counter. It had been delivered by a man from the church who'd asked Lettie, among other things, if the family planned to sell Seth's Chevrolet pickup truck. Lettie had no idea but promised to pass along the inquiry. She did not.

She had seriously considered tossing the cake into a ditch along the route home, but couldn't bring herself to be so wasteful. Her mother was battling diabetes and did not need another load of sugar, if she in fact wanted to sample the cake.

Lettie parked in the gravel drive and noted that Simeon's old truck was not there. She did not expect it since he'd been away for several days. She preferred him to be away, but she never knew from one day to the next. It was not a happy house in good times, and her husband rarely made things better.

The kids were still on the school bus somewhere, headed home. Lettie entered through the kitchen and placed the cake on the table. As always, she found Cypress in the den, watching television for the umpteenth hour in a row.

Cypress smiled and stretched her arms upward. "My baby," she said. "How was your day?"

Lettie leaned down and gave her a polite hug. "Pretty busy. How was yours?"

"Just me and the shows," Cypress replied. "How are the Hubbards dealin' with their loss, Lettie? Please sit down and talk to me."

Lettie turned off the television, sat on the stool next to her mother's wheelchair, and talked about her day. Not a dull moment as Herschel and the Dafoes arrived and walked through their childhood home, with their father gone for the first time. Then the traffic, the neighbors and food and the endless parade. Quite an exciting day altogether, as Lettie spun things, careful to avoid any hint of trouble. Cypress's blood pressure was barely held in check by a collection of medications, and it could spike at the slightest hint of trouble. At some point, and soon, Lettie would gently break the news that she was losing her job, but not now. There would be a better time later.

"And the funeral?" Cypress asked, stroking her daughter's arm. Lettie gave the details, said she planned to attend, and relished the fact that Mr. Hubbard insisted that blacks be allowed inside the church.

"Probably make you sit on the back row," Cypress said with a grin.

"Probably so. But I'll be there."

"Wish I could go with you."

"So do I." Because of her weight and lack of mobility, Cypress rarely left the house. She'd been living there for five years, and gaining weight and becoming less mobile by the month. Simeon stayed away for many reasons, not the least of which was Lettie's mother.

Lettie said, "Mrs. Dafoe sent us a cake. Would you like a small piece?"

"What kind?" Though she weighed a ton, Cypress could be a picky eater.

"Well, it's a pineapple something or other, not sure I've seen it before, but it might be worth a try. Would you like some coffee with it?"

"Yes, and just a small piece."

"Let's sit out back, Momma, and get some fresh air."

"I'd like that." The wheelchair could barely squeeze between the sofa and the television, and it fit tightly in the narrow hallway into the kitchen. It rubbed alongside the table, inched through the rear door, and with Lettie pushing gently it rolled onto the sagging wooden deck Simeon had thrown together years earlier.

When the weather was nice, Lettie liked a late afternoon coffee or iced tea outside, away from the noise and stuffiness of the cramped house. There were too many people for a small house with only three tiny bedrooms. Cypress had one. Lettie and Simeon—whenever he was home—shared another, usually with a grandchild or two. Their daughters somehow survived shoulder to shoulder in the third bedroom. Clarice, age sixteen, was in high school and had no children. Phedra, age twenty-one, had a kindergartner, a first grader, and no husband. Their younger son, Kirk, fourteen, slept on the sofa in the den. It was not at all uncommon for nieces and nephews to stay a few months while their parents sorted things out.

Cypress took a sip of instant coffee and picked at the cake with a fork. Slowly, she took a bite, and chewed and frowned. Lettie didn't like it either, so they drank their coffee and talked about the Hubbard family and how confused it was. They poked fun at white folks and their funerals, and how they got in such a hurry to bury their dead, often within two or three days of death. Black folks took their time.

"You seem distant, honey, what's on your mind?" Cypress asked softly.

The kids would be home shortly from school, then Phedra from work. This would be the last quiet moment until bedtime. Lettie took a deep breath and said, "I heard them talkin',

Momma, and they're gonna let me go. Probably this week, not long after the funeral."

Cypress shook her large round head and looked ready to cry. "But why?"

"No need for a housekeeper, I guess. They'll sell the house because neither of them wants it."

"Heavens."

"They can't wait to get their hands on his money. They never had time to come see him, but now they're circlin' like buzzards."

"White people. Do it ever' time."

"They think he paid me too much, so they're in a hurry to cut me off."

"How much he pay you?"

"Now Momma." Lettie had never told anyone in her family that Mr. Hubbard was paying $5 an hour, and in cash. Such a wage was indeed on the high end for domestic help in rural Mississippi, and Lettie knew better than to cause trouble. Her family might want a little extra. Her friends might talk. "Keep secrets, Lettie," Mr. Hubbard had told her. "Never talk about your money." Simeon, sorry as he was, would lose all motivation to bring home anything. His earnings were as erratic as his presence, and he needed no prompting to earn even less.

Lettie said, "I heard them refer to me as a servant."

"A servant? Ain't heard that in a long time."

"They're not nice people, Momma. I doubt if Mr. Hubbard was a good father, but his kids are sorry."

"And now they get all his money."

"I suppose. They're sure countin' on it."

"How much he got?"

Lettie shook her head and took a sip of cold coffee. "I have no idea. Not sure anybody does."

6

The parking lot of the Irish Road Christian Church was half-full when Ozzie's relatively unmarked car turned in to it at five minutes before four on Tuesday afternoon. There were no words or numbers painted boldly on the car—Ozzie preferred a lower profile—but one glance and you knew it was the high sheriff. A collection of antennas; a small round blue light on the dash, partially hidden; a big brown Ford with four doors and black wheels, same as virtually every other high sheriff in the state.

He parked it next to the red Saab, which was parked away from the other cars. Ozzie got out as Jake was getting out and together they crossed the parking lot. "Anything new?" Jake asked.

"Nothing," Ozzie said. He was wearing a dark suit with black cowboy boots. Jake, the same, minus the boots. "You?"

"Nothing. I guess the shit'll hit the fan tomorrow."

Ozzie laughed and said, "I can't wait."

The church, originally, was a redbrick chapel with a squatty steeple above a set of double front doors. Over time, though, the congregation had added the obligatory metal buildings—one beside the chapel that dwarfed it, and one behind it where the youth played basketball. On a small knoll nearby there was a cemetery under shady trees, a quiet and pretty place to be buried.

A few smokers were getting their last-minute drags, country men in old suits reluctantly worn. They were quick to speak to the sheriff. They nodded politely to Jake. Inside, there was a respectable crowd scattered throughout the dark-stained oak pews. The lights were low. An organist softly played a mournful dirge, priming the crowd for the sorrow to come. Seth's closed casket was draped in flowers and situated below the pulpit. His pallbearers sat grim-faced and shoulder to shoulder off to the left near the piano.

Jake and Ozzie sat alone on a back row and began looking around. Grouped together not far away were some black folks, five in total.

Ozzie nodded at them and whispered, "Green dress, that's Lettie Lang."

Jake nodded and whispered back, "Who are the others?"

Ozzie shook his head. "Can't tell from here."

Jake stared at the back of Lettie's head and tried to imagine the adventures they were about to share. He had yet to meet this woman, had never heard her name until the day before, but they were about to become well acquainted.

Lettie sat unknowing, her hands folded in her lap. That morning she had worked for three hours before being asked by Herschel to leave. On her way out, he informed her that her employment would be terminated as of 3:00 p.m. Wednesday, the following day. At that point, the house would be locked up and deserted until further orders from the court. Lettie had $400 in her checking account, one she kept away from Simeon, and she had $300 in a pickle jar hidden in the pantry. Beyond that, she was broke and had slim prospects for meaningful work. She had not spoken to her husband in almost three weeks. Occasionally, he would return home with a paycheck or some cash; usually, though, he was just drunk and needed to sleep it off.

Soon to be unemployed, with bills and people to feed, Lettie could have sat there listening to the organ and fretted over her future, but she did not. Mr. Hubbard had promised her more than once that when he died, and he knew his death was imminent, he would leave a little something for her. How little, or how much? Lettie could only dream. Four rows behind her, Jake thought to himself, If she only knew. She had no idea he was there, or why. She would later claim she recognized his name because of the Hailey trial, but she had never actually seen Mr. Brigance.

In the center, on the row directly in front of the casket, Ramona Dafoe sat with Ian to her left and Herschel to her right. None of their children, Seth's grandchildren, had been able to make the drive. Their lives were just too busy; not that their parents had pushed too hard. Behind them was a row of relatives so distant they had to introduce themselves in the parking lot, and their names were quickly forgotten. Seth Hubbard's parents had been dead for decades. His only sibling, Ancil, was long gone. There had never been much family to begin with and the years had decimated the rest.

Behind the family, and throughout the dim sanctuary, there were several dozen other mourners—employees of Seth's, friends, fellow church members. When Pastor Don McElwain stepped to the pulpit precisely at 4:00 p.m., he and everyone else knew the service would be brief. He led them in prayer and recited a quick obituary: Seth was born May 10, 1917, in Ford County, where he died on October 2, 1988. Preceded in death by parents so-and-so; two surviving children, some grandchildren, et cetera.

Jake spotted a familiar profile several rows up and to his left, a man in a nice suit. Same age, same law class. Stillman Rush, attorney-at-law, third-generation prick from a family of same, blue bloods from the big leagues of corporate and insurance law, or as big as they could possibly be in the rural South. Rush & Westerfield, the largest firm in north Mississippi, based in Tupelo with offices coming soon to a shopping center near you. Seth Hubbard mentioned the Rush firm in his letter to Jake, and also in his handwritten will, so there was little doubt Stillman Rush and the other two well-dressed gentlemen with him had come to check on their investment. Typically, the insurance boys worked in pairs. It took two to perform even the most mundane legal tasks: two to file papers in court; two to answer a docket call; two for an uncontested hearing; two to drive here and there; and, of course, two to jack up the billing and pad the file. Big law firms vigorously worshipped inefficiencies: more hours meant more fees.

But three? For a quick funeral out in the boonies? This was impressive, and exciting. It meant money. There was no doubt in Jake's hyperactive mind that the three had turned on their meters when they'd left their offices in Tupelo and were now sitting over there pretending to mourn at $200 an hour per man. According to Seth's final words, a Mr. Lewis McGwyre had drafted a will in September of 1987, and Jake figured he was one of the three. Jake did not know McGwyre, but then the firm had so many lawyers. Since they prepared the will, they naturally assumed they would probate it.

Tomorrow, he thought, they'll drive over again, at least two but maybe another trio, and they'll take their paperwork to the offices of the Chancery Court clerk, on the second floor of Jake's courthouse, and they'll smugly inform either Eva or Sara that they have arrived for the purposes of opening the estate of Mr. Seth Hubbard for probate. And either Eva or Sara will suppress a grin while appearing confused. Papers will be shuffled, questions asked, then a big surprise—you're a bit late, sirs. That estate has already been opened!

Either Eva or Sara will show them to the new filings, where they will gawk at the thin, handwritten will, one that specifically revoked and denounced the thick one they so cherished, and the war will begin. They will curse Jake Brigance, but once they settle down they will realize that the war could be profitable for all the lawyers.

Lettie wiped a tear and realized she was probably the only person crying.

In front of the lawyers were some business types, one of whom turned around and whispered something to Stillman Rush. Jake thought this might be one of the higher-ups who worked for Seth. He was particularly curious about Mr. Russell Amburgh, described in the handwritten will as once the vice president of Seth's holding company and the man with the knowledge of the assets and liabilities.

Mrs. Nora Baines sang three stanzas of "The Old Rugged Cross," a somber, surefire tearjerker at any funeral, but at Seth's it failed to provoke emotion. Pastor McElwain read from Psalms and dwelled on the wisdom of Solomon, then two teenage boys with pimples and a guitar strummed and hummed through something contemporary, a strained song Seth would not have appreciated. Ramona finally broke down and was comforted by Ian. Herschel just stared at the floor in front of the casket, never blinking, never moving. Another woman sobbed loudly in response.

Seth's cruel plan was to withhold knowledge of his last will until after the funeral. In his letter to Jake, his exact words were: "Do not mention my last will and testament until after the funeral. I want my family to be forced to go through all the rituals of mourning before they realize they get nothing. Watch them fake it—they're very good at it. They have no love for me." As the service dragged on, it became apparent that there was little faking going on. What was left of his family didn't care enough to even fake it. What a sad way to go, thought Jake.

At Seth's instructions, there were no eulogies. No one spoke but the pastor, though it was easy to get the impression there might be no volunteers if they opened up the mike. The pastor finished with a marathon of a prayer, one obviously designed to burn some clock. Twenty-five minutes after he started, he dismissed them with the invitation to walk next door to the cemetery for the interment. Outside, Jake managed to dodge Stillman Rush and the lawyers. Instead, he bumped into the nearest man in a business suit and said, "Excuse me, but I'm looking for a Russell Amburgh."

The man politely pointed and said, "Right there."

Russell Amburgh was standing ten feet away, lighting a cigarette, and he heard Jake's inquiry. The two shook hands grimly and gave their names. Jake said, "Could I have a moment alone?"

Mr. Amburgh half shrugged and said softly, "Sure, what's up?"

The crowd was drifting slowly in the general direction of the cemetery. Jake had no plans to watch the burial; he was on another mission. When he and Amburgh were far enough away not to be heard, he said, "I'm a lawyer in Clanton, never met Mr. Hubbard, but I received a letter from him yesterday. A letter, along with his last will and testament in which he names you as his executor. It is imperative that we talk as soon as possible."

Amburgh stopped cold and jammed the cigarette into a corner of his mouth. He glared at Jake, then glanced around to make sure they were alone. "What kinda will?" he said, exhaling smoke.

"Handwritten, last Saturday. He was clearly contemplating his death."

"Then he was probably out of his mind," Amburgh said, sneering, the first rattle of a saber in the coming war.

Jake had not expected this. "We'll see. I guess that will be determined later."

"I was a lawyer once, Mr. Brigance, a long time ago before I found honest work. I know the game."

Jake kicked a rock and looked around. The first mourners were nearing the front entrance of the cemetery. "Can we talk?"

"What's in the will?"

"I can't tell you now but I can tell you tomorrow."

Amburgh cocked his head back and glared down along his nose. "How much do you know about Seth's business?"

"Let's say nothing. In his will he writes that you have a good knowledge of his assets and liabilities."

Another draw, another sneer. "There are no liabilities, Mr. Brigance. Only assets, and plenty."

"Please, let's meet and have a chat. All secrets are about to be revealed, Mr. Amburgh, I just need to know where it's going. Under the terms of his will, you're the executor and I'm the lawyer for the estate."

"That doesn't sound right. Seth hated the lawyers in Clanton."

"Yes, he made that very clear. If we can meet in the morning, I'll be happy to show you a copy of his will and shed some light."

Amburgh started walking again and Jake tagged along, for a few steps anyway. As they approached the cemetery, Ozzie was waiting by the gate. Amburgh stopped again and said, "I live in

Temple. There's a café on Highway 52, west of town. Meet me there at 7:30 in the morning."

"Okay. What's the name of the café?"

"The Café."

"Got it."

Amburgh disappeared without another word. Jake looked at Ozzie, shook his head in disbelief, then pointed to the parking lot. Both of them eased away from the cemetery. They'd had enough of Seth Hubbard for one day. Their farewell was complete.

Twenty minutes later, at exactly 4:55 p.m., Jake jogged into the offices of the Chancery Court clerk and smiled at Sara. "Where you been?" she snapped, waiting.

"It's not even five o'clock," he shot back as he zipped open his briefcase.

"Yes, but we stop working at four, on Tuesdays anyway. Five on Monday. Three on Wednesday and Thursday. On Friday you're lucky if we show up." The woman talked nonstop and had a quick tongue. After twenty years of daily give-and-take with a bunch of lawyers, she had honed her retorts and one-liners.

Jake laid the papers on the counter in front of her and said, "I need to open the estate of Mr. Seth Hubbard."

"Testate or intestate?"

"Oh, he has a will, more than one. That's where the fun's coming from."

"Didn't he just kill himself?"

"You know damned well he just killed himself because you work in this courthouse where rumors fly and gossip is created and nothing is secret."

"I'm offended," she said, stamping the petition. She flipped a few pages, smiled and said, "Ooh, nice, a handwritten will. A boon to the legal profession."

"You got it."

"Who gets everything?"

"My lips are sealed." As Jake bantered he pulled more papers from his briefcase.

"Well, Mr. Brigance, your lips may be sealed but this court file certainly is not." She stamped something dramatically and said, "It is now officially a public record, under the laws of this great state, unless of course you have a written motion requesting the file to be sealed."

"I do not."

"Oh good, so we can talk about all the dirt. There is some dirt, right?"

"Don't know. I'm still digging. Look, Sara, I need a favor."

"Anything you want, baby."

"This is a race to the courthouse and I've just won. Sometime soon, perhaps tomorrow, I expect two or three pompous-ass lawyers in dark suits to show up and hand over their version of a petition to open Mr. Hubbard's estate. More than likely they'll be from Tupelo. There's another will, you see."

"I love it."

"So do I. Anyway, you're not required to inform them they've just finished second, but it might be fun to watch their faces. Whatta you think?"

"I can't wait."

"Great, show them the court file, have a laugh, then call me with a full report. But please, bury this until tomorrow."

"You got it, Jake. This could be fun."

"Well, if things unfold the way I expect, this case could keep us amused for the next year."

As soon as he left, Sara read the handwritten will that was attached to Jake's petition. She summoned the other clerks to her desk where they read it too. A black lady from Clanton said she'd never heard of Lettie Lang. No one seemed to know Seth Hubbard. They chatted awhile, but it was now after 5:00 p.m. and everyone had places to go. The file was put in its place, the lights were turned off, and the clerks quickly forgot things related to work. They would resume their speculation the following day and get to the bottom of the matter.

Had the petition and will been filed during the morning, the entire courthouse would have been buzzing by noon; the entire town by late afternoon. Now, though, the gossip would have to wait, but not for long.

Simeon Lang was drinking but he was not drunk, a distinction that was often blurred but generally understood by his family. Drinking meant behavior that was somewhat controlled and not threatening. It meant he was slowly sipping beer with glassy eyes and a thick tongue. Being drunk meant harrowing times with people running from the house and hiding in the trees. And, to his credit, he was often cold sober, the preferred state, even for Simeon.

After three weeks on the road, hauling loads of scrap iron throughout the Deep South, he had returned with a paycheck intact, tired and clear-eyed. He offered no explanation of where he had been; he never did. He tried to appear content, even domesticated, but after a few hours of bumping into other people, and of listening to Cypress, and of deflecting the rejections of his wife, he ate a sandwich and moved outdoors with his beer, to a spot under a tree beside the house where he could sit in peace and watch the occasional car go by.

Returning was always a struggle. Out there, on the open road, he would dream for hours of a new life somewhere, always a better life alone and unbothered. He'd been tempted a thousand times to keep driving, to drop his freight at its destination and never slow down. His father left them when he was a kid, left a pregnant wife and four children and was never heard from. For days Simeon and his older brother sat on the porch, hiding tears, waiting. As he grew, he hated his father, still did, but now he too was feeling the urge to run away. His kids were much older; they would survive.

On the road he often asked himself why he felt the pull of home. He hated living in a cramped rental house with his mother-in-law, two rotten grandkids he didn't ask for, and a wife who nagged him for more out of life. Lettie had threatened divorce a hundred times in the past twenty years, and to him it was a miracle they were together. You wanna split, then let's have a split, he said as he took a sip. But he'd said that a hundred times too.

It was almost dark when she stepped out of the house onto the rear patio and slowly made her way across the grass to his tree. He sat in one of two mismatched lawn chairs, his feet propped on an old milk crate, his beer cooler next to him. He offered her the other chair but she declined.

"How long you home?" she asked softly as she stared at the road, like him.

"I just got home and you're ready for me to leave."

"I didn't mean it that way, Simeon. Just curious, that's all."

He wasn't about to answer the question so he took another sip. They were rarely alone together, and when they were they couldn't remember how to talk. A car passed slowly on the county road and they watched it as though fascinated. Finally, she said, "I'm probably gonna lose my job tomorrow. I told you Mr. Hubbard killed himself, and his family don't want me around past tomorrow."

Simeon had mixed feelings about this. It made him feel superior because once again he would be the principal breadwinner, the head of the house. He despised the way Lettie took on airs when she was earning more than he was. He resented her bitching and chirping when he was out of work. Even though she was only a housekeeper, she could get arrogant when acting like a white man trusted her so thoroughly. But, the family needed the money, and losing her wages would inevitably lead to trouble.

He struggled to say "I'm sorry."

There was another long, silent gap. They could hear voices and noise from inside the house. "Any word from Marvis?" he asked.

She dropped her head and said, "No, it's been two weeks and no letter."

"Did you write him?"

"I write him every week, Simeon, you know that. When's the last time you wrote him?"

Simeon seethed but held his fire. He was proud of himself for coming home sober, and he wouldn't ruin it with a fight. Marvis

Lang, age twenty-eight, two years in the pen with at least ten to go. Drug trafficking, assault with a deadly weapon.

A car approached and slowed, then slowed some more as if the driver wasn't sure. It moved a few feet, then turned in to their driveway. There was enough sunlight left to reveal it to be an odd make, definitely foreign, and red in color. The engine was turned off and a young white man got out, alone. He was wearing a white shirt with a loosened tie. He carried nothing, and after walking a few feet seemed uncertain of where he was.

"Over here," Simeon called out, and the young man stiffened as if scared. He had not seen them under the tree. He proceeded cautiously across the small front yard. "Looking for Ms. Lettie Lang," he said loud enough for them to hear.

"I'm over here," she said as he came into view. He walked to within ten feet and said, "Hello, my name is Jake Brigance. I'm a lawyer in Clanton and I need to speak to Lettie Lang."

"You were at the funeral today," she said.

"I was, yes."

Simeon reluctantly climbed to his feet and the three exchanged awkward handshakes. Simeon offered him a beer, then returned to his seat. Jake declined the beer, though he would have enjoyed one. He was, after all, there on business.

Lettie said, without being edgy, "I'm sure you're not just passin' through our little corner of the world."

"No, no I'm not."

"Brigance," Simeon said, sipping. "Didn't you represent Carl Lee Hailey?"

Aw, the old icebreaker, at least with black folks. "I did," Jake said modestly.

"I thought so. Good job. Great job."

"Thanks. Look, I'm actually here on business, and, well, I need to speak with Lettie here in private. No offense or anything, but I have to tell her something confidential."

"What is it?" she asked, confused.

"Why is it private?" Simeon asked.

"Because the law says it is," Jake replied, fudging a bit. The law had nothing to do with this situation. In fact, as he muddled through this encounter he began to realize that his big news perhaps wasn't so confidential after all. There was no doubt Lettie would tell her husband everything before Jake pulled out of the driveway. The last will and testament of Seth Hubbard was now a public record and would be scrutinized by every lawyer in town within twenty-four hours. Where was the privacy, the confidentiality?

Simeon angrily tossed a beer can against the tree, sending a line of foam across the trunk. He bolted to his feet, growling, "All right, all right," as he kicked the milk crate. He reached into the cooler, grabbed another beer, and stomped away, mumbling and cursing under his breath. The shadows consumed him as he moved deeper into the trees, no doubt watching and listening.

Lettie, almost whispering, said, "Very sorry about that, Mr. Brigance."

"No problem. Look, Ms. Lang, there is a very important matter we need to discuss as soon as possible, preferably tomorrow in my office. It's about Mr. Hubbard and his last will and testament."

Lettie bit her bottom lip as she stared wild-eyed at Jake. Tell me more.

Jake continued: "The day before he died, he made a new will, one that he dropped in the mail so I would receive it after his death. It appears to be a valid will, but I'm sure it will be contested by his family."

"Am I in his will?"

"You certainly are. In fact, he left a sizable portion of his estate to you."

"Oh God."

"Yes. He wants me to be the lawyer for his estate, and I'm sure that will be contested too. That's why we need to talk."

Her right hand covered her mouth as she mumbled, "Oh my Lord."

Jake looked at the house where the light from its windows cut through the darkness. A shadow moved beyond it, probably Simeon circling around. Jake had the sudden desire to hop in the old Saab and cut a trail quickly back to civilization.

She asked, nodding, "Should I tell him?"

"That's up to you. I would have included him but I've heard stories about his drinking. Didn't know what shape he's in right now. But, to be honest, Ms. Lang, he's your husband and he should come with you tomorrow. That is, if he's in good shape."

"He'll be in good shape, I promise."

Jake handed her a business card and said, "Anytime tomorrow afternoon. I'll be in my office waiting."

"We'll be there, Mr. Brigance. And thank you for comin' here."

"It's very important, Ms. Lang, and I felt like I needed to meet you. We could be in for a long, hard fight together."

"I'm not sure I understand."

"I know. I'll explain it tomorrow."

"Thank you, Mr. Brigance."

"Good night."

7

After a quick, late supper of grilled cheese and tomato soup, Jake and Carla cleared the table and cleaned the dishes (there was no dishwasher), and eventually settled in the den, which began where the kitchen left off, some six feet away from the dining table. Three years (plus) in tight living quarters required a constant reassessment of priorities and attitudes, along with a vigilance against edginess. Hanna helped tremendously. Small children care little for the material things that so impress adults; as long as both parents are doting, little else matters. Carla helped her with spelling and Jake read her stories, and as they tag-teamed through the evening they also caught up with the daily papers and the cable news. At 8:00 p.m. on the dot, Carla gave her a bath, and thirty minutes later Hanna was tucked snugly into bed by both parents.

Alone at last and wrapped together under a quilt on the rickety sofa, Carla said, "Okay, what's up?"

Jake, flipping through a sports magazine, replied, "What do you mean 'What's up?'"

"Don't play dumb. Something's up. A new case maybe? A new client who can pay a decent fee, or perhaps even a huge fee that might rescue us from poverty? Please."

Jake flung the quilt onto the floor and jumped to his feet. "Well, as a matter of fact, my dear, there's a good chance we've just stiff-armed poverty."

"I knew it. I can always tell when you sign up a good car wreck. You get twitchy."

"It's not a car wreck." Jake was thumbing through his briefcase. He pulled out a file and handed her some papers. "It's a suicide."

"Oh that."

"Yes, that. Last night I told you about the unfortunate demise of Mr. Seth Hubbard, but what I didn't tell you was that before he died he did a quickie will, mailed it to my office, and designated me as the lawyer for his estate. I probated it late this afternoon. It's now public record, so I can talk about it."

"And this is the guy you never met?"

"Correct."

"A guy you never met but you went to his funeral this afternoon?"

"You got it."

"Why did he pick you?"

"Brilliant reputation. Just read the will, please."

One glance and she said, "But it's handwritten."

"No kidding?"

Jake re-entangled himself with his wife on the sofa and watched her intently as she read the two-page will. Slowly, her mouth dropped open, her eyes widened, and when she finished she looked at Jake in disbelief and mumbled, "'Perish in pain'? What a jerk."

"Evidently so. Never met the man, but Harry Rex handled his second divorce and he doesn't think much of Mr. Hubbard."

"Most people don't think much of Harry Rex."

"This is true."

"Who's Lettie Lang?"

"His black housekeeper."

"Oh my gosh, Jake. This is scandalous."

"I sure hope so."

"Does he have money?"

"Did you read the part where he says, 'My estate is substantial'? Ozzie knew him and seems to agree. I'm driving to Temple early in the morning to meet with Mr. Russell Amburgh, the executor. I'll be a lot smarter by noon."

She sort of waved the two sheets of paper and asked, "Is this valid? Can you make a will like this?"

"Oh yes. Wills and Estates 101, taught for fifty years by

Professor Robert Weems at the Ole Miss Law School. He gave me an A. As long as every word is written by the deceased, and signed and dated, it's a real will. I'm sure it'll be contested by his two kids, but that's where the fun starts."

"Why would he leave virtually everything to his black house-keeper?"

"I guess he liked the way she cleaned his house. I don't know. Maybe she did more than clean."

"Meaning?"

"He was sick, Carla, dying of lung cancer. I suspect Lettie Lang cared for him in a lot of ways. Obviously, he was fond of her. His two kids will lawyer up and howl about undue influ-ence. They'll claim she got too close to him, whispered in the old guy's ear, and maybe more. It'll be up to the jury."

"A jury trial?"

Jake was smiling, dreaming. "Oh yes."

"Wow. Who knows about this?"

"I filed the petition at five this afternoon, so the gossip hasn't started. But I reckon by nine in the morning the courthouse will be alive."

"This'll blow the top off the courthouse, Jake. A white man with money cuts out his family, leaves it all to his black house-keeper, then hangs himself. Are you kidding?"

He was not. She read the will again as her husband closed his eyes and thought about the trial. When she finished, she placed the two sheets of paper on the floor, then glanced around the room. "Just curious, dear, but how are your fees determined in a case like this? Forgive me for asking." She sort of waved a loose arm as she took in the narrow room, the flea market furni-ture, the cheap bookshelves sagging and overloaded, the fake Persian rug, the secondhand curtains, the stack of magazines piled on the floor, the general shabbiness of renters with better taste but no way to prove it.

"What? You want nicer digs? Maybe a duplex, or a double-wide?"

"Don't start with me."

"The fees could be substantial, not that I've considered the subject."

"Substantial?"

"Sure. The fees are based on actual work, billable hours, something we know so little about. The attorney for the estate gets to punch the clock each day and actually get paid for his time. This is unheard-of for us. All fees must be approved by the judge, who in this case is our dear friend, the Honorable Reuben Atlee, and since he knows we're starving he'll probably be in a generous mood. A big estate, a pile of money, a hotly contested will, and we just might avoid bankruptcy."

"A pile of money?"

"Just a figure of speech, dear. We shouldn't get greedy at this point."

"Don't patronize me," she said as she looked into the twinkling eyes of a hungry lawyer.

"Right." But Carla was mentally packing boxes and preparing to move. She had made the same mistake a year earlier when the law offices of Jake Brigance attracted a young couple whose newborn died in a Memphis hospital. A promising case of medical malpractice wilted under the scrutiny of expert review, and Jake had no choice but to settle for nuisance value.

She asked, "And you went to see Lettie Lang?"

"I did. She lives out from Box Hill in a community called Little Delta; not too many white folks around. Her husband is a drunk who comes and goes. I didn't go in the house but I got the impression it's crowded in there. I checked the land records; they don't own the place. It's a cheap little rental, similar—"

"Similar to this dump, right?"

"Similar to our home. Probably built by the same hack, who no doubt went bankrupt. But, anyway, there are only three of us here and probably a dozen in Lettie's house."

"Is she nice?"

"Nice enough. We didn't talk long. I got the impression she's a fairly typical black woman for these parts, with a houseful of kids, a part-time husband, a minimum-wage job, a hard life."

"That's pretty harsh."

"Yes, but it's also pretty accurate."

"Is she attractive?"

Under the quilt, Jake began massaging her right calf. He thought for a moment, then said, "I couldn't really tell; it was getting dark in a hurry. She's about forty-five, seemed to be in fairly good shape, certainly not unattractive. Why do you ask? You think sex could be behind Mr. Hubbard's last will and testament?"

"Sex? Who mentioned sex?"

"That's exactly what you're thinking. Did she screw her way into his will?"

"All right, sure, that's what I'm thinking, and that's what the entire town will be buzzing about by noon tomorrow. This has sex written all over it. He was a dying man and she was his caregiver. Who knows what they did?"

"You have a filthy mind. I love it."

His hand moved to her thigh but there it was blocked. The phone rang, startling both of them. Jake walked to the kitchen, answered it, then hung up. "It's Nesbit, outside," he said to her. He found a cigar and a box of matches and left the house. At the end of the short driveway, by the mailbox, he lit the cigar and blew a cloud of smoke into the cool, crisp evening air. A minute later, a patrol car turned onto the street and rolled to a quiet stop near Jake. Deputy Mike Nesbit grappled his overweight self out of the car, said, "Evenin' Jake," and lit a cigarette.

"Evenin' Mike."

Both blowing smoke, they leaned against the hood of the patrol car. Nesbit said, "Ozzie's found nothin' on Hubbard. He ran a search through Jackson and came up dry. Looks like the ol' boy kept his toys somewhere else; ain't no records in this state except for his house, cars, acreage, and the lumber yard up near Palmyra. Beyond that, not a trace. I mean nothin'. No bank accounts. No corporations. No LLCs. No partnerships. A couple of insurance policies where you'd expect to find them, but that's all. Rumors that he did business in other states, but we ain't got that far yet."

Jake nodded and smoked. By now, he was not surprised. "And Amburgh?"

"Russell Amburgh is from Foley, Alabama, way down south close to Mobile. He was a lawyer there until he got himself disbarred about fifteen years ago. Commingling client funds, but no indictment. No criminal record. Freed from the legal profession, he went into the timber business and it's safe to assume that's where he met Seth Hubbard. As far as we can tell, everything's on the up-and-up. Not sure why he moved to a dead-end place like Temple."

"I'm driving to Temple in the morning. I'll ask him."

"Good."

An elderly couple walked by with an elderly poodle. They exchanged pleasantries without slowing down. When they were gone, Jake blew more smoke and asked, "Any luck with Ancil Hubbard, the brother?"

"Not a peep. Nothin'."

"No surprise."

"It's funny. I've lived here all my life, never heard of Seth Hubbard. My dad's eighty, lived here all his life, and he's never heard of Seth Hubbard."

"There are thirty-two thousand people in this county, Mike. You can't know all of them."

"Ozzie does."

They had a quick laugh. Nesbit flipped his cigarette butt into the street and stretched his back. "Guess I need to get home, Jake."

"Thanks for stopping by. I'll talk to Ozzie tomorrow."

"You do that. See ya."

He found Carla in the empty bedroom, sitting in a chair facing the window with a view of the street. The room was dark. He entered quietly, then stopped, and when she knew he was listening she said, "I'm so sick of seeing police cars in front of my house, Jake."

He took a deep breath and a step closer. This conversation was too familiar, and a wrong word could send it spiraling down. "So am I," he said softly.

"What did he want?" she asked.

"Not much, just some background on Seth Hubbard. Ozzie's been asking around but hasn't found much."

"He couldn't call you tomorrow? Why does he have to drive over and park in front of our house so everyone can see that the Brigances can't make it through the night without the police showing up again?"

Questions with no answers.

Jake bit his tongue and eased out of the room.

8

Russell Amburgh hid behind a newspaper in a booth in the rear of The Café. He was not a regular, nor was he well known in the small town of Temple. He had moved there because of a woman, his third wife, and they stayed to themselves. He also worked for a man who valued discretion and secrecy, and this suited Amburgh fine.

He secured the booth a few minutes after 7:00, ordered some coffee, and started reading. On the subject of Seth Hubbard's will or wills, he knew nothing. Though he had worked for Mr. Hubbard for almost a decade, he knew little about his private life. He could put his finger on most of the man's assets, certainly not all, but he had learned early on that his boss loved secrets. And he liked to play games, and hold grudges, and keep people guessing. The two had traveled extensively together throughout the Southeast as Mr. Hubbard pieced his holdings together, but they had never been close. No one was close to Seth Hubbard.

Jake walked in at exactly 7:30 and found Amburgh back in a booth. The Café was half-full, and Jake, the foreigner, got some looks as he walked through it. He and Amburgh shook hands and exchanged pleasantries. Based on their conversation the day before, Jake was expecting a cool reception and grudging cooperation, though he was not overly concerned with Mr. Amburgh's initial reactions. Jake had been directed by Seth Hubbard to do a job, and, if he was challenged, the court would stand behind him. Amburgh, though, seemed relaxed and sufficiently receptive. After a few minutes of football and weather, he got down to business. "Has the will been probated?" he asked.

"Yes, as of 5:00 p.m. yesterday. I left the funeral and hurried back to the courthouse in Clanton."

"Did you bring me a copy of it?"

"I did," Jake said, without reaching for a pocket. "You are named as executor. It is now a public record, so you can have a copy."

Amburgh showed both palms and asked, "Am I a beneficiary?"

"No."

He nodded grimly and Jake could not tell if this was expected. "I get nothing in the will?" Amburgh asked.

"Nothing. Is this a surprise?"

Amburgh swallowed hard and glanced around. "No," he said unconvincingly. "Not really. With Seth, there are no surprises."

"You're not surprised he killed himself?"

"Not at all, Mr. Brigance. The last twelve months have been a nightmare. Seth just got tired of the pain. He knew he was dying. We knew he was dying. So no, no real surprise."

"Wait till you read the will."

A waitress blew by, barely slowing long enough to top off both cups of coffee. Amburgh took a sip and said, "Tell me your story, Mr. Brigance. How did you know Seth?"

"Never met him," Jake said. He rattled off the short version of why he was now sitting at the table. Amburgh listened intently. He had a small round head that was slick on top, and his nervous habit was to start above the eyebrows with his right hand and sweep back, as if the few thick strands of dark hair needed to be continually plastered down. He wore a golf shirt, old khakis, and a light windbreaker, and looked more like a retiree than the businessman from the funeral.

Jake was saying, "Is it safe to assume you're his most trusted lieutenant?"

"No, not at all. In fact, I'm not sure why Seth wants me involved in this. I can think of others who were closer." A long sip of coffee, then, "Seth and I didn't always get along. Several times I thought about leaving. The more money he made, the more risks he took. More than once I became convinced Seth was determined to flame out in some glorious bankruptcy, with the loot hidden offshore, of course. He became fearless, and it was frightening."

"Now that we're on the subject, let's talk about Seth's money."

"Sure. I'll tell you what I know, but I don't know everything."

"Okay," Jake said calmly, as if they were back on the weather. For almost forty-eight hours he had been consumed with the burning question of what did Seth possess? Finally, he was about to hear it. He had no legal pad, no pen at the ready, just a cup of black coffee before him.

Amburgh glanced around again, but no one was listening. "What I'm about to tell you is not well known. It's not confidential, but Seth did a good job of keeping things hidden."

"It's all about to come out, Mr. Amburgh."

"I know." He took a sip of coffee as if he needed fuel, then leaned in a bit lower. "Seth had a lot of money, and he made it all in the past ten years. After his second divorce, he was bitter, angry at the world, broke, and also determined to make some money. He really liked his second wife, and after she ditched him he wanted revenge. To Seth, revenge meant making more money than what she got in the divorce."

"I know her lawyer very well."

"The big fat guy, what's his name?"

"Harry Rex Vonner."

"Harry Rex. I've heard Seth cuss him a few times."

"He's not the only one."

"That's what I hear. Anyway, Seth got his house and land, and he borrowed heavily against them to buy a big lumber mill near Dothan, Alabama. I was working there, buying timber, and that's how I came to know Seth. He got it cheap, good timing. This was late 1979, the price of plywood spiked, and we were doing pretty well. We had a good hurricane season, lots of damage, lots of demand for plywood and lumber. He borrowed against the mill and bought a furniture factory near Albany, Georgia. The place made these oversized rocking chairs you see on the front porches of Griddle restaurants, coast-to-coast. Seth negotiated a contract with the chain and overnight they couldn't make the rocking chairs fast enough. He pledged the stock, borrowed some more, and bought another furniture factory near Troy, Alabama. About that time he found a banker in Birmingham who was trying to grow his small bank into something much bigger, and he was aggressive. He and Seth were on the same page, and the deals came one after the other. More factories, more lumber mills, more timber leases. Seth had a nose for sniffing out businesses that were undervalued or in trouble, and his banker rarely said no. I warned him against so much debt, but he was too reckless to listen. He had something to prove. He bought an airplane, kept it in Tupelo so no one around here would know, and stayed in the air."

"Does this have a happy ending?"

"Oh yes. Over the past ten years or so, Seth bought about three dozen companies, primarily furniture plants in the South, some of which he moved to Mexico, but also lumber yards and sawmills, along with thousands of acres of timber. All with borrowed money. I mentioned the one banker in Birmingham, but there were others. The bigger he got the easier it became to borrow more. As I said, it was at times frightening, but the guy never got burned. He didn't sell a single thing he bought, just held on, looking for the next deal. Deals and debts were like an addiction to Seth. Some men gamble, some drink, some chase women. Seth loved the smell of somebody else's money as he bought another company. He also liked women.

"Then, sadly, he got sick. It was about a year ago when the doctors told him he had lung cancer. He was ripping along at full speed until he went to the doctor. They told him he had a year, max. Needless to say, he was devastated. Without consulting anyone, he decided to sell out. A few years ago, we found the Rush law firm in Tupelo, and Seth finally had some guys he could trust. He hated lawyers and fired them as fast as he hired them. But the Rush firm convinced him to consolidate everything into one holding company. Last November, he sold the holding company to a leveraged buyout group in Atlanta for

$55 million. He happily repaid his debts, to the tune of $35 million."

"He netted twenty?"

"He netted twenty, give or take. There were a few other loose ends, including me. I had some stock in the holding company and so I walked away in good shape. I retired at the end of last year. I don't know what Seth has done with the money since then, probably buried it in the backyard. Plus, he accumulated other assets that he kept out of the holding company. There's a cabin in the mountains of North Carolina, and quite a few other assets. There's probably an offshore bank account or two."

"Probably?"

"I can't say for certain, Mr. Brigance. Just things I've heard over the years. As I said, Seth Hubbard loved his secrets."

"Well, Mr. Amburgh, you as his executor and I as his lawyer have the job of tracking down all assets."

"Shouldn't be too hard. We'll need access to his office."

"And where is that?"

"At the lumber yard near Palmyra. That was his only office. There's a secretary there, Arlene, who runs the show. I spoke to her Sunday night and suggested that she keep everything locked up until she hears from the lawyers."

Jake took another sip of coffee and tried to digest it all. "Twenty million bucks, huh? I can't think of anyone else in Ford County with that kinda money."

"I can't help you there, Mr. Brigance. I've never lived there. I assure you, though, there's no one here in Milburn County worth even a fraction of that."

"It's the rural South."

"Indeed it is. That's the greatness of Seth's story. He woke up one day at the age of sixty and said I'm broke, tired of being broke, and damned if I'm not gonna make something. He got lucky on his first two deals, then discovered the beauty of using other people's money. He mortgaged his own house and land a dozen times. Talk about brass balls."

The waitress delivered oatmeal for Mr. Amburgh and scrambled eggs for Jake. As they sprinkled salt and sugar, Amburgh asked, "Did he cut out his kids?"

"He did."

A smile, a nod, no surprise.

"You expected this?" Jake asked.

"I expect nothing, Mr. Brigance, and nothing surprises me," he replied smugly.

"I have a surprise for you," Jake said. "He cut out both of his kids, both of his ex-wives, who, by the way, are not entitled to anything, and he cut out everybody else except for his long-lost brother, Ancil, who's probably dead, but if not gets 5 percent, his church, also on board at 5, which leaves a grand total of 90 percent left to his black housekeeper of three years, one Lettie Lang."

Amburgh stopped chewing as his jaws sagged and his eyes squinted. Deep wrinkles broke out across his forehead.

"Don't tell me you're not surprised," Jake said, victorious, then tossed back a forkful of eggs.

Amburgh took a deep breath and reached out an empty hand. Jake pulled a copy of the will out of a pocket and gave it to him. The deep wrinkles hardened as both pages were read. He began to shake his head in disbelief. He read it a second time, then folded it and placed it aside.

"Did you by chance know Lettie Lang?" Jake asked.

"Never met her. I've never seen Seth's home, Mr. Brigance. Never heard him say a word about it, really, or about anyone who worked there. Seth kept things in compartments, most of which were off-limits to everyone. Do you know this woman?"

"I met her yesterday for the first time. She'll be in my office this afternoon."

With his fingertips, Amburgh slowly pushed the platter and bowl away; breakfast was over, the appetite gone. "Why would he do this, Mr. Brigance?"

"I was thinking of asking you the same question."

"Well, it obviously makes no sense, and that's why this will is in serious trouble. He was out of his mind. You can't make a valid will if you lack testamentary capacity."

"Of course not, but little is clear right now. On the one hand, he seems to have planned his death in meticulous detail, as if he knew exactly what he was doing. On the other hand, leaving it all to his housekeeper is hard to figure."

"Unless she influenced him."

"I'm sure that'll be argued."

Amburgh reached for a pocket and said, "Mind if I smoke?"

"No."

He lit a menthol and flicked ashes into his oatmeal. His mind was spinning, nothing made sense. Finally, he said, "I'm not sure I have the stomach for this, Mr. Brigance. I may be named as the executor, but that doesn't mean I have to serve."

"You said you were a lawyer once. You sound like it."

"In the day, I was a small-town hack, same as a million others. Over in Alabama, but probate laws don't vary much from state to state."

"You're right—you don't have to serve as executor."

"Who would want to get involved in this mess?"

Me, for one, thought Jake, but he bit his tongue. The waitress cleared the table and topped off the coffee cups. Amburgh read the will again and lit another cigarette. When he'd emptied his lungs, he said, "Okay, Mr. Brigance, allow me to think out loud. Seth mentions a prior will, one prepared last year by the Rush law firm in Tupelo. I know those guys and it's safe to assume that will is much thicker, much smarter, and put together in such a way as to take advantage of proper estate tax planning, gift exclusions, generation-skipping transfers, the whole nine yards, okay, whatever is available to protect the estate and legally avoid as much in taxes as possible. Are you with me?"

"Yes."

"Then, at the last minute, Seth prepares this crude document that revokes the proper will, leaves virtually everything to his black housekeeper, and guarantees that much of what he's trying to give away will be eaten up in estate taxes. Still with me?"

"About 50 percent will go for taxes," Jake said.

"Half, blown away just like that. Does that sound like a man who's thinking clearly, Mr. Brigance?"

It did not, though Jake was not ready to yield an inch. He said, "I'm sure that argument will be made in court, Mr. Amburgh. My job is to probate the estate and pursue the wishes of my client."

"Spoken like a true lawyer."

"Thank you. Are you gonna serve as the executor?"

"Will I get paid?"

"Yes, there will be a fee, to be approved by the judge."

"How much time will be involved?"

"Could be a lot. If there is a will contest, which seems likely, we could be in court for hours, for days. As executor, you'll have to be there, listening to every witness."

"But, Mr. Brigance, I don't like this will. I don't approve of what Seth did. I have not seen the other will, the thick one, but I'm pretty damned certain I like it better. Why should I be an advocate for this slipshod, last-minute, handwritten piece of crap that gives everything to an undeserving black housekeeper who probably had too much influence over the old boy. Know what I mean?"

Jake nodded slightly and frowned with great suspicion. After thirty minutes with this guy, he was fairly certain he didn't want to spend the next year with him. Replacing an executor was generally no big deal, and Jake knew he could convince the judge that this guy needed to go. Amburgh glanced around again and said softly, "It makes no sense. Seth worked like a dog the last ten years of his life to build a fortune. He took enormous risks. He got lucky. And then, he dumps it all in the lap of some woman who didn't have a damned thing to do with his success. Kinda makes me sick, Mr. Brigance. Sick and very suspicious."

"Then don't serve as executor, Mr. Amburgh. I'm sure the court can find someone else to do the job." Jake picked up the will, creased the folds, and stuck it back into his pocket. "But sleep on it. There's no rush."

"When does the war start?"

"Soon. The other lawyers will show up with the other will."

"Should be fascinating."

"Thanks for your time, Mr. Amburgh. Here's my card." Jake left his business card and a $5 bill on the table and hurried out. He sat in his car for a moment, thinking, trying to collect his thoughts and get his mind focused on a contested estate worth $20 million.

A year earlier, Clanton had gossiped its way through a lawsuit over an insurance policy covering a fertilizer plant that had mysteriously burned to the ground. Its owner was a local shyster named Bobby Carl Leach, a shifty operator with a history of burned buildings and lawsuits. Fortunately, Jake was not involved in the litigation; he avoided Leach at all costs. But during the trial, it was revealed that Leach had a net worth of about $4 million. There was nothing liquid about his balance sheet, but when his liabilities were subtracted from his assets, there was an impressive figure for his equity. This had led to countless discussions and arguments over who, exactly, was the richest person in Ford County. The debates had raged over early morning coffee around the square, and in bars where bankers met after hours, and throughout the courthouse where lawyers huddled to exaggerate the latest testimony, all over town, literally.

Bobby Carl, with $4 million, was certainly at the top of the list. The Wilbanks clan would have been had Lucien not squandered the family fortune decades earlier. Several farmers were mentioned, but only out of habit. They had "family money," which, by the late 1980s, meant they owned sections of land but struggled to pay their bills. A man named Willie Traynor had sold *The Ford County Times* eight years earlier for $1.5 million, and there were rumors he'd doubled his money in the stock market. However, few rumors about Willie had ever been taken seriously. A ninety-eight-year-old woman held bank stock worth $6 million. As the contest wore on, an anonymous list appeared in a court clerk's office and was soon faxed all over town. It was cleverly labeled "Forbes Top Ten List of Richest Ford Countians." Everybody had a copy, and this fueled the gossip. The list was edited, enlarged, detailed, amended, and modified and even fictionalized, but through it all there was no mention of Mr. Seth Hubbard.

The town's exercise in speculation went on with enthusiasm for several weeks before running out of gas. Not surprisingly, Jake had never seen his own name on the list.

He chuckled to himself as he thought of Ms. Lettie Lang and her forthcoming and rather dramatic entry onto the list.

9

For her last day on the job Lettie arrived half an hour early, and she did so in the hopeless belief that such punctuality might impress Mr. Herschel and Mrs. Dafoe; that they might somehow reconsider and allow her to stay on. At 7:30, she parked her twelve-year-old Pontiac next to Mr. Seth's pickup truck. She had stopped calling him Mr. Seth months earlier, when they were alone anyway. Around other people she used the "Mister," but only for appearances. She took a deep breath and clutched the wheel and hated the thought of seeing those people again. They would be leaving soon, as soon as possible. She'd heard them gripe about being forced to spend two nights there. Their worlds back home were crumbling, and they were desperate to get away. Burying their father was such a nuisance. They despised Ford County.

She had slept little. Mr. Brigance's words "sizable portion of his estate" had rattled noisily around her brain throughout the night. She had not told Simeon. Perhaps she would later. Perhaps she would let Mr. Brigance do it. Simeon had badgered her about what the lawyer wanted, what he'd said, but Lettie had been too bewildered and too frightened to try and explain anything. And how could she explain what she didn't under-stand? As confused as she was, Lettie knew the most foolish thing she could do was to believe in a positive outcome. The day she saw any money would be the day she believed, and not a moment before.

The kitchen door off the garage was unlocked. Lettie entered quietly and paused to listen for sounds of activity. The television was on in the den. Coffee was brewing on the counter. She coughed as loudly as possible, and a voice called, "Is that you, Lettie?"

"It is," she said sweetly. She stepped into the den behind a fake smile and found Ian Dafoe on the sofa, still in his pajamas, surrounded by paperwork, lost in the details of some looming deal.

"Good mornin', Mr. Dafoe," she said.

"Good morning, Lettie," he replied with a smile. "How are you?"

"Fine, thanks, and you?"

"As well as can be expected. Up most of the night with this," he said, sweeping an arm over his beloved paperwork, as if she knew exactly what it all meant. "Get me some coffee, would you? Black."

"Yes sir."

Lettie took him coffee, which he accepted without a nod or a word, lost once more in his deal. She returned to the kitchen, poured herself some coffee, and when she opened the refrigerator to get the cream she saw a bottle of vodka, almost empty. She had never seen liquor in the house; Seth didn't keep it. Once a month he brought home a few beers, stuck them in the fridge, and then usually forgot about them.

The sink was full of dirty dishes—how could they possibly be expected to load the dishwasher with a servant on the payroll? Lettie got busy with the cleaning, and presently Mr. Dafoe stopped at the door and said, "I think I'll get a shower now. Ramona is not feeling well, probably caught a cold."

Cold or vodka? Lettie thought. But she said, "I'm sorry. Can I do anything for her?"

"Not really. But some breakfast would be nice, eggs and bacon. Scrambled for me, not sure about Herschel."

"I'll ask him."

Since they were leaving, as was the servant, and since the house was about to be locked up, then sold or somehow disposed of, Lettie decided to clean out the pantry and refrigerator. She fried bacon and sausage, whipped up pancakes, scrambled eggs and made omelets and cheese grits and warmed up store-bought biscuits, Seth's favorite brand. The table was covered with steaming bowls and platters when the three sat down for breakfast, complaining the entire time about all the food and fuss. But they ate. Ramona, puffy-eyed and red-faced and unwilling to say much, seemed to especially crave the grease. Lettie hung around for a few minutes, properly serving them, and the mood was tense. She suspected they'd had a rough night, drinking and arguing and trying to survive one last night in a house they hated. She eased back into the bedrooms, happy to see their bags were packed.

From the shadows, she heard Herschel and Ian discussing a visit by the lawyers. Ian argued it was easier for the lawyers to come to Seth's house than for the three of them to troop over to Tupelo.

"Damned right they can come to us," Ian said. "They'll be here at ten."

"Okay, okay," Herschel conceded, then they lowered their voices.

After breakfast, as Lettie cleared the table and stacked the dishes, the three moved outdoors again, to the patio where they settled around the picnic table and drank their coffee in the morning sun. Ramona seemed to perk up. Lettie, who lived with a drunk, figured that most mornings started slow for Mrs. Dafoe. There was laughter as they momentarily shook off last night's harsh words, whatever they were.

The doorbell rang; it was a locksmith from Clanton. Herschel showed him around and explained loudly, for the benefit of Lettie, that they wanted new locks on the home's four exterior doors. As the man went to work, starting with the front door, Herschel stopped in the kitchen and said, "We're getting all new locks, Lettie, so the old keys won't work."

"I've never had a key," she said with an edge because she'd already said it once.

"Right," Herschel replied, not believing. "We'll leave one key with Calvin down the road, and we'll keep the others. I suspect I'll be back from time to time to check on things."

Whatever, Lettie thought, but she said, "I'll be happy to come over and clean the place whenever you want. Calvin can let me in."

"Won't be necessary, but thanks. We're meeting with the lawyers at ten o'clock, here, so make some fresh coffee. After that we'll be leaving for home. I'm afraid we won't be needing you after that, Lettie. Sorry, but Dad's death changes everything."

She clenched her jaws and said, "I understand."

"How often did he pay you?"

"Every Friday, for forty hours."

"And he paid you last Friday?"

"That's right."

"So we owe you for Monday, Tuesday, and half of today, right?"

"I suppose."

"At five bucks an hour."

"Yes sir."

"I still can't believe he paid you that much," Herschel said as he opened the door and walked outside onto the patio.

Lettie was stripping the beds when the lawyers arrived. In spite of the dark suits and serious faces, they might as well have been Santa Claus delivering sacks of toys to well-behaved children. In the moments before they pulled in to the driveway, Ramona, in heels and pearls and a dress much prettier than the one she'd worn to the funeral, peeked out the front window a dozen times. Ian, now in coat and tie, paced around the den, checking his watch. Herschel, clean shaven for the first time since arriving, was in and out of the kitchen door.

In the past three days, Lettie had overheard enough to know that expectations were high. They did not know how much money old Seth had in the bank, but they were perceptive enough to believe something was there. And it was all a windfall anyway, right? The house and land alone were worth at least half a million, according to Ian's latest guess. How often are you lucky enough to split $500,000. And there was the lumber yard, and who knew what else?

They gathered in the den. Three lawyers, three potential beneficiaries, all well dressed with perfect manners and light moods. The servant, in her best white cotton dress, served them coffee and cake and then retired into the shadows to listen.

Grave condolences were offered by the lawyers. They had known Seth for several years and were great admirers. What a man. It was entirely possible the lawyers thought more of Seth than did his own children, but at that moment this was not contemplated. Herschel and Ramona performed well, even admirably, as the conversation passed through its first phase. Ian seemed bored with the preliminaries and ready to get down to business.

"I have an idea," Herschel said. "There could be other ears listening right now. It's a lovely day, so let's move outside to the patio where things are, shall I say, more confidential."

"Really, Herschel," Ramona protested, but Ian was already standing. The group moved en masse through the kitchen and onto the patio where they re-situated around the picnic table. An hour earlier, Lettie, in anticipation, had cracked a bathroom window. She now sat on the edge of the bathtub and could hear better than ever.

Mr. Lewis McGwyre popped open his heavy briefcase and removed a file. He passed around three copies of a multipage document and began: "Our firm prepared this for your father over a year ago. There's a lot of boilerplate in there, sorry, but that's always required." Ramona, nervous and still red-eyed, said, "I'll read it later. Please, just tell us what's in the will."

"Very well," Mr. McGwyre said. "To skin it all down, each of you, Herschel and Ramona, gets 40 percent of the estate. Some of it's outright, some of it's tied up in trusts, but the bottom line is that you will inherit 80 percent of Mr. Hubbard's estate."

"And the other 20?" Ian demanded.

"Fifteen percent goes into trusts for the grandchildren, and 5 percent is an outright gift to the Irish Road Christian Church."

"What's in the estate?" Herschel asked.

Stillman Rush calmly replied, "The assets are substantial."

★   ★   ★

When Lettie emerged half an hour later with a pot of fresh coffee, the mood had changed in startling ways. Gone was the nervousness, the anticipation, the initial round of gloom and loss, all replaced by a giddiness that only instant and unearned wealth can create. They had just won the lottery; now their only concern was how to collect it. With so much money floating around, the six clammed up immediately when Lettie appeared. Not a word was spoken as she poured the coffee. When the kitchen door closed behind her, all six began chattering away again.

Lettie was listening and growing more confused by the minute.

The will on the table named Lewis McGwyre as the executor of the estate, so not only did he prepare the will, but he also bore the principal responsibility for its probate and administration. The third lawyer, Mr. Sam Larkin, had been the principal business adviser to Seth and seemed quick to take credit for his incredible success. Larkin waxed on about one deal after another, regaling his audience with Seth's fearless exploits when borrowing reckless amounts of money, or so it seemed. Turns out, Seth was smarter than them all. Only Ian tired of this narrative.

Mr. McGwyre explained that, since they were already in Ford County, they planned to run by the courthouse and file the necessary paperwork to initiate the probate proceedings. A notice to creditors would run in the county newspaper for ninety days and invite claims from anyone Seth might owe. Frankly, Mr. McGwyre said, he doubted if there were unknown creditors out there. Seth was aware of his impending death. The two had spoken less than a month earlier.

Stillman Rush said, "All in all, we see this as a fairly routine probate, but it will take time."

More fees, thought Ian.

"In a few months we'll submit to the court an accounting and inventory of all your father's assets and liabilities. To do so, we'll be required to hire a CPA firm, and we know several, to track down the assets. All real estate must be appraised. All personal property listed. It's a process."

"How long?" Ramona asked.

The three lawyers squirmed in unison, the usual reaction when an effort is made to solicit exact information. Lewis McGwyre, the most senior, shrugged and offered a noncommittal "I'd say twelve to eighteen months."

Ian grimaced as he absorbed this and thought of all the loans coming due in the next six months. Herschel frowned while trying not to, while trying to act as though his bank accounts were stuffed and there was no pressure. Ramona shook her head angrily and asked, "Why so long?"

Mr. McGwyre replied, "Fair question."

"Oh thank you."

"Twelve months is not really a long time in these matters. A lot of groundwork has to be laid. Fortunately, your father had significant assets. Few estates do. If he'd died with nothing, then his probate could be complete in ninety days."

"In Florida the average probate takes thirty months," Mr. Larkin said.

"This ain't Florida," Ian said with a cold stare.

Stillman Rush added quickly, "And there is a provision in the law for partial distributions; that is, you might be allowed to take some of your share along the way, before the actual closing of the estate."

"I like the sound of that," Ramona said.

"Can we talk about taxes?" Ian insisted. "What's the ballpark figure?"

Mr. McGwyre leaned back and confidently crossed his legs. Smiling and nodding, he said, "With an estate of this size, with no surviving spouse, the taxes would be brutal, slightly more than 50 percent. But, because of Mr. Hubbard's foresight, and our expertise, we were able to arrive at a plan"— he lifted a copy of the will—"and by the use of some trusts and other devices we have reduced the effective tax rate to about 30 percent."

Ian, the number cruncher, did not need a calculator. Twenty million and change in the net estate, minus 30 percent would knock it down to about $14 mill. Forty percent of that for his dear wife and their share would be around $5.6 million, give or take. And clean, no taxes since all of those nasties, state and federal, would be slapped onto the estate. At that moment, Ian and his various partners and companies owed a plethora of banks in excess of $4 million, about half of which was past due.

As Herschel's internal calculator stuttered along, he caught himself humming under his breath. Seconds later, he too arrived at something around $5.5 million. He was so sick of living with his mother. And his kids—no more worries about tuition.

Ramona turned evil and cast a vicious smile at her husband. She said, "Twenty million, Ian, not too bad for, what did you like to call him, an uneducated logger."

Herschel closed his eyes and exhaled while Ian said, "Come on, Ramona." The lawyers were suddenly interested in their shoes.

She pressed on, "You won't make twenty million in your entire life, and Daddy did it in ten years. And your family, with all the banks they once owned, never had that kind of money. Don't you find that unbelievable, Ian?"

Ian's mouth fell open and he could only stare at her. Alone, he would have certainly gone for her throat, but he was helpless. Be cool, he told himself as he fought his anger. Damn right you'd better be cool because that smirking bitch sitting five feet away is about to inherit several million, and though the money will probably blow up the marriage, there will be something for me.

Stillman Rush closed his briefcase and said, "Well, we need to be moving along. We'll run by the courthouse and kick things off, and we'll need to meet again very shortly, if that's okay." He was standing as he spoke, suddenly eager to leave the family behind. McGwyre and Larkin bounced up too, slapping closed their briefcases and making the same phony farewells. They insisted on showing themselves to the front, and were practically scrambling when they disappeared around the house.

After they left, there was a long, lethal vacuum of silence on the patio as all three avoided eye contact and wondered who would speak next. The wrong word could start another fight, or something worse. Finally, Ian, the angriest, asked his wife, "Why'd you say that in front of the lawyers?"

Herschel jumped in: "No, why did you say it, period?"

She ignored her brother and snarled at her husband, "Because I've been wanting to say it for a long time, Ian. You've always looked down on us, especially my father, and now, suddenly, you're counting his money."

"Aren't we all?" Herschel asked.

"Shut up, Herschel," she snapped.

She ignored him and didn't take her eyes off Ian. "I'll divorce you now, you know that."

"Didn't take long."

"No, it didn't."

"Come on, guys," Herschel pleaded. This was not the first divorce threat he'd witnessed. "Let's go inside, finish packing, and get out of here."

The men stood slowly and walked away. Ramona stared at the trees in the distance, beyond the backyard and into a forest where she played as a child. She had not felt such freedom in years.

Another cake arrived before noon and Lettie tried to decline it. She eventually sat it on the kitchen counter where she was wiping pots for the last time. The Dafoes said a quick good-bye, but only because they really couldn't leave without doing so. Ramona promised to keep in touch and so on. Lettie watched them get in the car without saying a word. It would be a long drive back to Jackson.

At noon, Calvin arrived as planned, and at the kitchen table Herschel handed over a key to the new door locks. Calvin was to check on the house every other day, keep the grass cut, leaves blown, the usual.

When Calvin was gone, Herschel said, "So, Lettie, I figure we owe you for eighteen hours, at five bucks each, right?"

"Whatever you say."

He was writing a check as he stood by the counter. "Ninety dollars," he mumbled with a frown, still wanting to gripe over her excessive pay. He signed it, tore it out, handed it over, and said, "There you are," as if it were a gift.

"Thank you."

"Thanks, Lettie, for taking care of Dad and the house and everything. I know this is not easy."

Firmly, she said, "I understand."

"The way things go, I'm sure we'll never see you again, but I just want you to know how much we appreciate what you did for our dad."

Such a load of crap, Lettie thought, but she said, "Thank you." Her eyes were watering as she folded the check.

After an awkward pause, he said, "Well, Lettie, I'd like for you to leave now so I can lock up."

"Yes sir."

hree well-dressed lawyers from out of town strutting
through the courthouse on a dull Wednesday morning were
bound to attract attention, which didn't seem to bother them at
all. One lawyer could have easily performed the menial task, but
three could charge triple for it. They ignored the local lawyers
and the clerks and the courthouse regulars in the hallways and
purposefully entered the office of the Chancery Clerk. There
they were met by Sara, who'd been alerted by Jake Brigance,
who'd been alerted by a surprise call from Lettie Lang, then still
at Seth's house, with the news that an entire pack of lawyers had
just left and was headed for Clanton.

Stillman Rush flashed a killer smile at Sara, who was slowly
chewing gum and glaring at the men as if they were trespassers.
"We're from the Rush law firm in Tupelo," he announced, and
not one of the other three clerks looked up. The soft music from
a radio failed to stop.

"Congratulations," Sara said. "Welcome to Clanton."

Lewis McGwyre had opened his fine briefcase and was
removing papers. Stillman said, "Yes, well, we need to file a petition to probate an estate." With a flurry, the paperwork landed
on the counter in front of Sara, who, chewing, looked at it without touching it. "Who died?" she asked.

"A man named Seth Hubbard," Stillman said, an octave
higher but still not loud enough to draw the attention of anyone
in the office of the Ford County Chancery Clerk.

"Never heard of him," Sara deadpanned. "He lived in this
county?"

"He did, up near Palmyra."

She finally touched the papers, picked them up, and immediately began frowning. "When'd he die?" she asked.

"Last Sunday."

"They buried him yet?"

Stillman almost blurted, "Is that really any of your business?" but he caught himself. He was on foreign soil and alienating the underlings could only cause trouble. He swallowed, managed a smile, and said, "Yesterday."

Sara's eyes rolled up the wall as if she were bothered by something. "Seth Hubbard? Seth Hubbard?" Over her shoulder she said, "Hey Eva, didn't we get something already on Seth Hubbard?" From thirty feet away Eva replied, "Late yesterday. A new file in the rack over there."

Sara took a few steps, yanked out a file, and scanned it as the three lawyers froze and watched every move. Finally, she said, "Yep, got a petition to probate the last will and testament of Mr. Henry Seth Hubbard, filed at 4:55 yesterday afternoon."

Each of the three lawyers attempted to say something at once, but none could do so. Finally, Stillman managed a weak "What the hell?"

"I didn't file it," Sara said. "I'm just a lowly clerk."

"Is that a public record?" Mr. McGwyre asked.

"It is." She slid the file onto the counter and all three heads grouped over it, ear to ear to ear. Sara turned around, winked at the other girls, and returned to her desk.

Five minutes later, Roxy buzzed Jake on his phone intercom. "Mr. Brigance, there are some gentlemen here to see you." From the terrace, Jake had watched them storm out of the courthouse and march in his direction.

"Do they have an appointment?"

"No sir, and they say it's urgent."

"I'm in a meeting which will take another thirty minutes," Jake said in his empty office. "They're welcome to wait."

Roxy, who'd been quickly briefed, put the phone down and delivered the message. The lawyers frowned and exhaled and fidgeted and finally decided to step out for some coffee. At the door, Stillman said, "Please explain to Mr. Brigance that this is an urgent matter."

"That's already been done."

"Yes, well, thanks."

Jake heard the door close solidly and smiled to himself. They would be back and he looked forward to the meeting. He returned his attention to the latest weekly edition of *The Ford County Times*, published early each Wednesday morning and a rich source of local news. On the front page, below the fold, there was a brief story about the death of Mr. Seth Hubbard, an "apparent suicide." The reporter had followed leads and done some digging. Unnamed sources whispered that Mr. Hubbard had once had extensive holdings in lumber, furniture, and timber rights throughout the Southeast. He had unloaded most of his assets less than a year ago. No one from his family had returned calls. There was a portrait photo of Seth as a much younger man. He looked nothing like the poor guy hanging from a rope in Ozzie's grisly death scene photos. But, then, who would?

Twenty minutes later the lawyers were back. Roxy parked them in the conference room on the first floor. They stood by the window and watched the languid prelunch traffic around the square and waited. Occasionally, they would whisper to one another, as if the room had bugs and someone else might be listening. Finally, Mr. Brigance entered and welcomed them. There were forced smiles and stiff but courteous handshakes, and when they were finally seated Roxy asked about coffee or water. Everyone declined, and she closed the door and disappeared.

Jake and Stillman had finished law school at Ole Miss ten years earlier, and though they had known each other during that ordeal, and often had classes together, they ran in different circles. As the favored son in a family who owned a law firm claiming to be a hundred years old, Stillman's future was secure before he briefed his first case in Contracts. Jake and virtually all of the others were forced to scramble for employment. To his credit, Stillman worked hard to prove himself and graduated in the top 10 percent. Jake was not far behind. As lawyers, their paths had crossed once since law school when Lucien ordered Jake to file an unpromising sex discrimination case against an employer, one represented by the Rush law firm. The outcome was a draw, but during the process Jake came to despise Stillman. He'd been tolerable in law school, but a few years in the trenches had made him a big shot in a big firm with the requisite ego. He wore his blond hair a bit longer now and it flipped up around his ears, contrasting nicely with the fine black wool suit he was wearing.

Jake had never met Mr. McGwyre or Mr. Larkin, but he knew them by reputation. It was a small state.

"To what do I owe this honor, gentlemen?" Jake began.

"Oh, I think you've figured it out by now, Jake," Stillman replied smugly. "I saw you at Mr. Hubbard's funeral yesterday. We've read his holographic will and it's rather self-explanatory."

"It's deficient in many ways," Lewis McGwyre inserted gravely.

"I didn't prepare it," Jake shot across the table.

"But you're offering it for probate," Stillman said. "Obviously you must think it's valid."

"I have no reason to think otherwise. The will came to me in the mail. I was directed to probate it. Here we are."

"But how can you advocate for something as shoddy as this?" Sam Larkin asked, gently lifting a copy of the will. Jake glared at him with all the contempt he could generate. Typical big-firm asshole. Far superior to the rest of us because you bill by the hour and get paid for it. In your well-educated and learned opinion this will is "shoddy" and thus invalid; therefore, everyone else's opinion should fall in line.

Jake kept his cool and said, "It's a waste of time for us to sit here and debate the merits of Mr. Hubbard's handwritten will. Let's save that for the courtroom." And with that, Jake delivered the first salvo. The courtroom was, after all, where he'd made his reputation, whatever it happened to be. Mr. McGwyre prepared wills and Mr. Larkin prepared contracts, and, as far as Jake could tell, Stillman's specialty was defending commercial arson cases, though he fancied himself an aggressive courtroom lawyer.

The courtroom, Jake's courtroom, the one across the street in his courthouse, was where the great Hailey trial had raged barely three years earlier, and though the other three would not admit it, they too had watched that trial keenly from a distance. Like every lawyer in the state, they had been green with envy at Jake's exposure.

"Is it fair to ask about your relationship with Seth Hubbard?" Stillman asked politely.

"Never met the man. He died Sunday and his will arrived in my mailbox on Monday."

They were fascinated by this and took a moment to absorb it. Jake decided to press on: "I'll admit I've never had a case like this, never probated a handwritten will. I assume you have plenty of copies of the old one, the one your firm prepared last year. Don't suppose I could have a copy, could I?"

They shifted and glanced at each other. Stillman said, "Well, Jake, if that will had been admitted to probate, then it would be public and we'd give you a copy. However, we withdrew it once we learned another will was already in play. So I guess our will is still a confidential document."

"Fair enough."

The three continued to exchange nervous looks and it was apparent none of them knew exactly what to do next. Jake said nothing but enjoyed watching their discomfort. Stillman, the litigator, said, "So, uh, Jake, we ask you to withdraw the handwritten will and allow us to proceed with the authentic one."

"The answer is no."

"No surprise. How do you suggest we proceed?"

"It's very simple, Stillman. Let's file a joint request with the court to have a hearing to address the situation. Judge Atlee will look at both wills, and, believe me, he'll devise a game plan. I practice in his court every month and there's no doubt who'll be in charge."

"I was thinking the same thing," Lewis McGwyre said. "I've known Reuben for many years, and I think we should start with him."

"I'll be happy to arrange things," Jake said.

"So you haven't spoken to him yet?" Stillman asked.

"Of course not. He knows nothing about this. The funeral was yesterday, remember?"

They managed to exchange cordial good-byes and separate peacefully, though all four knew they were in for a brawl.

Lucien was sitting on his front porch, drinking what appeared to be lemonade, which he occasionally did when his body and his life became so overwhelmed with sour mash that he managed to break free for a week or so and suffer the horrors of detox. The porch wrapped around an old house on a hill just outside Clanton, with a view of the town below and the courthouse cupola square in the middle. The house, like most of Lucien's assets and burdens, was a hand-me-down from ancestors he deemed wretched, but who, with hindsight, had done an admirable job of securing for him a comfortable life. Lucien was sixty-three but an old man, his face grizzled and whiskered gray to match his long unkempt hair. The whiskey and cigarettes were adding patches of wrinkles to his face. Too much time on the porch was adding a thickness to his waist and a gloominess to his always complicated moods.

He'd lost his license to practice nine years earlier, and, according to the terms of his disbarment, he could now apply for reinstatement. He'd dropped that bomb on Jake a couple of times to gauge his response, but got nothing. Nothing visible anyway, but just under the surface Jake was mortified at the thought of reacquiring a senior partner who owned the building and was impossible to work with, or under. If Lucien became a lawyer again, and moved back in his office, Jake's current one, and started suing everyone who crossed him and defending pedophiles and rapists and capital murderers, Jake wouldn't last six months.

"How are you, Lucien?" Jake said as he climbed the steps.

Sober, clear-eyed, and feeling fresh, Lucien replied, "I'm fine, Jake. Always a pleasure to see you."

"You offered lunch. Have I ever said no to lunch?" Weather permitting, they ate at least twice a month on the porch.

"Not that I recall," Lucien said, standing in his bare feet and offering a hand. They shook heartily, did the quick shoulder-pat thing that men do when they really don't want to hug one another, and took their seats in aging white wicker chairs that had not been moved more than six inches since Jake's first visit a decade earlier.

Sallie eventually appeared and said hi to Jake. He said iced tea would be fine and she strolled away, never in a hurry. She had been hired as a housekeeper, then promoted to a nurse to care for Lucien when he threw a bender and checked out for two weeks. At some point, she moved in, and for a while the gossip rippled through Clanton. It died soon enough, though, because nothing Lucien Wilbanks could do would really shock anyone.

Sallie brought the iced tea and poured more lemonade. When she was gone, Jake said, "On the wagon?"

"No, never. Just taking a break. I'd like to live for twenty more years, Jake, and I worry about my liver. I don't want to die and I don't want to give up Jack Daniel's, so I'm in a constant quandary. I worry about this all the time, and the worry and stress and pressure eventually become too much and can only be alleviated by the Jack."

"Sorry I asked."

"Are you drinking?"

"Not really. An occasional beer, but we don't keep it around the house. Carla frowns on it, you know."

"My second wife frowned on it too and she didn't last a year. But, then, she didn't look like Carla."

"Thanks, I guess."

"Don't mention it. Sallie's cooking vegetables if that's okay."

"Delicious."

There was an unwritten checklist of topics they always covered and usually in an order that was so predictable Jake often suspected that Lucien had notes tucked away somewhere. The family—Carla and Hanna; the office and the current secretary and any profitable cases that had popped up since the last visit; the lawsuit against the insurance company; the investigation into the Klan; the latest on Mack Stafford, the attorney who had disappeared and taken his clients' money; gossip about other lawyers, and judges; college football; and, of course, the weather.

They moved to a small table at the other end of the porch where Sallie was arranging lunch——butter beans, squash, stewed tomatoes, and corn bread. They filled their plates, and she disappeared again.

After a few bites, in total silence, Jake asked, "Did you ever know Seth Hubbard?"

"I saw it in the paper this morning. Quite sad. I met him once or twice fifteen years ago, some trifling legal matter. Never sued him, though, so I'll always regret that. He might've had some assets. I tried to sue everyone with assets, which, as you know, is a pretty damned small class around here. Why?"

"I have a hypothetical for you."

"Can't it wait? I'm eating."

"No, listen. You have some assets, no wife, no kids, some distant relatives, and you have a lovely black housekeeper who gives appearances of being something a little more than just a housekeeper."

"This sounds like meddling. Where are we going?"

"If you wrote a new will today, who might get your assets?"

"Damned sure wouldn't be you."

"No surprise, and I can assure you you're not mentioned in my will either."

"No loss. By the way, you haven't paid last month's rent."

"Check's in the mail. Can you answer my question?"

"No. I don't like your question."

"Come on. Play along. Humor me. If you wrote a new will right now, who would get everything?"

Lucien shoved corn bread into his mouth and chewed slowly. He glanced around to make sure Sallie wasn't listening. Finally, he said, "None of your business. Why?"

Jake reached into his coat pocket and whipped out some papers. "Get a load of this. The last will and testament of Seth Hubbard, written last Saturday in thoughtful consideration of what he was about to do on Sunday. The original arrived in my office mailbox on Monday."

Lucien adjusted his reading glasses, sipped some lemonade, and read Seth's will. As he flipped to the second page, his face relaxed considerably and he began to smile. He was nodding along with old Seth by the time he finished. "I like it," he said, lowering it and grinning at Jake. "I'm assuming Lettie is the black housekeeper."

"Correct. I met her yesterday for the first time. Name ring a bell?"

Lucien thought for a moment as he held the will and forgot about lunch. "I don't recall any Taybers, perhaps a Lang or two. Box Hill is a strange part of the county and I never spent any time up there." He read it again as Jake continued eating.

"What's he worth?" Lucien asked as he refolded the sheets of paper and handed them back to Jake.

"Twenty million, give or take," Jake said nonchalantly, as if that was the typical estate in Ford County. "He did well in furniture and timber."

"Evidently."

"Now it's all in cash, for the most part."

Lucien began laughing. "Just what this town needs," he said as he shook. "A brand-new black millionaire with more money than anyone else."

"She doesn't have it yet," Jake said, enjoying the levity. "I just met with some lawyers from the Rush firm and they basically promised a war."

"Of course. Wouldn't you fight over that kind of money?"

"Sure. I'd fight over a lot less."

"So would I."

"Did you ever handle a nasty will contest?"

"Oh, so that's where we're going. You need some free legal advice from a disbarred lawyer."

"These cases are pretty rare."

Lucien worked a mouthful and scratched his beard. He shook his head and said, "No, nothing. Look, the Wilbanks family has fought over its land and stocks and deposits for a hundred years; everything has been fought over, bitterly at times. There have been fistfights, divorces, suicides, duels, threats of murder, you name it and a Wilbanks has done it. But, we've always managed to keep it out of the courts."

Sallie appeared and topped off their glasses. They ate in silence for a few minutes. Lucien was staring at the front lawn, his eyes glowing, his mind racing. "Fascinating, isn't it, Jake?"

"It is indeed."

"And either side can demand a trial by jury, right?"

"Yes, the law has not been changed. And, the request for a jury trial must be made before any hearing, so it must be dealt with soon. That's what I want you to ponder, Lucien. That's the big issue of the day. Do I play it before a jury, or do I trust Judge Atlee with the decision?"

"What if Atlee recuses himself?"

"He won't because this case will be too much fun. The largest estate he'll ever see, a packed courtroom, high drama, and, if there's a jury, then Atlee gets to preside over the circus while hiding behind its verdict."

"You may be right."

"The question is, Can you trust a Ford County jury? Three blacks, four at the most."

"The Hailey jury was all white as I recall."

"This is not Carl Lee Hailey, Lucien. Far from it. That was all about race. This is all about money."

"Everything is about race in Mississippi, Jake, don't ever forget that. A simple black woman on the verge of inheriting what might be the largest fortune this county has ever seen, and the decision rests with a jury that's predominantly white. It's race and money, Jake, a rare combination around here."

"So you wouldn't risk a jury?"

"I didn't say that. Allow me to consider this for a spell, okay? My valuable advice, though still free to you, often needs proper reflection."

"Fair enough."

"I might stop by this afternoon. I'm looking for an old book that might be in the attic."

"You own the place," Jake said, shoving away his plate.

"And you're late with the rent."

"Sue me."

"I'd love to but you're broke. You're living in a rental house and your car has almost as many miles as mine."

"I guess I should've gone into the furniture business."

"Anything but the law. I like this case, Jake. I might want to work on it."

"Sure, Lucien," Jake managed to say without hesitation. "Stop by late this afternoon and we'll chat." He stood and dropped his napkin on the table.

"No coffee?"

"No, I need to run. Thanks for lunch and pass along my regards to Sallie."

11

A nosy paralegal sniffing through old land records down the hall heard the gossip as it drifted over from a watercooler, and went to make copies of the latest will to be filed for probate in Ford County. Back at the office, he showed it to his bosses, made even more copies, and began faxing here and there. His bosses faxed it too, and by noon Wednesday copies of Seth's two-page will were popping up all over the county. The "perish in pain" wish was a favorite touch, but speculation about the deceased's net worth soon dominated the discussion.

As soon as Herschel left his father's home, he called his lawyer in Memphis to pass along the wonderful news that he would soon be inheriting "several" million dollars. Of particular concern was his ex-wife—he was still bleeding from the divorce—and he was curious if she could make a claim. No she could not, his lawyer assured him. The lawyer called a lawyer friend down in Tupelo for no reason other than to spread rumors, and in doing so managed to include the bit about Seth Hubbard having a net worth "in excess of $20 million." The lawyer in Tupelo called some friends. The size of the estate began to grow.

As soon as Ian Dafoe got on the Natchez Trace Parkway and headed south, he set his cruise control on fifty and settled in for the pleasant drive. Traffic was light; the sun was up; the leaves were beginning to change and some were dropping in the breeze. Though his wife, as always, was complicating his life, he had reason to smile. He had managed to defuse the divorce talk, at least for the moment. She was hungover and she had just buried her father and her nerves were shot anyway, and even on a good day Ramona dealt poorly with adversity. He could pacify her, bring her around, kiss her ass enough to gloss over their problems, and set about the task of managing their new wealth. Together. He was certain he could handle this.

She was lying across the rear seat, on her back with a forearm over her eyes, trying to sleep it off. She had stopped talking and her breathing was heavy. He turned around often to make sure she was out of it, then he carefully reached for his new car phone and called the office. Speaking as softly as possible, he offered only the minimum to Rodney, his partner: "The old boy's gone . . . estate's somewhere north of twenty mill . . . furniture and lumber . . . pretty amazing . . . had no idea . . . just saw the will . . . 40 percent, after taxes . . . not bad . . . about a year . . . not kidding . . . more later."

Ian drove on, smiling at the foliage and dreaming of a better life. Even if they got a divorce, he'd still get a piece of her inheritance, right? He thought about calling his lawyer, but wisely decided to wait. The phone rang suddenly, startling him and waking up Ramona. "Hello," he said.

On the other end, a stiff male voice said, "Yes, hello, Ian, Stillman Rush here, hope I didn't disturb. We're on our way back to Tupelo."

"Not at all. We're on the Trace with a couple of hours to go. Nothing to do but talk."

"Yes, well, look, there's been a slight complication, so I'll just go ahead and get right to the point." His voice had a nervous tinge to it, and Ian knew immediately that something was wrong. Ramona sat up in the rear seat and rubbed her swollen eyes.

Stillman went on: "We didn't get the chance to open Mr. Hubbard's estate after we saw you this morning because another will has already been presented. Seems as though a lawyer in Clanton hustled over to the courthouse late yesterday afternoon and filed a handwritten will that Mr. Hubbard purportedly wrote last Saturday, the day before he died. Handwritten wills are still valid, if they meet certain criteria. This will is just awful. It leaves nothing to the family—Ramona and Herschel are specifically cut out—and instead gives 90 percent of the estate to Lettie Lang, the housekeeper."

"Lettie!" Ian managed to gasp as he veered across the center line. He caught himself and yanked the wheel.

"What is it?" Ramona snarled from the backseat.

"Yes, Lettie Lang," Stillman repeated. "I guess he was quite fond of her."

"This is ridiculous!" Ian said sharply, his voice already several octaves higher, his eyes glaring wildly into the rearview mirror. "Ninety percent? Did you say 90 percent?"

"I did, yes. I have a copy of the will and it clearly says 90 percent."

"Handwritten? Is it a forgery?"

"We don't know at this point. Everything is preliminary."

"Well, obviously, Stillman, this can't stand up, can it?"

"Of course not. We met with the attorney who probated the will, and he's not going to withdraw it. So we've agreed to meet with the judge soon and work things out."

"Work things out? What does that mean?"

"Well, we'll ask the judge to toss out this handwritten will and probate the legitimate one we looked at this morning. If for some reason he says no, then we'll go to court and fight over which will should stand."

"When do we go to court?" Ian asked belligerently, but there was also a noticeable layer of desperation in his voice, as if he could feel the fortune beginning to slide.

"We're not sure right now, but I'll call in a few days. We'll work this out, Ian."

"Damned right you will or I'll bring in the Lanier firm from Jackson, the big boys, been representing me for a long time. Those guys know how to litigate. In fact, I'll probably call Wade Lanier as soon as we hang up."

"No need for that, Ian, not yet anyway. The last thing we need at this point is more lawyers. I'll call you in a couple of days."

"You do that." Ian slammed the phone down and glared at his wife, who said, "What's going on, Ian?"

Ian took a deep breath, exhaled, and said, "You're not going to believe it."

Herschel was sitting behind the wheel of his small Datsun listening to the end of a Springsteen song when the call came. The Datsun was parked near the main entrance of the BMW dealer in East Memphis. Dozens of shiny new BMWs glistened in perfect rows along the street. He'd fought himself over this ridiculous stop, and made peace only with a compromise that was to include a chat with a salesman but certainly no test-drive. Not yet anyway. As he reached to turn off the radio, his car phone rang.

It was Stillman Rush. He began with a nervous "Herschel, there's a new wrinkle."

Lettie arrived alone. Jake followed her up the stairs to the big office, where he closed the door and directed her to a small sitting area with a sofa and chairs. He took off his tie and poured coffee and tried to ease her apprehension. She explained that Simeon had already left again. She had told him nothing about Seth's will, and this angered him. They had fought briefly, with every word echoing around the crowded house, and so he left.

Jake handed her a copy of Seth's will. She read it and began crying. He placed a box of tissues next to her chair. She read it again, and when she finished she laid it on the coffee table before her and sat for a long time with her face in her hands. When the tears stopped, she wiped her cheeks and sat straighter, as if the shock was gone and she was ready for business.

"Why would he do this, Lettie?" Jake asked firmly.

"I don't know, I swear I don't know," she said, her voice low and hoarse.

"Did he discuss this will with you?"

"No."

"Have you seen this before?"

She was shaking her head. "No, no."

"Has he ever mentioned his will to you?"

A pause as she tried to unscramble her thoughts. "Twice, maybe, in the past few months, he said he would leave a little something behind for me, but he never said what. Of course I was hoping he would, but I never brought it up. I never had no will. My momma never had one. Not something we think about, you know, Mr. Brigance?"

"Please call me Jake."

"I'll try."

"Did you call him Mr. Hubbard, Mr. Seth, or just Seth?"

Deliberately, she said, "When it was just the two of us, I called him Seth because that's what he wanted. If anybody else was around, I always called him Mr. Seth or Mr. Hubbard."

"What did he call you?"

"Lettie. Always."

He quizzed her about Seth's last days, his illness, treatments, doctors, nurses, appetite, daily rituals, and her employment. She knew almost nothing about his business and said that he kept his papers locked up tight around the house; most had been moved to his office over the past few months. He never discussed business with her, or in her presence. Before he got sick, and afterward when he felt well, he traveled a lot and preferred to be out of town. His home was quiet, lonely, and not a happy place. Often she would arrive at 8:00 a.m. with nothing to do for the next eight hours, especially if Seth were out of town. When he was there, she cooked and cleaned. When he was sick, and dying, she stayed by his side. She fed him, and, yes, she bathed him and cleaned up after him when necessary. There had been dark periods, especially during the chemo and radiation, when he was bedridden and too weak to feed himself.

Jake delicately explained the concept of undue influence. The legal assault on the handwritten will would be an assault on Lettie, with allegations that she was too close to Seth, had too much influence; that she manipulated him into including her. For Lettie to prevail, it would be important for her to prove otherwise. As they talked, and as she began to relax, Jake could envision her deposition in the near future, in a room full of hyped-up lawyers all clamoring for the floor and the chance to grill her about what she and Mr. Hubbard did and did not do. He already felt sorry for her.

When she was composed and under control, he said, "I need to explain the relationships here, Lettie. I am not your lawyer. I am the lawyer for Mr. Hubbard's estate, and in that capacity it's my job to advocate in favor of this will and to follow its terms. I have to work with the executor, and we're assuming it will be Mr. Amburgh, to do certain things the law requires, such as notifying potential creditors, protecting assets, preparing an inventory of everything he owned, and so forth. If the will is contested, and I'm sure it will be, then it's my job to go into court and fight to uphold this will. I'm not your lawyer because you are a beneficiary of the will—the same as his brother, Ancil Hubbard, and the same as his church. However, you and I are on the same side here because we both want this will to prevail. Does this make any sense?"

"I suppose. Do I need a lawyer?"

"Not really, not at this point. Don't hire a lawyer until you need one." The vultures would soon be circling and the courtroom would get crowded. Drop $20 million on the table and get out of the way.

"Will you tell me if I need one?" she asked innocently.

"Yes, I will," Jake said, though he had no idea how he would give such advice. He poured more coffee and noticed she had not touched hers. He glanced at his watch. They had been together for thirty minutes and she had yet to ask about the size of the estate. A white person wouldn't have made it five minutes without such an inquiry. At times she seemed to absorb each word, and at times she seemed to deflect them, as if overwhelmed.

She cried again and wiped her cheeks.

"Are you curious about how much?" Jake asked.

"I figured you'd tell me sooner or later."

"I've seen nothing in the way of financial statements. I've not been inside his office, though that should happen soon. But, according to Mr. Amburgh, Seth Hubbard recently sold his company and cleared about $20 million. Mr. Amburgh thinks this is probably sitting in a bank somewhere. Cash. Plus there are a few other assets, maybe some real estate here and there. One of my jobs is to locate everything and inventory it for the court, and for the beneficiaries."

"And I'm one of those—a beneficiary?"

"Oh yes, very much so. Ninety percent."

"Ninety percent of twenty million?"

"Yes, give or take."

"Oh my God, Jake." She reached for the tissues and collapsed again.

Over the next hour, they managed some progress. Between her emotional meltdowns, Jake laid out the basics of estate administration—time, the people involved, court appearances, taxes, and lastly, the transfer of assets. The more he talked, though, the more confused she became, and he suspected that much of what he was saying would be repeated soon. He dumbed down the issues involved in a will contest and made cautious predictions as to what might happen. Knowing Judge Atlee and his distaste of lingering cases and slow lawyers, Jake believed a trial, assuming there was one, would take place within the next twelve months, probably sooner. With so much at stake, the losing party would certainly appeal, so tack on two more years before a final outcome. As Lettie began to grasp the ordeal and how long it might take, her resolve stiffened and she gathered her emotions.

Twice she asked if there was any way to keep it all quiet. No, Jake explained patiently, that would not be possible. She feared Simeon and his family of outlaws and wondered if she should move away. Jake had no advice on that matter, but he had already envisioned the coming chaos in her life as kinfolks materialized and new friends came out of the woods.

After two hours, she reluctantly left. Jake escorted her to the front door where she looked through the glass, across the sidewalk and the street, as if she preferred to stay inside where she knew it was safe. She had been jolted by the will, then overwhelmed by the law, and at that moment Jake was the only person she trusted. Her eyes were wet again when she finally stepped out.

"Are those tears of joy or is she scared to death?" Roxy asked after Jake closed the door.

"Both, I would say."

She waved a pink phone message slip and said, "Doofus Lee called. He's hot on the trail."

"Oh come on."

"Not kidding. Said he might stop by this afternoon and poke around in Seth Hubbard's dirty laundry."

"What's dirty about it?" Jake asked as he took the slip.

"Everything's dirty to Doofus."

Dumas Lee wrote for *The Ford County Times* and was famous for screwing up the facts and barely dodging libel suits. While sloppy and easily avoidable, his errors were usually minor and harmless and had never risen to the level of outright defamation. He butchered dates and names and places but had never seriously embarrassed anyone. He had an ear for the street, an uncanny nose for picking up a story immediately after it happened, or while it was unfolding, and though he was too lazy for prolonged digging he could be counted on to stir things up. He preferred to cover the courthouse, primarily because it was across the street from the newspaper's offices and many of its records were public.

He strode into the law offices of Jake Brigance late Wednesday afternoon, took a chair near Roxy's desk, and demanded to see the lawyer. "I know he's here," he said with a killer smile that Roxy ignored. He liked the ladies and labored under the permanent illusion that every woman was eyeing him.

"He's busy," she said.

"So am I." He opened a magazine and began whistling softly. Ten minutes later, Roxy said, "He'll see you now."

Jake and Dumas had known each other for years and never had a problem. Jake was one of the few lawyers around the square who had never threatened to sue him, and Dumas appreciated it.

"Tell me about Seth Hubbard," he said, pulling out his note-pad and uncapping his pen.

"I assume you've seen the will," Jake replied.

"Got a copy. They're everywhere. How much is he worth?"

"Nothing. He's dead."

"Ha-ha. His estate then."

"I can't say anything, Dumas, at this time. I don't know much and I can't say anything."

"Okay, let's go off the record." With Dumas, nothing was off the record, and every lawyer, judge, and clerk knew it.

"I'm not off the record. I'm not on the record. I'm not talking, Dumas. It's that simple. Maybe later."

"When are you going to court?"

"The funeral was yesterday, okay? There's no rush."

"Oh really? No rush? Why did you file your petition twenty minutes after the funeral was over?"

Jake paused, nailed, busted, great question. "Okay, maybe I had a reason to rush my petition."

"The old race to the courthouse, huh?" Dumas said with a goofy smirk as he scribbled something on his pad.

"No comment."

"I can't find Lettie Lang. Any idea where she is?"

"No comment. And she will not talk to you, or any other reporter."

"We'll see. I tracked down a guy in Atlanta, writes for a business magazine, said an LBO group bought a holding company owned by Mr. Seth Hubbard for fifty-five million. Happened late last year. Ring a bell?"

"No comment, Dumas," Jake said, impressed that the notoriously lazy reporter had been working the phones.

"I'm not much when it comes to business, but you gotta figure the old guy had some debts, you know? No comment, right?" Jake nodded, yes, no comment. "But I can't locate his banks. The more I dig, the less I learn about your client."

"Never met the man," Jake said, then wished he hadn't. Dumas wrote it down.

"Do you know if he had any debts? Mr. Amburgh clammed up, then he hung up."

"No comment."

"So if I say that Mr. Hubbard sold out for fifty-five million and don't mention any debts because I have no sources, then my readers will get the impression that his estate is worth a lot more than it really is, right?"

Jake nodded. Dumas watched him, waited, then scribbled. Shifting gears, he asked, "So the great question, Jake, is, Why would a man who's worth millions change his will the day before his suicide, screwing his family with the update and leaving everything to his housekeeper?"

You got it, Dumas. That is the great question. Jake kept nodding but said nothing.

"And perhaps number two might be, What did Seth and his little brother witness that left such an impression that Seth mentions it decades later? Right?"

Jake replied, "That's indeed a great question, but I'm not sure it's number two."

"Fair enough. Any idea where Ancil Hubbard is these days?"

"None whatsoever."

"I found a cousin in Tupelo who says the family has assumed he's been dead for decades."

"I have not had time to search for Ancil."

"But you will?"

"Yes, he's a beneficiary under the will. It's my job to locate him if possible, or find out what happened to him."

"And how will you go about this?"

"I have no idea. Haven't really thought about it yet."

"When's the first court date?"

"It has not been set."

"Will you get your girl to contact me when a date has been set?"

"Yes, unless it's a closed hearing."

"Fair enough."

★   ★   ★

Jake's last visitor of the afternoon was his landlord. Lucien was in the conference room on the first floor where the law books were kept. He'd covered the table with them, obviously lost somewhere deep in his own world. When Jake walked in, said hello, and saw a dozen books opened, he took a deep breath as a sense of dread hit him in the gut. He could not remember the last time Lucien dug through law books. The disbarment had happened not long after Jake hired on, and Lucien had kept his distance from the office and from the law. Now, he was back.

"Some light reading?" Jake asked as he fell into a leather chair.

"Just brushing up on probate law. Never did much of it. Pretty dull stuff, unless of course you get a case like this. I can't decide if you want a jury or not."

"I'm leaning toward a jury, but everything is premature."

"Of course." Lucien closed a book and slid it away. "You said you were meeting with Lettie Lang this afternoon. How did it go?"

"Fine, Lucien, and you know as well as I do that I cannot talk about our confidential discussions."

"Oh sure. Do you like her?"

Jake paused a second and reminded himself to be patient. "Yes, she's a nice person who's easily overwhelmed. This is overwhelming, to say the least."

"But will a jury like her?"

"You mean white jurors?"

"I don't know. I understand black people far better than most whites. I'm not a racist, Jake. I'm one of at least a dozen whites in this county not blinded by racism. I was the first, and only, white member of the NAACP here. At one time, almost all of my clients were black. I know black people, Jake, and having blacks on this jury could cause trouble."

"Lucien, the funeral was yesterday. Isn't this a bit premature?"

"Maybe, but these conversations will take place eventually. You're lucky to have someone like me on your side, Jake. Humor me. Talk to me. A lot of blacks will be jealous of Lettie Lang because now she's one of them, but if she gets the money she'll be the richest person in Ford County. There are no rich black people around here. It's unheard-of. She won't be black anymore. She'll be uppity and rich and she'll look down on everybody, especially her people. Do you follow me, Jake?"

"To some degree, yes, but I'd still rather have blacks on the jury. They'll be more sympathetic than a bunch of rednecks who can barely pay their mortgages."

"No rednecks either."

Jake laughed and asked, "Well, if you eliminate the blacks and the rednecks, who, exactly, will you seat on your perfect jury?"

"I'm still working on that. I like this case, Jake. I've thought about nothing else since lunch. It has reminded me of why I once loved the law." He leaned forward on his elbows and looked at Jake as if he might get choked up. "I want to be in that court-room, Jake."

"You're getting ahead of yourself, Lucien. A trial, if it happens, is months away."

"Sure, I know that. But you'll need some help and lots of it. I'm bored, Jake, tired of sitting on the porch and drinking, and I've got to cut back on the booze. I'm worried about it, Jake, I'll be honest with you."

And with good reason.

"I'd like to hang out around here. I'll stay out of the way. I know most people avoid me, and I understand why. Hell, I'd avoid me if I could. It'll give me something to do, keep me away from the bottle, at least during the day, and I know so much more about the law than you do anyway. And, I want to be in that courtroom."

This, for the second time, and Jake knew it would not go away. The courtroom was a large, stately room with different sections and lots of seating. Did he want to sit with the specta-tors and watch the show? Or was he thinking of a seat at the table with the other lawyers, because if he was then Jake's life was about to become messy. If Lucien wanted to be a lawyer again, he would be required to suffer through the ordeal of the bar exam. If successful, he would have a license to practice, which, of course, would usher him back into Jake's professional life.

The image of Lucien sitting at counsel table, not fifteen feet from the jury box, was frightening. To most whites, he was a toxic legend, a crazy old drunk who had embarrassed a once proud family and now shacked up with his housekeeper.

"We'll see," Jake said cautiously.

12

The Honorable Reuben V. Atlee was recovering from his third heart attack, with the recovery expected to be "full," if one can physically feel complete after so much cardiac damage. He was gaining strength and endurance and there was evidence of this in the flow of his docket. There were clear signs he was regaining his stride. Lawyers were getting barked at. Deadlines were being enforced. Long-winded witnesses were being cut off. Perjurers were being threatened with jail. Litigants pursuing frivolous claims were finding themselves bounced out of court. Along the hallways of the courthouse, lawyers and clerks and even janitors were saying, "He's back."

He had been on the bench for thirty years and now ran unopposed every four years. He was neither a Democrat nor a Republican, liberal nor conservative, Baptist nor Catholic; he pulled for neither State nor Ole Miss. He had no favorites, no leanings, no preconceived notions about anything or any person. He was a judge, as open, tolerant, and fair-minded as he could possibly be, given his upbringing and genetic composition. He ran his courtroom with a heavy hand, quick to scold an unprepared lawyer, but equally quick to help a struggling one. He could show incredible compassion when it was needed, and he had a mean streak that terrified every lawyer in the county, perhaps with the exception of Harry Rex Vonner.

Nine days after Seth hung himself, Judge Atlee assumed the bench in the main courtroom and said good morning. In Jake's opinion, he looked as fit as ever, which was not altogether that healthy but fine given his history. He was a big man, over six feet tall with a protruding midsection that he hid well under his black robe.

"A nice crowd," Judge Atlee said with amusement as he scanned the courtroom. With so many lawyers, seating had been a problem. Jake had arrived early and staked his claim to the plaintiff's table, where he now sat with Russell Amburgh, who had informed Jake that morning that he wanted out. Close behind them, and on their side but not exactly on their team, was Lettie Lang. On each side of Lettie there was a lawyer, both black, both from Memphis.

Jake's world had been rattled the day before when he heard the news that Lettie had hired Booker Sistrunk, an infamous bomb thrower whose entry into this case would greatly complicate matters. Jake had tried to call her. He was still stunned by her decision. It was an extremely unwise one.

Across the way and tucked tight around the defense table was an assemblage of lawyers in nice suits. Beyond the bar and scattered across the rows of ancient wooden pews, there was an impressive crowd, its collective curiosity piqued.

Judge Atlee said, "Before we get started, it's best to understand where we are and what we'd like to accomplish here today. We're not here because of a motion filed by anyone. That'll happen later. Today our goal is to put together a plan to proceed. As I understand it, Mr. Seth Hubbard left two wills. One offered for probate by you, Mr. Brigance, a handwritten will dated October 1 of this year." Jake nodded but did not stand. If a lawyer spoke to Judge Atlee, that lawyer had better be on his or her feet. Nodding from a chair was acceptable, barely. "And a second will dated September 7 of last year, though this will was expressly revoked by the handwritten will. Now, does anyone know of another will? Any chance Mr. Hubbard left another surprise?" He paused for only a second as his large brown eyes swept around the courtroom. A pair of cheap thick-rimmed reading glasses stuck to the end of his nose. "Good. Didn't think so."

He shuffled some papers and made a note. "Okay, let's start over here. Please stand, give me your name, and let's meet one another." He was pointing at Jake, so he stood and stated his name. Russell Amburgh stood next and gave his name.

"And you're the executor in the handwritten will?" Judge Atlee asked as a formality.

"Yes sir, but I'd prefer to skip all this," Amburgh said.

"We'll have plenty of time to deal with it later. And you, in the light gray suit?"

The taller black lawyer stood purposefully and buttoned the top button of his tailored suit. "Yes, Your Honor, my name is Booker Sistrunk, and along with my partner here, Mr. Kendrick Bost, we represent the interests of Ms. Lettie Lang." Sistrunk touched her shoulder. Bost stood and both lawyers towered over her. She shouldn't have been there, not at this stage. She belonged beyond the bar on the benches with the rest of the spectators, but Sistrunk and Bost had jostled her into position and dared anyone to object. Had it been a proper motion hearing, Judge Atlee would have quickly put her in her place, but he wisely ignored the impropriety.

"I don't believe I've had the honor of seeing you gentlemen in my courtroom before," Judge Atlee said in a suspicious tone. "Where are you from?"

"Our firm is in Memphis," Sistrunk replied, though everyone knew it. These days in the Memphis press their firm was getting more ink than the next five combined. They were at war with the Memphis Police Department and were winning brutality cases monthly, it seemed. Sistrunk was riding a wave of notoriety. He was loud, brash, divisive, and was proving to be a highly effective race baiter in a city that had produced many.

Jake knew Simeon had kinfolks in Memphis. One thing had evidently led to another, and Jake had received the dreadful call from Booker Sistrunk. They were "entering" the case, which meant another layer of intense scrutiny of Jake's work, along with another finger in the pie. There were already troubling stories of cars parked in Lettie's front yard and vultures lounging on the front porch.

Judge Atlee continued, "I'm assuming, then, that you have a license to practice law in this state."

"No sir, not as of this morning. But we will associate local counsel."

"That would be a wise move, Mr. Sistrunk. The next time you appear in my court, I expect to know the lawyer you're with."

"Yes sir," Sistrunk said stiffly, almost with a sneer. He and Bost sat down and squeezed next to their valuable client. Before the hearing began, Jake had tried to say good morning to Lettie, but her lawyers had shielded her. She would not make eye contact.

"Over here," Judge Atlee said, pointing to the crowded defense table. Stillman Rush was quick to rise and say, "Yes, Your Honor, I'm Stillman Rush with the Rush firm in Tupelo, and I'm here with Sam Larkin and Lewis McGwyre." Both men stood on cue and nodded politely to the bench. They knew Judge Atlee; longer introductions were not needed.

"And your firm prepared the 1987 will, is that correct?"

"That is true," Stillman said with a generous, sappy smile.

"Very well. Next."

A large man with a round hairless head stood and growled, "Your Honor, I'm Wade Lanier, of the Lanier firm in Jackson. I'm here with my associate, Lester Chilcott, and we represent the interests of Ms. Ramona Dafoe, daughter of the deceased. Her husband, Ian Dafoe, is a longtime client of our firm and—"

"That's enough, Mr. Lanier," Judge Atlee barked, rudely cutting him off. Welcome to Ford County. "I didn't ask about your other clients or your firm."

The presence of Wade Lanier was also disturbing. Jake knew him by reputation only, but that was enough to dread dealing with him. Big firm, hardball tactics, enough success to fuel the ego and keep it hungry.

Judge Atlee pointed again and said, "And you, sir?"

A man in a gaudy sports coat jumped up and announced, "Yes, well, Your Honor, my name is D. Jack O'Malley, and I represent Mr. Herschel Hubbard, surviving son of the deceased. My client lives in Memphis and that's where I'm from but I will most certainly associate local counsel the next time I'm here."

"Good idea. Next?"

Wedged into a spot behind O'Malley was a thin, rat-faced young man with wild, wiry hair. He stood timidly as if he'd never addressed a judge before and said, in a squeaky voice, "Sir, I'm Zack Zeitler, also from Memphis, and I've been hired to represent the interests of the children of Herschel Hubbard."

Judge Atlee nodded and said, "So, the grandkids have lawyers too?"

"Yes sir. They are beneficiaries under the prior will."

"Got it. And I'm assuming they are in the courtroom."

"They are."

"Thank you, Mr. Zeitler, and if you haven't already figured things out, next time you're here please bring a local lawyer— God knows we'll need some more. Unless, of course, you are licensed in this state."

"I am, Your Honor."

"Very well. Next."

Leaning against a railing in a corner, chairless, a lawyer glanced around and said, "Yes, Your Honor, I'm Joe Bradley Hunt with the Skole firm in Jackson, and—"

"Which firm?"

"Skole, Your Honor. Skole, Rumky, Ratliff, Bodini, and Zacharias."

"Sorry I asked. Continue."

"And we represent the interests of the two minor children of Ramona and Ian Dafoe, grandchildren of the deceased."

"Okay. Anyone else?"

Necks craned and eyes scanned the crowd. Judge Atlee did some quick math and said, "A dozen. I count eleven lawyers so far, and there is no reason to believe there won't be more." He shuffled some papers and looked at the spectators in the courtroom. To his left, behind Jake and Lettie, there was a crowd of black people, including Simeon, their kids and grandkids, some cousins and aunts, Cypress, a preacher, and a lot of friends, old and new, who were there to provide moral support for Lettie as she took the first step in fighting for what was rightfully hers. To His Honor's right, across the aisle, behind the throng of lawyers gearing up to oppose the last will, there was a crowd of white people, including Ian and Ramona and their two children;

Herschel and his two kids; his ex-wife, though she was on the back row as far away as possible; Dumas Lee and another reporter; and the usual collection of courthouse regulars who rarely missed a trial or a contested hearing. Deputy Prather stood at the main door, sent there by Ozzie to hear it all and report back later. Lucien Wilbanks sat on the back row on the black side, partially hidden by a beefy young man in front of him. He and Atlee went back many years, and Lucien did not want to be a distraction.

Minutes before they began, Jake had attempted to politely introduce himself to Herschel and Ramona, but they had rudely turned their backs. He was the enemy now, not their father. Ian in particular looked as if he might throw a punch. Their teenage children were turned out in the finest preppy fashions and gave every impression of bearing the arrogance of inherited wealth. Herschel's two children, on the contrary, were ill-kempt and grungy. Just days earlier, the four had been too busy to attend the funeral of their beloved grandfather. Now, though, their priorities had suddenly shifted.

Jake figured the lawyers had impressed upon the families the need for the kids to be there, to be seen, to be closely identified with the consequences of the court's actions. A waste of time, in his opinion, but then the stakes were high.

At the moment, in a crowded courtroom, Jake felt very alone. Next to him, Russell Amburgh was uncooperative, hardly civil, and planning a quick exit from the proceedings. Behind him, only inches away, sat Lettie, a person he thought he could talk to. She, though, was being guarded by a couple of pit bull lawyers who were ready for an alley fight over the fortune. And these were the people on his side of the room! Across the aisle, an entire pack of hyenas was waiting to pounce.

Judge Atlee said, "I've read both wills. We will proceed with the last one, the handwritten will dated October 1. A petition to probate it was filed on October 4. Mr. Brigance, you will begin the administration of the estate as required by law—posting the notification to creditors, filing a preliminary inventory, and so

on. I expect this to be done promptly. Mr. Amburgh, I understand you wish to step aside."

Amburgh slowly stood and said, "That's right, Judge. I have
no stomach for this. As the executor I would be required to take
an oath in which I swear that this is the valid last will and testament of Seth Hubbard, and I simply refuse to take that oath. I
don't like this will and I want no part of it."

"Mr. Brigance?"

Jake stood next to his soon-to-be-ex-client and said, "Your
Honor, Mr. Amburgh was once a lawyer and he knows the basics
of probate. I will prepare an order allowing him to withdraw, and
at the same time I'll submit names for his replacement."

"Please make this a priority. I want the administration to
proceed while we sort out other matters. Regardless of what
happens to the holographic will, or the prior one, the estate of
Mr. Hubbard needs tending to. I assume there are several parties
who intend to contest this will, am I right?"

A squad of lawyers stood, nodding, and Judge Atlee held up
his hand. "Thank you. Please be seated, everyone. Mr. Amburgh,
you may be excused." Amburgh managed a terse "Thanks" as he
scampered from the plaintiff's table and hurried down the aisle.

Judge Atlee adjusted his glasses and said, "We will proceed as
follows. Mr. Brigance, you have ten days to find a substitute executor, and, according to the wishes of the deceased, let's make sure
it's not a lawyer from this county. Once the executor is in place,
you and he will begin the task of locating assets and identifying
liabilities. I would like a preliminary inventory as soon as possible.
In the meantime, the rest of you should file your objections to this
will. Once all parties have properly joined in opposition, we will
meet again and map out a plan for the trial. As you know, either
side may demand a trial by jury. If you so wish, then please make
this demand timely, when you file your objection. Will contests
proceed like all other civil trials in Mississippi, so the rules of
evidence and procedure will apply." He removed his glasses and
chewed on a stem as he surveyed the lawyers. "Since we are
headed for a trial, I'll tell ya'll right now that I will not preside over

one with a dozen lawyers. I cannot envision such a nightmare, nor will I subject a jury, if we do in fact have one, to such abuse. We will define the issues, streamline the procedure, and try the case in an efficient manner. Any questions?"

Oh, a thousand questions, but there would be plenty of time to ask them later. Suddenly, Booker Sistrunk rose, and in his booming baritone said, "Your Honor, I'm not sure what's appropriate at this time, but I would like to suggest that my client, Lettie Lang, be appointed as the substitute executor to take the place of Mr. Amburgh. I have reviewed the law of this state and have found no provision requiring a lawyer or an accountant or the like to serve in this role. Indeed, the law sets forth no requirements for training or experience for one to serve as either an administrator, in the case of an estate with no will, or an executor, in a case like this."

Sistrunk spoke slowly, carefully, with perfect diction, and his words boomed around the courtroom. Judge Atlee and the rest of the lawyers listened and watched. The words were true. Technically, anyone could be named to take the place of Russell Amburgh: any sane person over the age of eighteen. Not even criminals were excluded. However, given the size of the estate and the complex issues facing it, a more experienced, dispassionate hand would be needed. The notion of putting Lettie in charge of a $20 million estate, with Sistrunk whispering in her ear, was shocking, at least to the white people in the courtroom. Even Judge Atlee seemed frozen for a second or two.

Sistrunk wasn't finished. He paused just long enough for the initial shock to register, then continued, "Now, Your Honor, I know that virtually all the probate work is done by the estate's lawyer, under the strict supervision of the court, of course, and for that reason I'd suggest that my firm be designated as counsel of record in this matter. We will work closely with our client, Ms. Lettie Lang, to follow the precise dictates of Mr. Hubbard's wishes. If necessary, we will consult with Mr. Brigance, a fine young lawyer in his own right, but most of the heavy lifting will be done by me and my staff."

And with that, Booker Sistrunk accomplished his goal. The war would now be defined in terms of black versus white.

Herschel and Ramona and their families glared with hatred across the aisle at the group of blacks, who eagerly and some- what smugly returned the looks. Their girl Lettie had been chosen to receive the money, and they were there to fight for her. But the money belonged to the Hubbards. Seth had been out of his mind.

Jake, stunned, shot a fierce look over his shoulder but was ignored by Sistrunk. Jake's first reaction was, How stupid! A predominantly white county means a predominantly white jury. They were a long way from Memphis, where Sistrunk had proven skillful at getting his people on federal juries and winning huge verdicts. But Memphis was another world.

Put nine or ten white folks from Ford County on the jury, make them suffer through a week with Booker Sistrunk, and Ms. Lettie Lang would leave with nothing.

The horde of white lawyers sat as stunned as Jake, but Wade Lanier quickly saw the opportunity. He jumped to his feet and blurted, "We have no objection, Your Honor."

Judge Atlee snapped, "You have no standing to object to anything."

Jake's second thought was, Fine, get me out of here. With this pack of vultures, there will be nothing left. Life is too short to waste a year dodging bullets in a race war.

Judge Atlee said, "Anything else, Mr. Sistrunk?"

"Well, not at this time, Your Honor." Sistrunk turned and looked smugly at Simeon and the family. He had just proven his backbone. He was fearless, could not be intimidated, and was ready for a street brawl. They had hired the right lawyer. Before he sat, he shot a glance at Herschel Hubbard, and with a smirk seemed to say, "Game on, old boy."

Judge Atlee calmly said, "You need to keep researching, Mr. Sistrunk. Our probate laws give supreme deference to the wishes of the person who wrote the will. Mr. Hubbard clearly stated his intentions with regard to the attorney he wanted. There will be no change in that regard. Any other requests you may have should be dealt with by proper motion; that is, once you have associated a lawyer recognized by this court and are duly before it."

Jake began to breathe normally again, though he was still shaken by the brazenness of Sistrunk and his ideas. And his greed. There was little doubt he had signed up Lettie to some form of contingency agreement that gave him a cut of her take. Most plaintiffs' lawyers took one-third of a settlement, 40 percent of a jury verdict, and half where the case was appealed. An ego like Sistrunk, and, admittedly, one with a history of winning, would doubtless be at the top end of those percentages. And if that were not enough, he was craving another pile of cash to be earned by the hour as the probate attorney.

Judge Atlee was finished. He picked up his gavel, said, "We'll meet again in thirty days. Adjourned," and slammed it onto the surface of his bench.

Lettie was immediately engulfed by her attorneys, who whisked her away, through the railing of the bar and to the front row where she was circled by her family and other clingers. As if her life were in danger, they huddled around, stroking her, cooing, offering encouragement. Sistrunk was admired and congratulated for his bold assertions and positions, while Kendrick Bost kept an arm on Lettie's shoulder as she whispered gravely to her loved ones. Cypress, her mother, sat in a wheelchair and wiped tears from her cheeks. What an awful thing they were putting the family through.

Jake was in no mood for small talk, not that anyone tried to engage him. The other lawyers broke off into small pockets of conversation as they repacked their briefcases and prepared to leave. The Hubbard heirs clung together and tried to avoid glaring at the blacks who were after their money. Jake ducked through a side door and was headed for the back stairs when Mr. Pate, the ancient courtroom deputy, called, "Say, Jake, Judge Atlee wants to see you."

In the small cramped room where lawyers gathered for coffee and judges held their off-the-record meetings, Judge

Atlee was removing his robe. "Close the door," he said when Jake walked in.

The judge was no raconteur, no teller of tall legal tales, no jokester. There was little bullshit and rarely was there humor, though, as a judge, he had an audience eager to laugh at anything. "Have a seat, Jake," he said, and both sat at a small desk.

"What an ass," Judge Atlee said. "That might work in Memphis, but not here."

"I think I'm still stunned."

"Do you know Quince Lundy, lawyer down in Smithfield?"

"I've heard of him."

"Older guy, maybe even semiretired. He's done nothing but probate work for a hundred years, really knows his stuff, and straight as an arrow. Old friend of mine. File a motion suggesting Quince and two others—you pick 'em—as the substitute executor, and I'll appoint Quince. You'll get along fine with him. As for you, you're on board until the end. What's your hourly rate?"

"I don't have one, Judge. My clients work for ten bucks an hour if they're lucky. They can't afford to pay a lawyer a hundred."

"I think one fifty is a fair rate in today's market. You agree?"

"One fifty sounds fine, Judge."

"Okay, you're on the clock at one fifty an hour. I'm assuming you have the time."

"Oh yes."

"Good. Because this will eat up your life for the near future. Every sixty days or so, file a petition and ask for attorney's fees. I'll make sure you get paid."

"Thanks, Judge."

"There are a lot of rumors about the size of the estate. Any idea what's true?"

"Russell Amburgh says it's at least twenty million, with most of that in cash. Hidden out of state. Otherwise, everyone in Clanton would know exactly."

"We'd better move fast to protect it. I'll sign an order giving you the authority to take possession of Mr. Hubbard's financial records. Once Quince Lundy is on board, you guys can start digging."

"Yes sir."

Judge Atlee took a long sip of coffee from a paper cup. He looked through a dirty window, seemed to gaze upon the courthouse lawn, and finally said, "I almost feel sorry for that poor woman. She's lost all control, surrounded by people who smell money. She won't have a dime when Sistrunk gets finished with her."

"Assuming the jury finds in her favor."

"Will you request a jury, Jake?"

"I don't know yet. Should I?" The question was far out-of-bounds, but at the moment it didn't seem so. Jake braced himself for the reprimand, but instead Judge Atlee managed a tight grin as he continued staring at nothing outside. "I'd rather have a jury, Jake. I don't mind making tough decisions. That goes with the job. But, in a case like this, it'll be nice to have twelve of our good and faithful citizens in the hot seat. I'd like that, for a change." His grin became a smile.

"I don't blame you. I'll make the request."

"You do that. And Jake, there are a lot of lawyers out there and few that I really trust. Don't hesitate to stop by and say hello and drink coffee if something needs to be discussed. I'm sure you appreciate the significance of this case. There's not much money around here, Jake, never has been. Now, suddenly, there's a pot of gold, and a lot of people want some of it. You don't. I don't. But there are plenty of others. It's important that you and I stay on the same page."

Jake's muscles relaxed for the first time in hours, and he breathed deeply. "I agree, Judge, and thanks."

"I'll see you around."

13

Dumas Lee owned the front page of *The Ford County Times* on Wednesday, October 12. The hearing the day before was evidently the only news in the county. A bold headline announced, **BATTLE LINES DRAWN OVER HUBBARD WILL**, and Dumas kicked off the lead story in his finest tabloid fashion: "A courtroom full of expectant heirs and their eager lawyers squared off yesterday in front of Chancellor Reuben Atlee as the opening shots were fired in what promises to be an epic battle for the fortune of the late Seth Hubbard, who hung himself on October 2."

A photographer had been busy. In the center of the front page was a large photo of Lettie Lang as she was walking into the courthouse, with both Booker Sistrunk and Kendrick Bost tugging at her as if she were an invalid. Under the photo, she was described as "Lettie Lang, age 47 of Box Hill, former housekeeper of Seth Hubbard and presumed beneficiary under his last, handwritten, and suspicious will, accompanied by her two lawyers from Memphis." Next to it were two smaller, candid shots of Herschel and Ramona, also walking somewhere near the courthouse.

Jake read the paper at his desk early Wednesday morning. He sipped coffee, read every word twice looking for mistakes, and was surprised to see Dumas got his facts straight for a change. But he cussed him for using the word "suspicious." Every registered voter in the county was a potential juror. The majority would either read the paper or hear someone talking about it, and out of the gate Dumas had declared the will to be suspicious. The scowling, smirking faces of the well-dressed intruders from Memphis didn't help matters either. As Jake stared at the photo, he tried to imagine a jury of nine whites and three blacks trying to find sympathy for Lettie as $20 million hung in the balance. They would find little. After a week in the courtroom with Booker Sistrunk, they would see through his intentions and void the will. A jury might grow to dislike Herschel and Ramona, but at least they were white and weren't being led by a shyster with the appeal of a TV preacher.

Jake reminded himself that they were, for the moment, on the same team, or at least the same side of the courtroom. He vowed to quit. If Judge Atlee allowed Sistrunk to stay in the game, Jake would withdraw and go look for an ambulance to chase. Anything would be better than a brutal trial in which he was destined to lose. He needed the fees but not the headaches.

There was a commotion downstairs, then footsteps. There was an unmistakable rhythm and clatter to the way Harry Rex climbed the old wooden stairs to Jake's office. His steps were slow and heavy and each seemed determined to shatter boards. The stairwell shook. Roxy called after him, protesting. Badly overweight and pathetically out of shape, he was almost gasping when he kicked open Jake's door and began with a friendly "Damn woman's gone crazy." He tossed a copy of the newspaper onto Jake's desk.

"Morning Harry Rex," Jake said as his friend collapsed in a chair and worked on his heavy breathing, each gasp a bit softer, each exhalation delaying cardiac arrest.

"She tryin' to piss off everybody?" he asked.

"It sure looks that way. You want some coffee?"

"Got a Bud Light?"

"It's nine o'clock in the morning."

"So? I'm not goin' to court today. On days off, I'm startin' earlier."

"Do you think you're drinking too much?"

"Hell no. With my clients, I'm not drinkin' enough. Neither are you."

"I don't keep beer in the office. Don't keep it at home."

"What a life." Harry Rex suddenly reached forward, grabbed the newspaper, held it up, and pointed to the photo of Lettie. "Tell me something, Jake, what does the average white person in this county say when he sees this photo. You got a black house-keeper, who's lookin' all right, and she somehow got herself inserted into the old boy's will, and now she's hired these slick African lawyers from the big city to come down here and grab the money. How does this play over at the Coffee Shop?"

"I think you know."

"Is she stupid?"

"No, but they got to her. Simeon has kinfolks in Memphis, and somehow a connection was made. She has no idea what she's doing and she's getting bad advice."

"You're on her side, Jake. Can't you talk to her?" He tossed the paper back onto the desk.

"No. I thought I could, then she hired Sistrunk. I tried to speak to her in court yesterday, but they were guarding her too closely. Tried to speak to the Hubbard kids, too, but they weren't too friendly."

"You're a popular man these days, Jake."

"I didn't feel too popular yesterday. But Judge Atlee likes me."

"I heard he wasn't too impressed with Sistrunk."

"No, he wasn't. The jury won't be either."

"So you're askin' for a jury?"

"Yes, His Honor wants one, but you didn't hear it from me."

"I did not. You gotta figure out a way to get to her. Sistrunk'll piss off everybody in the state and she won't get a dime."

"Should she?"

"Hell yeah. It's Seth's money, if he wants to leave it to the Communist Party then it's his business. He made it all by himself, he can damned sure give it away as he pleases. Wait till you deal with those two kids, a couple of sacks-a-shit if you ask me, and you'll understand why Seth picked somebody else."

"I thought you hated Seth."

"I did ten years ago, but then I always hate the jerk on the other side. That's what makes me so mean. I get over it eventually. Hate him or love him, he wrote a will before he died and the law has got to support that will, if in fact it's valid."

"Is it valid?"

"That's up to the jury. And it'll be attacked from every direction."

"How would you attack the will?"

Harry Rex sat back and swung an ankle over a knee. "Been thinkin' about that. First, I'd hire me some experts, some medical guys who'll testify that Seth was drugged up with painkillers, that his body was ravaged by lung cancer and because of all the chemo and radiation and medications that he'd been hit with over the past year he couldn't've been thinkin' clearly. He was in horrible pain, and I'd hire me another expert to describe what pain can do to the thought process. Don't know where these experts are, but, hell, you can hire an expert to say anything. Keep in mind, Jake, the average juror in this county barely finished high school. Not that sophisticated. Get a slick expert or a whole team of them and the jury can really get confused. Hell, I could make Seth Hubbard look like a slobbering idiot as he was stickin' his head through that noose. Don't you have to be crazy to hang yourself?"

"Can't answer that."

"Second. Seth had zipper problems, couldn't keep his pants on. Don't know if he ever crossed the color line, but maybe he did. If a white jury sniffs even the slightest suspicion that Seth was gettin' somethin' more than hot food and starched shirts from his housekeeper, then they'll be quick to turn against Miss Lettie."

"They can't drag up a dead man's sex life."

"True, but they can nibble around the edges of Lettie's. They can imply, infer, exaggerate, and use all manner of loose language. If she takes the witness stand, which she's bound to do, she becomes fair game."

"She has to testify."

"Of course she does. And here's the kicker, Jake. It really doesn't matter what is said in court or who says it. The truth is that if Booker Sistrunk is in that courtroom rantin' and showin' his black ass in front of a white jury, then your chances are zero."

"I'm not sure I care that much."

"You have to care. It's your job. It's a big trial. And it's a fat fee. You're workin' by the hour now, and gettin' paid, and that's rare in our world, Jake. If this thing goes to trial, then an appeal and so on, you'll make a half-million bucks over the next three years. How many DUIs you gotta do to make that kinda money?"

"Hadn't thought about the fee."

"Well, every other ambulance chaser in town certainly has. It'll be generous. A windfall for a street lawyer like you. But you need to win, Jake, and to win you gotta get rid of Sistrunk."

"How?"

"I'm thinkin' about that too. Just give me some time. Some damage has already been done with that damned picture in the paper, and you can bet Doofus'll do it again next hearing. We gotta get Sistrunk bounced as soon as possible."

To Jake, it was significant that Harry Rex was now using the word "we." There was no one more loyal, no one he'd rather have in the foxhole. Nor was there another legal mind as cunning and devious. "Give me a day or two," he said as he climbed to his feet. "I need a beer."

An hour later, Jake was still at his desk when the Booker Sistrunk matter took a turn for the worse. "There's a lawyer named Rufus Buckley on the phone," Roxy announced through the intercom.

Jake took a deep breath and said, "Okay." He stared at the blinking light and racked his brain for any idea as to why Buckley would be calling. They had not spoken since the trial of Carl Lee Hailey, and if their paths never again crossed both would have been content. A year earlier, during Buckley's reelection, Jake had quietly supported his opponent, as had most of the lawyers in Clanton, if not the entire Twenty-Second Judicial District. Over a twelve-year career, Buckley had managed to alienate almost every lawyer in the five-county district. The payback was sweet, and now the former hard-charging DA with statewide ambitions was stuck at home in Smithfield, an hour down the road, where he was rumored to be puttering around a small office on Main Street doing wills and deeds and no-fault divorces.

"Hello Governor," Jake said in a deliberate effort to resume hard feelings. Three years had not diminished his low regard for the man.

"Well, hello, Jake," Buckley said politely. "I was hoping we could forgo the cheap shots."

"Sorry, Rufus, didn't mean anything by it." But of course he did. At one point not too long ago a lot of people called him Governor. "What are you up to these days?"

"Just practicing law and taking it easy. I do more oil and gas than anything else."

Sure you do. Buckley had spent most of his adult life trying to convince folks that his wife's family's natural gas leases were the source of immense wealth. They were not. The Buckleys lived far below their pretensions.

"That's nice. What's on your mind?"

"Just got off the phone with a Memphis lawyer named Booker Sistrunk. I believe you've met him. Seems to be a nice guy. Anyway, he's associating me as Mississippi counsel in the Seth Hubbard case."

"Why would he pick you, Rufus?" Jake asked impulsively as his shoulders sagged.

"Reputation, I guess."

No, Sistrunk had done his homework and found the one lawyer in the entire state who hated Jake with a passion. Jake could only imagine the vile things Buckley had said about him.

"I'm not sure where you fit, Rufus."

"We're working on that. Booker wants you off the case to begin with so he can take over. He mentioned perhaps requesting a change of venue for the trial. He says Judge Atlee has an obvious bias against him, so he'll ask the judge to step aside. These are just preliminary matters, Jake. As you know, Sistrunk is a high-powered litigator with plenty of resources. I suppose that's why he wants me on his team."

"Well, welcome aboard, Rufus. I doubt if Sistrunk told you the rest of the story, but he has already tried to get me kicked off. Didn't work because Judge Atlee can read as well as anyone. The will specifically names me as the attorney for the estate. Atlee is not going to recuse himself, nor will he move the trial out of Clanton. You boys are pissing in the wind and pissing off every potential juror in the county. Pretty stupid, in my opinion, Rufus, and the stupidity is killing our chances."

"We'll see. You're inexperienced, Jake, and you need to step aside. Oh sure, you've had a handful of nice verdicts in criminal cases, but this ain't criminal, Jake. This is complicated, high-dollar civil litigation, and you're already in over your head."

Jake bit his tongue and reminded himself how much he despised the voice on the other end. Slowly, deliberately, he said, "You were a prosecutor, Rufus. When did you become an expert in civil litigation?"

"I'm a litigator. I live in the courtroom. In the past year I've tried nothing but civil cases. Plus, I've got Sistrunk at the table. He nailed the Memphis Police Department three times last year for more than a million dollars."

"And they're all on appeal. He hasn't collected a dime."

"But he will. The same way we'll kick ass with the Hubbard matter."

"What are you guys raking off the top, Rufus? Fifty percent?"

"Confidential, Jake. You know that."

"It should be made public."

"Don't be envious, Jake."

"Later, Rufus," Jake said and hung up.

He took a deep breath, jumped to his feet, and walked downstairs. "Back in a minute," he said to Roxy as he passed her desk. It was 10:30 and the Coffee Shop was empty. Dell was drying forks at the counter when Jake walked in and sat on a stool nearby. "A time-out?" she asked.

"Yes. Decaf coffee please." Jake often appeared at odd hours, and it was usually in an effort to get away from the office and the phone. She poured him a cup and eased closer, still drying the flatware.

"What do you know?" Jake asked as he stirred in sugar. With Dell, there was a fine line between what she knew and what she'd heard. Most of her customers thought she would repeat anything, but Jake knew better. After twenty-five years at the Coffee Shop, she had heard enough false rumors and outright lies to know how damaging they could be; so, in spite of her reputation, she was generally careful.

"Well," she began slowly, "I don't believe Lettie helped herself by bringing in those black lawyers from Memphis." Jake nodded and took a sip. She went on, "Why did she do that, Jake? I thought you were her lawyer." She spoke of Lettie as if she'd known her a lifetime, though they'd never met. This was not unusual now in Clanton.

"No, I'm not her lawyer. I'm the lawyer for the estate, for the will. She and I are on the same side, but she couldn't hire me."

"Does she need a lawyer?"

"No. My job is to protect the will and follow its wishes. I do my job, and she gets her money. There's no reason for her to hire a lawyer."

"Did you explain this to her?"

"I did, and I thought she understood it."

"What happened? Why are they involved?"

Jake took another sip and reminded himself to be careful. The two often swapped inside information, but delicate matters were still off-limits. "I don't know, but I suspect somebody in Memphis heard about the will. Word filtered up to Booker Sistrunk. He smelled money, so he made the drive down, pulled up in front of her house in his black Rolls-Royce, and swooped her away. He promised her the moon, and in return he gets a piece."

"How much?"

"Only they know. It's a confidential matter that's never revealed."

"A black Rolls-Royce? Are you kidding, Jake?"

"Nope, they spotted him yesterday as he arrived in court; parked in front of Security Bank. He was driving, his co-counsel was riding shotgun. And Lettie was in the rear seat with a guy in a dark suit, probably a bodyguard of some variety. They're putting on a show and Lettie's fallen in with them."

"I don't get it."

"Neither do I."

"Prather was saying this morning that they might try and change venue. Move it to another county where they can get more black jurors. Any truth to it?"

"Just a rumor, I guess. You know Marshall. I swear I think he starts half the gossip in town. Any more rumors?"

"Oh yes, Jake. They're buzzing everywhere. The guys lay off when you walk in, but as soon as you're gone it's all they talk about." The door opened and two clerks from the tax collector's office walked in and sat at a table nearby. Jake knew them and nodded politely. They were close enough to hear, and they would indeed absorb everything.

He leaned toward Dell and said softly, "Keep your ears open, okay?"

"Jake, honey, you know I miss nothing."

"I know." Jake left a dollar for the coffee and said good-bye.

Still unwilling to return to his desk, Jake strolled around the square and stopped at the office of Nick Norton, another sole practitioner who had graduated from the Ole Miss Law School the year Jake started. Nick had inherited the law office from his uncle and was, in all likelihood, somewhat busier than Jake. They referred clients back and forth across the square, and in ten years had managed to avoid any unpleasant disagreements.

Two years earlier, Nick had represented Marvis Lang when he pleaded guilty to drug trafficking and assault with a deadly weapon. The family had paid a fee of $5,000 in cash, less than what Nick wanted but more than what most of his clients could pay. Marvis had been dead guilty and there had been little wiggle room; plus, he had been unwilling to squeal on his co-defendants. Nick negotiated a twelve-year sentence. Four days earlier, over lunch, Nick had told Jake everything he could about the Lang family and Marvis.

He was with a client, but his secretary had pulled the file. Jake promised to copy what he wanted and return it soon. No rush, said the secretary. It's been closed for some time.

Wade Lanier's favorite lunch spot was Hal & Mal's, an old Jackson haunt a few blocks from the state capitol and a ten-minute walk from his office on State Street. He took his favorite table, ordered a glass of tea, and waited impatiently for five minutes until Ian Dafoe walked through the door and joined him. They ordered sandwiches, covered the weather and football, and soon enough got down to business. "We'll take the case to trial," Lanier said gravely, his voice barely above a whisper, as if delivering an important secret.

Ian sort of nodded and shrugged and said, "That's good to hear." Anything to the contrary would have been a surprise. There weren't too many jackpots in the state and lots of lawyers were circling around this one.

"But we don't need any help," Lanier said. "Herschel has that clown from Memphis, unlicensed of course in Mississippi, and he'll just get in the way. There's not a damned thing that boy can do to help us, and he can do plenty to irritate me. Can you talk to Herschel and convince him that he and his sister are on the same team and I can handle it?"

"I don't know. Herschel has his own ideas and Ramona doesn't always agree."

"Well, figure it out. The courtroom is already crowded, and I suspect Judge Atlee will start whittling down the lineup pretty soon."

"What if Herschel says no, wants to keep his own lawyer?"

"We'll deal with it then. First, though, try and convince him that his lawyer is not needed, that's just another finger in the pie."

"Okay, along those same lines, what's your fee proposal?"

"We'll take it on a contingency. One-third of the recovery. The legal issues are not overly complex and the trial should last less than a week. We would normally suggest 25 percent of any settlement, but that looks highly unlikely, in my opinion."

"Why not?"

"It's all or nothing, one will or the other. No room for compromise."

Ian considered this but didn't fully grasp it. The sandwiches arrived and they spent a few minutes arranging the food on their plates. Lanier said, "We're in, but only if both Ramona and Herschel sign on. We—"

"So you prefer a third of fourteen million as opposed to a third of only seven," Ian interrupted in a half-baked attempt to add a little humor. But it fell flat. Lanier ignored it and took a bite; he didn't smile very often anyway. He swallowed and said, "You got it. I can win this case, but I'm not going to have some jackass from Memphis looking over my shoulder, getting in the way, and alienating the jury. Plus, Ian, you gotta understand that we, my partners and I, are extremely busy. We've vowed to stop taking new cases. My partners are reluctant to commit the firm's time and resources to a will contest. Hell, we got three trials against Shell Oil scheduled for next month. Offshore oil rig injuries."

Ian filled his mouth with fries so he wouldn't be able to speak. He also held his breath for a second in the hopes that the lawyer would not launch into yet another round of war stories about some of his greatest cases and trials. It was an obnoxious habit most trial lawyers were afflicted with, and Ian had suffered through the routine before.

But Lanier resisted the temptation and kept going. "And you're right, if we're taking the case, we want both heirs, not only you. It's the same amount of work; actually, it's less work for us because we won't waste time dealing with that boy from Memphis."

"I'll see what I can do," Ian said.

"We'll bill you each month for the expenses, and there'll be some, mainly expert witnesses."

"How much?"

"We've worked up a litigation budget. Fifty thousand should cover the expenses." Lanier glanced around, though no other diner could possibly hear a word they were saying. In a lower voice, he said, "Plus, we need to hire an investigator, and not just your average run-of-the-mill gumshoe. We gotta spend some money on a guy who can infiltrate the world of Lettie Lang and find some dirt, and it won't be easy."

"How much?"

"Strictly a guess, but I'd say another twenty-five."

"I'm not sure I can afford this lawsuit."

Finally, a smile from Lanier, but a forced one. "You're about to get rich, Ian, just stick with me."

"What makes you so confident? When we met last week you were pretty cautious, even doubtful."

Another gruff smile. "That was our first conversation, Ian. The surgeon is always reserved when confronted with a complicated procedure. Now, things are getting clearer. We were in court yesterday morning. I got the lay of the land. I heard the opposition. And, most important, I got a good look at Lettie Lang's lawyers, those slick-ricks from Memphis. They are the key to our victory. Put them before a jury in Clanton, and the handwritten will becomes a bad joke."

"Got that. Let's get back to the seventy-five grand in expense money. I thought some law firms fronted the expense money and took a reimbursement out of the verdict or settlement."

"We've done that."

"Come on, Wade. You do it all the time because most of your clients are broke. They're working stiffs who get mangled in job injuries, stuff like that."

"Yes, but that's not you, Ian. You can afford to finance the lawsuit; others cannot. Ethics dictate that a client must cover the expenses if he's financially able."

"Ethics?" Ian asked with a smirk. It was almost an insult, but Lanier took no offense. He was well versed in the ethics of his profession when they could be beneficial; otherwise, he ignored them.

Lanier said, "Come on, Ian. It's only seventy-five grand, and it'll be spread over the next year or so."

"I'll pay up to twenty-five. Beyond that, you can cover it and we'll settle at the end."

"All right. Whatever. We'll figure it out later. We've got bigger problems. Start with Herschel, if he doesn't ditch his lawyer and sign up with me, then I've got bigger fish to fry. Clear enough?"

"I guess. All I can do is try."

14

The Berring Lumber Company was a compound of mismatched metal buildings encircled with chain link eight feet tall and secured behind heavy gates partially opened, as if visitors weren't really that welcome. It was hidden at the end of a long asphalt drive, unseen from Highway 21 and less than a mile from the Tyler County line. Once inside and just past the main gate, office buildings were to the left and acres of raw timber were to the right. Straight ahead was a series of semi-attached buildings where the pine and hardwoods were cleaned, sized, cut, and treated before being stored in warehouses. A parking lot to the right was filled with well-worn pickup trucks, a sign that business was booming; folks had jobs, which were always scarce in this part of the country.

Seth Hubbard lost the lumber yard in his second divorce, only to get it back a few years later. Harry Rex engineered the forced sale, for $200,000, and made off with the money, for his client, of course. Seth, true to form, waited patiently in the bushes until a downturn, then squeezed the desperate owner for a quick sale. No one knew where the name Berring came from. As Jake was learning, Seth pulled names randomly from the air and stuck them on his corporations. When he owned it the first time around, it was Palmyra Lumber. To confuse anyone who might be watching, he selected Berring for the second go.

Berring was his home office, though he had others at various times. After he sold out, and after he was diagnosed with lung cancer, he consolidated his records and spent more time at Berring. The day after his death, Sheriff Ozzie Walls stopped by and had a friendly chat with the office employees. He strongly suggested that nothing be touched. The lawyers would soon follow and from there things would only get complicated.

Jake had spoken twice on the phone with Arlene Trotter, Seth's secretary. She had been pleasant enough, though certainly not eager to help. On Friday, almost two weeks after the suicide, Jake walked through the front door and into a reception area with a desk in the center of it. Behind the desk was a heavily made-up young lady with wild black hair, a tight sweater, and the unmistakable look of a woman who was fast and loose. A brass plate gave only her first name—Kamila— and Jake's second or third impression was that the exotic name matched the person. She offered a comely smile and Jake was already thinking about the comment "Seth had zipper problems."

He introduced himself. She did not stand but gave a soft handshake. "Arlene's waiting," she cooed as she pushed a button to someone's office.

"I'm very sorry about your boss," Jake said. He did not remember seeing Kamila at the funeral, and he was certain he would have remembered the face and figure had she been there.

"It's very sad," she said.

"How long have you worked here?"

"Two years. Seth was a nice man, and a good boss."

"I never had the pleasure of meeting him."

Arlene Trotter appeared from a hallway and offered a hand. She was around fifty but completely gray; a little heavy but fighting it. Her matching pantsuit was a decade out of style. They chatted as they walked deeper into the hodgepodge of offices. "That's his," she said, pointing to a closed door. Her desk was right beside the door, literally guarding it. "His records are over there," she added, pointing to another door. "Nothing has been touched. Russell Amburgh called me the night he died and said to secure everything. Then the sheriff stopped by the next day and said the same thing. It's been very quiet around here." Her voice cracked for a second.

"I'm sorry."

"You'll probably find his books in good order. Seth kept good records of everything, and as he got sicker he spent more time organizing everything."

"When did you last see him?"

"The Friday before he died. He was not feeling well and he left around 3:00 p.m. Said he was going home to rest. I heard he wrote that last will here. Is that right?"

"That appears to be correct. Did you know anything about it?"

She paused for a moment and seemed unable, or unwilling, to answer. "Can I ask you a question, Mr. Brigance?"

"Sure."

"Whose side are you on? Are we supposed to trust you, or do we need our own lawyers?"

"Well, I don't think more lawyers is a good idea. I am the attorney for the estate, chosen by Mr. Hubbard, and instructed by him to make sure his last will, the handwritten will, is honored and followed."

"And that's the will that gives everything to his maid?"

"Basically, yes."

"Okay, what's our role in this?"

"You don't have a role in the administration of his estate. You might be called as a witness if the will is contested by his family."

"As in a trial, in a courtroom?" She took a step back and seemed frightened.

"It's possible, but it's too early to worry about it. How many people here worked with Seth on a daily basis?"

Arlene wrung her hands and collected her thoughts. She leaned back and situated herself on the corner of her desk. "Me, Kamila, and Dewayne. That's about it. There are some offices on the other side, but those guys didn't see much of Seth. To be honest, we didn't see much of him either, not until the past year when he was sick. Seth preferred to be on the road, checking his factories, his timber, running after his deals, flying to Mexico to open another furniture plant. He really didn't like to stay at home."

"Who kept up with him?"

"That was my job. We talked every day by phone. I made some of his travel arrangements, but he usually preferred to do that himself. He was not one to delegate. He paid all of his personal bills, wrote every check, balanced every account, kept up with every dime. His CPA is a guy in Tupelo—"

"I've spoken to him."

"He has boxes of records."

"I'd like to speak to you, Kamila, and Dewayne later, if possible."

"Sure. We're all here."

The room had no windows and poor lighting. An old desk and chair indicated that it once might have been used as an office, but not recently. A thick layer of dust covered everything. One wall was lined with tall, black, metal file cabinets. Another wall had nothing but a 1987 Kenworth Truck calendar, hanging by a nail. Four imposing cardboard boxes were stacked on the desk, and that's where Jake began. Careful to keep things in order, he flipped through the files in the first box, noting what was in them but not exactly crunching the numbers. That would come later.

The first box was labeled "Real Estate," and it was filled with deeds, canceled mortgages, appraisals, tax bills, tax assessments, paid invoices from contractors, copies of checks written by Seth, and closing statements from lawyers. There were records for Seth's home place on Simpson Road; a cabin near Boone, North Carolina; a condo in a high-rise near Destin, Florida; and several parcels of what appeared at first glance to be raw land. The second box was labeled "Timber Contracts." The third was "Bank—Brokerage," and Jake's interest rose somewhat. A Merrill Lynch portfolio in an Atlanta office had a balance of almost $7 million. A bond fund at UBS in Zurich was valued at just over $3 million. A cash account at the Royal Bank of Canada on the island of Grand Cayman had $6.5 million. But all three of these rather exotic and exciting accounts had been closed in late September. Jake dug deeper, followed the trail that Seth had carefully left behind, and soon found the money sitting in a bank in Birmingham, earning 6 percent annually and just waiting for probate: $21.2 million, cash.

Such figures made him dizzy. For a small-town lawyer living in a rented house and driving a car with almost 200,000 miles on the odometer, the scene was surreal: he, Jake, poking through cardboard boxes in a dusty, semi-lit storage room in a prefabricated office building at a backwoods sawmill in rural Mississippi, and casually looking at sums of money that greatly exceeded the combined lifetime earnings of every lawyer now working in Ford County. He started laughing.

The money was really there! He shook his head in amazement and suddenly had a profound admiration for Mr. Seth Hubbard.

Someone rapped on the door and Jake almost jumped out of his skin. He closed the box, opened the door, and stepped outside. Arlene said, "Mr. Brigance, this is Dewayne Squire. His official title is vice president, but in reality he just does what I tell him." Arlene managed a laugh, the first one. Jake and Dewayne exchanged a nervous handshake while shapely Kamila watched close by. The three employees stared at him, obviously wishing to discuss something important. Dewayne was a wiry, hyper sort, who, as it turned out, chain-smoked Kools with little regard for where his fumes drifted.

"Can we talk to you?" asked Arlene, the unquestioned leader. Dewayne fired up a Kool, his hands palsy-like as he arranged the cigarette. Talk, as in a serious conversation, not just a chat about the weather.

"Sure," Jake said. "What's on your mind?"

Arlene thrust forward a business card and asked, "Do you know this man?" Jake looked at it. Reed Maxey, Attorney-at-Law, Jackson, Mississippi. "No," Jake said. "Never heard of him. Why?"

"Well, he dropped by last Tuesday, said he was working on Mr. Hubbard's estate, and that the court was concerned about the handwritten will that you've filed or whatever it's called; said the will is probably invalid because Seth was obviously doped up and out of his mind when he was planning to kill himself and at the same time writing that will; said that the three of us would be crucial witnesses because we saw Seth the Friday before the suicide and it would be up to us to testify as to how doped up he was; and, to boot, the real will, the one prepared by real lawyers and such, leaves some money to us as friends and employees; so, he said, it would be in our best interests to tell the truth, tell how Seth lacked—what was the term—"

"Testamentary capacity," Dewayne said from deep within the menthol fog.

"That's it—testamentary capacity. He made it sound like Seth was crazy."

Stunned, Jake managed to maintain a grim face and give away nothing. His first reaction was anger—how dare another lawyer step into his case, tell lies, and tamper with witnesses. There were so many ethical violations Jake couldn't think of them all. His second reaction, though, was more restrained—this lawyer was a fraud, a fake. No one would do this.

He kept his cool and said, "Well, I'll have a talk with this lawyer and tell him to butt out."

"What's in the other will, the real one?" Dewayne asked.

"I haven't seen it. It was prepared by some lawyers in Tupelo, and they have not yet been required to show it."

"Do you think we're in it?" Kamila asked without the slightest effort at subtlety.

"Don't know."

"Can we find out?" she asked.

"I doubt it." Jake wanted to ask if such knowledge might affect their testimony, but he decided to say as little as possible.

Arlene said, "He asked a lot of questions about Seth and how he was acting that Friday. He wanted to know how he was feeling and all about his medications."

"And what did you tell him?"

"Not much. To be honest, he was not the kind of person I wanted to talk to. He was shifty-eyed and—"

"A real fast talker," Dewayne added. "Too fast. At times I couldn't understand him and I kept thinking, This guy's a lawyer? Hate to see him in court, in front of a jury."

Kamila said, "He got pretty aggressive, too, almost demanding that we tell our stories a certain way. He really wanted us to say that Seth was unbalanced because of all the drugs."

Dewayne, smoke pouring from his nostrils, said, "At one point he placed his briefcase on Arlene's desk, upright, in an odd position, and made no effort to open it. He's trying to tape this, I said to myself. He's got a recorder in there."

"No, he wasn't too smooth," Arlene said. "We believed him at first, you know. Guy comes in wearing a nice dark suit, says he's a lawyer, hands over his card, and seems to know a lot about Seth Hubbard and his business. He insisted on talking to the three of us at the same time, and we didn't know how to say no. So we talked, or, rather, he talked. We did most of the listening."

"How would you describe this guy?" Jake asked. "Age, height, weight, so on."

The three looked at each other with great reluctance, certain that there would be little agreement. "How old?" Arlene asked the others. "I'd say forty."

Dewayne nodded and Kamila said, "Yes, maybe forty-five. Six feet, thick, I'd say two hundred pounds."

"At least two hundred," Dewayne said. "Dark hair, real dark, thick, kinda shaggy—"

"Needed a haircut," Arlene said. "Thick mustache and sideburns. No glasses."

"He smoked Camels," Dewayne said. "Filters."

"I'll track him down and find out what he's up to," Jake said, though by then he was fairly certain there was no lawyer named Reed Maxey. Even the dumbest of lawyers would know that such a visit would lead to sure trouble and an ethics investigation. Nothing added up.

"Should we talk to a lawyer?" Kamila asked. "I mean, this is something new for me, for us. It's kinda scary."

"Not yet," Jake said. He planned to get them one-on-one and hear their stories. A group talk might sway the narrative. "Perhaps later, but not now."

"What'll happen to this place?" Dewayne asked, then noisily filled his lungs.

Jake walked across the open space and roughly yanked open a window so he could breathe. "Why can't you smoke outside?" Kamila hissed at the vice president. It was obvious the smoking issue had been roiling for some time. Their boss had been dying of lung cancer and his office suite smelled like burned charcoal. Of course smoking was permitted.

Jake walked back, stood before them, and said, "Mr. Hubbard, in his will, directed his executor to sell all of his assets for fair value and reduce everything to cash. This business will continue operating until someone buys it."

"When will that happen?" Arlene asked.

"Whenever the right offer comes along. Now, or two years from now. Even if the estate gets bogged down in a will contest, Mr. Hubbard's assets will be protected by the court. I'm sure word is out in these parts that this business will go on the block. We might get an offer in the near future. Until then, nothing changes. Assuming, of course, that the employees here can continue to run things."

"Dewayne's been running it for five years," Arlene said graciously.

"We'll carry on," he said.

"Good. Now, if there's nothing else, I need to get back into the records." The three thanked him and left.

Thirty minutes later, as Arlene puttered at her desk, Jake walked over and said, "I'd like to see his office." She waved her arm and said, "It's unlocked." Then she stood and opened the door for Jake. It was a long narrow room, with a desk and chairs at one end and a cheap conference table at the other. Not surprisingly, there was a lot of wood on display: heart-pine walls and flooring, stained to a bronze-like finish; darker oak book-shelves along the walls, many of them empty. There was no ego wall—no diplomas because Seth had earned none; no civic club awards; no photos with politicians. In fact, there was not a single photo anywhere in the office. The desk appeared to be a custom-made table with drawers, and the top of it was virtually bare. One stack of papers and three empty ashtrays.

On the one hand, it was what you would expect from a country boy who had managed to put together some assets in his later years. On the other hand, it was hard to believe that a man worth $20 million wouldn't have a nicer office.

"Everything's neat and tidy," Jake said, almost to himself.

"Seth liked things in order," Arlene said. They walked to the far end where Jake pulled a chair away from the conference table and said, "Got a minute?" She sat down too as if she had been expecting a conversation and was looking forward to it.

Jake pulled over a phone and said, "Let's call this Reed Maxey guy, okay?"

"Okay. Whatever." You're the lawyer.

Jake dialed the number on the business card, and to his surprise got a receptionist, who announced the name of a large, well-known Jackson law firm. Jake asked for Mr. Reed Maxey, who evidently worked there because she said, "One moment please." The next female voice said, "Mr. Maxey's office." Jake gave his name, and asked to speak to the lawyer. "Mr. Maxey is out of town and won't be back until Monday," she said. Turning on the charm, Jake explained the basics of what he was doing and, with a hint of gloom, said he was afraid someone might be impersonating Mr. Reed Maxey. "Was he in Ford County last Tuesday?" he asked.

"Oh, no. He's been in Dallas on business since Monday." Jake said he had a physical description of her boss, and proceeded to describe the impostor. At one point, the secretary chuckled and said, "No, no, there's some mistake. The Reed Maxey I work for is sixty-two years old, bald, and is shorter than me and I'm five nine."

"Do you know of another lawyer in Jackson named Reed Maxey?" he asked.

"No, sorry."

Jake thanked her and promised to call her boss next week for a more in-depth discussion. When he hung up he said, "Just what I thought. The guy was lying. He was not a lawyer. He may be working for one, but he's a fake."

Poor Arlene just stared at him, unable to put words together. He went on, "I have no idea who the guy is and we'll probably never see him again. I'll try and find out, but we may never know. I suspect he was sent by someone involved in the case, but I can only speculate."

"But why?" she managed to ask.

"To intimidate you, confuse you, frighten you. In all likelihood, the three of you, and perhaps others who work here, will be called to testify about Seth's behavior in the days before he died. Was he of sound mind? Was he acting strange? Was he heavily medicated? If so, were the drugs affecting his judgment? These will be crucial questions down the road."

She seemed to ponder them as Jake waited. After a long pause, he said, "So, Arlene, let's have some answers. He wrote the will right here in this office on Saturday morning. He had to mail it before noon for me to receive it Monday. You saw him Friday, right?"

"Yes."

"Did you notice anything unusual?"

She pulled a tissue from a pocket and touched her eyes. "I'm sorry," she said, crying before she'd really said anything. This could take some time, Jake thought. She pulled herself together, stiffened her spine, and smiled at Jake. "You know, Mr. Brigance, I'm not certain who to trust in this situation, but, to be perfectly honest, I trust you."

"Thanks, I guess."

"You see, my brother was on that jury."

"Which jury?"

"Carl Lee Hailey."

All twelve names were forever etched in Jake's memory. He smiled and asked, "Which one?"

"Barry Acker. My youngest brother."

"I'll never forget him."

"He has a lot of respect for you, because of that trial and all."

"And I have a lot of respect for him. They were very courageous, and they reached the right verdict."

"When I heard that you were the lawyer for Seth's estate, I felt better. But then, when we heard about his last will, well, it's pretty confusing."

"I understand. Let's trust each other, okay? Drop the 'Mister' stuff. Call me Jake, and tell me the truth. Fair enough?"

Arlene placed the tissue on the table and relaxed in her chair. "Fair enough, but I don't want to go to court."

"Let's worry about that later. For now, just give me some background."

"Okay." She swallowed hard, braced herself, and let it rip. "Seth's last days were not pleasant. He'd been up and down for a month or so, post-chemo. He had two rounds of chemo and radiation, lost his hair and a lot of weight, so weak and sick he couldn't get out of bed. But he was a tough old guy and wouldn't quit. It was lung cancer, though, and when the tumors came back he knew the end was near. He stopped traveling and spent more time here. He was in pain, taking a lot of Demerol. He would come in early, drink some coffee, and feel okay for a few hours, but then he would fade. I never saw him take the painkillers but he told me about them. At times he was drowsy and dizzy, and even nauseous. He insisted on driving and that worried us."

"Worried who?"

"The three of us. We took care of Seth. He never allowed people to get close. You said you never met him. I'm not surprised because Seth avoided people. He hated small talk. He was not a warm person. He was a loner who didn't want anyone knowing his business or doing things for him. He'd get his own coffee. If I took it to him he wouldn't say thanks. He trusted Dewayne to run his business, but they didn't spend much time together. Kamila's been here a couple of years and Seth really liked to flirt with her. She's a tart, but a sweet girl, and he liked her. But that's it. Just the three of us."

"In his last days, did you see him do anything out of the ordinary?"

"Not really. He felt bad. He napped a lot. He seemed upbeat on that Friday. We've talked about it, the three of us, and it's not unusual for people who've made the decision to commit suicide to become relaxed, even look forward to the end. I think Seth knew on that Friday what he was about to do. He was tired of it all. He was dying anyway."

"Did he ever discuss his will?"

She found this funny and uttered a quick laugh. "Seth didn't talk about his private matters. Never. I've worked here for six years and I've never heard him say a word about his children, grandchildren, relatives, friends, enemies—"

"Lettie Lang?"

"Not a word. I've never been to his house, never met that woman, know nothing about her. I saw her picture in the paper this week, first time I've seen her face."

"It's rumored Seth liked the ladies."

"I've heard those rumors, but he never touched me, never came on. If Seth Hubbard had five girlfriends, you'd never know it."

"Were you aware of what he was doing with his businesses?"

"Most of it. A lot of stuff crossed my desk. It had to. He warned me many times about confidentiality. But I never knew it all; not sure anybody did. When he sold out last year, he gave me a bonus of $50,000. Dewayne and Kamila got bonuses too, but I have no idea how much. He paid us well. Seth was a fair man who expected his people to work hard and he didn't mind paying them. And there's something else you should know. Seth was not a bigot like most white people around here. We have eighty employees on this yard: half white, half black, all paid the same scale. I've heard all of his furniture factories and lumber yards work the same way. He wasn't much for politics, but he despised the way black people have been treated in the South.

He was just a fair man. I came to respect him a great deal." Her voice cracked and she went for the tissue.

Jake glanced at his watch and was surprised to see it was almost noon. He'd been there for two and a half hours. He said he had to go, but would return early the following week with a Mr. Quince Lundy, the new court-appointed administrator. On the way out, he spoke to Dewayne and got a pleasant good-bye from Kamila.

As he drove back to Clanton, his mind spun with the possible scenarios that involved some thug posing as a big-firm Jackson lawyer and trying to intimidate potential witnesses; and doing so just days after the suicide and before the first court hearing. Whoever he was, he would never be seen again. More than likely, he worked for one of the lawyers representing Herschel or Ramona or their kids. Wade Lanier was Jake's top suspect. He ran a ten-man litigation firm with a reputation for aggressive and creative tactics. Jake had spoken to a classmate who mixed it up often with the Lanier firm. The scouting report was impressive but also disheartening. When it came to ethics, the firm was notorious for breaking the rules, then running to the judge and pointing fingers at the other guys. "Don't turn your back," Jake's friend had said.

For three years, Jake had carried a gun to protect himself from Klansmen and other crazies. Now, he was beginning to wonder if he needed protection from the sharks swimming after the Hubbard fortune.

15

Sleep was fleeting these nights as Lettie found herself yielding even more space to her family. Simeon had not left home in over a week, and he took up half the bed. Lettie shared the other half with her two grandchildren. Two nephews were sleeping on the floor.

She awoke as the sun was rising. She was on her side, looking at her husband wrapped in a blanket and snoring off last night's beer. Without moving, she watched him for a while as her thoughts drifted unpleasantly. He was getting fat and gray, and his paychecks were shrinking as the years clicked along. Hey big boy, time for a road trip, huh? Time to disappear as only you can do and give me a break around here for a month or two. You're good for nothing but sex, but who can do that with grandkids in the room?

Simeon, though, was not leaving. No one was leaving Lettie nowadays. She had to admit that his behavior had improved dramatically in the past couple of weeks, since, of course, Mr. Hubbard had passed and altered things. Simeon still drank every night, but not to excess, not like before. He was kind to Cypress, offering to run errands for her and refraining from his usual insulting manner. He was showing patience with the children. He had cooked twice on the grill and cleaned the kitchen, a first. Last Sunday, he went to church with the family. The most obvious change was his gentle and thoughtful nature when he was around his wife.

He hadn't hit her in several years, but when you've been beaten you never forget it. The bruises go away but the scars remain, deep, hidden, raw. You stay beaten. It takes a real coward to beat a woman. Eventually, he had said he was sorry. She said she forgave him, but she did not. In her book some sins cannot be forgiven, and beating your wife is one of them. She had made a vow that she was still determined to keep—one day she would walk away and be free. It might be ten years or twenty, but she would find the courage to leave his sorry ass.

She was not sure if Mr. Hubbard had made a divorce more or less likely. On the one hand, it would be far more difficult to leave Simeon when he was fawning over her and following every command. On the other, the money would mean independence.

Or would it? Would it mean a better life in a bigger house with nicer things and fewer worries and perhaps freedom from a husband she did not like? Surely these were possible. But would it also lead to a lifetime of running from family and friends and strangers, all with their hands out? Already, Lettie was feeling the urge to run. She had felt trapped for years in her boxlike house with too many people and not enough beds, too few square feet. Now, though, the walls were really closing in.

Anthony, the five-year-old, shifted in his sleep down by her feet. Lettie quietly eased out of bed, picked up her bathrobe from the floor, put it on, and left the room without making a sound. The hall floor creaked under the worn and dirty carpet. Next door, Cypress was asleep in her bed, her mammoth body too big for the scrawny blanket. Her wheelchair sat folded next to the window. On the floor were two kids who belonged to a sister of Lettie's. She peeked into the third bedroom where Clarice and Phedra slept together in a single bed, arms and legs dangling. Lettie's sister had the other bed, and for almost a week now. Another kid lay knotted, knees to chest, on the floor. In the den, Kirk had the floor while an uncle snored on his sofa.

Bodies were everywhere, it seemed to Lettie as she turned on the kitchen light and stared at the mess from last night's dinner. She would do the dishes later. She made coffee, and while it was brewing she checked the refrigerator and found what she was anticipating. Other than a few eggs and a pack of lunch meat, there was little in the way of food, certainly not enough to feed the masses. She would send her dear husband to the store as soon as he was up. And the groceries would be paid for not by wages earned by Simeon or her, nor by a government check, but by the generosity of their new hero, the Honorable Booker Sistrunk. Simeon had asked him for a loan of $5,000. ("A man drives a car like that ain't worryin' 'bout no five thousand bucks.") It really wasn't a loan, Simeon had said, but more like an advance. Booker said sure and they'd both signed the promissory note. Lettie kept the cash hidden in a saltine box in the pantry.

She put on sandals, tightened the bathrobe, and walked outside. It was October 15, and the air was chilly again. The leaves were turning and fluttering in the breeze. She sipped from her favorite cup and ambled across the grass to a small shed where they stored their lawn mower and other necessities. Behind the shed a swing hung by ropes from a hemlock, and Lettie sat down. She kicked off the sandals, shoved back with her feet, and began flowing through the air.

She had already been asked and the questions would return again and again. Why did Mr. Hubbard do what he did? And, did he discuss it with her? The latter was the easier—no, he never discussed anything with her. They would talk about the weather, repairs around his house, what to buy at the store and what to cook for dinner, but nothing important. That was her standard response, for the moment. The truth was that on two occasions he had casually and unexpectedly mentioned leaving something behind for her. He knew he was dying and that death was near. He was making plans for his exit and wanted to assure her that she would get something.

But why did he leave her so much? His kids were not nice people but they didn't deserve such a harsh penalty. Lettie certainly didn't deserve what he left her. None of it made sense. Why couldn't she sit down with Herschel and Ramona, just the three of them without all those lawyers, and work out a deal where they split the money in some reasonable manner? Lettie had never had anything and she wasn't greedy. It wouldn't take much to satisfy her. She would yield most of the estate to the Hubbards. She just wanted enough to start another life.

A car approached on the county road in front of the house. It slowed, then kept going, as if the driver needed a long look at the home of Lettie Lang. Minutes later, another one came from the other direction. Lettie recognized it: her brother Rontell and his passel of rotten kids and bitch of a wife. He'd called and said they might be coming over, and here they were, dropping in too early on a Saturday morning to see their beloved Aunt Lettie, who'd gotten her picture on the front page and was everybody's favorite topic now that she had wormed her way into that old white man's will and was about to be rich.

She scampered into the house and began yelling.

As Simeon hovered over his grocery list at the kitchen counter, he caught a glimpse of Lettie reaching her hand into a box of saltines in the pantry. She withdrew cash. He pretended not to notice, but seconds later, as she went to the den, he grabbed the box and pulled out ten $100 bills.

So that's where she's hiding "our money."

At least four of the kids along with Rontell said they wanted to go to the store, but Simeon needed some quiet time. He managed to sneak out the back door, hop in his truck, and leave without being seen. He was headed to Clanton, fifteen minutes away, and enjoying the solitude. He realized he missed the open road, the days away from home, the late-night bars and lounges and women. He would leave Lettie eventually, and move far away, but it damned sure wouldn't happen now. No sir. For the foreseeable future, Simeon Lang planned to be the model husband.

Or so he told himself. He often did not know why he did the things he did. An evil voice came from nowhere, and Simeon listened to it. Tank's Tonk was a few miles north of Clanton, at the end of a dirt road that was used only by those looking for trouble. Tank had no liquor license, no permit, and no Chamber of Commerce sticker in the front window. Drinking, gambling, and whoring were illegal in other parts of the county. The coldest beer in the area was kept in Tank's coolers, and Simeon suddenly had a craving as he puttered innocently down the road with his wife's grocery list in one pocket and their lawyer's borrowed cash in another. Ice-cold beer and Saturday morning dice and cards. What could be better?

Last night's smoke and debris were being cleared as a one-armed boy they called Loot mopped around the tables. Broken glass littered the dance floor, evidence of the inevitable fight. "Anybody get shot?" Simeon asked as he popped the top of a sixteen-ounce can. He was alone at the bar.

"Not yet. Got two in the hospital with cracked skulls," replied Ontario, the one-legged bartender who'd been to prison for killing his first two wives. He was now single. Tank had a soft spot for amputees and most of his employees were missing a limb or two. Baxter, the bouncer, was minus an ear.

"Sorry I missed it," Simeon said, gulping.

"I hear it was a right good scrape."

"Looks like it. Benjy in?"

"I think so." Benjy dealt blackjack in a locked, windowless room behind the bar. Next to it, in a similar room, they were shooting dice at the moment and anxious voices could be heard. A comely white woman, with all limbs and other critical body parts intact and exposed, walked in and said to Ontario, "I'm here."

"I thought you slept all day," he replied.

"Expecting some customers." She kept walking, and when she passed behind Simeon she gently raked her long, fake, pink fingernails across his shoulder. "Ready for business," she cooed into his ear, but he pretended not to hear. Her name was Bonnie, and for years she'd worked the back room where many of the young black men of Ford County first crossed the line. Simeon had been there several times, but not today. When she was out of sight, he drifted to the rear and found the blackjack dealer.

Benjy closed the door and asked, "How deep, man?"

"A thousand," Simeon said, cocky with the cash, a big player. He quickly spread the ten bills across the felt surface of the blackjack table. Benjy's eyes widened. "Good God, man, you clear this with Tank?"

"No. Don't tell me you ain't seen a thousand bucks before."

"A minute." He took a key out of his pocket and opened the cash box under the table. He counted, pondered, worried, then said, "I guess I can do it. As I recall, you ain't much of a threat anyway."

"Just shut up and deal."

Benjy exchanged the cash for ten black chips. The door opened and Ontario hopped in with a fresh beer. "You got any peanuts?" Simeon asked. "Bitch didn't fix breakfast."

"I'll find somethin'," he mumbled as he left.

Benjy, shuffling, said, "I wouldn't be callin' that woman no names, from what I hear."

"You believe everything you hear?"

They split the first six hands, then Bonnie arrived with a platter of mixed nuts and another cold beer in a frosted mug. She had changed costumes and was wearing skimpy, see-through lingerie with black stockings and kinky platform high heels that would make a tart blush. Simeon took a long look. Benjy mumbled, "Oh boy." Bonnie inquired, "Anything else you want?"

"Not right now," Simeon said.

An hour and three beers later, Simeon looked at his watch, knew he should leave, but couldn't force himself. His home was packed with freeloading kinfolk. Lettie was impossible. And he hated Rontell on a good day. All those damn kids running around.

Bonnie was back with another beer, one she delivered topless. Simeon called a time-out, said he'd be back shortly.

The fight started after Simeon doubled down on a hard 12, a stupid move in anyone's how-to book. Benjy dealt him a queen, busted him, and pulled away his last two chips. "Loan me five hundred," Simeon demanded immediately.

"Ain't no bank round here," Benjy said, predictably. "Tank don't do no credit."

Simeon, drunk, slapped the table and yelled, "Give me five chips, a hundred each!"

The game had attracted another player, a burly young man with biceps as round as basketballs. They called him Rasco and he'd been playing $5 chips as he watched Simeon throw around the big money until it was all gone. "Watch it!" Rasco snapped as he grabbed his chips.

Simeon had been irritated by Rasco's presence to begin with. A high roller like himself should be able to play alone, one-on-one with the dealer. In a flash, Simeon knew there would be a fight, and in these situations he had learned that it was best to draw first blood, to land the initial and maybe decisive blow. He swung wildly, missed badly, and as Benjy was yelling, "Stop that nonsense! Not in here you don't!" Rasco bounced from his chair—he was much taller than he appeared sitting down—and pummeled Simeon with two brutal shots to the face.

Simeon woke up later in the parking lot, where they had dragged him to his truck and laid him on the tailgate. He sat up, looked around, saw no one, gingerly touched his right eye, which was closed, and delicately rubbed his left jaw, which was quite tender. He glanced at his watch but it wasn't there. In addition to blowing the $1,000 he'd stolen from Lettie, he realized he'd lost $120 he'd planned to use for the groceries. All cash and coins had been pilfered. They had left behind his wallet, though it contained nothing of value. For a moment, Simeon thought about rushing into the tonk, grabbing one-legged Ontario or one-armed Loot, and demanding to be reimbursed for the stolen money. After all, he'd been robbed on their premises. What kind of tonk were they running?

He changed his mind, though, and drove away. He'd come back later and meet with Tank, get things settled. Ontario was watching, and when Simeon's truck was out of sight, he called the sheriff's office. They stopped him at the Clanton city limits, arrested him for drunk driving, handcuffed him, and gave him a ride to jail. He was thrown in the drunk tank and informed he could not use a telephone until he sobered up.

He wasn't too eager to call home anyway.

In time for lunch, Darias arrived from Memphis with his wife, Natalie, and a carload of kids. They were hungry, of course, and Natalie had at least brought a large platter of coconut squares. Rontell's wife had brought nothing. No sign of Simeon and the groceries. Other plans were made, with Darias dispatched by Lettie to the store. As the afternoon dragged on, the crowd moved outdoors where the boys played tackle football and the men sipped beer. Rontell fired up the grill and the rich aroma of barbecue ribs settled like a fog over the backyard. The women sat on the porch and talked and laughed. Others arrived—two cousins from Tupelo and some friends from Clanton.

They all wanted to spend time with Lettie. She loved the spotlight, the admiration, the fawning, and even though she was suspicious of their motives, she couldn't deny the pleasure of being the center of attention. No one mentioned the will, the money, or Mr. Hubbard, at least not in her presence. The figure of $20 million had been tossed around so much, and with such authority, that it was now accepted fact, established and well known. The money was there and Lettie was all set to collect 90 percent of it. At one point, though, Darias couldn't resist. When he and Rontell were alone by the grill, he asked, "You see the paper this morning?"

"Yep," Rontell replied. "Don't see how that can help much."

"That's what I was thinkin'. But it sure makes Booker Sistrunk look good."

"I'm sure he called the newspaper, planted the story."

Front page, Mid-South section of the Memphis morning paper. A nice, gossipy story about Mr. Hubbard's suicide and his unusual will, with the same photo of Lettie all dressed up in her courtroom best with Booker Sistrunk and Kendrick Bost pawing at her.

"They'll be comin' out of the woods," Darias said.

Rontell grunted and laughed and waved his arm. "They already here," he said. "Lined up, just waitin'."

"How much you reckon Sistrunk'll take?"

"I asked her but she ain't tellin'."

"He won't get half, will he?"

"Don't know. He ain't cheap."

A nephew stopped by to check on the ribs, and the two uncles changed the subject.

Late in the afternoon, Simeon was removed from the drunk tank and led by a deputy to the small windowless room used by the lawyers to huddle with their clients. He was given an ice pack for his face and a cup of fresh coffee. "What now?" he asked.

"You got a visitor," the deputy said.

Five minutes later Ozzie walked in and sat down. He was wearing blue jeans and a sports coat, with a badge on his belt and holster on his hip. He said, "Don't think we've ever met."

"I voted for you twice," Simeon said.

"Thank you, but they all say that after you win." Ozzie had checked the records and knew damned well Simeon Lang was not registered to vote.

"I swear I did."

"Got a call from Tank; said stay away, okay? No more trouble out of you."

"They cleaned my pockets."

"It's a tough place. You know the rules because there are no rules. Just stay away."

"I want my money back."

"You can forget that money. You wanna go home or you wanna stay here tonight?"

"I'd rather go home."

"Let's go."

Simeon rode in the front seat of Ozzie's car, no handcuffs. A deputy followed in Simeon's pickup. Nothing was said for the first ten minutes as they listened to the squawking on the sheriff's radio. Ozzie finally turned it down and said, "None of my business, Simeon, but those Memphis lawyers got no business down here. Your wife's already lookin' bad, at least in the eyes of the rest of the county. This all comes down to a trial by jury, and ya'll are pissin' everybody off."

Simeon's first thought was to tell him to butt out, but his brain was numb and his jaw was aching. He didn't want to argue. Instead, he thought how cool it was, riding shotgun in the big car and being escorted home.

"You hear me?" Ozzie asked. In other words, say something.

"What would you do?" Simeon asked.

"Get rid of those lawyers. Jake Brigance will win the case for you."

"He's a kid."

"Go ask Carl Lee Hailey."

Simeon couldn't think quick enough for a response, not that there was one. For blacks in Ford County, the Hailey verdict meant everything.

Ozzie pressed on. "You ask what I would do. I'd clean up my act and stay out of trouble. What you mean drinkin' and whorin' and losin' money at cards on a Saturday mornin', or any other day for that matter? Your wife's gettin' all this attention. White folk already suspicious, and you're lookin' at a jury trial down the road. Last thing you need is your name in the paper for drunk drivin' or fightin' or whatever. What're you thinkin'?"

Drinking, whoring, and gambling, but Simeon fumed without speaking. He was forty-six years old and unaccustomed to being reprimanded by a man who was not his boss.

"Clean your act up, okay?" Ozzie said.

"What about the drunk drivin' charge?"

"I'll put it off six months, see how you behave. One more screwup and I'll have you in court. Tank'll call the minute you walk through his door. Understand?"

"I got it."

"There's somethin' else. That truck you been drivin', from Memphis to Houston and El Paso, who owns it?"

"Company in Memphis."

"This company got a name?"

"My boss got a name, I don't know who his boss is."

"I doubt that. What's in the truck?"

Simeon went quiet and gazed through the side window. After a heavy pause he said, "It's a storage company. We haul a lot of stuff."

"Any of it stolen?"

"Of course not."

"Then why is the FBI askin' questions?"

"I ain't seen no FBI."

"Not yet, but they called me two days ago. They had your name. Look, Simeon, you get your ass busted by the Feds, and you and Lettie can forget about a jury trial in this county. Can't you see this, man? Front-page news. Hell, everybody in town is talkin' 'bout Lettie and Mr. Hubbard's will anyway. You screw up, and you get no sympathy from any jury. I'm not even sure the black folk'll stick with you. You gotta think, man."

The Feds, Simeon almost said, but he held his tongue and continued looking through the window. They rode in silence until they were close to his home. To spare him the indignity, Ozzie allowed him to get in his truck and drive. "Be in court at 9:00, Wednesday morning," he said. "I'll get Jake to handle the paperwork. We'll bump it down the road for a while."

Simeon thanked him and drove away, slowly.

He counted eight cars parked in his driveway and around his front yard. Smoke lifted from the grill. Kids were everywhere. A regular party as they closed ranks around their dear Lettie.

He parked on the road and began walking toward the house. This might get ugly.

16

Since the arrival of Mr. Hubbard's last will and testament two weeks earlier, the morning mail had become far more interesting. Each day brought a new wrinkle as more lawyers piled on and scrambled for position. Wade Lanier filed a petition to contest the will on behalf of Ramona and Ian Dafoe, and it proved inspirational. Within days, similar petitions were filed by lawyers representing Herschel Hubbard, his children, and the Dafoe children. Since petitions were allowed to be liberally amended, the early drafts followed the same basic strategy. They claimed that the handwritten will was invalid because (1) Seth Hubbard lacked testamentary capacity and (2) he was unduly influenced by Lettie Lang. Nothing was offered to substantiate these allegations, but that was not unusual in the suing business. Mississippi held to the practice of "notice pleading," or, in other words, just lay out the basics and try to prove the specifics later.

Behind the scenes, Ian Dafoe's efforts to convince Herschel to join ranks with the Wade Lanier firm proved unproductive and even caused a rift. Herschel had not been impressed with Lanier and thought he would be ineffective with a jury, though he had little to base this on. In need of a Mississippi lawyer, Herschel approached Stillman Rush with the idea of representing his interests. As the attorneys for the 1987 will, the Rush firm was facing a declining role in the contest. It would have little to do but watch, and it looked doubtful Judge Atlee would tolerate its presence, even from the sideline, with the meter ticking, of course. Herschel made the shrewd decision to hire the highly regarded Rush firm, on a contingency basis, and said good-bye to his Memphis attorney.

While the contestants of the will jockeyed for position, the proponents fought among themselves. Rufus Buckley made an official entry into the case as local counsel for Lettie Lang. Jake filed a trivial objection on the grounds that Buckley did not have the necessary experience. The bombs landed when Booker Sistrunk, as promised, filed a motion to remove Jake and replace him with the firm of Sistrunk & Bost, with Buckley as the Mississippi attorney. The following day, Sistrunk and Buckley filed another motion asking Judge Atlee to remove himself on the vague, bizarre grounds that he held some sort of bias against the handwritten will. Then they filed a motion requesting a change of venue to another, "fairer" county. In other words, a blacker one.

Jake spoke at length to a litigator in Memphis, a stranger connected by a mutual acquaintance. This lawyer had tangled with Sistrunk for years, was no fan, but had come to grudgingly admire the results. Sistrunk's strategy was to blow up a case, reduce it to a race war, attack every white person involved, including the presiding judge if necessary, and haggle over jury selection long enough to get enough blacks on the panel. He was brash, loud, smart, fearless and could be very intimidating in court and out. When necessary, he could turn on the charm in front of a jury. There were always casualties in a Sistrunk trial, and he showed no concern for who got hurt. Litigating against him was so unpleasant that potential defendants had been known to settle quickly.

Such tactics might work in the racially charged atmosphere of the Memphis federal court system, but never in Ford County, not in front of Judge Reuben V. Atlee anyway. Jake had read and reread the motions filed by Sistrunk, and the more he read the more he became convinced that the big lawyer was causing irreparable damage to Lettie Lang. He showed copies to Lucien and Harry Rex, and both agreed. It was a boneheaded strategy, guaranteed to backfire and fail.

Two weeks into the case, and Jake was ready to walk away if Sistrunk stayed in the game. He filed a motion to exclude the motions filed by Sistrunk and Buckley, on the grounds that they had no standing in court. He was the attorney for the will proponents, not them. He planned to lean on Judge Atlee to put them in their place; otherwise, he would happily go home.

Russell Amburgh was discharged and disappeared from the matter. He was replaced by the Honorable Quince Lundy, a semiretired lawyer from Smithfield, and an old friend of Judge Atlee's. Lundy had chosen the peaceful career of a tax adviser, thus avoiding the horrors of litigation. And as the substitute executor or administrator, as he was officially known, he would be expected to perform his tasks with little regard for the will contest. His job was to gather Mr. Hubbard's assets, appraise them, protect them, and report to the court. He hauled the records from the Berring Lumber Company to Jake's office in Clanton and stored them in a room downstairs next to the small library. He began making the one-hour commute and arrived promptly each morning at ten. Luckily, he and Roxy hit it off and there was no drama.

Drama, though, was brewing in a different part of the office. Lucien seemed to be acquiring the habit of stopping by each day, nosing around in the Hubbard matter, digging through the library, barging into Jake's office, offering opinions and advice, and pestering Roxy, who couldn't stand him. Lucien and Quince had mutual friends, and before long they were drinking pots of coffee and telling stories about colorful old judges who'd been dead for decades. Jake stayed upstairs with his door closed while little work was being done downstairs.

Lucien was also being seen in and around the courthouse, for the first time in many years. The humiliation of his disbarment had faded. He still felt like a pariah, but he was such a legend, for all the wrong reasons, that people wanted to say hello. Where you been? What're you up to these days? He was often seen in the land records, digging through dusty old deed books late in the afternoon, like a detective searching for clues.

★   ★   ★

Late in October, Jake and Carla awoke at 5:00 on a Tuesday morning. They quickly showered, dressed, said good-bye to Jake's mother, who was babysitting and sleeping on the sofa, and took off in the Saab. At Oxford, they zipped through a fast-food drive-in and got coffee and biscuits. An hour west of Oxford, the hills flattened into the Delta. They raced along highways that cut through fields white with late cotton. Giant, insect-like cotton pickers crept through the fields, devouring four rows at a time while trailers waited to collect their harvest. An old sign announced, "Parchman 5 Miles Ahead," and before long the fencing of the prison came into view.

Jake had been there before. During his last semester as a law student, a professor of criminal procedure organized his annual field trip to the state's infamous penitentiary. Jake and his classmates spent a few hours listening to administrators and gawking at death row inmates in the distance. The highlight had been a group interview with Jerry Ray Mason, a condemned killer whose case they'd studied and who was scheduled to make a final walk to the gas chamber in less than three months. Mason had stubbornly maintained his innocence, though there was no proof of this. He had arrogantly predicted the State would fail in its efforts, but he'd been proven wrong. On two occasions since law school, Jake made the drive to visit clients. At the moment, he had four at Parchman and three locked away in the federal system.

He and Carla parked near an administration building and went inside. They followed signs and found a hallway filled with people who looked as though they'd rather be elsewhere. Jake signed in and was given a document titled "Parole Hearings— Docket." His man was number three on the list. Dennis Yawkey—10:00 a.m. Hoping to avoid the Yawkey family, Jake and Carla climbed the stairs to the second floor and eventually found the office of Floyd Green, a law school classmate now working for the state prison system. Jake had called ahead and was asking a favor. Floyd was trying to help. Jake produced a letter from Nick Norton, the Clanton lawyer who represented

Marvis Lang, currently residing in Camp No. 29, maximum security. Floyd took the letter and said he would try to arrange a meeting.

The hearings began at 9:00 a.m. in a large, bare room with folding tables arranged in a square, and behind them dozens of folding chairs in haphazard rows. Along the front table, the chairman of the Parole Board and its four other members sat together. Five white men, all appointed by the Governor.

Jake and Carla entered with a stream of spectators and looked for seats. To his left, Jake caught a glimpse of Jim Yawkey, father of the inmate, but they did not make eye contact. He took Carla by the arm and they moved to the right, found seats, and waited. First on the docket was a man who'd served thirty-six years for a murder committed during a bank robbery. He was brought in and his handcuffs were removed. He quickly scanned the audience looking for family members. White, age about sixty, long neat hair, a nice-looking guy, and, as always, Jake marveled at how anyone could survive for so long in a brutal place like Parchman. His parole investigator went through a report that made him sound like a model prisoner. There were some questions from the Parole Board. The next speaker was the daughter of the bank teller who'd been murdered, and she began by saying this was the third time she had appeared before the Parole Board. The third time she'd been forced to relive the nightmare. Choking back her emotions, she poignantly described what it was like being a ten-year-old girl and learning that her mother had been blown away by a sawed-off shotgun at her place of employment. From there, it only got worse.

Though the Parole Board took the issue under advisement, parole for the killer seemed unlikely. He was led away after the thirty-minute hearing.

Next, a young black kid was brought in and his handcuffs removed. He was placed in the hot seat, and introduced to the board. He had served six years for carjacking and had been an exemplary prisoner, finishing high school, racking up college credits, and staying out of trouble. His parole investigator recommended release, as did his victim. There was an affidavit signed by the victim in which she urged the Parole Board to show mercy. She had not been injured during the crime, and over the years had corresponded with her carjacker.

While her affidavit was being read, Jake noticed others from the Yawkey clan inching along the walls on the far left. He'd found them to be harsh people, lower class, rednecks, with a fondness for violence. He had stared them down in open court on two occasions, and now here they were again. He despised them as much as he feared them.

Dennis Yawkey walked in with a cocky smile and began looking for his people. Jake had not seen him in twenty-seven months, and he preferred to never see him again. His investigator clicked off the relevant facts: In 1985, Dennis Yawkey pled guilty in Ford County to one count of conspiracy to commit arson. It was alleged that Yawkey and three other men conspired to burn the home of one Jake Brigance, in the town of Clanton. His three co-conspirators actually carried out the firebombing and were serving time in the federal prison system. One of them testified on behalf of the government; thus, the guilty pleas. The investigator had no recommendation as to whether Yawkey should be paroled, which, according to Floyd Green, meant that a release was unlikely.

Jake and Carla listened and fumed. Yawkey got off light only because Rufus Buckley botched the prosecution. If Buckley had stayed out of the way and allowed the Feds to handle it, Yawkey would have been sent away for at least ten years, like his buddies. Because of Buckley, here they were twenty-seven months later staring at parole for a little thug who'd been trying to impress the Klan. His sentence was five years. Barely halfway through, he was trying to get out.

As Jake and Carla walked hand in hand to the cheap lectern sitting on a folding table, Ozzie Walls and Marshall Prather made a noisy entry into the room. Jake nodded at them, then turned his attention to the Parole Board. He began by saying, "I know we only have a few minutes, so I'll hurry along. I'm Jake

Brigance, owner of the house that no longer exists, and this is my wife, Carla. Both of us would like to say a few words in opposition to this request for parole." He stepped aside and Carla assumed the lectern. She unfolded a sheet of paper and tried to smile at the members of the Parole Board.

She glared at Dennis Yawkey, then cleared her throat. "My name is Carla Brigance. Some of you might remember the trial of Carl Lee Hailey in Clanton in July of 1985. My husband defended Carl Lee, a zealous defense that cost us dearly. We received anonymous phone calls; some were outright threats. Someone burned a cross in our front yard. There was even an attempt to kill my husband. A man with a bomb was caught trying to blow up our house while we were asleep—his trial is still pending while he pretends to be insane. At one point, I fled Clanton with our four-year-old daughter to stay with my parents. My husband carried a gun, still does, and several of his friends acted as bodyguards. Finally, when he was at the office one night, during the trial, these people"—and she pointed at Dennis Yawkey—"torched our house with a gasoline bomb. Dennis Yawkey might not have been there in person, but he was a member of the gang, he was one of the thugs. Too cowardly to show his face, always hiding in the night. It is hard to believe that we are here, only twenty-seven months later, watching as this criminal tries to free himself from prison."

She took a deep breath and flipped a page. Beautiful women rarely appeared at parole hearings, which were 90 percent male anyway. Carla had their complete attention. She stiffened her back and continued: "Our home was built in the 1890s by a railroad man and his family. He died the first Christmas Eve in the house and his family owned it until it was finally abandoned twenty years ago. It was considered a historic home, though when we bought it there were holes in the floor and cracks in the roof. For three years, with every dime we could borrow, Jake and I poured our lives into that house. We would work all day and then paint until midnight. Our vacations were spent hanging wallpaper and staining floors. Jake bartered legal fees for plumbing work and landscaping and building supplies. His father added a guest room in the attic, and my father laid the brick on the rear patio. I could go on for hours, but time is scarce. Seven years ago, Jake and I brought our daughter home and put her in the nursery." Her voice cracked slightly, but she swallowed hard and lifted her chin. "Luckily, she was not in the nursery when our home was destroyed. I've often wondered if these men would have cared. I doubt it. They were determined to do as much damage to us as possible." Another pause and Jake put a hand on her shoulder. She continued, "Three years after the fire, we still think of all the things we lost, including our dog. We're still trying to replace things that can never be replaced, still trying to explain to our daughter what happened, and why. She's too young to understand. Often, I think we're still in a state of disbelief. And I find it hard to believe that we're here today, forced to relive this nightmare, like all victims, I guess, but here to stare at the criminal who tried to destroy our lives, and to ask you to enforce his punishment. A five-year sentence for Dennis Yawkey was much too light, too easy. Please, make him serve all of it."

She stepped to her right as Jake assumed the lectern. He glanced over at the Yawkey family and noticed that Ozzie and Prather were now standing near them, as if to say, "You want trouble, here it is." Jake cleared his throat and said, "Carla and I thank the Parole Board for this opportunity to speak. I'll be brief. Dennis Yawkey and his pathetic little band of thugs were successful in burning our home and seriously disrupting our lives, but they were not successful in harming us, as they had planned. Nor were they successful in achieving their bigger goal, which was to destroy the pursuit of justice. Because I represented Carl Lee Hailey, a black man who shot and killed the two white men who raped and tried to kill his daughter, they—Dennis Yawkey and his ilk and various known and unknown members of the Klan—tried repeatedly to intimidate and harm me, my family, my friends, even my employees. They failed miserably. Justice was served, fairly and wonderfully, when an all-white jury ruled in favor of my client. That jury also ruled against nasty little thugs like Dennis Yawkey and his notions of violent racism. That jury has spoken, loud and clear and forever. It would be a shame if this Parole Board gave Yawkey a slap on the wrist and sent him home. Frankly, he needs all the time here at Parchman you folks can possibly give him. Thank you."

Yawkey was staring at him with a smirk, still victorious over the firebombing and wanting more. His cockiness was not missed by several members of the Parole Board. Jake returned the stare, then backed away and escorted Carla back to their seats.

"Sheriff Walls?" the chairman said, and Ozzie strutted to the lectern, his badge glistening over his coat pocket.

"Thank you, Mr. Chairman. I'm Ozzie Walls, sheriff of Ford County, and I don't want this boy back home causin' trouble. Frankly, he should be in a federal pen servin' a much longer sentence, but we don't have time to get into that. I have an ongoin' investigation into what happened three years ago, as does the FBI over in Oxford. We ain't through, okay? And it would be a mistake to release him. In my opinion, he'll just pick up where he left off. Thank you."

Ozzie walked away, and walked as close to the Yawkey family as possible. He and Prather stood against the wall behind them, and when the next case was called, they eased out with a few other spectators. Jake and Carla met them outside the room and thanked them for making the trip. They had not expected the sheriff to appear. They chatted a few minutes before Ozzie and Deputy Prather left to check on an inmate who was headed back to Clanton.

Floyd Green found Jake and Carla and seemed somewhat agitated. "I think it'll work," he said. "Follow me, and you owe me one." They left one building and entered another. Beside the office of an assistant warden, two armed guards stood by a door. A man with a short-sleeve shirt and clip-on tie said gruffly, "You got ten minutes."

And a pleasure to meet you, Jake thought. One of the guards opened the door. "Wait here," Jake said to Carla.

"I'll stay with her," Floyd Green said.

The room was tiny, windowless, more of a closet than an office. Handcuffed to a metal chair was Marvis Lang, age twenty-eight, wearing the standard prison whites with a faded blue stripe down each leg. He seemed quite relaxed, low in the chair, one leg crossed over the other. He had a bushy Afro and a goatee.

"Marvis, I'm Jake Brigance, a lawyer from Clanton," Jake said as he slid the other chair close and sat down.

Marvis smiled politely and awkwardly offered his right hand, which was secured to the chair arm just like his left. They managed a firm handshake in spite of the restraints. Jake asked, "You remember your lawyer, Nick Norton?"

"Sort of. Been a while. I ain't had much reason to talk to him."

"I have a letter in my pocket signed by Nick giving me the authority to talk to you, if you want to see it."

"I'll talk. Let's talk. What you wanna talk about?"

"Your mother, Lettie. Has she been to see you recently?"

"She was here last Sunday."

"Did she tell you about her name being mentioned in the last will of a white man named Seth Hubbard?"

Marvis looked away for a second, then nodded slightly. "She did. Why you wanna know?"

"Because in that will Seth Hubbard named me as the attorney to handle his assets and property. He gave 90 percent of it to your mother and it's my job to make sure she gets it. Follow?"

"So you're a good guy?"

"Damned right. In fact, I'm the best guy in the entire fight right now, but your mother doesn't think so. She's hired some Memphis lawyers who are in the process of robbing her blind while they screw up the case."

Marvis sat up straight, tried to raise both hands, and said, "Okay, I'm officially confused. Slow down and talk to me."

Jake was still talking when someone knocked on the door. A guard stuck his head in and said, "Time's up."

"Just finishing," Jake said as he politely shoved the door closed. He leaned even closer to Marvis and said, "I want you to call Nick Norton, collect, he'll take the call, and he'll verify what I'm saying. Right now every lawyer in Ford County will tell you the same thing—Lettie is making a terrible mistake."

"And I'm supposed to fix things?"

"You can help. Talk to her. We, she and I, have a tough fight to begin with. She's making it much worse."

"Let me think about it."

"You do that, Marvis. And call me anytime, collect."

The guard was back.

17

The usual white-collar crowd gathered at the Tea Shoppe for breakfast and coffee, never tea, not at such an early hour. At one round table there was a lawyer, a banker, a merchant, and an insurance agent, and at another there was a select group of older, retired gentlemen. Retired, but not dull, slow, or quiet. It was called the Geezer Table. The conversation was picking up steam as it rolled through the feeble efforts of the Ole Miss football team—last Saturday's loss to Tulane at homecoming was unforgivable—and the even feebler efforts down at Mississippi State. It was gaining momentum as the geezers finished trashing Dukakis, who'd just been thrashed by Bush, when the banker said, loudly, "Say, I heard that woman has rented the old Sappington place and is moving to town, with her horde, of course. They say she's got kinfolks moving in by the carload and needs a bigger place."

"The Sappington place?"

"You know, up north of town, off Martin Road, just down from the auction yard. Old farmhouse you can barely see from the road. They've been trying to sell it ever since Yank Sappington died, what, ten years ago?"

"At least. Seems like it's been rented a few times."

"But they've never rented to blacks before, have they?"

"Not to my knowledge."

"I thought it was in pretty good shape."

"It is. They painted it last year."

This was considered for a moment and was the cause of great consternation. Even though the Sappington place was on the edge of town, it was in an area still considered white.

"Why would they rent to blacks?" asked one of the geezers.

"Money. None of the Sappingtons live here anymore, so why should they care? If they can't sell it, might as well rent it. The money's green regardless of who sends it over." As soon as the banker said this, he waited for it to be challenged. His bank was notorious for avoiding black customers.

A realtor walked in, took his seat at the white-collar table, and was immediately hit with "We were just talking about that woman renting the Sappington place. Any truth to it?"

"Damned right," he replied smugly. He took pride in hearing the hot gossip first, or at least appearing to. "They moved in yesterday, from what I hear. Seven hundred dollars a month."

"How many carloads?"

"Don't know. Wasn't there and don't plan on dropping by. I just hope it don't affect the property values in the neighborhood."

"What neighborhood?" asked one of the geezers. "Down the road is the auction barn that's smelled like cow dung since I was a kid. Across the road is Luther Selby's scrap yard. What kinda neighborhood you talking about?"

"You know, the housing market," the realtor fought back. "If we get these folks moving into the wrong areas, then property values will go down all over town. It could be bad for all of us."

"He's right about that," the banker chimed in.

The merchant said, "She ain't working, right? And her husband is a deadbeat. So how does she afford $700 a month in rent?"

"She can't get Hubbard's money this soon, can she?"

"No way," the lawyer said. "The money is locked up in the estate until the lawsuits are gone. It'll take years. She can't get a penny."

"Then where's the money coming from?"

"Don't ask me," said the lawyer. "Maybe she's charging everybody some rent."

"The house has got five bedrooms."

"And I'll bet they're all full."

"And I'll bet nobody's paying her any rent."

"They say he got picked up for drunk driving, couple of weeks back."

"He did indeed," the lawyer said. "Saw it on the docket, Simeon Lang. Caught him on a Saturday morning. He put in a first appearance and Jake represented him. Got it postponed for a while. I figure Ozzie's involved some way."

"Who's paying Jake?"

The lawyer smiled and said, "Oh, we'll never know for sure, but you can bet your ass it'll come out of the estate, by hook or crook."

"If there's anything left in the estate."

"Which looks doubtful."

"Very doubtful."

The merchant said, "So back to my question. How does she afford the rent?"

"Come on, Howard. They get checks. They know how to play the system. Food stamps, Aid to Dependent Children, welfare, housing, unemployment—they make more sitting on their asses than most folks do working forty hours. You get five or six of 'em in one house and all drawing checks—ain't gotta worry about the rent."

"True, but the Sappington place ain't exactly subsidized housing."

The lawyer said, "Her Memphis lawyer is probably front-loading the expenses. Hell, he probably paid her to get the case. Think about it. If he forks over fifty or a hundred grand, cash, up front, to get the case, then rakes off half of the estate when the ship comes in, then it's a good deal. Plus, he probably charges interest."

"He can't do that ethically, can he?"

"You mean a lawyer would cheat?"

"Or chase a case?"

The lawyer calmly said, "Ethics are determined by what they catch you doing. If you don't get caught, then you haven't violated any ethics. And I doubt if Sistrunk spends too much time reading the latest ethical guidelines from the American Bar Association."

"He's too busy reading his own press clippings. When's he coming back to town?"

The lawyer replied, "Judge Atlee has a hearing scheduled for next week."

"What're they gonna do?"

"Bunch of motions and such, probably another circus."

"He's a fool if he shows up again in a black Rolls-Royce."

"I bet he does."

The insurance agent said, "I got a cousin in Memphis, works in the court system. He says Sistrunk owes money all over town. He makes a lot, spends even more, always running from banks and creditors. He bought an airplane two years ago and it damned near broke him. The bank repossessed it, then sued him. He's claiming it's a racist conspiracy. He threw a big birthday party for his wife, number three, rented a big tent, brought in a circus, rides for all the little kids, then a fancy dinner with fresh lobster and crab and wines flown in. When the party was over, all his checks bounced. He was threatening to file for bankruptcy when he settled some barge case for ten million and paid everybody off. He's up and down."

This had their attention and they mulled it over. The waitress refilled their cups with scalding coffee.

The realtor looked at the lawyer and said, "You didn't really vote for Michael Dukakis, did you?" It was an act of outright provocation.

"I did and I'd do it again," the lawyer said, and this was met with some guffaws and some fake laughter. The lawyer was one of two Democrats present. Bush carried Ford County by 65 percent.

The other Democrat, one of the geezers, redirected things by asking, "When do they file Hubbard's inventory? We need to know what's in the estate, right? I mean, look at us here, gossiping and bickering over his estate and his last will and so on. Don't we have the right, as citizens and taxpayers and beneficiaries under the Freedom of Information Act, to know exactly what's in the estate? I certainly think so."

"It's none of your business," said the merchant.

"Maybe so, but I really want to know. And you don't?"

"I couldn't care less," replied the merchant, who was then ridiculed.

When the heckling died down, the lawyer said, "The administrator is required to file an inventory whenever the judge tells him to do so. There is no statutory deadline. Just guessing, in an estate of this size, the administrator will be given plenty of time to find everything and have it appraised."

"What size are you talking about?"

"The same size everybody else is talking about. We won't know for sure until the administrator files his inventory."

"I thought he was called the executor."

"Not if the executor quits, as he did here. The court then appoints an administrator to handle everything. The new guy is a lawyer from Smithfield named Quince Lundy, an old friend of Judge Atlee's. I think he's semiretired."

"And he gets paid out of the estate?"

"Where else would the money come from?"

"Okay, so who all gets paid out of the estate?"

The lawyer thought for a moment, then said, "The estate lawyer, which is Jake for the time being, though I don't know if he'll last. Rumor is he's already fed up with the Memphis lawyers and thinking of quitting. The administrator gets paid from the estate. Accountants, appraisers, tax advisers, folks like that."

"Who pays Sistrunk?"

"I'm assuming he has a contract with that woman. If she wins, he'll take a percentage."

"What the hell is Rufus Buckley doing slinking around the case?"

"He's the local counsel for Sistrunk."

"Hitler and Mussolini. They trying to offend every single person in Ford County?"

"Apparently so."

"And it will be a jury trial, right?"

The lawyer answered, "Oh yes. Seems like everyone wants a jury trial, including Judge Atlee."

"Why Judge Atlee?"

"It's simple. Takes the monkey off his back. He doesn't have to make the decision. You're gonna have big winners and big losers, and with a jury verdict no one can blame the judge."

"I'll lay ten-to-one odds right now the jury finds against that woman."

The lawyer said, "Let's wait, okay? Let's give it a few months so Judge Atlee will have time to put everyone in their box, get things organized and planned and set for a trial. Then right before it starts we'll set up a pool and lay odds. I enjoy taking your money. What, four Super Bowls in a row now?"

"How they gonna find twelve people who know nothing about this case? Everybody I know's got an opinion, and you can be damned certain every African within a hundred miles is angling for a cut. I heard Sistrunk wants to move the trial to Memphis."

The lawyer said, "It can't be moved out of state, knucklehead. But he has requested a change of venue."

"Didn't Jake try and move the Hailey case? To a friendlier county, one with more black voters?"

"He did, but Judge Noose declined. Hailey was a far bigger case than this one, though."

"Maybe. It didn't have twenty million bucks on the line."

The Democratic geezer asked the lawyer, "You think Jake can win this case for that woman?"

Everyone stopped talking for a second and looked at the lawyer. He'd been asked the same question at least four times in the past three weeks while sitting at the same table. "Depends," he said gravely. "If Sistrunk is in the courtroom, there's no way they win. If it's just Jake, then I'd give him a fifty-fifty chance." And this from a lawyer who never went to court.

"I hear he's got a secret weapon these days."

"What kind?"

"They say Lucien Wilbanks has returned to the bar. And not for drinking. He's supposedly hanging around Jake's office."

The lawyer said, "He's back. I've seen him in the courthouse digging through old land records and wills. Hasn't changed a bit."

"That's sad to hear."

"Did he appear to be sober?"

"Somewhat."

"Surely Jake won't let him near the jury."

"I doubt if Judge Atlee will allow him in the courtroom."

"He can't practice law, can he?"

"No, he was permanently disbarred, which means, in his case, he has to wait eight years before he can apply for reinstatement."

"It's permanent, but for eight years?"

"Yep."

"That makes no sense."

"That's the law."

"The law, the law."

"Who said, 'The first thing we should do is kill all the lawyers'?"

"I think it was Shakespeare."

"I thought it was Faulkner."

To which the lawyer replied, "When we start quoting Shakespeare, it's time for me to leave."

The phone call came from Floyd Green at Parchman. By a vote of 3 to 2, the Parole Board had decided to release Dennis Yawkey. There was no explanation. Floyd made some vague references to the mysterious workings of the Parole Board. Jake knew the State had a long, sordid tradition of cash for pardons, but he refused to believe the Yawkey family could have been sophisticated enough to pull off a bribe.

Ten minutes later, Ozzie called with the same news. He conveyed his disbelief and frustration. He told Jake that he, Ozzie, would personally drive to Parchman the following day to retrieve Dennis, and that he would have two hours alone with the boy in the car. He would make every threat possible, and forbid the kid to enter the city limits of Clanton.

Jake thanked him and called Carla.

18

Rufus Buckley parked his weathered Cadillac on the other side of the square, as far from Jake's office as possible. For a moment he sat in his car and remembered how much he loathed the town of Clanton, its courthouse, its voters, and especially his history there. There was a time, not too many years earlier, when the voters adored him and he considered them part of his base, the foundation from which he would launch a statewide race for governor, and from there, well, who knew? He'd been their district attorney, a young hard-charging prosecutor with a gun on each hip, a noose in hand, and no fear of the bad guys. Find 'em, haul 'em in, then watch Rufus string 'em up. He campaigned hard on his 90 percent conviction rate, and his people loved him. Three times they had voted for him in overwhelming numbers, but the last time around, last year with the bitter Hailey verdict still fresh on their minds, the good people of Ford County turned him out. He also lost badly in Tyler, Milburn, and Van Buren Counties, pretty much the entire Twenty-Second District, though his home folks in Polk County limped to the polls and gave him a pathetic sixty-vote margin.

His career as a public servant was over—though, at the age of forty-four, he could at times almost convince himself there was a future, that he was still needed. By whom and for what he wasn't certain. His wife was threatening to leave if he ever again declared himself a candidate for anything. After ten months of puttering around a small quiet office and watching the paltry traffic on Main Street, Rufus was bored, defeated, depressed, and going out of his mind. The phone call from Booker Sistrunk had been a miracle, and Rufus leapt at the chance to plunge into some controversy. The fact that Jake was the enemy only made the case richer.

He opened the door, got out, and hoped no one would recognize him. How the mighty had fallen.

The Ford County Courthouse opened at 8:00 a.m., and five minutes later Rufus walked through the front door, as he had done so many times before in another life. Back then he was respected, even feared. Now he was ignored, except for the slightly delayed glance from a janitor who almost said, "Say, don't I know you?" He hustled upstairs and was pleased to find the main courtroom unlocked and unguarded. The hearing was set for 9:00 a.m. and Rufus was the first one there. This was by design because he and Mr. Sistrunk had a plan.

It was only his third visit back since the Hailey trial, and the horror of losing hit low in the bowels. He stopped just inside the large double doors and took in the vastness of the empty, awful courtroom. His knees were spongy and for a second he felt faint. He closed his eyes and heard the voice of the court clerk, Jean Gillespie, read the verdict: "As to each count of the indictment, we the jury find the defendant not guilty by reason of insanity." What a miscarriage! But you can't gun down two boys in cold blood and then say you did it because they deserved it. No, you have to find a legal reason for doing so, and insanity was all Jake Brigance had to offer.

Evidently, it was enough. Carl Lee Hailey was as sane as any man when he killed those boys.

Moving forward, Rufus remembered the pandemonium in the courtroom as the Hailey family and all their friends went crazy. Talk about insanity! Seconds later, the mob surrounding the courthouse exploded when a kid yelled to them, "Not guilty! Not guilty!"

At the bar, Rufus managed to collect himself and his thoughts. He had work to do and little time to prepare for it. Like every courtroom, between the bar, or railing, and the judge's bench there were two large tables. They were identical but radically different. The table on the right was the home of the prosecutor in a criminal case—his old turf—or the plaintiff in a civil case. This table was close to the jury box so that during a trial he, Rufus, always felt nearer to his people. Ten feet away, the other table was the home of the defense, both in criminal and civil cases. In the opinions of most lawyers who spent their careers in courtrooms, seating was important. It conveyed power, or lack thereof. It allowed certain lawyers or litigants to be seen more, or less, by the jurors, who were always watching. On occasion it could set the stage for a David and Goliath struggle as a solitary lawyer and his crippled client faced a throng of corporate suits, or a beaten-down defendant faced the power of the State. Seating was important to comely female lawyers with short skirts and a jury box filled with men, and it was equally important to drugstore cowboys with pointed-toe boots.

As a prosecutor, Rufus never worried about seating because it was never an issue. Will contests, though, were rare, and he and Mr. Sistrunk had made a decision. If possible, they would commandeer the table used by the prosecution and plaintiff, the one closest to the jury, and assert themselves as the true voice of the proponents of the will. Jake Brigance would probably throw punches, but bring it on. It was time to establish proper roles, and since their client was the beneficiary of the quite valid last will and testament of Seth Hubbard, they would stake their claim.

Personally, privately, Rufus wasn't so sure about this strategy. He was well versed in the legend of the Honorable Reuben V. Atlee, who, like most old, seasoned, and often cranky Chancellors in Mississippi, ruled with an iron fist and was often skeptical of outsiders. Sistrunk, though, was itching for a fight and calling the shots. Regardless of what happened, it would be exciting and he, Rufus, would be in the middle of it.

He quickly rearranged the chairs around the table on the right, leaving three and moving the rest off to one side. He unpacked a thick briefcase and scattered papers and pads all over the table, as if he'd been there for hours with a full day of labor ahead of him. He spoke to Mr. Pate, a courtroom deputy, as he filled pitchers with ice water. Once upon a time he and Mr.

Pate would have chatted about the weather, but Rufus was no longer interested in rainfall.

Dumas Lee entered quietly and, recognizing Buckley, went straight for him. He had a camera around his neck and a notepad ready for a quote, but when he asked, "Say, Mr. Buckley, what brings you here?" he was ignored.

"I understand you're local counsel for Lettie Lang, right?"

"No comment," Rufus said as he carefully arranged some files, humming.

Things have really changed, Dumas thought. The old Rufus would break his neck to talk to a reporter, and no one stood between Rufus and a camera.

Dumas drifted away and said something to Mr. Pate, who said, "Get that camera outta here." So Dumas left and went outside where he and a colleague waited hopefully for the possible sighting of a black Rolls-Royce.

Wade Lanier arrived with his associate, Lester Chilcott. They nodded at Buckley, who was too busy to speak, and were amused by his takeover of the plaintiff's table. They, too, went about the urgent task of unpacking heavy briefcases and preparing for battle. Minutes later, Stillman Rush and Sam Larkin appeared at the bar and said hello to their semi-colleagues. They were on the same side of the courtroom, and would press many of the same arguments, but at this early stage of the conflict they were not yet ready to trust each other. Spectators drifted in and the courtroom buzzed with the low rumble of anxious greetings and gossip. Several uniformed deputies milled about, cracking jokes and saying hello to the visitors. Ian and Ramona and their kids arrived in a pack and sat on the far left, behind their lawyers and as far away as possible from those on the other side. Nosy lawyers loitered about the bench as if they had business before the court. They laughed with the clerks. Drama finally arrived when Booker Sistrunk and his entourage crowded through the door and clogged the aisle and swept into the courtroom as if it had been reserved for them. Arm in arm with Lettie, he led his crowd down the aisle, scowling at everyone else, daring anyone to speak, and, as always, looking for conflict. He parked her on the front row, with Simeon and the kids next to her, and he positioned a thick-necked young black man in a black suit with a black shirt and tie at guard in front of her, as if either assassins or admirers might rush from nowhere. Around Lettie there were various cousins, aunts, uncles, nephews, neighbors, along with assorted well-wishers.

Buckley watched this parade and could barely suppress his suspicion. For twelve years he had faced juries in this part of the world. He could pick them, read them, predict them, talk to them and lead them, for the most part, and he knew in an instant that Booker Sistrunk and his Big & Black & Bad routine would not fly in this courtroom. Seriously, a bodyguard? Lettie was a lousy actress. She had been coached to appear somber, even sad, in mourning, as if her dear departed friend was gone and had left her a rightful inheritance that the greedy white folks now wanted. She tried to look mistreated, abused.

Sistrunk and his partner, Kendrick Bost, walked through the bar and exchanged solemn greetings with their co-counsel, Mr. Buckley. They added to his pile of debris on the coveted table while they totally ignored the lawyers on the other side. The audience grew as the clock approached 8:45.

Jake entered from a side door and immediately noticed his place had already been taken. He shook hands with Wade Lanier, Stillman Rush, and the other lawyers for the contestants. "Looks like we have a bit of a problem," he said to Stillman, nodding at Buckley and the lawyers from Memphis. "Good luck," Stillman said.

Jake made the snap decision to avoid a confrontation. He eased out of the courtroom and worked his way back to the judge's chambers. Herschel Hubbard arrived with his two children and some friends. They sat near Ian and Ramona. As the clock approached 9:00, the courtroom settled down. It was almost perfectly segregated—blacks on one side, whites on the other. Lucien, of course, sat on the black side, back in the rear.

Jake returned and stood alone near a door next to the jury box. He spoke to no one, but instead managed to flip nonchalantly through a   document. At 9:05, Mr. Pate barked, "All rise for the court," and Judge Atlee made his entrance, his old faded black robe trailing behind him. He took his place, said, "Please be seated," then looked around the courtroom. He looked and looked, frowned and frowned, but said nothing. He glanced at Jake, glared at Buckley and Sistrunk and Bost, and then picked up a sheet of paper. He called the roll of lawyers; all were present and accounted for, a total of ten.

He pulled his microphone even closer and said, "First a bit of housekeeping. Mr. Buckley, you have filed a notice of entry into this matter as local counsel for the Memphis firm of Sistrunk & Bost, is that correct?"

Buckley, ever eager to stand and be heard, bounced to his feet and said, "That's correct, Your Honor. I—"

"And after that it appears as though you and your associated counsel filed a boatload of motions, all to be considered here today. Is that correct?"

"Yes, Your Honor, and I would like to—"

"Excuse me. And Mr. Brigance has filed a motion objecting to your entry into this case based on your lack of experience, skill, and knowledge in these matters, correct?"

"A completely frivolous objection, Your Honor, as you can plainly see. A lawyer in this state is not required to—"

"Excuse me, Mr. Buckley. You filed your notice of entry, Mr. Brigance objected, and so that means I need to rule on his objection. I have not yet done so, and until then you are not properly recognized as an attorney of record in this matter. Follow me?"

"Your Honor, Mr. Brigance's objection is so frivolous it deserves to be sanctioned. In fact, I am in the process of preparing a demand for sanctions."

"Don't waste your time, Mr. Buckley. Sit down and listen to me." He waited until Buckley sat down. Judge Atlee's dark eyes narrowed and the deep wrinkles in his forehead grew tighter. He never lost his cool but he could show a flash of anger that frightened every lawyer within fifty yards. "You are not properly before this court, Mr. Buckley, so neither are you, Mr. Sistrunk, nor you, Mr. Bost. However, you have assumed control of my courtroom by taking your positions. You are not the lawyers for this estate. Mr. Brigance is, duly and officially ordered by me. You may one day become the attorneys for the proponents of this will, but you're not there yet." His words were slow, pointed, harsh, and quite easy to follow. They echoed around the courtroom and had the complete attention of everyone who heard them.

Jake couldn't suppress a smile. He had no idea his frivolous, obnoxious, even sophomoric objection to Buckley's entry would prove to be so useful.

Judge Atlee went on at full throttle. "You're not officially here, Mr. Buckley. Why have you assumed such a position of authority?"

"Well, Your Honor—"

"Please stand when you address the court!"

Buckley lurched upward, cracking a knee on the table ledge as he struggled for some dignity. "Well, Your Honor, I've never seen a case in which a duly licensed lawyer had his appearance objected to on such baseless grounds, and so I figured you would dispense with it on sight and we could proceed to much more pressing matters."

"You figured wrong, Mr. Buckley, and you assumed you and your Memphis co-counsel could march in here and take control of the proponents' case. I resent that."

"Well, Chancellor, I assure the court—"

"Sit down, Mr. Buckley. Gather your things and have a seat over here in the jury box." Judge Atlee was pointing a long bony finger in Jake's general direction. Buckley didn't move. His co-counsel, however, did.

Booker Sistrunk stood, spread his hands wide, and said in his deep, rich, booming voice, "Your Honor, if it please the court, I must say this is rather absurd. This is a routine matter that we can certainly dispose of in short shrift. It does not need this type of overreaction. We're all reasonable people here, all trying to pursue justice. May I suggest we confront the initial question of

Mr. Buckley's right to enter this case as local counsel? Surely Your Honor can see that the objection filed by young Mr. Brigance here has no merit and should be summarily overruled. You can see this, Judge, right?"

Judge Atlee said nothing and gave nothing away with his eyes. After a few, heavy seconds, he looked down at a clerk and said, "See if Sheriff Walls is in the courthouse."

That directive might have frightened Rufus Buckley, and it might have amused Jake and the lawyers on the other side, but it angered Booker Sistrunk. He stiffened his spine and said, "Your Honor, I have the right to speak."

"Not yet, you don't. Please sit down, Mr. Sistrunk."

"I object to your tone, Your Honor. I represent the beneficiary of this will, Ms. Lettie Lang, and I have the duty to protect her interests at every turn."

"Sit down, Mr. Sistrunk."

"I will not be silenced, Your Honor. Not too many years ago, lawyers like me were not allowed to speak in this very courtroom. For years they could not enter, and once inside they were not allowed to speak."

"Sit down before I hold you in contempt."

"Don't threaten me, Judge," Sistrunk said as he stepped from behind the table. "I have the right to speak, to advocate for my client, and I will not be silenced by some arcane technicality in your rules of procedure."

"Sit down before I hold you in contempt."

Sistrunk took another step forward as the lawyers and everyone else stared in disbelief. "I will not sit down," he snapped angrily, and Jake thought he was losing his mind. "This is the very reason I filed a motion asking you to recuse yourself. It's obvious to me and many others that you have a racial bias in this case and there's no way my client can get a fair trial. This is also the reason we filed a motion demanding a change of venue. Finding an impartial jury in this, this town here, well, it will be impossible. Justice demands that this trial be held in another courtroom in front of another judge."

"You're in contempt, Mr. Sistrunk."

"I don't care. I'll do whatever it takes to fight for my client, and if I have to go to federal court to make sure we get a fair trial, then that's what I'm willing to do. I'll file a federal lawsuit against anybody who gets in my way." Two courtroom deputies were slowly making their way toward Sistrunk. Suddenly, he spun and pointed a finger at one. "Don't touch me unless you want to be named in a federal lawsuit. Stay away!"

"Where is Sheriff Walls?" Judge Atlee asked.

A clerk nodded and said, "Here." Ozzie was coming through the door. He stormed down the aisle with Deputy Willie Hastings behind him. Judge Atlee rapped his gavel and said, "Mr. Sistrunk, I find you in contempt and order you into the custody of the Ford County sheriff. Sheriff Walls, please take him away."

"You can't do this!" Sistrunk yelled. "I'm a duly licensed lawyer, admitted to practice before the U.S. Supreme Court. I'm here on behalf of my client. I'm here with local counsel. You can't do this, Your Honor. This is discriminatory and highly prejudicial to my client." By then, Ozzie was within striking distance, and ready to pounce if necessary. He was also three inches taller, ten years younger, thirty pounds heavier, armed, and the look on his face left little doubt he would enjoy a good rumble in front of the home crowd. He grabbed Sistrunk's elbow, and for a brief second there was resistance. Ozzie squeezed and said, "Hands behind your back."

At that point, Booker Sistrunk was exactly where he wanted to be. With a fine effort at drama, he lowered his head, swung his hands behind his back, and suffered the indignity of being arrested. He looked at Kendrick Bost. Some of those nearby would later claim they saw a nasty little grin; others did not. Surrounded by deputies, Sistrunk was jostled through the bar and down the aisle. As he passed near Lettie, he said loudly, "I'll get 'em, Lettie. Don't you worry. These racists will never get your money. Just trust me." They shoved him farther down the aisle and out the doors.

For reasons no one would ever understand, Rufus Buckley felt compelled to say something. He stood in the deathly silent courtroom and said, "Your Honor, if it please the court, I must say this puts us at a distinct disadvantage."

Judge Atlee looked at one of the remaining deputies, pointed at Buckley, and said, "Take him too."

"What?" Buckley gasped.

"I find you in contempt, Mr. Buckley. Please take him away."

"But why, Your Honor?"

"Because you are contemptuous, along with presumptuous, disrespectful, arrogant, and a lot of other things. Leave!"

They slapped the handcuffs on Rufus, who had turned pale and wild-eyed. He, Rufus Buckley, former district attorney and symbol of the highest standards of law abidance, morality, and ethical conduct, was being hauled away like a common criminal. Jake fought the urge to applaud.

"And put him in the same cell with his co-counsel," Judge Atlee roared into the microphone as Rufus stutter-stepped down the aisle, his desperate face searching for friends.

When the door slammed, everyone gasped for what little oxygen was left in the room. The lawyers began exchanging humorous glances, certain they had just witnessed something they would never see again. Judge Atlee pretended to be taking notes while everyone tried breathing. Finally, he looked up and said, "Now, Mr. Bost, do you have anything to say?"

Mr. Bost did not. There was plenty on his mind, but given the current mood of the court, he wisely shook his head no.

"Good. Now you have about thirty seconds to clear that table and move yourself right over here to the jury box. Mr. Brigance, would you assume your proper position in my courtroom?"

"Be glad to, Your Honor."

"On second thought, let's take a ten-minute recess."

Ozzie Walls had a sense of humor. In the circular drive behind the courthouse there were four fully decorated patrol cars, all heavily painted with words and numbers and laden with antennas and lights. As he gathered his men around the two contemptuous lawyers in the rear hallway, he made the quick decision that they should ride together. "Put 'em in my car," he ordered.

"I'll sue you for this," Sistrunk threatened for the tenth time.

"We got lawyers," Ozzie fired back.

"I'll sue every one of you redneck clowns."

"And our lawyers are outta jail."

"In federal court."

"I love federal court."

Sistrunk and Buckley were shoved outside and jostled into the rear seat of Ozzie's big brown Ford. Dumas Lee and a cohort fired away with cameras.

"Let's give 'em a parade," Ozzie said to his men. "Lights, no sirens."

Ozzie got behind the wheel, started the engine, and pulled away, ever so slowly. "You been in the backseat before, Rufus?"

Buckley refused to answer. He sat as low as possible directly behind the sheriff and peered out the window as they crept around the square. Three feet to his right, Booker Sistrunk sat awkwardly with his hands behind him and continued the mouthing: "You oughtta be ashamed of yourself, treating a brother like this."

"The white guy's gettin' the same treatment," Ozzie said.

"You're violating my civil rights."

"And you're violatin' mine with your mouth. Now shut up or I'll lock you under the jail. We got a little basement down there. You seen it, Rufus?"

Again, Rufus chose not to respond.

They looped twice around the square, then zigzagged a few blocks with Ozzie in the lead and followed by the other cars. Ozzie was giving Dumas time to set up at the jail, and when they arrived, the reporter was snapping away. Sistrunk and Buckley were extracted from Ozzie's car and led slowly along the front walkway and into the jail. They were treated like all fresh arrestees—photographed, fingerprinted, asked a hundred questions for the record, relieved of all belongings, and given a change of clothes.

Forty-five minutes after raising the ire of the Honorable
Reuben V. Atlee, Booker Sistrunk and Rufus Buckley, in matching county jail overalls, faded orange with white stripes on the
legs, sat on the edges of their metal beds and looked at the black-
stained and dripping toilet they were expected to share. A jailer
peeked through the bars of their narrow cell and asked, "Get
you boys anything?"

"What time is lunch?" Rufus asked.

With Bost banished to the jury box while his cohorts were being
processed, the hearing commenced and concluded with amazing speed. With no one present to argue for a change of venue
or removal of the judge, those motions were denied. The motion
to replace Jake with Rufus Buckley was rejected with hardly a
word. Judge Atlee granted the motions for a trial by jury, and
gave the parties ninety days to begin and complete discovery.
He explained in clear language that the case had top priority
with him and he would not allow it to drag on. He asked the
attorneys to pull out their calendars and forced them to agree on
a trial date of April 3, 1989, almost five months away.

He adjourned the hearing after thirty minutes and disappeared from the bench. The crowd stood and began buzzing
while the lawyers huddled and tried to confirm what had just
happened. Stillman Rush whispered to Jake, "I guess you're
lucky you're not in jail."

"Unbelievable," Jake said. "You wanna go visit Buckley?"

"Maybe later."

Kendrick Bost led Lettie and her people off to a corner where
he tried to assure them things were going as planned. Most seemed
skeptical. He and the bodyguard hurried away as soon as possible
and darted across the courthouse lawn. They jumped into the
black Rolls-Royce—the bodyguard was also the driver—and sped
away to the jail. They were told by Ozzie that visitation had not
been approved by the court. Bost cursed, left, and took off in the
direction of Oxford, home of the nearest federal courthouse.

★   ★   ★

Dumas Lee cranked out a thousand words before lunch and faxed the story to a reporter he knew at the Memphis paper. He also wired plenty of photographs. Later in the day, he sent the same materials to the newspapers in Tupelo and Jackson.

19

The word was leaked from a legitimate source and it spread like wildfire through the courthouse and around the square. Come 9:00 a.m., Judge Atlee would reconvene and allow his prisoners the opportunity to apologize. The very notion of seeing Rufus Buckley and Booker Sistrunk dragged into court, hopefully in chains and rubber shower shoes and orange county overalls, was impossible to resist.

Their story had gained traction and was the source of enthusiastic gossip and speculation. For Buckley, it was an enormous humiliation. For Sistrunk, it was nothing but another chapter.

The Memphis morning paper ran every word of Dumas's report on the front page of the Metro section, and accompanied it with a huge photo of the two handcuffed co-counsels leaving the courthouse the day before. The headline alone was worth it for Sistrunk: **PROMINENT MEMPHIS LAWYER JAILED IN MISSISSIPPI**. In addition to Dumas's startlingly accurate story, there was a smaller one about the petition for habeas corpus relief filed by the Sistrunk & Bost firm in federal court in Oxford. A hearing was scheduled for 1:00 that afternoon.

Jake sat on his balcony overlooking the square, sipping coffee with Lucien and waiting for the patrol cars to arrive. Ozzie had promised to call with a heads-up.

Lucien, who hated early mornings and with good reason, looked surprisingly fresh and clear-eyed. He claimed he was drinking less and exercising more, and he was certainly working harder. Jake was finding it increasingly difficult to avoid him around his (their) office.

Lucien said, "I never thought I would see the day when Rufus Buckley was hauled away in handcuffs."

"Beautiful, just beautiful, and still hard to believe," Jake said. "I'm going to call Dumas and see if I can buy the photo of Buckley being led into the jail."

"Please do, and make me a copy."

"Eight-by-ten, framed. I could probably sell them."

Roxy was forced to climb the stairs, enter Jake's office, and walk to the balcony where she found her boss. She said, "That was Sheriff Walls. They're on the way over."

"Thanks."

Jake and Lucien hurried across the street, and it was impossible to miss the fact that other law offices were being vacated as attorneys from around the square suddenly had urgent business in the courthouse. Poor Buckley had made so many enemies. The courtroom was far from packed, but quite a few of those enemies were milling about. It was blatantly obvious they were there for only one reason. A bailiff called things to order and Judge Atlee swept onto the bench. He nodded at a deputy and said, "Bring him in." A side door opened and Buckley walked in, his wrists and ankles free. Except for the stubble and a bad hair day, he looked much the same as he had the day before. Judge Atlee had shown compassion and allowed him to change clothing. It would have been a bit too much of an embarrassment to parade him over in inmate's attire. Given the coverage in the morning's papers, Judge Atlee simply could not allow an officer of his court to be seen in such garb.

There was no sign of Sistrunk. The door closed and it became apparent he was not there to take part. "Over here, Mr. Buckley," Judge Atlee said, pointing to a spot directly in front of the bench. Buckley complied and stood rather helplessly, quite alone, humiliated and defeated. He swallowed hard and looked up at the judge.

Judge Atlee shoved his microphone aside and said in a low voice, "I trust you survived the night in our fine jail."

"I did."

"And Sheriff Walls treated you well?"

"He did."

"Did you and Mr. Sistrunk have a restful night together?"

"I wouldn't call it restful, Your Honor, but we got through it."

"Can't help but notice that you're here alone. Any word from Mr. Sistrunk?"

"Oh yes, he has a lot to say, Your Honor, but I'm not authorized to repeat any of it. I don't think it would help his cause."

"I'm sure of that. I don't like being called names, Mr. Buckley, especially a name as harsh as 'racist.' It's one of Mr. Sistrunk's favorite words. I authorize you, as his co-counsel, to explain this to him and promise that if he ever calls me that again he, and you, will be barred from my courtroom."

Buckley nodded and said, "I'll be happy to pass that along, Judge."

Jake and Lucien were seated four rows from the back, on a long mahogany bench that hadn't been moved in decades. At the far end, a young black woman eased into view and took a seat. She was in her mid-twenties, attractive, vaguely familiar. She looked around quickly as if uncertain as to whether it was permissible to be there. She looked at Jake and he smiled. It's okay. The courtroom is open to the public.

Judge Atlee said, "Thank you. Now the purpose of this little hearing this morning is to review matters and hopefully get you released from my order of contempt. I found you in contempt, Mr. Buckley, you and your co-counsel, because of what I considered a flagrant disrespect for my courtroom, and thus me. I admit I became angry, and I try to avoid making decisions when I'm emotional. I have learned over the years that those are always bad decisions. I do not regret what I did yesterday and I would take the same actions again today. Having said that, I would offer you the chance to respond."

A deal had already been brokered by Ozzie. A simple acknowledgment, a simple apology, and the contempt orders would be lifted. Buckley had quickly agreed; Sistrunk was defiant.

Buckley shifted weight and looked at his feet. He said, "Yes, well, Your Honor, I realize we were out of line yesterday. We were presumptuous and disrespectful, and for that I apologize. It will not happen again."

"Very well. The contempt order is hereby nullified."

"Thank you, Your Honor," Buckley said meekly, his shoulders sagging with relief.

"Now, Mr. Buckley, I've set a trial date for April 3. There is a lot of work to be done, a lot of meetings when you lawyers get together, and I suppose quite a few more hearings in this courtroom. We cannot have a brawl or a circus every time we're in the same room. Things are very tense. We all acknowledge there's a lot at stake. And so my question for you is this: How do you see your role in this case, you and your Memphis co-counsel?"

Suddenly a free man, and given the chance to speak, Rufus Buckley cleared his throat and seized the moment with confidence. "Well, Your Honor, we will be here to protect the rights of our client, Ms. Lettie Lang and—"

"I get that. I'm talking about the trial, Mr. Buckley. It seems to me that there's simply not enough room for Mr. Brigance, the lead attorney for the proponents of the will, and all the lawyers representing the beneficiary. It's just too crowded, know what I mean?"

"Well, not really, Your Honor."

"Okay, I'll be blunt. A person who wishes to contest a will has the right to hire a lawyer and file a petition," he said as he waved an arm at the lawyers on the other side. "That lawyer is then involved in the case from start to finish. On the other hand, the proponents of the will are represented by the attorney for the estate. In this case, it's Mr. Brigance. The individual beneficiaries sort of ride his coattails."

"Oh, I disagree, Your Honor, we—"

"Hold on. What I'm saying, Mr. Buckley, with all due respect, is that I'm not sure you're really needed. Maybe you are, but you'll have to convince me later. We have plenty of time. Just think about it, okay?"

"Well, Judge, I think—"

Judge Atlee showed him his palms and said, "That's enough. I'll not argue this. Maybe another day."

For an instant, Buckley seemed ready for an argument, then quickly remembered why he was there. No sense irritating the judge again. "Sure, Judge, and thank you."

"You're free to go."

Jake glanced at the young woman again. Tight jeans, a red sweater, well-worn yellow running shoes, short hair and stylish glasses. She appeared lean and fit and did not look like the typical twenty-five-year-old black woman in Ford County. She glanced at him and smiled.

Thirty minutes later, she was standing before Roxy's desk, politely inquiring as to whether she might have a few minutes with Mr. Brigance. Name please? Portia Lang, daughter of Lettie. Mr. Brigance was very busy, but Roxy knew this might be important. She made her wait ten minutes, then found a gap in his schedule.

Jake welcomed her into his office. He offered coffee but she declined. They sat in a corner, Jake in an ancient leather chair and Portia on the sofa, as if she were there for therapy. She could not help but gaze around the big room and admire its handsome furnishings and organized clutter. She admitted that it was her first visit to a lawyer's office. "If you're lucky it'll be your last," he said and got a laugh. She was nervous and at first reluctant to say much. Her presence could be crucial, and Jake worked to make her feel welcome.

"Tell me about yourself," he said.

"I know you're busy."

"I have plenty of time, and your mother's case is the most important one in this office."

She smiled, a nervous grin. She sat on her hands, the yellow running shoes twitching. Slowly, she began to talk. She was twenty-four, the oldest daughter, and had just left the Army after six years. She had been in Germany when she got the news that her mother had been mentioned in Mr. Hubbard's will, though that had nothing to do with her discharge. Six years was enough. She was tired of the military and ready for civilian life. She had been a good student at Clanton High, but with her father's sketchy work history there was no money for college. (She frowned when she talked about Simeon.) Eager to leave home, and Ford County, she joined the Army and traveled the world. She had been back now for almost a week, though she had no plans to stay in the area. She had enough credits for three years of college, wanted to finish, and she was dreaming of law school. In Germany, she had worked in the JAG Corps as a clerk and watched court-martial proceedings.

She was staying with her parents and family, who, by the way, had moved to town. They were renting the old Sappington place, she said with a trace of pride. "I know," Jake said. "It's a small town. Word travels fast." Anyway, she doubted she would stay there much longer because the house, though much larger, was a circus with relatives coming and going and people sleeping everywhere.

Jake listened intently, waiting on an opening, certain it would come. Occasionally, he asked a question about her life, but she needed little prompting. She was warming up nicely and chattering away. Six years in the military had erased the drawl and twang and sloppy grammatical habits. Her diction was perfect, and not just by accident. She'd learned German and French in Europe and worked as a translator. Now she was studying Spanish.

Out of habit, he wanted to take notes, but that seemed rude.

She had gone to Parchman last weekend, to see Marvis, and he had told her about Jake's visit. She talked about him for a long time and occasionally wiped a tear. He was her big brother, had always been her hero, and it was such a waste. If Simeon had been a better father, Marvis would not have gone bad. Yes, he told Portia to tell their momma to stick with Jake, said he'd talked to his lawyer, Nick Norton, who said those Memphis lawyers would screw it all up.

"Why were you in court this morning?" Jake asked.

"I was in court yesterday, Mr. Brigance."

"Please call me Jake."

"Okay. Jake. I saw that fiasco yesterday, and I came back this morning to look through the court file in the clerk's office. That's when I heard the rumor that they were bringing the lawyers over from jail."

"Your family's lawyers."

"Right." She took a deep breath and spoke much slower. "That's what I wanted to talk to you about. Is it okay if we talk about the case?"

"Of course. Technically, we're on the same side. It doesn't feel that way, but for now we're allies."

"Okay." Another deep breath. "I have to talk to someone, okay? Look, Jake, I was not here during the Hailey trial, but I heard all about it. I came home that Christmas and there was a lot of talk about the trial and Clanton and the Klan and National Guard and all that, and I sort of felt bad for missing the fun. But your name is well known in our parts. My mother told me a few days ago that she felt like she could trust you. That's not easy for black folks, Jake, especially in a situation like this."

"We've never seen a situation like this."

"You know what I mean. With all this money being thrown around, well, we just sort of naturally expect to get the short end."

"I think I understand."

"So, when we got home yesterday, there was another fight. A big one, between Momma and Dad with a few other unwanted opinions thrown in. You see, I don't know everything that happened before I came home, but evidently they've been fighting over some pretty serious stuff. I think my dad accused her of sleeping with Mr. Hubbard." Her eyes watered quickly and she stopped to wipe them. "My mother is not a whore, Jake, she is a great woman who raised five kids practically alone. It hurts to know that so many people around here think she somehow screwed her way into that old man's will. I'll never believe it.

Never. But my father is another story. They've been at war for twenty years and when I was in high school I begged her to leave him. He criticizes everything she does and now he's criticizing her for something she didn't do. I told him to shut it up." Jake handed her a tissue, but the tears were gone. She said, "Thanks. Anyway, on one hand he accuses her of sleeping with Mr. Hubbard, and on the other hand he's secretly happy she did, if she did, because it might pay off. She can't win. So, after we got home yesterday from court, my momma tore into him about the Memphis lawyers."

"So he hired them?"

"Yes, he's a big shot now, and he has to protect his asset—my momma. He's convinced the white folks around here will conspire to invalidate the will and keep the money. It will all come down to race, so why not hire the biggest race baiter in these parts? And here we are. And there he is, sitting over there in jail."

"What do you think about that?"

"Sistrunk? He wants to be in jail right now. Got his picture in the paper with a nice headline. Another black man wrongfully jailed by the racists in Mississippi. It's perfect for him. He could not have scripted it any better."

Jake nodded and smiled. This woman could see around corners.

"I agree," he said. "It was all an act. By Sistrunk, at least. I can assure you Rufus Buckley had no plans to go to jail."

"How did we end up with these clowns?" she asked.

"I was planning to ask you the same question."

"Well, from what I gather, my dad went to Memphis and met with Sistrunk, who, no surprise, smelled a big payday. So he hustled down here to Ford County, put on his show, and my mother fell for it. She really likes you, Jake, and she trusts you, but Sistrunk convinced her no white people can be trusted in this case. For some reason, he brought in Buckley."

"If those guys stay in the case, we're going to lose. Can you imagine them before a jury?"

"No, I cannot, and that's what the fight was all about. My momma and I argued that we're screwing up the case right now. Simeon, always the expert, argued that Sistrunk will take the case to federal court and win it there."

"There's no way, Portia. There's no federal question here."

"I didn't think so."

"How much is Sistrunk getting?"

"Half. And the only reason I know this is because it spilled out during the fight. My momma said giving half of her share to Sistrunk was ridiculous. My dad said, 'Well, half of nothing is nothing.'"

"Have they borrowed money from Sistrunk?"

"You don't mind asking questions, do you?"

Jake smiled and shrugged, said, "It will all come out eventually, believe me."

"Yes, there was a loan. I don't know how much."

Jake took a sip of cold coffee as both pondered the next question. "This is serious business, Portia. There's a fortune at stake, and our side is losing right now."

She smiled and said, "A fortune? When word got out that this poor black woman in rural Mississippi was about to inherit twenty million, the lawyers went crazy. Had one call from Chicago, making all kinds of promises. Sistrunk was on board by then and he fought them back, but they're still calling. White lawyers, black lawyers, everybody's got a better deal."

"You don't need them."

"Are you sure?"

"My job is to enforce the provisions of Mr. Hubbard's last will, plain and simple. That will is under attack from his family, and that's where the fight should be. When we go to trial, I want her to be sitting right there, at my table, with Mr. Quince Lundy, the administrator of the estate. He's white and I'm white, and between us will be Lettie, looking pretty and happy. This is about money, Portia, but it's also about race. We don't need a courtroom that's black on one side and white on the other. I'll take the case all the way to the jury, and—"

"And you'll win?"

"Only an idiot lawyer predicts what a jury might do. But I'll swear that my chances of winning the case are far greater than Booker Sistrunk's. Plus, I'm not getting a cut of Lettie's inheritance."

"How do you get paid?"

"You don't mind asking questions, do you?"

"Sorry. There's just so much I don't know."

"I'm working by the hour and my fees come from the estate. All reasonable and court approved."

She nodded as if she heard this all the time. She coughed and said, "My mouth is dry. Do you have a soft drink or something?"

"Sure. Follow me." They went downstairs to the small kitchen where Jake found a diet soda. To impress her, he took her into the small conference room and showed her where Quince Lundy was currently doing his work and digging through the Hubbard records. Lundy had not yet arrived for the day. "How much of the money is in cash?" she asked timidly, as if she might be out-of-bounds. She stared at the boxes of records as if they were filled with cash.

"Most of it."

She admired the shelves packed with thick law books and treatises, few of which had been touched in years. "You have a nice office here, Jake," she said.

"It's a hand-me-down. It belongs to a man named Lucien Wilbanks."

"I've heard of him."

"Most people have. Have a seat."

She eased into a thick, leather chair at the long table as Jake closed the door. Roxy, of course, was nearby and on full radar alert.

Jake sat across from her and said, "So, tell me, Portia, how do you get rid of Sistrunk?"

In the best military tradition, she instantly blurted, "Keep his big ass in jail."

Jake laughed and said, "That's only temporary. Your mother has to fire him. Your father doesn't matter; he's not a party."

"But they owe him money."

"They can pay him later. If she'll listen to me, I'll walk her through it. But, first, she has to tell Sistrunk he's fired. And Buckley too. In writing. I'll draft a letter if she'll sign it."

"Give me some time, okay?"

"There's not much time. The longer Sistrunk hangs around the more damage he does. He's a publicity hound and loves the attention. Unfortunately, he's getting the attention of all the white people in Ford County. Those will be our jurors, Portia."

"An all-white jury?"

"No, but at least eight or nine of the twelve."

"Wasn't the Hailey jury all white?"

"Indeed it was, and it seemed to grow whiter each day. But that was a different trial."

She took a sip from the can and looked again at the rows of important books covering the walls. "It must be pretty cool being a lawyer," she said in awe.

"Cool" was not an adjective Jake would use. He was forced to admit to himself that it had been a long time since he viewed his profession as something other than tedious. The Hailey trial had been a great triumph, but for all the hard labor, harassment, physical threats, and raw emotions, he had been paid $900. For that, he'd lost his home and almost his family.

"It has its moments," he said.

"Tell me, Jake, are there any black female lawyers in Clanton?"

"No."

"How many black lawyers are there?"

"Two."

"Where's the nearest black woman with her own law office?"

"There's one over in Tupelo."

"Do you know her? I'd like to meet her."

"I'll be happy to make the phone call. Her name is Barbara McNatt, a nice lady. She was a year ahead of me in law school.

Does primarily family law but also mixes it up with the cops and prosecutors. She's a good lawyer."

"That'd be great, Jake."

She took another sip as they waited through an uncomfortable gap in the conversation. Jake knew where he wanted to go but couldn't be in a hurry. "You mentioned law school," he said, and this grabbed her attention. They talked about it at length, with Jake careful not to make his description as dreadful as the three-year ordeal itself. Occasionally, like all lawyers, Jake was asked by students if he would recommend the law as a profession. He had never found an honest way to say no, though he had many reservations. There were too many lawyers and not enough good jobs. They were packed along Main Streets in countless small towns, and they were stacked on top of each other in the tall buildings downtown. Still, at least half of all Americans who need legal help can't afford it, so more lawyers are needed. Not more corporate lawyers or insurance lawyers, and certainly not more small-town street lawyers like himself. He had a hunch that if Portia Lang became a lawyer, she would do it the right way. She would help her people.

Quince Lundy arrived and broke up the conversation. Jake introduced Portia to him, and then walked her to the front door. Outside, under the terrace, he invited her to supper.

The hearing on Kendrick Bost's petition for habeas corpus relief was held on the second floor of the federal courthouse in Oxford, as scheduled at 1:00 that afternoon. By then, the Honorable Booker F. Sistrunk had been wearing the county-jail coveralls for over twenty-four hours. He was not present at the hearing, nor was his presence expected.

A U.S. magistrate presided and did so with little interest. There was no precedent, at least not in the Fifth Circuit, for a federal court to get involved in a contempt ruling in state court. The magistrate asked repeatedly for some authority, from anywhere in the nation, but there was none.

Bost was permitted to rant and pant for half an hour, but said almost nothing of substance. His ill-grounded claim was that Mr. Sistrunk was the victim of some vague plot by the authorities in Ford County to remove him from the will contest, and so on. What was not said was the obvious: Sistrunk expected to be released simply because he was black and felt mistreated by a white judge.

The petition was denied. Bost immediately prepared an appeal to the Fifth Circuit in New Orleans. He and Buckley had also filed an appeal challenging the contempt order to the Mississippi Supreme Court.

Meanwhile, Mr. Sistrunk played checkers with his new cell mate, a hot-check artist.

The maternal side of Carla's family claimed some German roots, and for this reason she studied German in high school and for four years at Ole Miss. Clanton rarely provided the opportunity to practice the language, so she was delighted to welcome Portia to their modest rental home, even though Jake forgot to tell her about his invitation until almost 5:00 p.m. "Relax," he'd said. "She's a nice girl who might play a crucial role, plus she's probably never been invited to a white person's house for dinner." As they had this discussion, a bit tense at first, they finally realized and admitted that they had never invited a black person to dinner.

Their guest arrived promptly at 6:30, and she brought a bottle of wine, one with a cork. Though Jake had stressed that the evening was "as casual as possible," Portia had changed and was wearing a long, loose, cotton dress. She greeted Carla in German, but quickly switched to English. She apologized for the bottle of wine—a cheap red from California—and they had a good laugh over the paltry selections in the local liquor stores. Jake explained that all wine and booze in the state were in fact purchased by the State, then doled out to privately owned liquor stores. This led to a lively discussion about the ridiculous liquor laws in Mississippi, where in some towns you can buy 180-proof rum but not a single can of beer.

Jake, holding the bottle, said, "We don't keep alcohol in the house."

"Sorry," Portia said, embarrassed. "I'll be happy to take it home."

"Why don't we just drink it?" Carla asked. A great idea. As Jake rummaged for a corkscrew, the women moved to the stove and looked at dinner. Portia said she'd rather eat than cook, though she had learned a lot about food in Europe. She had also grown fond of Italian wines, bottles of which were scarce in Ford County. "You'll have to go to Memphis," Jake said, still searching. Carla had thrown together a pasta sauce with spicy sausage, and as it simmered she began practicing with a few elementary sentences in German. Portia responded slowly, sometimes repeating, often correcting. Hanna heard the strange words and came from the rear of the house. She was introduced to their guest, who greeted her with "Ciao."

"What does 'ciao' mean?" Hanna asked.

"Among friends it means hello and good-bye in Italian, also in Portuguese, I think," Portia said. "It's a lot easier than 'guten Tag' or 'bonjour.'"

"I know some words in German," Hanna said. "My mother taught me."

"We'll practice later," Carla said.

Jake found an old corkscrew and managed to wrestle the bottle open. "We once had real wineglasses," Carla said as she pulled out three cheap water goblets. "Like everything else, they went up in the fire." Jake poured; they clinked glasses, said "Cheers," and sat at the kitchen table. Hanna left them and went to her room.

"Do you talk about the fire?" Portia asked.

"Not much," Jake said. Carla shook her head slightly and looked away. "However, if you've seen the paper, you know that one of the thugs is now back on the streets, or somewhere around here."

"I saw that," Portia said. "Twenty-seven months."

"Yep. Granted, he didn't light the match, but he was in on the planning."

"Does it worry you, now that he's out?"

"Of course it does," Carla said. "We sleep with guns around here."

"Dennis Yawkey doesn't bother me that much," Jake said. "He's just a stupid little punk who was trying to impress some other guys. Plus, Ozzie is watching him like a hawk. One bad move, and Yawkey goes back to Parchman. I'm more concerned with the bad boys out there who've never been nailed. There were a lot of men, some local, some not, who were involved. Only four have been prosecuted."

"Five if you count Blunt," Carla said.

"He hasn't been prosecuted. Blunt was the Klucker who tried to blow up the house a week before they burned it. He currently resides at the state mental hospital where he's doing a good job of acting crazy."

Carla stood and went to the stove where she stirred the sauce and turned on the burner to boil the water.

"I'm sorry," Portia said softly. "Didn't mean to bring up an unpleasant subject."

"It's okay," Jake said. "Tell us about Italy. We've never been there."

Over dinner, she talked about her travels throughout Italy, Germany, France, and the rest of Europe. As a high school student, she had made the decision to see the world, and to get as far away from Mississippi as possible. The Army gave her the chance, and she took full advantage of it. After boot camp, her top three choices were Germany, Australia, and Japan. While stationed at Ansbach, she spent her money on railway passes and student hostels, often traveling alone as she saw every country from Sweden to Greece. She was stationed on Guam for a year, but missed the history and culture, and especially the food and wines, of Europe, and managed a transfer.

Jake had been to Mexico and Carla had been to London. For their fifth anniversary, they saved and scraped together enough money for a low-budget trip to Paris, one they still talked about. Beyond those trips, they had been homebound. If they were lucky, they sprang for a week at the beach at Destin in the summer. Listening to Portia trot the globe made them envious. Hanna was mesmerized. "You've seen the pyramids?" she asked at one point.

Indeed she had; in fact, it seemed as though Portia had seen everything. The bottle was empty after the salads, and they needed more wine. Instead, Carla poured iced tea and they managed to finish the meal. After Hanna was in bed, they sipped decaf coffee, ate cookies, and talked about worldly matters.

Of Lettie and the will and its related issues, not one word was uttered.

20

Ancil Hubbard was no longer Ancil Hubbard. The old name and self had been discarded in a hurry years earlier when a pregnant woman found him and made allegations and demands. She wasn't the first to cause him trouble, or a name change. There was an abandoned wife in Thailand, some jealous husbands here and there, the IRS, some type of police in at least three countries, and a cranky drug dealer in Costa Rica. And these were just the most memorable highlights of a chaotic and sloppily lived life, one he would have happily traded long ago for something more traditional. But traditional was not in the cards for Ancil Hubbard.

He was working in a bar in Juneau, Alaska, in a seedy section of town where sailors and deckhands and roustabouts gathered to drink and shoot dice and blow off steam. A couple of ferocious bouncers kept the peace, but it was always fragile. He went by Lonny, a name he'd noticed in an obituary in a newspaper in Tacoma two years earlier. Lonny Clark. Lonny knew how to game the system, and if Lonny had so chosen he could have obtained a Social Security number, a driver's license in any state he wanted, even a passport. But Lonny was playing it safe, and there were no records of his existence in any government file or computer. He did not exist, though he had some fake papers in the event he got cornered. He worked in bars because he was paid in cash. He rented a room in a flophouse down the street and paid cash. He rode bikes and buses, and if he needed to vanish, which was always a possibility, he would pay cash for a Greyhound ticket and flash a fake driver's license. Or hitchhike, something he'd done for a million miles.

He worked behind the bar and studied every person who came and went. Thirty years on the run and you learn how to watch, to look, to catch the prolonged glance, to spot someone who doesn't fit. Because his misdeeds involved no bodily harm to others, nor did they, regretfully, involve huge sums of money, there was a good chance he wasn't being chased at all. Lonny was a small-time operator whose principal weakness was an attraction to flawed women. No real crime there. There were some crimes—petty drug dealing, pettier gunrunning—but, hell, a man's gotta make a living somehow. Perhaps a couple of his crimes were more serious. Nonetheless, after a lifetime of drifting, he had become accustomed to looking over his shoulder.

The crimes were now behind him, as were the women, for the most part. At sixty-six, Lonny was accepting the fact that a fading libido might just be a good thing after all. It kept him out of trouble, kept him focused on other things. He dreamed of buying a fishing boat, though it would be impossible to save enough from his meager earnings. Because of his nature and habits, he often thought of pulling one last drug deal, one grand slam that would net him a bundle and set him free. Prison, though, terrified him. At his age, and caught with the quantity he was dreaming about, he would die behind bars. And, he hated to admit, his previous drug deals had not gone well.

No thanks. He was happy tending bar, chatting up sailors and hookers and dispensing well-earned advice. He closed the bar each morning at 2:00 and walked, half-sober, to his cramped room where he lay on a dirty bed and recalled with great nostalgia his days on the open seas, first in the Navy and later on cruise ships, yachts, even tankers. When you have no future, you live in the past, and Lonny would be stuck there forever.

He never thought about Mississippi, or his childhood there. As soon as he left, he somehow trained his mind to instantly negate any thoughts of the place. Like the click of a camera, he changed scenery and images effortlessly, and after decades he

had convinced himself that he had never lived there at all. His
life began when he was sixteen; nothing happened before then.
Nothing at all.

Early on his second morning of captivity, and not long after a
breakfast of cold scrambled eggs and even colder white toast,
Booker Sistrunk was fetched from his cell and led, without
restraints, over to the office of the high sheriff. He went inside
while a deputy waited at the door. Ozzie greeted him warmly
and asked if he would like fresh coffee. Indeed he did. Ozzie also
offered fresh doughnuts, and Sistrunk dove right in.

"You can be out in two hours if you want to," Ozzie said.
Sistrunk listened. "All's you gotta do is walk into court and apologize to Judge Atlee. You'll be in Memphis long before lunch."

"I kinda like it here," Sistrunk said with a mouth full.

"No, Booker, what you like is this." Ozzie slid across the
Memphis paper. Front page, Metro, beneath the fold, a stock
photo under a headline that read, **SISTRUNK DENIED
FEDERAL HABEAS RELIEF; REMAINS BEHIND
BARS IN CLANTON**. He read it slowly as he chomped on
another doughnut. Ozzie noticed a slight grin.

"Another day, another headline, huh Booker? Is that all you're
after here?"

"I'm fighting for my client, Sheriff. Good versus evil. I'm
surprised you can't see that."

"I see everything, Booker, and this is what's obvious. You're
not gonna handle this case in front of Judge Atlee. Period. You've
ripped it with him and he's tired of you and your foolishness.
Your name's on his shit list and it's not comin' off."

"No problem, Sheriff. I'm taking it to federal court."

"Sure, you can file some bullshit civil rights crap in federal
court, but it won't stick. I've talked to some lawyers, some guys
who do federal work, and they say you're full of shit. Look,
Booker, you can't bully these judges down here the way you can
in Memphis. We got three federal judges here in the Northern
District. One's a former Chancellor, like Atlee. One's an

ex–district attorney, and one used to be a federal prosecutor. All white. All fairly conservative. And you think you can walk into federal court down here and start slingin' all your racist shit, and somebody's gonna buy it. You're a fool."

"And you're not a lawyer, Mr. Sheriff. But thanks for the legal advice anyway. It'll be forgotten by the time I get back to my cell."

Ozzie rocked back and flung his feet upon his desk, his cowboy boots impressive with a new shine. He gazed at the ceiling, frustrated, and said, "You're makin' it easy for the white folks to hate Lettie Lang, you know that, Booker?"

"She's black. They hated her long before I came to town."

"That's where you're wrong. I've been elected twice by the white folks in this county. Most of them are good people. They'll give Lettie a fair shake, or at least they would have until you showed up. Now it's black versus white and we don't have the votes. You're an idiot, you know that, Booker? I don't know what kinda law you do up in Memphis, but it ain't workin' down here."

"Thanks for the coffee and doughnuts. Can I go now?"

"Please go."

Sistrunk stood and walked to the door, where he stopped and said, "By the way, I'm not sure your jail complies with federal law."

"Sue me."

"A lot of violations."

"It might get worse."

Portia was back before noon. She waited and chatted with Roxy while Jake finished a long phone call, then she went up the stairs. Her eyes were red, her hands shook, and she looked like she hadn't slept in a week. They managed some small talk about the dinner the night before. Finally, Jake asked, bluntly, "What's going on?"

She closed her eyes, rubbed her forehead and began talking. "We were up all night, one big nasty fight. Simeon was drinking, not bad, but enough to get himself riled up. Momma and I said that Sistrunk had to go. He, of course, didn't like that, and so we fought. A houseful of people, and we're fighting like a bunch of idiots. He finally left and we haven't seen him since. That's the bad news. The good news is that my mother will sign whatever it takes to get rid of the Memphis lawyers."

Jake walked to his desk, picked up a sheet of paper, and handed it to her. "It just says that she fires him. That's all. If she signs it, then we're in business."

"What about Simeon?"

"He can hire all the lawyers he wants, but he's not named in the will; therefore, he's not an interested party. Judge Atlee will not recognize him, nor his lawyers. Simeon's game is over. This is between Lettie and the Hubbard family. Will she sign it?"

Portia stood and said, "I'll be right back."

"Where is she?"

"Outside in the car."

"Please ask her to come in."

"She doesn't want to. She's afraid you're upset with her."

Jake couldn't believe it. "Come on, Portia. I'll make some coffee and we'll have a chat. Go get your mother."

Sistrunk was reading and resting comfortably on his lower bunk, a stack of motions and briefs balanced on his stomach, his cellie sitting nearby with his nose stuck in a paperback. Metal clanged, the door unlatched, Ozzie appeared from nowhere and said, "Let's go Booker." He handed him his suit, shirt, and tie, all on one hanger. His shoes and socks were in a paper grocery bag.

They sneaked out a rear door where Ozzie's car was parked. A minute later they stopped behind the courthouse and hustled inside. The halls were empty and no one suspected anything. On the third floor they entered Judge Atlee's cramped outer room. His court reporter doubled as his secretary. She pointed to another door and said, "They're waiting."

"What's going on?" Sistrunk mumbled for at least the fourth time. Ozzie did not reply. He pushed open the door. Judge Atlee sat at the end of a long table, in his standard black suit, minus the robe. To his right sat Jake, Lettie, and Portia. He motioned to his left and said, "Gentlemen, please have a seat." They did, with Ozzie sitting as far away from the action as possible.

Sistrunk glared across the table at Jake and Lettie. It was difficult for him to hold his tongue, but he managed to do so. His habit was to shoot first and ask questions later, but common sense told him to take it easy, hold his fire, and try not to anger the judge. Portia, in particular, seemed ready to pounce on him. Lettie studied her hands while Jake scratched on a legal pad.

"Please review this," Judge Atlee said to Sistrunk as he slid over a single sheet of paper. "You've been fired."

Sistrunk read the one short paragraph, then looked at Lettie and said, "Did you sign this?"

"I did."

"Under duress?"

"Absolutely not," Portia said boldly. "She has made the decision to terminate your services. It's right there in black and white. Do you understand?"

"Where's Simeon?"

"Gone," Lettie said. "Don't know when he'll be back."

"I still represent him," Sistrunk said.

"He's not an interested party," Judge Atlee said. "Thus, he will not be allowed to take part, nor will you." He picked up another sheet of paper and passed it over. "This is an order I just signed lifting the contempt citation. Since you are no longer involved in this matter, Mr. Sistrunk, you are free to go." It was more of a command than an observation.

Sistrunk looked angrily at Lettie and said, "I'm allowed to be paid for my time and expenses, plus there is the matter of the loans. When can I expect the money?"

"In due course," Jake said.

"I want it now."

"Well, you're not getting it now."

"Then I'll sue."

"Fine. I'll defend."

"And I'll preside," Judge Atlee said. "I'll give you a trial date in about four years."

Portia could not suppress a chuckle. Ozzie said, "Judge, are we finished? If so, I need to drive Mr. Sistrunk back to Memphis. Seems he's stranded down here. Plus, he and I have a few things to discuss."

"You'll hear from me again. This is not the last word," Sistrunk growled at Lettie.

"I'm sure of that," Jake said.

"Take him away," Judge Atlee said. "Preferably to the state line."

The meeting was adjourned.

21

The Law Offices of Jake Brigance had never used an intern. Other lawyers around the square occasionally allowed them in; they were usually local college kids who were considering law school and looking for something to stick on a résumé. In theory, they were good sources of either free or cheap labor, but Jake had heard more bad stories than good. He had never been tempted, until Portia Lang came along. She was bright, bored, unemployed, and talking about law school. She was also the most sensible person now residing in the old Sappington house, and her mother trusted her implicitly. And, obviously, her mother was still on track to become the richest black woman in the state, though Jake saw formidable hurdles ahead.

He hired Portia for $50 a week and gave her an office upstairs, away from the distractions of Roxy, Quince Lundy, and especially Lucien, who by Thanksgiving was showing up every day and warming up to his old habits. It was, after all, his office, and if he wanted to smoke a cigar and fog up everybody's space, then so be it. If he wanted to walk around the reception area with a late-afternoon bourbon and harass Roxy with dirty jokes, then so be it. If he wanted to pester Quince Lundy with questions about Seth Hubbard's assets, then who could stop him?

Jake was spending more and more time refereeing among his expanding staff. Two months earlier he and Roxy had existed quietly in a rather dull but productive manner. Now, there was tension, sometimes conflict, but also a lot of laughs and teamwork. Overall, Jake was enjoying the noise, though he was terrified Lucien was serious about returning to the practice. On the one hand, he loved Lucien and treasured his advice and insights. On the other, he knew any new arrangement wouldn't last. Jake's trump card was a key provision in Mississippi law that required a disbarred lawyer to take the bar exam before being reinstated. Lucien was sixty-three years old, and from around 5:00 p.m. each day, and sometimes earlier, until late in the night, he was under the influence of Jack Daniel's. There was no way such an old drunk could study and pass the bar exam.

Portia arrived for her first day of work at five minutes before 9:00, her appointed hour. She had timidly asked Jake about the office dress code. He had quietly explained that he had no idea what interns wore, but he guessed things were casual. If they were going to court, she might want to step it up a little, but he really didn't care. He was expecting jeans and running shoes, but instead Portia presented herself in an attractive blouse, skirt, and heels. The woman was ready for work, and within minutes Jake had the impression she was already thinking of herself as a lawyer. He showed her to her office, one of three empty ones upstairs. It had not been used in many years, not since the old Wilbanks firm was in its glory. Portia was wide-eyed as she took in the fine wooden desk and handsome but dusty furnishings. "Who was the last lawyer here?" she asked, looking at a faded portrait of an ancient Wilbanks.

"You'll have to ask Lucien," Jake replied. He had not spent five minutes in the room in the last ten years.

"This is awesome," she said.

"Not bad for an intern. The phone guy is coming today to get you plugged in. After that, you'll be in business."

They spent half an hour going over the rules: phone use, lunch breaks, office protocol, overtime, et cetera. Her first task was to read a dozen Mississippi cases involving will contests that were tried before juries. It was important that she learn the law and the lingo, and to understand how her mother's case would be handled. Read the cases, then read them again. Take notes. Absorb the law and become well versed in it so conversations with Lettie would be more meaningful. Lettie would be by far the most crucial witness at the trial, and it was important to begin laying the groundwork for her testimony. The truth was paramount, but as every trial lawyer knew, there were various ways of telling the truth.

As soon as Jake turned his back, Lucien barged into her office and made himself at home. They had met the day before; introductions were not necessary. He rambled on about how wise it was to ditch the Memphis lawyers and go with Jake, though in his opinion it would be a tough case to win. He remembered he'd represented one of her father's cousins, a Lang, twenty years earlier in a criminal matter. Kept the boy out of prison. Great lawyering. That led to another story about a shooting that involved four men, none of them remotely related to Portia, as far as she could tell. By reputation, she knew Lucien, like everyone else, as the old drunk lawyer who'd been the first white person to join the local NAACP and who now lived with his maid in the big house on the hill. Part legend, part scoundrel, he was a man she never thought she would meet, and here he was chatting with her (in her office!) as if they were old friends. For a while, she listened respectfully, but after an hour began wondering how often these visits might occur.

While she listened, Jake was locked in his office with Quince Lundy, reviewing a filing that would be known as the First Inventory. After a month of digging, Lundy was convinced the First Inventory would greatly resemble the final one. There were no hidden assets. Seth Hubbard knew when and how he would die, and he made certain he left behind adequate records.

The real estate appraisals were complete. At the time of his death, Seth owned (1) his home and 200 acres around it, valued at $300,000; (2) 150 acres of timberland near Valdosta, Georgia, valued at $450,000; (3) 400 acres of timberland near Marshall, Texas, valued at $800,000; (4) a vacant bay-front lot north of Clearwater, Florida, valued at $100,000; (5) a cabin and 5 acres outside Boone, North Carolina, valued at $280,000; and (6) a fifth-floor condo on the beach at Destin, Florida, valued at $230,000.

The total appraised value of Seth's real estate was $2,160,000. There were no mortgages.

A consulting firm from Atlanta valued the Berring Lumber Company at $400,000. Its report was attached to the inventory, along with the property appraisals.

Included also were statements listing the cash in the bank in Birmingham. Ticking along at 6 percent interest, the total was now $21,360,000 and change.

The small numbers were the most tedious. Quince Lundy listed as much of Seth's personal property as he thought the court could stand, beginning with his late-model vehicles ($35,000), and going all the way down to his wardrobe ($1,000).

The big number, though, was still astonishing. The First Inventory valued Seth's entire estate at $24,020,000. The cash, of course, was a hard number. Everything else would be subject to the market, and it would take months or even years to sell it all.

The inventory was an inch thick. Jake did not want anyone else in the office to see it, so he ran two copies himself. He left early for lunch, drove to the school, and had a plate of cafeteria spaghetti with his wife and daughter. He tried to visit once a week, especially on Wednesdays when Hanna preferred to buy rather than bring her lunch. She loved the spaghetti, but even more, she loved having her father there.

After she'd left for the playground, the Brigances walked back to Carla's classroom. The bell rang and class was set to resume.

"Off to see Judge Atlee," Jake said with a grin. "The first payday."

"Good luck," she said with a quick kiss. "Love you."

"Love you." Jake hustled away, wanting to clear the hall before the throng of little people came swarming in.

Judge Atlee was at his desk, finishing a bowl of potato soup, when Jake was escorted in by the secretary. Contrary to his doctor's orders, the judge was still smoking his pipe—he could not quit—and he loaded one up with Sir Walter Raleigh and struck a match. After thirty years of heavy pipe smoking, the entire office was tinged with a brownish residue. A permanent fog clung to the ceiling. A slightly cracked window offered some relief. The aroma, though, was rich and pleasant. Jake had always loved the place, with its rows of thick treatises and faded portraits of dead judges and Confederate generals. Nothing had changed in the twenty years Reuben Atlee had occupied this part of the courthouse, and Jake had the sense that little had changed in the past fifty years. The judge loved history and kept his favorite books in perfect order on custom-made shelves in one corner. The desk was covered with clutter, and Jake could swear that the same battered file had been sitting on the right front corner of it for the past decade.

They had first met at the Presbyterian church ten years earlier, when Jake and Carla arrived in Clanton. The judge ran the church in the same way he ran all the other aspects of his life, and he soon embraced the young lawyer. They became friends, though always at a professional level. Reuben Atlee was from the old school. He was a judge; Jake was just a lawyer. Boundaries must always be respected. He had sternly corrected Jake in open court on two occasions, with everlasting impressions.

With the pipe stem screwed into the corner of his mouth, Judge Atlee retrieved his black suit jacket and put it on. Except when he was in court, under a robe, he wore nothing but black suits. The same black suit. No one knew if he owned twenty, or just one; they were identical. And he always wore navy-blue suspenders and white starched shirts, most with a collection of tiny cinder holes from airborne tobacco embers. He took his position at the end of the table as they talked about Lucien. When Jake finished unloading his briefcase, he handed over a copy of the inventory.

"Quince Lundy is very good," Jake said. "I wouldn't want him looking through my finances."

"Probably wouldn't take that long," Judge Atlee observed wryly. To many he was a humorless man, but to those he liked he was occasionally a raging smart-ass.

"No. It wouldn't."

For a judge, he said little. Silently, and studiously, he went through the inventory, page by page as his tobacco burned out and he stopped puffing. Time was of no consequence because he controlled the clock. At the end, he removed his pipe, put it in an ashtray, and said, "Twenty-four million, huh?"

"That's the grand total."

"Let's lock this up, okay, Jake? No one should see it, not now anyway. Prepare an order and I'll seal this part of the file. God knows what would happen if the public knew this. It would be front-page news and probably attract even more lawyers. It'll come out later, but for now let's bury it."

"I agree, Judge."

"Any word from Sistrunk?"

"No sir, and I've got a good source now. In the spirit of full disclosure, I must tell you that I've hired a new intern. Portia Lang, Lettie's oldest daughter. A bright girl who thinks she might want to be a lawyer."

"Smart move, Jake, and I really like that girl."

"So, no problems?"

"None. I'm not in charge of your office."

"No conflicts of interest?"

"None that I can see."

"Me neither. If Sistrunk shows up, or comes slinking around, we'll know it soon enough. Simeon is still AWOL, but I suspect he'll come home eventually. He may be trouble but he's not stupid. She's still his wife."

"He'll be back. There's something else, Jake. The will leaves 5 percent to a brother, Ancil Hubbard. That makes him an interested party. I've read your report and the affidavits and I understand we're proceeding as if Ancil is dead. But that troubles me. Since we don't know for certain, then we should not assume he is dead."

"We've searched, Judge, but there are no clues anywhere."

"True, but you're not a pro, Jake. Here's my idea. Five percent of this estate is over a million dollars. It seems prudent to me to take a smaller sum, say fifty thousand or so, and hire a high-powered detective agency to find him, or find out what happened to him. What do you think?"

In situations like this, Judge Atlee did not really care what you thought. The decision was made, and he was just trying to be polite.

"A great idea," Jake said, something all judges like to hear.

"I'll approve it. What about the other expenses?"

"Well, Judge, delighted you asked. I need to get paid." Jake was handing over a summary of his time on the case. Judge Atlee studied it, frowned as if Jake were robbing the estate, then said, "One hundred and eighty hours. What rate did I approve?"

He knew exactly what he had approved. "One fifty per hour," Jake said.

"So a total of, let's see." He was peering down his nose through the thick reading glasses perched on the tip, still frowning mightily as if he'd been insulted. "Twenty-seven thousand dollars?" His voice rose with fake incredulity.

"At least that much."

"Seems a bit steep?"

"On the contrary, Judge. It's a bargain."

"It's also a nice start to the holiday season."

"Oh yes, that too." Jake knew Atlee would approve his fees if his hours had been doubled.

"Approved. Other expenses?" He reached into his coat pocket and removed a tobacco pouch.

Jake slid over more paperwork. "Yes, Judge, quite a few. Quince Lundy needs to get paid. He's showing 110 hours, at a hundred bucks per. And we need to pay the appraisers, the accountants, and the consulting firm. I have the documentation here, along with orders for you to sign. May I suggest that we move some cash from the bank in Birmingham to the estate account here at First National?"

"How much?" he asked, striking a match and waving it over the bowl of tobacco.

"Not much, because I don't like the idea of anybody at the

bank seeing the money. It's tucked away over in Birmingham, let's leave it there as long as we can."

"My thoughts exactly," Judge Atlee said, something he often said when confronted with a good idea. He discharged a blast of thick smoke that engulfed the table.

"I've already prepared the order," Jake said, shoving over even more paperwork and trying to ignore the smoke. Judge Atlee pulled the pipe from his teeth, a trail of smoke behind it. He began scribbling his name in his distinctive style, one that could never be deciphered but was recognizable nonetheless. He paused and looked at the order transferring the money. He said, "And with the stroke of my pen, I can move half a million bucks. Such power."

"That's more than I'll net in the next ten years."

"Not the way you're billing. You must think you're a big-firm lawyer."

"I'd rather dig ditches, Judge."

"So would I." For a few silent moments he smoked and signed his name, alternating between puffing and scribbling. When the stack was finished, he said, "Let's talk about next week. Is everything in order?"

"As far as I know. Lettie's deposition is set for Monday and Tuesday. Herschel Hubbard is Wednesday, his sister Thursday, and Friday we'll do Ian Dafoe. That's a pretty grueling week. Five straight days of depositions."

"And you're using the main courtroom?"

"Yes sir. There's no court, and I've asked Ozzie to give us an extra deputy to keep the doors closed. We'll have plenty of room, which of course we'll need."

"And I'll be right here in case there's trouble. I do not want any witnesses in the room while another witness is being deposed."

"That's been made clear to all parties."

"And I want them all on video."

"It's all arranged. Money is no object."

Judge Atlee chewed on the pipe stem and was amused by something. "My oh my," he mused. "What would Seth Hubbard think if he could look in next Monday and see a roomful of hungry lawyers fighting over his money?"

"I'm sure he'd be sick, Judge, but it's his own fault. He should've split things up, taken care of his kids and Lettie and anybody else he wanted, and we wouldn't be here."

"You think he was crazy?"

"No, not really."

"Then why'd he do it?"

"I have no idea."

"Sex?"

"Well, my new intern thinks not, and this girl has been around the world. It's her mother, but she's not naive."

There was actually a prohibition against such a conversation. Among the many antiquated sections of the Mississippi Code, one of the more famous, at least among lawyers, was titled Earwigging the Chancellor Prohibited. In simple English, it prohibited a lawyer from discussing sensitive areas of a pending case with the presiding judge in the absence of the lawyer for the other side. The rule was routinely violated. Earwigging was common, especially in the chambers of Chancellor Reuben V. Atlee, but only with a few preferred and trusted lawyers.

Jake had learned the hard way that what was said in chambers stayed there and was of no importance in open court. Out there, where it counted, Judge Atlee called them fair and straight, regardless of how much he'd been earwigged.

22

Just as Judge Atlee imagined the scene, old Seth would indeed have been upset, had he been a fly on the wall. No fewer than nine lawyers gathered in the courtroom early Monday morning to formally kick off discovery in the case now known on the docket as *In re Estate of Henry Seth Hubbard*. In other words, nine lawyers sharpening their knives for a slice of the pie.

In addition to Jake, those present were Wade Lanier and Lester Chilcott, from Jackson, representing Ramona Dafoe. Stillman Rush and Sam Larkin, from Tupelo, representing Herschel Hubbard. Lanier was still pressuring Ian to pressure Ramona to pressure Herschel to ditch the Tupelo lawyers and join forces, but such efforts so far had only led to more tension in the family. Lanier was threatening to bolt if the two allies could not join forces, but his threats were losing steam. Ian suspected there was simply too much money in the pot for any lawyer to walk away. Herschel's children were represented by Zack Zeitler, a Memphis lawyer also licensed in Mississippi. He brought along a useless associate whose only role was to fill a chair, scribble nonstop, and convey the impression that Zeitler had resources. Ramona's children were represented by Joe Bradley Hunt, from Jackson, and he dragged along an associate similar to Zeitler's. Ancil, also in at five, was still presumed dead, and thus unrepresented and not mentioned.

Portia was one of three paralegals in the courtroom. Wade Lanier and Stillman Rush brought the other two, both white males, same as everybody else except for the court reporter, who was a white woman. "The courtroom is owned by the taxpayers," Jake had told Portia. "So act like you own the place." She was trying, but she was still a nervous wreck. She was expecting tension, maybe harsh words, an atmosphere pervaded by competition and distrust. What she saw, however, was a bunch of white men shaking hands, swapping friendly insults, poking fun, laughing, and having a good time as they drank their coffee and waited on 9:00 a.m. If there was any edginess as they were about to begin their war over a fortune, it was not evident.

"It's just depositions," Jake had said. "You'll be bored out of your mind. Death by deposition."

In the center of the courtroom, between the bar and the bench, the tables had been joined together, with chairs crammed around them. The lawyers slowly found their places, though no seating was assigned. Since Lettie would be the first witness, Jake sat near the empty seat at the end. At the other end, the court reporter fiddled with a video camera as a clerk entered with a full pot of coffee and sat it on the table.

When everyone was in place and somewhat settled, Jake nodded at Portia who opened a side door and retrieved her mother. Lettie was dressed for church and looked great, though Jake had told her she could wear anything. "It's just a deposition."

She sat at the end of the table, with Jake close by on one side, the court reporter on the other side with her stenographic machine, and her daughter not far away. She looked down the long table, smiled at the horde of lawyers, and said, "Good morning." Every single lawyer returned the greeting with a smile. Off to a good start.

But only for a second. As Jake was about to start the preliminaries, the large main door opened and Rufus Buckley walked in, briefcase in hand as if he had business there. The courtroom was empty—not a single spectator—and it would remain so upon the order of Judge Reuben Atlee. Obviously, Buckley wasn't there to observe.

He walked through the swinging gate of the bar and took a seat at the table. The other nine lawyers watched suspiciously.

Jake was suddenly itching for a fight. He called out loudly, "Well, hello, Rufus. So nice to see you out of jail these days."

"Ha-ha, Jake. Such a comedian."

"What are you doing here?"

"I'm here for the deposition. Can't you see?" Buckley shot back.

"Who do you represent?"

"The same client I've had for a month. Simeon Lang."

"He's not an interested party."

"Oh, we think he is. We think it might need to be litigated, but our position is that Mr. Lang has a direct pecuniary interest in the will contest. That's why I'm here."

Jake stood and said, "Okay, let's stop right where we are. Judge Atlee is on standby in case there's trouble. I'll run fetch him." Jake left the courtroom in a hurry and Buckley settled into his seat, somewhat nervously.

Minutes later, Judge Atlee entered from behind the bench, minus his robe, and took his usual position. "Good morning, gentlemen," he said gruffly and without waiting for any response said, "Mr. Buckley, using as few words as possible, please tell me why you're here."

Buckley stood with his customary purpose, and said, "Well, Judge, we still represent Mr. Simeon Lang and—"

"Who's we?"

"Mr. Booker Sistrunk and myself, along—"

"Mr. Sistrunk will not be appearing in this courtroom, Mr. Buckley, not in this matter anyway."

"Okay, well, then our position hasn't changed. Mr. Simeon Lang is a party to these proceedings and—"

"He is not, nor will I allow him to become a party. Therefore, Mr. Buckley, you are not representing an interested party."

"But that has not been finally determined."

"It certainly has. By me. You have no business here, Mr. Buckley. And this deposition is closed."

"Come on, Judge, it's just a deposition, not some secret meeting. The testimony will be added to the court file and available to the public."

"That's for me to decide at some future date."

"Judge, what she says today will be sworn testimony, and it will become a part of the record in this case."

"Don't lecture me, Mr. Buckley."

"I'm sorry, I didn't—"

"These depositions will be sealed until I review them. Frankly, Mr. Buckley, I don't like being put in the position of having to argue with you. Need I remind you of what happened the last time you said too much in this courtroom?"

"No need for that, Judge," Buckley said.

"Good day, Mr. Buckley," the judge said at full volume.

Buckley stood helplessly, in disbelief, both arms outstretched as if stunned. "Seriously, Judge?"

"Dead serious, Mr. Buckley. Good day, sir."

Buckley nodded, reached for his briefcase, and made a hasty retreat from the courtroom. When the main door closed behind him, Judge Atlee said, "Carry on," and disappeared.

Everyone took a deep breath. Jake said, "Now, where were we?"

"I kinda miss Sistrunk," Wade Lanier drawled, and got a few laughs.

"I'm sure you do," Jake said. "He and Buckley would have scored well with a Ford County jury."

Jake introduced Lettie to the court reporter, the other lawyers, all names and faces blurred by the sheer number, and he went into a lengthy explanation of the purposes of a deposition. The instructions were fairly simple. Please speak clearly, slowly, and if a question isn't clear, ask that it be restated. If uncertain, say nothing. He, Jake, would object to anything objectionable, and please answer truthfully because you're under oath. The lawyers would take turns with their questioning. If you need a break, just say so. The court reporter would take down every word, and the video camera would record the entire deposition. If for some reason Lettie was not able to testify at trial, the video would be used as evidence.

The instructions were necessary, and then they were not. Jake, Portia, and Lucien had rehearsed with Lettie for hours in the conference room at the office. She was well prepared, though in a deposition it was impossible to predict what might be discussed. At trial, all testimony must be relevant. Not so in a deposition, which often turned into a prolonged fishing expedition.

Be polite. Be concise. Don't volunteer. If you don't know, then you don't know. Remember the camera catches everything. And I'll be right beside you for protection, Jake had said over and over. Portia had gone to the attic and found dozens of old depositions that she had spent hours poring over. She understood the technicalities, the strategies, and the pitfalls. She and her mother had talked for hours on the back porch of the old Sappington house.

Lettie was as prepared as possible. After she was sworn by the court reporter, Wade Lanier introduced himself with a sappy smile and began the questioning. "Let's start with your family," he said. Names, current residences, birth dates, birthplaces, education, employment, children, grandchildren, parents, brothers, sisters, cousins, aunts, uncles. Lettie and Portia had rehearsed thoroughly and the answers came easily. Lanier paused at one point when he realized Portia was her daughter. Jake explained, "She's an intern in my office. Paid." This caused some concern around the table. Stillman Rush finally asked, "Does this pose a conflict, Jake?"

Jake had thought it over long ago. "Not at all. I represent the estate. Portia is not a beneficiary under the will. I see no conflict. Do you?"

"Is she going to be a witness?" Lester Chilcott asked.

"No. She was away in the Army for the past six years."

Zack Zeitler asked, "Will she have access to certain information her mother perhaps should not see?"

"Such as?"

"I can't give you an example right now. I'm just speculating. I'm not saying there's a conflict here, Jake, I'm just sort of caught off guard."

"Have you informed Judge Atlee?" Wade Lanier asked.

"I did last week, and he approved."

End of conversation. Wade Lanier took off again with questions about Lettie's parents, and grandparents. His questions were soft and easy, quite conversational, as if he were truly interested in where her maternal grandparents once lived and what they did for a living. After an hour, Jake fought the temptation to daydream. It was important for him to take notes in the event another lawyer, hours from now, inadvertently stepped into the same territory.

Back to Lettie. She finished high school in 1959 in Hamilton, Alabama, at the old colored school. She ran away to Memphis and met Simeon. They married right away and Marvis was born the following year.

Wade Lanier spent some time on Marvis: his criminal record, convictions, incarceration. Lettie got choked up and wiped her cheeks, but did not break down. Next came Phedra and her problems: two children born out of wedlock, Lettie's first two grandkids; an employment history that was sketchy at best. Phedra was currently living at home; in fact she'd never really left. Her two children had different fathers who were out of the picture.

Portia flinched with questions about her older brother and her sister. These were not secrets, but they were not openly discussed either. The family whispered about such matters, yet here they were being kicked about by a bunch of white men, strangers all.

At 10:30, they broke for fifteen minutes and everyone scattered. The lawyers ran to find phones. Portia and Lettie headed for the ladies' room. A clerk brought in a fresh pot of coffee and a tray of store-bought cookies. The tables already resembled a landfill.

When they resumed, Stillman Rush took the handoff and dwelled on Simeon, whose family was more complicated. Lettie admitted she did not know as many details about his ancestors. His work history was filled with gaps, but she did recall stints as a truck driver, dozer operator, pulpwood cutter, painter, and brick mason's helper. He'd been arrested a couple of times, the most recent being last October. Misdemeanors, no felonies. Yes, they had separated several times, but never for more than two months.

Enough of Simeon, for now anyway; Stillman wanted to follow up with Lettie's résumé. She worked for Seth Hubbard off and on, part-time and full-time, for most of the past three years. Before that, she worked for three years as a house-keeper in the Clanton home of an old couple Jake had never heard of. Both died within three months of one another, and Lettie was out of work. Before that, she worked as a cook in the middle school cafeteria in Karaway. Stillman wanted dates, wages, raises, bosses, every minute detail, and Lettie did the best she could.

Seriously? Portia asked herself. How could the name of my mother's boss ten years ago possibly be important to this will contest? It would be a fishing expedition, Jake had said. Welcome to the mind-numbing dullness of deposition warfare.

Jake had also explained that depositions drag on for days because the lawyers are being paid by the hour, or at least the ones who are asking the banal and monotonous questions. With virtually no restrictions on what can be explored, and with their meters running, lawyers, especially those working for insurance companies and big corporations, have no interest in being concise. As long as they can keep the conversation close to a person, issue, or thing remotely connected to the lawsuit, then they can peck away for hours.

However, Jake had also explained that the Hubbard case was different because the only lawyer working by the hour was him. The others were there on a prayer and a percentage. If the hand-written will were to be invalidated, the money would revert to the family under the prior will, and all those lawyers would take a cut. Since the other lawyers had no guarantee they would be paid, he suspected their questions might not be so tedious.

Portia wasn't so sure about that. Tedium was closing in from all directions.

Stillman liked to bounce around, probably in an effort to keep the witness off balance. He woke up the crowd with "Now, did you borrow money from your former attorney, Booker Sistrunk?"

"I did." Lettie knew the question was coming and answered it without hesitation. There was no law or rule against such a loan, not on the receiving end anyway.

"How much?"

"Fifty thousand dollars."

"Did he write you a check or was it in cash?"

"Cash, and we, Simeon and I, signed a promissory note."

"Was this the only loan from Sistrunk?"

"No, there was a prior loan for $5,000."

"Why did you borrow money from Mr. Sistrunk?"

"Because we needed the money. I lost my job, and with Simeon you never know."

"Did you take the money and move into a larger house?"

"We did."

"And how many people now live in that house?"

Lettie thought for a moment, and said, "Usually around eleven, but the number varies. Some come and go."

Jake glared at Stillman as if to say, "Don't even think about wanting all eleven names. Can we just move along?"

Stillman was tempted, but moved along. "How much are you paying in rent?"

"Seven hundred a month."

"And you're unemployed as of today?"

"Correct."

"Where is your husband working right now?"

"He's not."

"Since Mr. Sistrunk is no longer your lawyer, how do you plan to repay him?"

"We'll worry about that later."

Roxy had sandwiches and chips ready for lunch, and they ate in the conference room where Lucien joined them. "How'd it go?" he asked.

"The usual first round of worthless questions," Jake said. "Lettie was great but she's already tired."

Lettie said, "I can't do this for another day and a half."

"Modern discovery," Lucien said in disgust.

"Tell us how it was back in the old days, Lucien," Jake said.

"Well, back in the old days, and the old days were much better than all these new rules you got now—"

"I didn't write them."

"You weren't required to divulge all of your witnesses and describe what they were going to say, no sir. It was trial by ambush. You get your witnesses, I'll get mine, and we'll show up at the courthouse and have us a trial. It made you a better lawyer too because you had to react on the fly. Nowadays, everything has to be fully disclosed and every witness has to be available for a deposition. Think of the time. Think of the expense. It was far better back then, I swear it was."

"Why don't you take a large bite of that sandwich?" Jake said. "Lettie needs to relax and no one can relax when you're on your soapbox."

Lucien took a small bite and asked, "What'd you think, Portia?"

She was nibbling on a chip. She laid it down and said, "It's pretty cool, I mean, being in a room full of that many lawyers. Makes me feel important."

"Don't be too impressed," Jake said. "Most of those guys couldn't try a shoplifting case in city court."

"I'll bet Wade Lanier can," Lettie said. "He's smooth. I get the impression he knows what I'm gonna say before I say it."

"He's very good," Jake admitted. "Believe me, Lettie, we will learn to despise him. He seems to be a nice guy now, but you won't be able to stand the sight of him before this is over."

The thought of a long fight seemed to deflate Lettie. Four hours into the initial skirmish, and she was already exhausted.

During lunch, two ladies from the clerk's office assembled a small artificial Christmas tree and placed it at the far rear corner of the courtroom. From where Jake was sitting at the table, he had a clear, unobstructed view of the tree. At noon each Christmas Eve, most of the Circuit and Chancery Court clerks and judges, and a few handpicked lawyers, gathered back there for egg nog and gag gifts. It was a gathering Jake tried his best to avoid.

The tree, though, reminded him that Christmas was only days away, and the thought of shopping had not yet crossed his mind, at least not until then. As Wade Lanier plowed ahead in a voice so low and dry that it was practically a sedative, Jake caught his mind drifting away to the holidays. For the past two years, they had struggled to decorate their rental and bring it alive for the holidays. Hanna helped tremendously. Having a child around the house kept everyone's spirits up.

Lanier moved into a sensitive area. Slowly, skillfully, he probed into Lettie's duties around the house when Mr. Hubbard was sick with the chemo and radiation and confined to his bed. Lettie explained that a home-health-care agency sent nurses over to tend to him, but these women were not good, not considerate enough, and Mr. Hubbard was quite rude. She didn't blame him. He ran them off and had fights with the agency. Eventually, Lettie took over his care. She cooked whatever he wanted, and fed him when he needed help. She helped him out of bed and to the bathroom, where he sometimes sat on the toilet for half an hour. He had accidents, and she cleaned his bed. On several occasions, he was forced to use a bedpan, and Lettie tended to him. No, it was not pleasant work and she was not trained in such ways, but she managed. He appreciated her kindness. He trusted her. Yes, on several occasions she bathed Mr. Hubbard in his bed. Yes, a complete bath, touching everywhere. He was so sick and hardly awake. Later, when they stopped the chemo and radiation for a while, he regained his strength and began moving around as soon as possible. He bounced back with an amazing determination. No, he never quit smoking.

Intimacy can kill our case, Jake had explained to Portia in blunt terms, which were then filtered through daughter to mother. If the jury believes Lettie got too close to Seth Hubbard, they'll have no trouble finding she unduly influenced him.

Was Mr. Hubbard affectionate with her? Was he one to hug, peck on the cheek, pat on the rear end? Not in the least, Lettie said. Never. Her boss was a hard man who kept to himself. He had little patience with other people and needed few friends. He did not shake Lettie's hand when she arrived for work in the morning, nor did he offer her even a semblance of an embrace when saying good-bye. She was his employee, nothing more: not a friend, nor confidante, nor anything else. He was polite and he thanked her when appropriate, but he was never a man of many words.

She knew nothing of his business, nor his social affairs. He never spoke of another woman and Lettie never saw one in his home. In fact, she could not remember a single incident when a friend or business acquaintance came to the house, not in the three years she worked there.

Perfect, Jake said to himself.

Bad lawyers tried to trick witnesses, or pin them down, or confuse them, all in an effort to win the deposition. Good lawyers preferred to win at trial, and used depositions as a means to gather information that could be used to set traps later. Great lawyers skipped depositions altogether, and orchestrated beautiful ambushes in front of the jury. Wade Lanier and Stillman Rush were good lawyers, and they spent the first day collecting data. During eight hours of direct examination, there was not the first cross word, not the first hint of disrespect for the witness.

Jake was impressed with his opponents. Later, in his office, he explained to Lettie and Portia that both Lanier and Rush were basically acting. They were presenting themselves as friendly guys who really liked Lettie and were just searching for the truth. They wanted Lettie to like them, to trust them, so that at the trial she might drop her guard. "They're a couple of wolves," he said. "At trial, they'll go for your throat."

Lettie, exhausted, asked, "Jake, I won't be on the stand for no eight hours, will I?"

"You'll be ready."

She had her doubts.

Zack Zeitler led off the following morning with a series of probing questions about Mr. Hubbard's last days. He struck pay dirt when he asked, "Did you see him on Saturday, October 1?"

Jake braced himself for what would follow. He had known it for several days, but there was no way to avoid it. The truth was the truth.

"I did," Lettie answered.

"I thought you said you never worked on Saturdays."

"That's right, but Mr. Hubbard asked me to come in that Saturday."

"And why was that?"

"He wanted me to go to his office with him, to clean it. The regular guy was off sick and the place needed cleaning." Around the table, Lettie's response was far more effective than the morning coffee. Eyes opened, spines stiffened, rear ends inched to the edges of chairs, a couple of telling glances were exchanged.

Smelling blood, Zeitler pressed on cautiously. "What time did you arrive at Mr. Hubbard's house?"

"Around nine that mornin'."

"And what did he say?"

"He said he wanted me to go with him to his office. So we got in the car and went to his office."

"Which car?"

"His. The Cadillac."

"Who drove?"

"I did. Mr. Hubbard asked me if I'd ever driven a new Cadillac. I said no. I had said somethin' earlier about how nice the car was, and so he asked me if I wanted to drive it. At first I said no, but he handed me the keys. So I drove it over to the office. I was a nervous wreck."

"You drove him over?" Zeitler repeated. Around the table all heads were low as the lawyers scribbled furiously, their minds spinning. In perhaps the most famous will contest in the history of the state, the beneficiary, who was not a blood relative, actually drove the dying person to the lawyer's office to sign a will that cut out all family and left everything to the beneficiary, the driver. The Supreme Court invalidated the last will on the grounds of undue influence, and gave as a significant reason the fact that the "surprise beneficiary" had been so involved in the making of the new will. Since that court decision thirty years earlier, it was not unusual for a lawyer to ask "Who drove him over?" when an unexpected will was discovered.

"Yes," she said. Jake watched the other eight lawyers as they reacted exactly as he anticipated. It was a gift to them, and a hurdle for him to clear.

Zeitler carefully arranged some notes, then said, "How long were you in his office?"

"I didn't look at no clock, but I'd say a couple of hours."

"Who else was there?"

"No one. He said they usually didn't work on Saturdays, at least not in the office."

"I see." For the next hour, Zeitler probed through that Saturday morning. He asked Lettie to draw a diagram of the office building to establish where she cleaned and where Mr. Hubbard spent the time. She said he never left his office and the door was shut. No, she did not go in there, not even to clean. She did not know what he was working on or what he was doing in his office. He came and went with his everyday briefcase, but she had no idea what was in it. He appeared to be clearheaded, certainly able to drive if he'd wanted, and she knew little about his pain medications. Yes, he was frail and weak, but he had gone to the office every day that week. If anyone else saw them at the office, she was not aware of it. Yes, she drove the Cadillac back to Mr. Hubbard's house, then she went home, arriving there around noon.

"And he never mentioned the fact that he was writing his last will?"

"Objection," Jake said. "She's already answered that twice."

"Okay, yes, well, I just wanted to make sure."

"It's in the record."

"Sure." Having scored big, Zeitler was reluctant to move on. He established that Lettie drove the Cadillac on that day only; she rarely saw pill bottles or drugs around the house; she suspected he kept his meds in his briefcase; at times he was in severe pain; he never talked about suicide; she never witnessed bizarre behavior that would suggest he was under the influence of medications; he was not a drinker but occasionally kept a few beers in the refrigerator; and he kept a desk in his bedroom but almost never worked at home.

By noon Tuesday, Lettie was ready to quit. She had a long lunch in Jake's office, again with Portia, then took a nap on a sofa.

Death by deposition continued on Wednesday as Jake took charge and quizzed Herschel Hubbard for several hours. The morning session dragged on with stultifying dullness, and it didn't take long to establish that Herschel had accomplished little and taken few chances in his career. His divorce had been the most exciting event in his life. Such hot topics as his education, work experiences, businesses, former homes and apartments, relationships, friends, interests, hobbies, religious convictions, and political leanings were covered in depth and proved to be stunningly boring. Several of the attorneys nodded off. Portia, in her third day of real legal action, struggled to stay awake.

After lunch, the lawyers reluctantly returned to the courtroom for another session. Jake managed to liven things up a bit when he began trying to pin down how much time Herschel had spent with his father in the past several years. Herschel tried to give the impression he and the old man were close, but had trouble recalling specific visits. If they spoke so often on the phone, what might the phone records reveal? Jake asked. Any cards and letters from Seth? Herschel was sure he had them but he wasn't so sure he could produce them. His lawyers had instructed him to be as vague as possible, and he succeeded beautifully.

On the subject of Lettie Lang, Herschel claimed to have been around her quite often, during his many visits to see his beloved father. In his opinion, Seth was quite fond of her. He admitted he never saw them touch in any way, but there was something in the way they looked at each other. What, exactly? Not sure, but just something between them. She was always listening, always in the shadows trying to eavesdrop. And as his father got sicker, he depended more and more on Lettie, and they grew closer. Jake asked if he was suggesting they were intimate. "Only Lettie knows that," Herschel replied, implying, of course, the obvious.

Portia fumed as she glanced around the table. She assumed that every person there, except for Jake, believed her mother was sleeping with a withered and decaying old white man, and doing so to get his money. But Portia kept her head low, and, as a professional, maintained a poker face as she filled another page with notes that would never be reviewed.

Seven hours of probing were more than enough to establish Herschel Hubbard was a less than interesting person who'd had a strained and distant relationship with his father. He was still living with his mother, still reeling from a bad divorce, and, at the age of forty-six, barely surviving on the income from a student hangout. What Herschel desperately needed was an inheritance.

As did Ramona. Her deposition kicked off at 9:00 on Thursday morning, and by then the lawyers were cranky and fed up with the case. Spending five consecutive days in deposition was a rare event, though not unheard-of. During a break, Wade Lanier told a story of deposing a dozen consecutive witnesses over ten straight days in an oil spill case in New Orleans. The witnesses were from Venezuela, most did not speak English, and the interpreters were not that fluent. The lawyers partied hard every night, suffered through the depositions with awful hangovers, and two of them entered rehab when the ordeal was over.

No one had more stories than Wade Lanier. He was the senior lawyer and had spent thirty years in courtrooms. The more Jake watched and listened, the more he respected Lanier. He would be a formidable foe before the jury.

Ramona turned out to be as dull as her brother. From their depositions, it slowly became apparent that Seth Hubbard was a neglectful father who viewed his children as little more than nuisances. In hindsight, and with the money on the line, they tried valiantly to prop up the old guy and make them all seem like a close, happy family, but Seth simply could not be reinvented. Jake poked and prodded and trapped her here and there, but he did so with a smile and tried not to offend her. Since she and Herschel spent so little time with their father, their testimony would not be that crucial at trial. They were not around him in the days before his death; thus, they had nothing to offer on the subject of his mental capacity. They had no firsthand knowledge of his alleged closeness to Lettie.

And these were only preliminary depositions. Jake and the other lawyers knew that in all likelihood Lettie, Herschel, Ramona, and Ian Dafoe would be deposed again. When the facts became clearer and the issues more narrowly defined, the lawyers would have more questions.

23

Leaving the courthouse in a hurry late Thursday afternoon, Jake was grabbed by Stillman Rush, who asked if he had time for a quick drink. It was a strange offer because the two had nothing in common except the Hubbard case. Sure, he said, why not? Stillman had something important to talk about; otherwise he wouldn't waste his time with a street lawyer like Jake.

They met in a bar in the basement of an old building just off the square, walking distance from the courthouse. It was already dark outside, and misting, a perfectly gloomy evening and a great time for a drink. Though Jake didn't frequent bars, he'd been there before. It was a shadowy, damp place with dark corners and booths and gave the impression that semi-legitimate deals were going down. Bobby Carl Leach, the town's most infamous shyster, owned a table next to the fireplace and was often seen there with politicians and bankers. Harry Rex Vonner was a regular.

Jake and Stillman got a booth, ordered draft beers, and began to unwind. After four straight days at the same table listening to endless and marginally useful testimony, they were almost numb with tedium. Stillman's innate cockiness seemed to vanish and he was almost likable. When the waiter dropped off the beers, he leaned in low and said, "Here's an idea, just me thinking with no authority from anyone else. But there's a pile of money here, we all know that. Not sure how much right now, but—"

"Twenty-four million," Jake interrupted. The lawyers would soon learn what was in the inventory, and there was no harm in revealing this to Stillman. Jake was just trying to keep it out of the newspapers.

Stillman paused, smiled, took a sip and shook his head. "Twenty-four million."

"And no debts."

"Hard to believe, isn't it?"

"It is."

"So there's twenty-four million, and by the time the tax collectors have their way, we'll be lucky if half of it's left."

Jake said, "That's right, according to the accountants."

"So we're down to twelve million, still a lot of money, more than you and I will ever see. So, here's my idea, Jake. Why don't we try and negotiate a settlement? There are three main players—Herschel, Ramona, and Lettie. Surely we can slice the pie and make everyone happy."

It was not an original idea. Jake and Lucien had kicked it around several times, and they were certain the opposing lawyers had done the same. Each side gives a little, or a lot, cut off the attorney's fees and expenses, stop the presses, avoid the stress and uncertainty of a trial, and everybody is guaranteed a nice slice of the pie. It made perfect sense. In every lawsuit, the potential of a settlement was always in the minds of the attorneys.

"Is this what your client wants to do?" Jake asked.

"I don't know. We haven't discussed it yet. But if it's a possibility, then I'll approach Herschel and lean on him."

"Okay. This pie you're talking about, how do you want to slice it?"

A long gulp, followed by a backhand wipe of the mouth, and Stillman lunged onward. "Let's be honest, Jake, Lettie Lang is entitled to very little. In the scheme of things, and in the normal transition of assets and estates, she just doesn't figure in. She's not family, and regardless of how screwed up a family might be, the money almost always gets handed down to the next generation. You know that. Ninety percent of all money that flows through wills goes to family members. Ninety percent in Mississippi, same in New York and California, where they have, shall we say, bigger estates. And look at the law. If a person dies with no will, then all money and assets go to blood kin and no one else. Keeping the money in the family is preferred by the law."

"True, but we can't settle this case if Lettie is told she gets nothing."

"Of course not, Jake. Give her a couple of million. Can you imagine that? Lettie Lang, unemployed, a career housekeeper, suddenly walks away with two million bucks, and that's after taxes? I'm not denigrating the woman, Jake; hell, I came to like her during her deposition. She's pleasant, even funny, a good person. I'm not being critical of her, but come on, Jake, do you know how many black people in Mississippi are worth seven figures?"

"Enlighten me."

"According to the 1980 census, seven black folks in this state claimed to be worth more than a million dollars. All men, most were in construction or real estate. Lettie would be the richest black woman in the state."

"And your client and his sister split the remaining ten million?" Jake asked.

"Something like that. Give a nice gift to the church, and we'll split the rest."

"That would be a good deal for you guys," Jake said. "You'll rake off a third of almost five million. Not a bad payday."

"I didn't say we're getting a third, Jake."

"But you're getting a percentage?"

"I can't say, but sure, it'll be a nice payday."

For some, thought Jake. If the case settled now, his fees would be severely reined in. "Have you discussed this with Wade Lanier?"

Stillman grimaced at the mention of his name. "That's another story. Lanier wants my client, who, for now, is sticking with me. I don't trust Lanier and I'll spend the next six months looking over my shoulder. What a snake."

"So the answer is no?"

"The answer is no. I haven't discussed it with anyone."

"I take it things are tense between your client and his client."

"I suppose. Herschel and Ramona can get along when they have to, but Ian is the problem. Herschel said he and Ian can't stand one another, never have. He sees Ian as a privileged little prick from a stuffy old family that managed to lose it all, and so he's trying hard to regain some status and play the big shot. He's always looked down on the Hubbards as something slightly above white trash, until now of course. Now he's suddenly enamored with the family and has deep concerns for its well-being."

It was not lost on Jake that Stillman referred to someone else as a "privileged little prick from a stuffy old family."

"What a surprise," he said. "Look, Stillman, I just spent eight and a half hours playing pitch and catch with Ramona, and if I didn't know better, I'd say the woman drinks too much. The red, leaky eyes, the puffiness partially hidden under makeup, the extra layer of wrinkles that seem too much for a woman of only forty-two. I'm an expert on drunks because I'm close to Lucien Wilbanks."

"Herschel says she's a lush who's been threatening to leave Ian for years," Stillman said, and Jake was impressed with his candor.

"Now, she can't run him off," Jake said.

"Oh no. I think Ian is once again madly in love with his wife. I have a pal in Jackson who knows some of Ian's drinking buddies. They say he likes the ladies."

"I'll ask him about it tomorrow."

"Do that. The point is, Herschel and Ian will never trust each other."

They ordered more beers and finished off their first round. Stillman said, "You don't seem too excited about the prospects of a settlement."

"You're ignoring what the old man wanted. He was very clear, both in his will and in his letter to me. He directed me to defend his handwritten will at all costs, to the bitter end."

"He directed you?"

"Yes. In a letter that accompanied the will. You'll see it later. He was very specific in his desire to cut out his family."

"But he's dead."

"It's still his money. How can we redirect his money when his wishes were quite clear? It's not right, and I doubt if Judge Atlee would approve it."

"And if you lose?"

"Then I'll lose doing what I was directed to do. Defend the will at all costs."

The second beers arrived just as Harry Rex lumbered by without speaking. He seemed preoccupied and did not look at Jake. It was not yet 6:00 p.m., too early for Harry Rex to leave the office. He crawled into a booth by himself in a corner and tried to hide.

Stillman wiped foam from his mouth again and asked, "Why'd he do it, Jake? Any clues so far?"

"Not really," Jake said with a shrug, as though he would honestly share inside dirt with his opponent. He wouldn't give Stillman Rush the time of day if it could possibly help his cause.

"Sex?"

Another casual shrug, a quick shake of the head, a frown. "I don't think so. The old guy was seventy-one, a heavy smoker, sick, frail, eaten up with cancer. It's hard to imagine him having the energy and stamina to get it on with any woman."

"He wasn't sick two years ago."

"True, but there's no way to prove it."

"I'm not talking about proof, Jake. Or evidence or trials or anything else. I'm just speculating. There's got to be a reason."

Then figure it out yourself, asshole, Jake thought but didn't say. He was amused at Stillman's clumsy effort at gossip, as if the two were old drinking buddies who often shared secrets. Loose lips sink ships, Harry Rex was fond of saying. Loose lips lose lawsuits.

Jake said, "It's hard to believe a little sex could be worth twenty-four million."

Stillman laughed and said, "Not so sure. Wars have been fought over it."

"True."

"No interest in pursuing a settlement?"

"No. I have my marching orders."

"You'll be sorry."

"Is that a threat?"

"Not at all. The way we see it, Booker Sistrunk has already pissed off every white person in Ford County."

"Didn't know you were such an expert on Ford County."

"Look, Jake, you got one huge, sensational verdict here. Don't let it go to your head."

"I wasn't looking for advice."

"Maybe you need it."

"From you?"

Stillman drained his mug and sat it hard on the table. "Gotta run. I'll pay at the bar." He was already out of the booth and reaching into a pocket. Jake watched him leave, cursed him, then eased deeper into the room and slid into the booth opposite Harry Rex.

"Sitting among your friends?" Jake asked.

"Well, well, so Carla let you out of the house." Harry Rex was working on a Bud Light and reading a magazine, which he put aside.

"I just had my first and last drink with Stillman Rush."

"How thrilling. Let me guess. He wants to settle."

"How'd you know?"

"Figures. A quick deal and those boys make out like bandits."

Jake described Stillman's version of a fair settlement, and they had a good laugh. A waiter delivered a platter of nachos and dip. "Is this your dinner?" Jake asked.

"Naw, this is high tea. I'm headed back to the office. You'll never guess who's in town."

"Who?"

"Remember Willie Traynor, used to own the *Times*?"

"Sort of. I met him once or twice, years ago. Seems like he sold the paper about the time I arrived here."

"That's right. Willie bought it in 1970 from the Caudle family. It was in bankruptcy and I think he paid something like fifty grand for it. Sold it ten years later for one point five mill." Harry

Rex loaded up a nacho and stuffed it in his mouth. Pausing only slightly, he continued, "He never really fit in around here, so he went back to Memphis, where he was from, and lost his ass in real estate. Then his grandmother died and left him another bundle. He's in the process of losing it too, I think. We were pretty close back in the day and he pops in from time to time, looking for a drink."

"Does he still own the Hocutt House?"

"Yep, and I think that's one reason he wants to talk. He bought it in 1972 after all the Hocutts died off. Talk about a weird bunch. Twins, Wilma and Gilma, plus a brother and a crazy sister, and none of them ever married. Willie bought the house because nobody else wanted it, then he spent a few years fixing it up. You ever seen it?"

"Only from the street. It's beautiful."

"It's one of the finest Victorians in these parts. Kinda reminds me of your old place, just a lot bigger. Willie has good taste and the interior is immaculate. Problem is, he hasn't spent three nights there in the past five years. He wants to sell it, probably needs the money, but, hell, can't nobody around here afford it."

"Whatever the price, it's way out of my range," Jake said.

"He thinks it's worth $300,000. I said maybe so, but he'll never get it. Not now, not ten years from now."

"Some doctor'll buy it."

"He mentioned you, Jake. He followed the Hailey trial, knows all about the Klan burning your house. He knows you're in the market."

"I'm not in the market, Harry Rex. I'm in litigation with the insurance company. But tell him thanks anyway. Too rich for my blood."

"You want some nachos?"

"No thanks. I need to get home."

"Tell Carla I love her and lust after her body."

"She knows it. Later."

Jake walked to his office in a cold drizzle. The streetlamps around the square were adorned with Christmas wreaths and silver bells. Carols rang out from a Nativity scene in front of the courthouse. The merchants were open late and the stores were busy. There was a slight chance of snow tomorrow and few things excited the town like such a forecast. The old-timers claimed there had been a white Christmas in 1952, and even the slightest chance of one now had kids staring out of windows and stores offering shovels and salt. Shoppers scurried about with great anticipation as if a blizzard was expected.

Jake took the long route home, driving slowly away from the square and into the shaded streets of central Clanton until he turned onto Market Street. A light was on in the Hocutt House, a rarity. Jake and Carla had passed it many times, always slowly, admiringly, and always aware that the lovely Victorian was hardly used. There had always been rumors that Willie Traynor was selling the place. He had abandoned Clanton after he sold the paper, and everyone knew it.

The house needed painting. In the summer, the flower beds were choked with weeds and the grass was rarely mowed. In the fall, the leaves gathered in drifts on the front porch and no one raked them.

For a moment, Jake was tempted to stop, knock on the door, barge in, have a drink with Willie, and talk business. But the temptation passed and he headed home.

24

On the morning of Christmas Eve, Jake slept late, or as late as possible. With Carla dead to the world, he eased out of bed at seven, and without a sound went to the kitchen. He brewed coffee, scrambled eggs, and toasted muffins, and when he returned with breakfast in bed she grudgingly came to life. They were eating slowly and talking quietly, thoroughly enjoying a rare moment, when Hanna bounded into the room full of anticipation and chattering nonstop about Santa Claus. She wedged herself between her parents and helped herself to a muffin. Without prompting, she reviewed everything she'd put in her letter to the North Pole, and seemed genuinely concerned that she might be asking for too much. Both parents patiently disagreed. She was, after all, the only child and usually got what she wanted. Plus, there was a surprise that would overshadow all of her requests.

An hour later, Jake and Hanna left for the square while Carla stayed home to wrap packages. Roxy was off for the day, and Jake needed to retrieve a gift for his wife. The office was always the best hiding place. He expected to find no one there, but was not too surprised when he saw Lucien in the conference room, digging through a stack of old files. He looked as though he'd been there for hours, and, more important, he looked clean and sober. "We need to talk," he said.

Hanna loved to rummage through her father's big office, so Jake turned her loose upstairs and went to find coffee. Lucien had already consumed half a pot and seemed sufficiently wired. "You're not gonna believe this," he said as he closed the conference room door. Jake fell into a chair, stirred his coffee, and asked, "Can this wait until Monday?"

"No, shut up and listen. The great question here is, Why would a man do what Seth Hubbard did? Right? Make a last-minute will, crude and handwritten, cut out his family, and leave everything to a person who has no claim to any of his fortune? This is the question that haunts you now, and it will only get bigger until we find the answer."

"Assuming there is an answer."

"Yes. So to unravel this mystery, and to hopefully help you win this case, we have to answer that question."

"And you've found it?"

"Not yet, but I'm on the trail." Lucien waved at a pile of debris on the table—files, copies of old deeds, notes. "I have examined the land records of the two hundred acres Seth Hubbard owned in this county when he died. A lot of the records were destroyed when the courthouse burned after the second war, but I've been able to reconstruct much of what I'm looking for. I've dug through every deed book, all the way back to the early 1800s, and I've scoured every copy of the local newspapers from the day they started printing. I've also done a fair amount of genealogical research, into the Hubbard, Tayber, and Rinds families. As you know, it's very difficult with these black folks. Lettie was raised by Cypress and Clyde Tayber, but she was never legally adopted. She didn't know it until she was thirty years old, according to Portia. Portia also believes, as do I, that Lettie was really a Rinds, a family that no longer exists in Ford County."

Jake took a sip of coffee and listened intently. Lucien propped up a large, hand-drawn map and began pointing. "This is the original Hubbard property, eighty acres, been in the family for a hundred years. Seth inherited it from his father, Cleon, who died thirty years ago. Cleon left a will giving everything to Seth, and Ancil was never mentioned. Next to it is another eighty-acre section, right here, at the bridge where they found Seth after he fell off his ladder. The other forty acres over here were purchased by Seth twenty years ago and are not important." Lucien was tapping the second parcel upon which he had crudely drawn a creek, a bridge, and a hanging tree. "Here's where it gets interesting. This second tract of eighty acres was purchased in 1930 by Cleon Hubbard. It was sold to him by Sylvester Rinds, or the wife of Sylvester Rinds. The land had been in the Rinds family for sixty years. What's unusual about this is that Rinds was black, and it appears as though his father was the son of a freed slave who took possession of the eighty acres around 1870, during Reconstruction. It's not clear how he managed to assume ownership, and I'm convinced we'll never know. The records simply do not exist."

"How did Cleon take ownership from Rinds?" Jake asked.

"By a simple quitclaim deed, signed by Esther Rinds, not by her husband."

"Where was her husband?"

"Don't know. I'm assuming he was either dead or gone because the land was in his name, not his wife's. For her to be able to convey property, it would've been necessary for her to inherit the land. So, he was probably dead."

"No record of his death?"

"None, yet, but I'm still digging. There's more. There are no records of the Rinds family in Ford County after 1930. They disappeared and there's not a single Rinds to be found today. I've checked phone books, voter registration records, tax rolls, you name it and I've been through it. Not a single Rinds anywhere. Pretty unusual."

"So?"

"So, they vanished."

"Maybe they all went to Chicago, like everybody else."

"Perhaps. From Lettie's deposition we learned that her mother was about sixteen when she was born, out of wedlock, and that she never knew her father. She says she was born near Caledonia, down in Monroe County. Her mother died a couple of years later—Lettie doesn't remember her—and an aunt took her in. Then another aunt. Then she finally landed over in Alabama with the Tayber family. She took their last name and got on with life. You heard the rest of it in her deposition. She's never had a birth certificate."

"What's the point here, Lucien?"

He opened another file and slid a copy of a single sheet of paper across the table. "A lot of Negro babies were born back then without birth certificates. They were born at home, with midwives and such, and nobody bothered with record keeping. But the health department in every county tried to at least record the births. That's a copy from a page in the 1941 Register of Live Births. It shows one Letetia Delores Rinds being born on May 16 to a young woman named Lois Rinds, age sixteen, in Monroe County, Mississippi."

"You went to Monroe County and dug this up?"

"I did, and I'm not finished. Looks like Lettie might be a Rinds."

"But she said she doesn't remember any of this, or at least she doesn't remember anything before her childhood in Alabama."

"Do you remember anything that happened before you were three years old?"

"Everything."

"Then you're a nutcase."

"So, what if Lettie's people came from Ford County?"

"Let's assume they did, just for the hell of it. And let's assume further that they once owned the same eighty acres that Cleon Hubbard took title to in 1930, the same that got handed down to Seth Hubbard. And the same he willed to Lettie. That closes the circle, doesn't it?"

"Maybe, maybe not. There are still some huge gaps. You can't assume that all black folks named Rinds in north Mississippi came from Ford County. That's a stretch."

"Granted. It's only a theory, but we're making progress."

"We?"

"Portia and I. I've got her digging through her family tree. She's been hounding Cypress for details, but she's not too talkative. And, like most families, there's a lot of crap back there that Portia wishes she'd never found."

"For example?"

"Cypress and Clyde Tayber never married. They had six kids and lived together for forty years, but never tied the knot, legally anyway."

"That was not that unusual. The common law protected them."

"I know that. There's a good chance that Cypress is not even blood kin. Portia thinks her mom might have been abandoned more than once before getting dumped on the Taybers' front doorstep."

"Does Lettie talk about it?"

"Not much, evidently. As you might guess, her family tree is not a pleasant subject."

"Wouldn't Lettie know if she was born a Rinds?"

"One would think so, but maybe not. She was thirty years old before Cypress told her the truth about being adopted; in fact, Cypress never met Lettie's mother. Think about that, Jake. For the first thirty years of her life she assumed Cypress and Clyde were her biological parents and the other six kids were her brothers and sisters. Portia said she was upset when she finally learned the truth, but she's never had any desire to dig into her past. The Taybers in Alabama are not even remotely related to the Rindses in Ford County, so I guess it's possible Lettie doesn't know where she came from."

Jake thought about this for a few minutes as he sipped coffee slowly and tried to think of all the angles. He said, "Okay, let's buy into your theory. Why, then, would Seth want to return the land to a Rinds?"

"My theory hasn't gotten that far yet."

"And why would he leave her everything—the eighty acres plus a helluva lot more—at the expense of his own family?"

"Still digging for that one."

"I like it. Let's keep digging."

"This could be crucial, Jake, because it could prove motive. The big question is, Why? And if we can answer it, then you might just win at trial. Otherwise, you're screwed."

"That's just your opinion, Lucien. As I recall, that was your general sentiment right before the Hailey trial."

"The sooner you forget that trial, the sooner you'll become a better lawyer."

Jake smiled and stood. "Some things you can't forget, Lucien. Now, if you'll excuse me, I have to go shopping with my daughter. Merry Christmas to you."

"Bah humbug."

"Are you coming over for dinner?"

"Bah humbug."

"That's what I figured. See you Monday."

Simeon Lang arrived home just after dark on Christmas Eve. He had been away for over two weeks, and his travels had taken him as far as Oregon, in an 18-wheeler packed with six tons of stolen appliances. He had a pocketful of cash, love in his heart, Christmas jingles on his tongue, and a nice bottle of bourbon hidden under the passenger's seat. He was cold sober at the moment, and he was promising himself he would not let the booze disrupt the holidays. All in all, Simeon was in a cheerful mood, at least until he pulled to a stop in front of the old Sappington place. He counted seven cars parked haphazardly in the driveway and around the front lawn. Three he recognized; the others, he wasn't so sure. He abruptly stopped "Jingle Bells" in mid-chorus and wanted to curse. All the lights were on in the house and it gave every impression of being filled with people.

One of the advantages of marrying Lettie was that her family lived far away, over in Alabama. She had no relatives in Ford County. On his side there were too many, and they caused trouble, but he took no flack from her people, at least not in the early years. He had secretly been delighted when she, at the age of thirty, learned that Cypress and Clyde Tayber were not her real parents and their six kids were not her siblings. This delight faded quickly, though, when Lettie carried on as if they were blood kin. Clyde died, the kids scattered, and Cypress needed a place to live. They took her in, temporarily, and five years later she was still there, bigger and needier than ever. The brothers and sisters were back, with their broods in tow and their hands out.

To be fair, there were some Langs in there too. A sister-in-law in particular had become a constant nuisance. She was out of work and needed a loan, preferably one accompanied by a verbal promise that could not be enforced. Simeon almost reached for the bottle, but he fought the urge and got out of his truck.

There were kids everywhere, a fire in the fireplace, and a kitchen full of women cooking and men tasting. Almost everyone was either happy to see him or good at pretending. Lettie smiled and they hugged. He had called the day before from Kansas and promised to be home in time for dinner. She pecked him on the cheek to see if he had been drinking, and when he passed that test she relaxed considerably. To her knowledge, there was not a drop of booze in the house, and she wanted desperately to keep it that way. In the den, Simeon hugged his kids—Portia, Phedra, Clarice, and Kirk, and his two grandchildren. From upstairs, a boom box was blasting "Rudolph" while three little boys pushed Cypress in her wheelchair up and down the hallway at a dangerous speed. Teenagers watched the television at full volume.

The old house almost shook with a chaotic energy, and after a few minutes Simeon was at peace again. The solitude of the open road had been dashed, but it was, after all, Christmas Eve, and he was surrounded by family. For sure, much of the love and warmth on display was being driven by greed and the desire to get closer to Lettie, but Simeon let it go. For a few hours anyway, just enjoy the moment.

If only Marvis could be there.

Lettie arranged two tables end to end in the dining room. The ladies then covered them with roasted turkeys, hams, sweet potatoes, half a dozen other vegetables and casseroles, and an impressive assortment of cakes and pies. It took a few minutes to gather everyone around the food, and when they were still Lettie offered a quick prayer of thanksgiving. But she had more to say. She unfolded a sheet of white notebook paper and said, "Please listen, this is from Marvis."

At the sound of his name, all movements stopped, all heads dipped lower. They all had their own memories of the oldest child, and most of them were heartbreaking, unpleasant.

Lettie read, "Hello Mom and Dad, brothers and sisters, nieces and nephews, aunts and uncles, cousins and friends. I wish you the happiest holiday greetings and hope everyone has a Merry Christmas. I'm writing this from my cell, at night. From here I can catch a glimpse of the sky and tonight there is no moon but plenty of stars. One is really bright, I think it's the North Star but I'm not sure. Anyway, right now I'm pretending it's the star over Bethlehem, leading the wise men to the baby Jesus. Matthew, Chapter 2. I love you all. I wish I could be there. I'm so sorry for my mistakes and the misery I've caused to my family and friends. I'll get out one day and when I'm free I'll be there at Christmas and we'll have a great time. Marvis."

Her voice stayed strong but tears streamed down her cheeks. She wiped them, managed a smile, then said, "Let's eat."

Because it was a special occasion, Hanna insisted on sleeping with her parents. They read Christmas stories until well past ten, with at least two breaks every half hour so she could sprint to the den and make sure Santa had not somehow sneaked into the house. She chattered and wiggled with usual nervous anticipation until she inadvertently grew still. When Jake awoke at sunrise, she was wedged under her mother, both of them sound asleep. But with a gentle "I think Santa Claus has been here," his girls sprang to life. Hanna dashed to the tree and squealed with amazement at the glorious loot Santa had left her. Jake made the coffee while Carla took photos. They opened gifts and laughed with Hanna as the wrappings and boxes piled up. What on earth was better than being a seven-year-old on Christmas morning? When the excitement began to wane, Jake stepped away and eased outside. In a small utility room next to the carport, he retrieved another package, a large square box wrapped in green paper with a large red bow. From inside, the puppy whimpered. It had been a long night, for both of them.

"Look what I found," he announced as he sat the box on the floor next to Hanna.

"What is it, Daddy?" Hanna asked, immediately suspicious. From inside, the frazzled puppy made not a sound.

"Open it," Carla said, and Hanna began ripping paper. Jake unfolded the top of the box, and Hanna looked inside. Sadie met her gaze with sad, tired eyes that seemed to say, "Get me outta here."

They would pretend Sadie came from the North Pole; in fact, she came from the county's rescue shelter, where, for $37, Jake bought her with all shots included and some future spaying thrown in. With hints of pedigree not even remotely possible, her handlers could not speculate on her size or temperament. One thought she had "a lot of terrier," while another disagreed sharply and said, "There's gotta be some schnauzer in there somewhere." Her mother had been found dead in a ditch, and she and her five siblings had been rescued at the age of about one month.

Hanna lifted her gently, cradled her, cuddled her, squeezed her next to her chest, and of course the dog began licking her face. She looked at her parents in speechless amazement, her beautiful eyes moist, her voice unable to work.

Jake said, "Santa called her Sadie, but you can choose any name you want."

Santa was a miracle worker, but at that moment all other gifts and toys he'd left behind were instantly forgotten. Hanna finally said, "Sadie's perfect."

Within an hour, the dog had taken over, as all three humans followed her around, making sure she got whatever she wanted.

The invitation to cocktails was a handwritten note from Willie Traynor. Six o'clock, the day after Christmas, at the Hocutt House. Holiday attire, whatever that meant. Carla insisted it meant a necktie at the least, and Jake eventually caved in. Initially, they went through the motions of pretending they did not want to go, when in reality there was absolutely nothing else to do on the day after Christmas. Well-done cocktail parties were rare in Clanton, and they suspected Willie, who grew up in Memphis amid money, might just know how to throw one. The biggest draw was the house. For years they had admired it from the street but had never managed to get inside.

"There's a rumor he wants to sell it," Jake said as they were discussing the invitation. He had not told his wife about the earlier conversation with Harry Rex, mainly because the price, whatever it happened to be, was far out of their range.

"That rumor has been around, hasn't it?" she replied, and from that moment on began dreaming about the house.

"Yes, but Harry Rex says Willie is serious now. He never stays there."

They were the first to arrive, fashionably late at ten minutes after, and Willie was all alone. His holiday attire included a red bow tie, black satin dinner jacket, and some modification of Scottish kilts. He was in his early forties, handsome with long hair and a graying beard, and perfectly charming, especially to Carla. Jake had to admit to some level of envy. Willie was only a few years older yet he had already made a million bucks. He was single, known to enjoy the ladies, and gave the impression of a man who'd been around the world.

He poured champagne into heavy, crystal flutes, offered a holiday toast, and after the first sip said with a smile, "I want to tell you something," as if they were family and important news had arrived.

He went on, "I have decided to sell this house. I've owned it for sixteen years, and I love the place, but I'm simply not here enough. It needs real owners, people who will treasure it, preserve it, and keep it just like it is." Another sip as Jake and Carla hung in midair. "And I'm not selling to just anyone. No realtor is involved. I'd like to avoid putting it on the market. I don't want the town talking about it."

Jake couldn't suppress a chuckle at this. The town was already talking.

"Okay, okay, there are no secrets around here, but folks don't have to know what we discuss. I would love for you two to have it. I actually saw your other house before it was destroyed, and I admire the way you restored it."

"Cut the price and we're in," Jake said.

Willie looked at Carla's soft brown eyes and said, "This place has your name written all over it."

"How much?" Jake asked. His spine stiffened and he vowed not to flinch when the figure was revealed.

"Two fifty," Willie said without hesitation. "I paid a hundred for it in 1972, then spent a hundred more fixing it up. Same house in midtown Memphis would push a million, but then that's a long way off. At two fifty it's a steal, but you can't ignore the market. If I advertised it for half a million it would sit here until the weeds took over. Frankly, I'd just like to get my money back."

Jake and Carla exchanged blank stares because there was nothing to say, not at that moment. Willie, ever the salesman, said, "Let's look around. The others get here at six thirty." He topped off their flutes and they headed for the front porch. Once the tour commenced, Jake knew there was no turning back.

According to Willie, the house was built around 1900 by Dr. Miles Hocutt, the town's leading physician for decades. It was a classic Victorian, with two high-gabled roofs, a turret that ran up four levels, and wide covered porches that swept around the house on both sides.

The price was not outrageous, Jake had to admit. It was certainly out of his range, but it could have been much worse. Jake suspected Harry Rex had advised Willie to be reasonable, especially if he wanted the Brigances to own it. According to Harry Rex, one rumor had Willie making another bundle in the stock market, another had him losing badly in Memphis real estate, and yet another had him inheriting a fortune from his grandmother, BeBe. Who knew? The price, though, seemed to indicate a need for quick cash. Willie knew Jake and Carla needed a house. He knew they were bogged down in insurance litigation. He knew (probably through Harry Rex) that Jake was in line to collect a generous fee in the Hubbard matter. As Willie chatted nonstop and guided Carla across the beautifully stained heart-pine floors, through the modern kitchen, up the winding staircase, and all the way into the circular reading room on the fourth level of the turret, with a view of the church steeples just blocks away, Jake dutifully followed along, wondering how in the world they could possibly afford it, let alone furnish it.

25

For those contesting the handwritten will of Seth Hubbard, Christmas came late. January 16, to be exact.

An investigator working for Wade Lanier struck gold. His name was Randall Clapp, and he finally found a potential witness named Fritz Pickering, who was living near Shreveport, Louisiana. Clapp was Wade Lanier's top investigator and had a well-trained nose for digging up information. Pickering was simply minding his own business and had no idea what Clapp wanted. But he was curious, so they agreed to meet at a delicatessen where Clapp said he'd buy lunch.

Clapp was in the process of interviewing Lettie Lang's former employers, almost all of whom were fairly affluent white homeowners accustomed to using black domestic help. In her deposition, Lettie had given as many of these names as she could remember, or so she testified. She was clear that there might have been one or two others over the past thirty years; she didn't keep records. Most housekeepers did not. She had failed, though, to mention working for Irene Pickering. The name surfaced when Clapp was interviewing another former boss.

Lettie had never worked for anyone longer than six years. There were various reasons for this, none of which had anything to do with incompetence. Indeed, almost all of her ex-employers gave her high marks. Pickering, though, would be different. Over soup and salad, he told his story.

About ten years earlier, either in 1978 or 1979, his mother, a widow named Irene Pickering, had hired Lettie Lang to clean and cook. Mrs. Pickering lived just outside the small town of Lake Village, in an old house that had been in the family forever.

At the time, Fritz Pickering lived in Tupelo and worked for an insurance company, the one that transferred him to Shreveport. He saw his mother at least once a month and came to know Lettie fairly well. Everyone was pleased with the relationship, especially Mrs. Pickering. In 1980, her health began a rapid decline and it became obvious that the end was near. Lettie worked longer hours and showed real compassion for the dying woman, but Fritz and his sister, the only other sibling, began to grow suspicious about their mother's routine financial affairs. Gradually, Lettie had taken control of collecting the bills and writing the checks, though it appeared as if Mrs. Pickering always signed them. Lettie kept up with the bank statements, insurance forms, bills, and other paperwork.

Fritz got an urgent call one day from his sister, who had found an astonishing document. It was a will handwritten by their mother, and in it she left $50,000 in cash to Lettie Lang. Fritz took off from work, sped over to Lake Village, met his sister after hours, and took a look at the will. It had been dated two months prior and signed by Irene Pickering. There was no doubt about the handwriting, though it was a much feebler version of what they had always known. His sister had found the will in a plain envelope stuffed in an old family Bible on a shelf with the kitchen cookbooks. They confronted their mother, who claimed to be too weak to discuss the matter.

At the time, Mrs. Pickering had $110,000 in a certificate of deposit and $18,000 in a checking account. Lettie had access to the monthly statements for these accounts.

The following morning, Fritz and his sister confronted Lettie when she arrived for work. During a nasty row, they claimed she had convinced or even coerced their mother into making the will. She denied any knowledge of it and seemed genuinely surprised, even hurt. They fired her anyway and made her leave the house immediately. They loaded up their mother and drove her to a lawyer's office in Oxford, where the sister lived. While they waited, the lawyer prepared a two-page will that made no mention of Lettie Lang and left everything to Fritz and his sister, in equal shares, just as they had discussed many times with their mother. She signed it on the spot, died a month later, and the probate went off without a hitch. Fritz and his sister sold the house and property and split the assets evenly without a cross word.

Before Irene died, they quizzed her several times about the handwritten will, but it always upset her and she wouldn't discuss it. They quizzed her about Lettie Lang, and this made her cry too. Eventually, they stopped these conversations. Truthfully, at the time she signed the will in the lawyer's office she was not really thinking clearly, and things did not improve before she died.

Over coffee, Clapp listened with growing excitement. With Fritz's permission, he was recording the conversation and couldn't wait to play it back for Wade Lanier.

"Did you keep a copy of the handwritten will?"

Fritz shook his head and said, "I don't recall doing that, and if we did keep it, it's long gone. I sure don't know where it would be."

"Did the lawyer in Oxford keep it?"

"I think so. When we took Mother to see him, we gave him her prior will, one that was prepared by a lawyer in Lake Village, plus the handwritten will, and I'm sure he kept both of them. He said it was important to destroy prior wills because they some-times show up and cause problems."

"Do you remember the name of the lawyer in Oxford?"

"Hal Freeman, an old guy who's since retired. My sister died five years ago and I was the executor of her estate. Freeman had retired by then but his son handled the probate."

"Did you and the son ever talk about the handwritten will?"

"I don't think so. I had very little contact with him, really. I try to avoid lawyers, Mr. Clapp. I've had some very unpleasant experiences with them."

Clapp was savvy enough to know he had discovered dyna-mite, and he was experienced enough to know it was time to back off. Take it slow, share it all with Wade Lanier, and let the lawyer call the shots. Pickering began to inquire into Clapp's reasons for pursuing Lettie, but was met with a wall of vagueness. They finished lunch and said good-bye.

Wade Lanier listened to the tape with his customary grim face and tight lips. But Lester Chilcott, his associate, could hardly suppress his enthusiasm. After Clapp was excused from Lanier's office, Chilcott rubbed his hands together and said, "This ball game is over!" Wade eventually smiled.

Step one: No further contact with Pickering. His mother and sister were dead, so he was the only person who could possibly testify about the handwritten will, other than Hal Freeman. Two quick phone calls to Oxford verified that Freeman was retired, still alive, and that his old office was run by his two sons, Todd and Hank. Ignore Pickering, for now. No contact between Lanier's office and Pickering because it would be important, at a later date, for Pickering to testify he had never spoken to the attorneys.

Step two: Find the handwritten will, at all costs. If it exists, find it, get it. But do so without alerting Hal Freeman, if possible. Find it, before Jake or somebody else does.

Step three: Bury this now and save it for later. The most dramatic and effective use of the handwritten will of Irene Pickering would come at trial, with Lettie Lang on the witness stand and denying any knowledge of the will. Produce it then. Make her a liar. And prove to the jury that conniving her way into wills handwritten by her old and vulnerable bosses was a devious pattern.

Such a strategy was loaded with hazards. The first and most obvious was the basic rules of discovery. Jake had filed interrogatories requiring his adversaries to divulge the identities of all potential witnesses. Lanier and the other lawyers had done the same; it was standard procedure in the new days of wide-open discovery where everything was supposedly transparent. To hide a witness like Fritz Pickering was not only unethical, but also dangerous. Attempting to produce a surprise at trial was often futile. Lanier and Chilcott needed time to plot ways around this rule. There were exceptions, but they were narrow. Just as troublesome was the plan to find Irene's handwritten will. There was a chance it had been destroyed, along with a thousand other worthless old files in the Freeman archives. But lawyers generally kept their retired files for longer than ten years, so the odds were decent that the will was still around.

Ignoring Fritz was also problematic. What if another lawyer tracked him down and asked the same questions? If the other lawyer happened to be Jake, then the element of surprise would be lost. Jake would have plenty of time to coach Lettie into testimony that might appease the jury. He could certainly spin the story. And he would rage at the violated discovery rules. Judge Atlee would not be sympathetic.

Lanier and Chilcott debated the idea of contacting Freeman directly. If the will was filed away and gathering dust, Freeman could certainly produce it without someone being forced to steal it. And, he would be a respectable witness at trial. But speaking to Freeman would blow their great secret. As a potential witness, his name would be revealed. The element of surprise would be lost. It might become necessary to approach him later, but for now Wade Lanier and Lester Chilcott were quite content to spin a web of silence and deceit. Cheating was often hard to cover and required meticulous planning, but they were skilled.

Two days later, Randall Clapp entered the Freeman Law Firm and informed the secretary he was there for a four o'clock appointment. The two-man shop was in a converted bungalow one block off the Oxford town square, next door to a savings and loan and just down the street from the federal courthouse. As Clapp waited in the reception area, he flipped through a magazine and took in the surroundings. No video cameras; no security sensors; a dead bolt on the front door; no chains; almost nothing to prevent even a half-witted cat burglar from sneaking in during the night and taking his time. And why would there be? Other than the usual mountain of paperwork, there was nothing of real value in the building.

It was a typical small-town law office, just like a hundred others Clapp had visited. He had already wandered through the rear alley and scoped out the back door. A dead bolt but nothing formidable. His man Erby could walk through either the front or the rear door faster than one of the employees using a key.

Clapp met with Todd Freeman and discussed some land he wanted to buy west of town, along the main highway. He used his real name, real job, and real business card, but lied when he said he and his brother wanted to put in an all-night truck stop. The legal work would be routine and Todd seemed sufficiently interested. Clapp asked to use the restroom and was sent down the narrow hall. Retractable staircase; at least two cluttered rooms chock-full of files; a small kitchen with a broken window, no lock. No security sensors anywhere. Piece of cake.

Erby entered the building just after midnight while Clapp sat low in his car across the street and watched for trouble. It was January 18, cold, a Wednesday, and the students were not out on the town. The square was dead, and Clapp's biggest fear was getting noticed by a bored policeman. Once Erby was inside, he checked in by radio. All was quiet and still. Using his trusty jack-blade, he had picked the rear door dead bolt in seconds. With an infrared penlight, he eased through the offices; not a single interior door was locked. The retractable stairs were flimsy and squeaked, but he managed to pull them down with little racket. He stood in the front window, spoke to Clapp by radio, and Clapp could not see his shadow inside. Wearing gloves and disturbing nothing, Erby began in one of the storage rooms. It would take hours and he was in no hurry. He opened drawers, looked at files, dates, names, and so on, and in doing so touched documents that had not been touched in weeks, months, maybe years. Clapp moved his car to a lot on the other side of the square and walked through the alleys. At 1:00 a.m., Erby opened the rear door and Clapp entered the building. Erby said, "Every room has file cabinets. Looks like the current files are kept in the lawyers' offices, some by the secretaries."

"What about these two rooms?" Clapp asked.

"The files date back about five years. Some are retired, some not. I'm still looking. I haven't finished the second room. There's a large basement filled with old furniture, typewriters, law books, and more files, all retired."

They found nothing of interest in the second room. The files were the typical assortment of retired cases one would find in any small-town law office. At 2:30, Erby carefully climbed the steps of the retractable stairs and disappeared into the attic. Clapp closed them behind him and went to the basement. The attic was windowless, pitch-black, and lined with neat rows of cardboard storage boxes stacked four-deep. With no chance of being seen from the outside, Erby increased the glow of his penlight and scanned the boxes. Each had a code handwritten in black marker: "Real Estate, 1/1/76–8/1/77"; "Criminal, 3/1/81–7/1/81"; and so on. He was relieved to find files dating back a dozen years, but frustrated at the absence of any related to wills and estates.

Those would be in the basement. After rummaging down there for half an hour, Clapp found a stack of the same types of storage boxes marked "Probate, 1979–1980." He pulled the box out of a stack, opened it carefully, and began leafing through dozens of files. Irene Pickering's was dated August 1980. It was an inch and a half thick, and tracked the legal work from the day Hal Freeman prepared the two-page will that Irene signed on the spot through the final order dismissing Fritz Pickering as her executor. The first entry was an old will prepared by the lawyer in Lake Village. The second was a handwritten will. Clapp read it aloud and slowly, the scrawl at times difficult to decipher. The fourth paragraph contained a $50,000 bequest to Lettie Lang.

"Bingo," he mumbled. He placed the file on a table, closed the box, gently put it back in its place, backtracked carefully, and left the basement. With the file in a briefcase, he stepped into the dark alley, and after a few minutes called Erby on the radio. Erby eased out of the rear door, stopping only to quickly relock the dead bolt. To their knowledge, they had disturbed nothing and left no marks. The offices needed a good cleaning to begin with, and a bit of dirt off a shoe or some rearranged dust was not going to attract attention.

They drove two and a half hours to Jackson and met Wade Lanier at his office before 6:00 a.m. Lanier had been a courtroom brawler for thirty years, and he could not remember a more beautiful example of "the smoking gun." But the question remained: How best to fire it?

Fat Benny's was at the end of the paved section of a county road; beyond it was all gravel. Portia had been raised in Box Hill, a dark and secluded community hidden by a swamp and a ridge with few whites anywhere near. Box Hill, though, was Times Square compared to the forbidding, backwater settlement of Prairietown on the backside of Noxubee County, less than ten miles from the Alabama line. If she'd been white, she would have never stopped. There were two gas pumps in the front and a few dirty cars parked on the gravel. A screen door slammed behind her as she nodded to a teenage boy behind the front counter. There were a few groceries, soft drink and beer coolers, and in the rear a dozen neat tables all covered with red-and-white checkerboard tablecloths. The smell of thick grease hung heavy in the air and hamburger patties sizzled and popped on a grill. A large man with an enormous belly held a spatula like a weapon and talked to two men sitting on stools. There was little doubt as to who was Fat Benny.

A sign said, "Order Here."

"What can I do for you?" the cook said with a friendly smile.

She gave him her best smile and said softly, "I'd like a hot dog, a Coke, and I'm looking for Benny Rinds."

"That's me," he said. "And you are?"

"My name is Portia Lang, from Clanton, but there's a chance I might be a Rinds. I'm not sure, but I'm looking for information."

He nodded to a table. Ten minutes later he placed the hot dog and the Coke in front of her, and sat across the table. "I'm

working on the family tree," she said, "and I'm finding a lot of
bad apples."

Benny laughed and said, "You should've come here and
asked me before you started."

Without touching the hot dog, she told him about her mother,
and her mother's mother. He had never heard of them. His
people were from Noxubee and Lauderdale Counties, more to
the south than the north. He'd never known a Rinds from Ford
County, not a single one. As he talked, she ate rapidly, and she
finished as soon as she realized it was another dead end.

She thanked him and left. Driving home, she stopped at
every small town and checked the telephone directories. There
were very few Rindses in this part of the world. Twenty or so in
Clay County. A dozen or so in Oktibbeha County, near the state
university. She had spoken by phone to a dozen in Lee County,
in and around Tupelo.

She and Lucien had identified twenty-three members of the
Rinds family who had been living in Ford County in the years
leading up to 1930, before they all vanished. Eventually, they
would find a descendant, an old relative who knew something
and might be willing to talk.

26

On the last Friday in January, Roxy arrived for work at 8:45, and Jake was waiting by her desk, nonchalantly scanning a document as if all was well. It was not. It was time for a performance review and it was not going to be pretty. Things began pleasantly enough when she barked, "Jake, I'm sick of this place."

"And good morning to you."

She was already crying. No makeup, unkempt hair, the frazzled look of a wife/mother/woman out of control. "I can't take Lucien," she said. "He's here almost every day and he's the rudest man in the world. He's vulgar, crude, profane, dirty, and he smokes the filthiest cigars ever made. I loathe that man."

"Anything else?"

"It's either him or me."

"He owns the building."

"Can't you do something?"

"Like what? Tell Lucien to be a nicer person, to stop smoking, cussing, insulting people, telling dirty jokes, to sober up? In case you haven't noticed, Roxy, no one tells Lucien Wilbanks to do anything."

She grabbed a tissue and wiped her cheeks. "I can't take it."

This was the perfect opening and Jake wasn't about to miss an opportunity. "Let's call it resignation," he said with compassion. "I'll be happy to provide a good reference."

"I'm being fired?"

"No. You're resigning, effective immediately. Leave now and you've got the day off. I'll send your last paycheck."

The emotion turned to anger as she looked around her desk. She was gone in ten minutes, slamming doors behind her. Portia walked in promptly at 9:00 and said, "I just passed Roxy on the street and she wouldn't speak to me."

"She's gone. Here's the offer. On a temporary basis, you can work down here as the secretary and receptionist. You'll be considered a paralegal, not a lowly intern. It's a big promotion all the way around."

She absorbed it coolly, said, "My typing is not great."

"Then practice."

"What does it pay?"

"A thousand dollars a month for two months, a trial run. After two months, we'll take a look and reevaluate."

"Hours?"

"Eight thirty to five, thirty minutes for lunch."

"What about Lucien?" she asked.

"What about him?"

"He's down here. I kinda like it up there, on the second floor, where it's safe."

"Has he bothered you?"

"Not yet. Look, Jake, I like Lucien and we work well together, but I sometimes get the feeling he would like to get a little closer, know what I mean?"

"I think so."

"If he touches me, I'll slap his ass across the room."

Jake laughed at the visual, and there was no doubt whatsoever Portia could take care of herself. He said, "I need to have a chat with Lucien. Let me handle it. I'll warn him."

Portia took a deep breath and looked around the office. She nodded, smiled, said, "But I'm not a secretary, Jake. I'm going to be a lawyer, just like you."

"And I'll help you in every way possible."

"Thank you."

"I want an answer. Now. On the spot."

"But I don't want to miss the trial. If I'm stuck at this desk, I'll miss the trial, right?"

"Let's worry about that later. Right now I need you down here."

"Okay."

"So we have a deal?"

"No. A thousand a month is too low for a secretary, receptionist, and paralegal all rolled into one."

Jake threw up his hands and knew he was beaten. "Well, then, what do you have in mind?"

"Two thousand is more in line with the market."

"What in hell do you know about the market?"

"Not much, but I know a thousand a month is too cheap."

"Okay. Fifteen hundred a month for the first two months, then we'll take a look."

She lunged forward, gave him a quick and proper hug, and said, "Thanks, Jake."

An hour later, Jake dealt with the second office personnel crisis of the morning. Lucien barged in with hardly a knock and fell into a chair. "Jake, son," he began in a tone that meant trouble, "I've made a decision. For months, even years now I've been wrestling with the decision about whether to begin the reinstatement process, sort of start my comeback, you know?"

Jake, who was hard at work drafting a response to a motion filed by Stillman Rush, slowly put down his pen and managed to look thoughtfully at Lucien. The word "comeback" had not been used until that point, but in the past three months Lucien had managed to drop every other possible hint that he wanted to become a lawyer again. Though he feared it was coming, this news still put Jake on a tightrope. He didn't want Lucien around, especially Lucien as a lawyer because Lucien as an untitled and unpaid adviser had already worn thin. Lucien as a lawyer meant Lucien, the Boss, and Jake wouldn't last. But, Lucien the friend was the man who'd given Jake a job, an office, a career, and was as loyal as anyone.

"Why?" Jake asked.

"I miss it, Jake. I'm too young to sit on the porch. Will you support me?"

The only answer was yes, and Jake quickly said, "Of course, you know I will. But how?"

"Moral support, Jake, at first anyway. As you know, before I

can be reinstated I have to pass the bar exam, no small feat for
an old fart like me."

"You've done it once before, you can do it again," Jake said
with requisite conviction. He seriously doubted if Lucien could,
starting from scratch, grind through a six-month cram session,
studying on his own while trying to lay off the sour mash.

"So, you're on board?"

"On board how, Lucien? After you're reinstated, what then?
You want this office back? You want me around as the flunky?
Do we go back to where we were eight, nine years ago?"

"I don't know, but we'll figure it out, Jake. I'm sure we can."

Jake shrugged and said, "Yes, I'm on board, and I'll help in
any way." And for the second time that morning, Jake lent his
assistance to a budding lawyer in his office. Who could be next?

"Thanks."

"While you're here, a couple of housekeeping matters. Roxy
quit and Portia is the interim secretary. She's allergic to cigar
smoke so please go outside. And keep your hands to yourself.
She spent six years in the Army, knows hand-to-hand combat,
plus karate, and she does not fancy the thought of a creepy old
white man pawing at her. Touch her, and she'll crack your teeth,
then sue me for sexual harassment. Got it?"

"She said this? I swear I've done nothing."

"It's just a warning, Lucien, okay? Don't touch her, don't tell her
dirty jokes or make suggestive comments, don't even swear in her
presence, and don't drink or smoke around her. She thinks she's
a lawyer and wants to become one. Treat her like a professional."

"I thought we were getting on just fine."

"Perhaps, but I know you. Keep it straight and clean."

"I'll try."

"Do more than try. Now, if you'll excuse me, I'll get back to
work."

Leaving, Lucien mumbled just loud enough for Jake to hear,
"She does have a nice ass."

"Drop it Lucien."

*   *   *

On a typical Friday afternoon, it was almost impossible to find a judge in the courthouse or a lawyer in his office. The weekend began early as they all sneaked away in various modes. A lot of fish were caught. A lot of beer consumed. A lot of legal business got delayed until Monday. And on dreary Friday afternoons in January, lawyers and nonlawyers alike quietly closed their offices early and left the square.

Judge Atlee was on the front porch under a quilt when Jake arrived around 4:00. The wind was still and a cloud of pipe smoke hung over the front steps. A sign at the mailbox gave the name of the place as Maple Run. It was a stately old semi-mansion with Georgian columns and sagging shutters, another of the many hand-me-downs in Clanton and Ford County. The roof of the Hocutt House was visible two blocks over.

Reuben Atlee earned $80,000 a year as a judge and spent little of it on his estate. His wife had been dead for years, and from the flower beds and the sagging wicker porch furniture and the torn curtains hanging in the upstairs windows, it was obvious the place was missing the feminine touch it was not getting. He lived alone. His longtime maid was dead too and he had not bothered with a replacement. Jake saw him in church every Sunday morning and had noticed a general decline in his appearance as the years went by. His suits were not as clean. His shirts were not as starched. The knots in his neckties were not as crisp. He was often in need of a good haircut. It had become obvious that Judge Atlee left the house each morning without getting properly inspected.

He wasn't much of a drinker but enjoyed a toddy most afternoons, especially Fridays. Without inquiring, he fixed Jake a generous whiskey sour and placed it on the wicker table between them. Doing business with the judge on his porch meant having a toddy. He kicked back in his favorite rocker, took a long soothing sip, and said, "Rumor has it Lucien's hanging around your office these days."

"It's his office," Jake said. They were gazing across the front lawn, brown and dismal in the dead of winter. Both wore their overcoats, and if the whiskey didn't kick in soon Jake, quiltless, might request a move inside.

"What's he up to?" Judge Atlee asked. He and Lucien went back many years, with many chapters in their history.

"I asked him to do some title work on Seth Hubbard's property, and some research, just basic legal stuff like that." Jake would never reveal what Lucien told him that morning, especially to Reuben Atlee. If word got out that Lucien Wilbanks was plotting a comeback, most judges in the area would resign.

"Keep him close," Judge Atlee said, once again dispensing advice that had not been sought.

"He's harmless," Jake said.

"He's never harmless." He rattled the ice around, seemed oblivious to the temperature. "What's the latest on the search for Ancil?"

Jake avoided his ice and tried to suck down some more bourbon. His teeth were starting to chatter. He replied, "Not much. Our guys found an ex-wife in Galveston who reluctantly admitted she married a man named Ancil Hubbard thirty-five years ago. They were married for three years, had two kids, then he skipped town. Owes a fortune in child support and alimony but she doesn't care. It looks like he stopped using his real name fifteen years ago and went underground. We're still digging."

"And these are the guys from D.C.?"

"Yes sir, it's a firm of ex-FBI types that specializes in finding missing persons. I don't know how good they are but I do know they're expensive. I have a bill we need to pay."

"Keep pushing. In the court's view, Ancil is not dead until we know he's dead."

"They're combing death records in all fifty states and in a dozen foreign countries. It takes time."

"How is discovery proceeding?"

"Rapidly. It's a strange case, Judge, because every lawyer involved wants a trial as soon as possible. How many times have you seen that?"

"Perhaps never."

"The case is a priority in every office, so there's a lot of cooperation."

"No one's dragging feet?"

"Not a single lawyer. Last week we took eleven depositions in three days, all from members of the church who saw Mr. Hubbard the morning before he died. Nothing particularly interesting or unusual. The witnesses are in general agreement that he seemed like himself, nothing bizarre or strange. So far we have deposed five people who work in his headquarters and were with him the day before he wrote the will."

"I've read those," Judge Atlee said, sipping. Move along.

"Everyone is busy lining up the experts. I've found my handwriting guy and—"

"A handwriting expert? They will not stipulate that it is Seth Hubbard's handwriting?"

"Not yet."

"Is there any doubt?"

"No, not really."

"Then bring it on for a hearing before the trial and I'll take a look. Perhaps we can settle this issue. My goal is to streamline the issues and try the case as smoothly as possible." Reuben Atlee wrote the book on "streamlining" a case. He hated wasting time as much as he loathed windy lawyers. Fresh out of law school, Jake had witnessed the mauling of an ill-prepared lawyer who was presenting a lame argument to Judge Atlee. When he repeated himself for the third time, the judge stopped him cold with "Do you think I'm stupid or deaf?" Stunned, and wisely avoiding a response, the lawyer could only look up in disbelief. Judge Atlee then said, "My hearing aids are working just fine and I'm not stupid. If you repeat yourself again, I'll rule in favor of the other side. Now move along, sir."

Are you stupid or deaf? It was a common question in Clanton legal circles.

The bourbon was finally warming things up and Jake told himself to slow down. One drink would be enough. Arriving home buzzed on Friday afternoon would not sit well with Carla.

He said, "As expected, there will be a fair amount of medical testimony. Mr. Hubbard was in severe pain and taking a lot of meds. The other side will try to prove this affected his judgment, so—"

"I understand, Jake. How many medical experts will the jury listen to?"

"I'm not sure at this point."

"How much medical testimony can a jury in this town understand? Out of twelve, we'll have two college graduates at most, a couple of dropouts, and the rest will have high school diplomas."

"Seth Hubbard was a dropout," Jake said.

"True, and I'll bet he was never asked to evaluate conflicting medical testimony. My point is, Jake, we must guard against overwhelming our jury with too much expert opinion."

"I understand, and if I were on the other side I would call plenty of experts in an effort to plant doubt. Confuse the jurors, give them a reason to suspect Seth was not thinking clearly. Wouldn't you, Judge?"

"Let's not discuss trial strategy, Jake. I don't like to be earwigged. It is against the rules, you know?" He said this with a smile but his point was well made.

There was a long, heavy pause in the conversation as they sipped their drinks and savored the quiet. Finally, the judge said, "You haven't been paid in six weeks."

"I brought the paperwork."

"How many hours?"

"Two hundred and ten."

"So, something north of thirty thousand?"

"Yes sir."

"Sounds reasonable. I know you're working very hard, Jake, and I'm happy to approve your fees. But I do have a slight concern, if you'll allow me to meddle in your business."

At this point, nothing Jake could say would stop the meddling. If the judge liked you, then he felt it necessary to offer unsolicited advice on a wide range of subjects. You were expected to consider yourself lucky to be so favored. "Go right ahead," Jake said as he braced himself.

A rattle of the ice, another sip, then, "Now, and in the near future, you will be well paid for your work and no one will begrudge it. As you've said, this mess was caused by Seth Hubbard, and he knew it was coming. So be it. However, I doubt the wisdom of you giving the impression you're suddenly in the money. Ms. Lang moved her family to town, into the Sappington house, which as we know is nothing special and has gone unsold for a reason, but nonetheless it's not in Lowtown. It's on our side of the tracks. There's been grumbling about this. It looks bad. A lot of folks think she's already tapped into the money, and there is resentment. Now there's talk that you have your eye on the Hocutt House. Don't ask how I know; it's a small town. Such a move at this time would get a lot of attention, and none of it favorable."

Jake was speechless. As he gazed at the highest gable of the Hocutt House in the distance, he tried in vain to think of who told whom and how the word leaked. Willie Traynor swore him to secrecy because he, Willie, did not want to be pestered by other buyers. Harry Rex was a confidant of both Jake and Willie, and though he loved to spread gossip maliciously, he would never rat out inside information like this. "We're only dreaming, Judge," Jake managed to say. "It's out of my range and I'm still tied up in litigation. But thanks."

Thanks for meddling once again, Judge. Though, as Jake breathed deeply and let the anger pass, he admitted to himself that he and Carla had had the same conversation. Such a conspicuous purchase would naturally lead many to suspect Jake was moving up at the expense of a dead man.

"Has the topic of a settlement been broached?" the judge asked.

"Yes, briefly," Jake answered quickly, eager to move away from real estate.

"And?"

"It went nowhere. In his letter to me, Seth Hubbard was explicit in his instructions. I believe his exact words were, 'Fight them, Mr. Brigance, to the bitter end. We must prevail.' That doesn't leave much room for settlement negotiations."

"But Seth Hubbard is dead. This lawsuit he created is not. What will you tell Lettie Lang when, and if, the jury rules against her and she gets nothing?"

"Lettie Lang is not my client. The estate is, and it's my job to enforce the terms of the will that created the estate."

Judge Atlee nodded as if he agreed, but he did not say so.

27

Charley Pardue's arrival benefited from fortunate timing. Simeon was gone again. Had he been around the house on that late Saturday morning, he and Charley would have locked horns immediately, and the fight would have been nasty.

As it was, though, Charley knocked on the door of the old Sappington place and found a houseful of women and children. The kids were eating cereal out of boxes and watching television, while the women loitered around a dirty kitchen drinking coffee and talking in bathrobes and pajamas. Phedra answered the door and managed to get him situated in the living room, then ran to the kitchen and gushed, "Momma, there's a man here to see you, and he's soooo fine!"

"Who is he?"

"Charley Pardue and he says he thinks he's a cousin."

"Never heard of no Charley Pardue," Lettie said, suddenly on the defensive.

"Well, he's here and he's really cute."

"Is he worth talkin' to?"

"Oh yes."

The women scrambled upstairs and changed quickly. Phedra sneaked out the back door and eased around to the front. Yellow Cadillac, late model, spotless, with Illinois plates. Charley himself was just as presentable. Dark suit, white shirt, silk tie, a diamond tie clasp, and at least two small, tasteful diamonds on his fingers. No wedding band. A gold chain on his right wrist and a serious watch on his left. He exuded big-city slickness, and Phedra knew he was from Chicago before he got through the front door. She insisted on sitting with her mother when

Lettie came back down to meet him. Portia and Clarice would join them later. Cypress stayed in the kitchen.

Charley began by dropping a few names, none of which meant much. He said he was from Chicago, where he worked as an entrepreneur, whatever that meant. He had a wide, easy grin, a glib manner, and his eyes twinkled when he laughed. The women warmed up considerably. In the past four months, many people had come to see Lettie. Many of them, like Charley, claimed blood kinship. Given the bareness of her family tree, it was easy to be cynical and to dismiss a lot of potential relatives. The truth was that Lettie had been unofficially adopted by Clyde and Cypress Tayber, after she had been abandoned more than once. She had no idea who her grandparents were. Portia had spent hours sifting through the sparse history of their ancestry, with little to show for her efforts. Charley rattled them when he said, "My maternal grandmother was a Rinds, and I think you are too, Lettie."

He produced some paperwork, and they moved to a dining room table where they huddled over him. He unfolded a flowchart that, from a distance, more closely resembled a pile of scrub brush than a properly developed tree. Crooked lines ran in all directions, with notes wedged into the margins. Whatever it was, someone had spent hours trying to decipher it.

"My mother helped me with this," Charley was saying. "Her mother was a Rinds."

"Where did Pardue come from?" Portia asked.

"My dad's side. They're from Kansas City, settled in Chicago a long time ago. That's where my parents met." He was pointing at his chart with an ink pen. "It goes back to a man named Jeremiah Rinds, a slave who was born around 1841 near Holly Springs. He had five or six kids, one of whom was Solomon Rinds, and Solomon had at least six kids, one of whom was Marybelle Rinds, my grandmother. She gave birth to my mother, Effie Rinds, in 1920, who was born in this county. In 1930, Marybelle Rinds and her husband and some more Rinds took off for Chicago and never looked back."

Portia said, "That's the same year the property of Sylvester

Rinds was transferred to the Hubbard family." The others heard this but it meant little. Portia was not even sure of the connection; there were too many missing details.

"Don't know about that," Charley said. "But my mother remembers a cousin who she thinks was the only child of Sylvester Rinds. As best we can tell, this cousin was born around 1925. They lost touch after 1930 when the family scattered. But through the years there was the usual family gossip. This girl supposedly had a baby when she was real young, the daddy caught a train, and the family never knew what happened to the baby. My mother remembers her cousin's name as Lois."

"I've heard that my mother's name was Lois," Lettie said cautiously.

"Well, let's look at your birth certificate," Charley said, as if he had finally arrived at a critical moment.

"Never had one," Lettie said. "I know I was born in Monroe County in 1941, but there's no official certificate."

"No listing of either parent," Portia added. "We found this recently, down in Monroe County. The mother is listed as L. Rinds, age sixteen. The father is H. Johnson, but that's the only mention of him."

Charley was instantly deflated. He had worked so hard and traveled so far to prove his lineage with his newfound cousin, only to hit a dead end. How can you be alive with no birth certificate?

Portia continued, "My mother was sort of adopted by Cypress and her husband, and she was thirty years old before she knew the truth. By then so many of her relatives were dead and scattered it really didn't matter anyway."

Lettie said, "I was married with three kids when I found out. I couldn't exactly take off and go chase down a buncha dead kinfolk. Besides, I really didn't care, still don't. I was a Tayber. Clyde and Cypress were my parents. I had six brothers and sisters." She was sounding a bit defensive and this irritated her. She owed no explanation to this stranger, cousin or not.

Portia said, "So, under your theory, it looks like my mother might be a Rinds from Ford County, but there's no way to prove it."

"Oh, I think she's definitely a Rinds," Charley said, hanging on in desperation. He thumped his paperwork as if it held the unquestioned truth. "We're probably seventh or eighth cousins."

"Same as ever' other black person in north Mississippi," Lettie said, almost under her breath. The women backed away from the table. Shirley, a sister and one of Cypress's daughters, arrived with the coffeepot and topped off their cups.

Charley seemed undaunted and kept up his barrage of chatter as the conversation drifted away from bloodlines and shaky family histories. He was there looking for money, and he had done his homework. His sleuthing had brought Lettie as close to her true ancestors as any efforts so far, but there was simply not enough hard evidence to tie up the loose ends. There were still too many gaps, too many questions that could never be answered.

Portia eased into the background and just listened. She was tiring of his diamonds and slickness, but she was enthralled by his research. She and Lucien, and now Lettie too, were laboring under the unfounded theory that Lettie was related to the Rindses who once owned the land the Hubbards took title to in 1930. If proven, this might help explain why Seth did what he did. And, it might not. It might also raise a hundred other questions, some of which could prove detrimental. Was any of it admissible in court? Probably not, in Lucien's opinion, but it was worth their determined pursuit.

"Where's the best place for lunch?" Charley asked boldly. "I'm taking you ladies out for lunch. My treat."

Such a Chicago idea! Black folks in Clanton rarely ate out, and to do so on a Saturday for lunch with such a charming young man, and one picking up the tab, was irresistible. They quickly decided on Claude's, the black-owned café on the square. Jake ate there every Friday and had even taken Portia. On Saturdays, Claude grilled pork chops and the place was packed.

The last time Lettie rode in a late-model Cadillac was the morning she drove Seth to his office, the day before he killed himself. He'd made her drive and she'd been a wreck. She remembered it well as she sat up front with Charley. Her three daughters sank into the lush leather of the rear seat and admired the well-appointed interior as they headed for the square. Charley talked nonstop, drove slowly so the locals could admire his car, and within minutes brought up the idea of a wildly profitable funeral home he wanted to buy on the South Side of Chicago. Portia glanced at Phedra, who glanced at Clarice. Charley caught them in the rearview mirror, but never stopped talking.

According to his mother, who was now sixty-eight and in good health with a fine memory, her branch of the Rinds family lived near the rest of them, and at one time made up a sizable community. With time, though, they joined the great migration and headed north in search of jobs and a better life. Once they left Mississippi, they had no desire to return. Those in Chicago sent money back to retrieve the ones left behind, and over time all the Rindses had either fled or died.

The funeral home could be a gold mine.

The little restaurant was almost full at noon. In a spotless white apron, Claude worked the front while his sister handled the kitchen. Menus were not needed. Daily specials were sometimes scrawled on a chalkboard, but for the most part you ate whatever the sister was cooking. Claude served the food, directed the traffic, worked the cash register, created more gossip than he filtered, and in general ran the place with a heavy hand. By the time Charley and the ladies settled into their seats and ordered iced tea, Claude had heard that they were all related. He rolled his eyes at this; wasn't everyone related to Lettie these days?

Fifteen minutes later, Jake and Lucien ambled in as if they had just been passing by. They were not. Portia had called Lucien thirty minutes earlier with the heads-up. There was a decent chance Charley could be a link to the past, to the mystery of the Rinds family, and she thought Lucien might want to meet him. Introductions were made, then Claude sat the two crackers off to themselves near the kitchen.

Over grilled pork chops and mashed potatoes, Charley continued to tout the dazzling benefits of the mortuary business in "a city of five million," though the women were losing interest. He'd been married but was now divorced; two kids, living with their mother; he'd gone to college. Slowly, the women extracted the details as they thoroughly enjoyed lunch. By the time the coconut cream pie arrived, the women were completely ignoring him and trashing a deacon who'd fled with another man's wife.

Late in the afternoon, Portia arrived at Lucien's home, for the first time. The weather had abruptly turned raw and windy and the porch was out of the question. She was intrigued to meet Sallie, a woman seldom seen around town but well known nonetheless. Her living arrangement was a source of endless condemnation on both sides of the tracks, but it didn't seem to bother either Sallie or Lucien. As Portia had learned quickly, nothing really bothered Lucien, at least nothing related to the thoughts and opinions of other people. He ranted about injustice or history or the problems of the world, but was happily oblivious to the observations of others.

Sallie was about ten years older than Portia. She had not been raised in Clanton and no one was quite certain where her people were from. Portia found her to be polite, gracious, and seemingly comfortable with another black female in the house. Lucien had a fire going in his study, and Sallie served them hot cocoa there. Lucien spiked his with cognac, but Portia declined. The thought of adding alcohol to such a comfort beverage seemed almost bizarre, but then Portia had long since realized that Lucien had never seen a drink that could not be improved with a shot or two of booze.

With Sallie in the room, and commenting occasionally, they spent an hour updating the family tree. Portia had taken notes of things Charley had said: important things like names and dates, and throwaways like deaths and disappearances of people who were not related to them. There were several strains of Rindses in the Chicago area, and another bunch in Gary. Charley had mentioned a distant cousin named Boaz who lived near Birmingham, but he had no contact information. He also had mentioned a cousin who'd moved to Texas. And so on.

Sitting by the fire in a fine old home, one with a history, and sipping hot cocoa made by someone else, and talking to such a noted rogue as Lucien Wilbanks, Portia at times couldn't believe herself. She was an equal. She had to constantly remind herself of this, but it was true because Lucien treated her as one. There was an excellent chance they were wasting their time chasing the past, but what a fascinating search. Lucien was obsessed with the puzzle. He was convinced Seth Hubbard did what he did for a reason.

And the reason wasn't sex or companionship. Portia had gently confronted her mother and, with all the trust and respect and love she could humanly muster, had asked her the big question. No, Lettie had said. Never. It was never considered, not on her part anyway. It was never discussed, never a possibility. Never.

Randall Clapp slid the envelope into a drop box outside the main post office in downtown Oxford. It was plain, white, legal-sized, no return info, and it was addressed to Fritz Pickering in Shreveport, Louisiana. Inside were two sheets of paper—a full copy of the will handwritten by Irene Pickering and signed by her on March 11, 1980. The other copy was locked away in Wade Lanier's law office. The original was in the file stolen from the Freeman Law Firm, two blocks down the street.

The plan was for Fritz Pickering to receive the anonymous letter, notice it postmarked in Oxford, open it, recognize the old will, and wonder who in the world had sent it to him. He would probably have a hunch but he would never know for sure.

It was late Saturday night, the college bars were rocking, and the police were more concerned with that activity than with the petty break-in of a small law office. With Clapp in the alley watching things, agent Erby entered the rear door, and within five minutes had returned the Pickering file to its proper and long-neglected resting place.

28

On Monday, February 20, Judge Atlee assembled the players for a progress report. Since it was not an official hearing of any variety, he locked the courtroom to keep reporters and spectators away. Most of the litigants were present: the Hubbards on one side, Lettie and Phedra on the other. Still no sign of Ancil, though Judge Atlee was not quite ready to declare him dead.

He assumed the bench, in his robe, managed a gruff "Good morning," and called the roll of lawyers. All present. It was soon obvious the judge was not in a good mood and probably felt bad. In a tired voice he said, "Gentlemen, this matter is scheduled for a jury trial six weeks from today. I am monitoring discovery and I see no reason why we can't be ready to go on as planned on April 3. Am I missing something here? Any reason to delay the trial?"

Serious head shaking followed. No sir. No reason at all. As Jake had said, it was indeed a strange case in that every lawyer was eager for a trial. If anyone wanted to stall, it might be Jake. He had every reason to drag things along, at $150 an hour, but he had Judge Atlee breathing down his neck too. The case officially known as *In re Estate of Henry Seth Hubbard* was barreling down the docket at record speed.

The judge continued: "Now, Mr. Brigance has copies of the First Inventory for your perusal. As I have instructed in writing, this is to be kept as confidential as possible." Portia began handing over copies to the other side. "I have sealed this section of the court file because nothing good can come from the dissemination of this sensitive material. You, as the attorneys, and your clients have the right to know what's in the estate, so take a look."

The lawyers snatched the copies of the inventory and flipped through the pages. Some had heard the alleged value, but they still wanted to see it in black and white. Twenty-four million and change. It validated what they were doing, why they were fighting.

The courtroom was deathly silent for a few moments as it sank in. More money than any of them could ever hope to earn in a long career. Then there were some whispers, and a chuckle over a wisecrack.

Judge Atlee said, "I address the contestants now. In reviewing the discovery, it seems as though you may have plans to challenge the validity of the handwriting. You have listed two experts in this field, and I assume the proponents will need to employ their own. I've looked at the handwriting samples, specifically the will, the burial instructions, the letter Mr. Hubbard left behind on his kitchen table, and the letter he addressed to Mr. Brigance, dated October 1. I have also seen the other samples of his handwriting that have been filed. Now, Mr. Lanier and Mr. Rush, do you plan to seriously contend that this will was written by someone other than Seth Hubbard?" His tone left little doubt about how he felt.

Rush and Lanier stood slowly, neither eager to respond. Lanier said, "Your Honor, we're still debating that point."

"Well hurry up," Judge Atlee said rudely. "It's a waste and you're wasting my time. A blind man can see it's his handwriting. Any expert who saunters into this courtroom and says otherwise will be laughed at by the jury and scorned by the court."

And with that, the handwriting issue was settled. They sat down. Lanier whispered to his sidekick, Lester Chilcott, "What else has he already decided?"

Judge Atlee looked at Jake and growled, "Mr. Brigance, any progress in the search for Ancil Hubbard? Five percent of this inventory is a lot of money."

Well, no shit, Judge, Jake wanted to say as he was jolted out of another thought and stood properly, though rattled. "Not really,

Your Honor. The search has turned up very little. It appears as though Ancil began using different names a long time ago. We've found no proof that he's dead, and certainly nothing to prove he's alive."

"Very well. Next on my list is a discussion about the jury pool. It's been over eight years since I presided over a trial involving a jury, and I admit to being a bit rusty. I've spoken to Judge Noose, Judge Handleford, and others, so I'm getting good advice. They seem to think a pool of one hundred will be sufficient. Gentlemen?"

Nothing.

"Good. I'll instruct the clerk to pull that many names at random from the voter registration rolls, and I'll make the list available two weeks before trial, the same procedure as in Circuit Court. There will be the standard precautions and warnings against unauthorized contact with the potential jurors. This is a high-profile case, gentlemen, and at times I'm almost convinced every person in this county already has an opinion."

Jake stood and said, "In that case, Your Honor, perhaps we should consider a change of venue."

"Requesting one is up to you, Mr. Brigance. I've seen nothing in writing."

"I haven't done so. I'm just speculating here. If most of our prospective jurors know about the case, then it seems like moving the case might be the proper thing to do."

"Mr. Lanier," Judge Atlee said, looking at the other lawyers. "Mr. Rush. Mr. Zeitler. Anybody?"

Wade Lanier straightened himself up with great frustration. "There's never been a change of venue in a will contest in Mississippi. Not a single case. We've done the research." Lester Chilcott was suddenly clawing his way through a thick briefcase. "And it seems a bit broad to declare that everyone in this county has formed an opinion before we've presented the evidence." Chilcott handed him a thick brief. "Here it is, if the court would like to take a look. Not a single case."

Jake was impressed with the research; Judge Atlee less so. He said, "I'll take your word for it, for now. I'll review the research later."

Jake wasn't serious about moving the case because he wanted it to stay in his courtroom, but there were advantages to having the trial in another county. These included (1) the possibility of more black jurors; (2) avoiding the lingering damage caused by Booker Sistrunk, his mouth, his race-baiting, and his black Rolls-Royce; (3) finding jurors who hadn't gossiped about Lettie and her family, their problems, and their new rental home outside Lowtown; and (4) selecting a jury untainted with endless speculation about Lettie and Seth Hubbard and what they were really up to. These factors and issues had been debated by Jake, Lucien, and, increasingly, Portia, as the weeks passed. They could debate all they wanted, but it was a waste of time. Judge Atlee was not moving the case, and he had said as much to Jake. So Jake was bluffing, and enjoying the sight of his opponents scrambling in opposition. He said, "Judge, if you think every person in Ford County has an opinion, then I'll file a motion to change venue."

Judge Atlee said, "I have a better idea, Mr. Brigance. Let's summon our pool and start the selection process. We should know immediately if we're wasting our time here. If it looks as though we can't pick an impartial jury, then we'll just move the trial somewhere else. There are lots of courtrooms in this state, at least one in every county."

Jake sat down, as did Lanier and Stillman Rush. Judge Atlee rustled some papers, then launched into a discussion about the remaining depositions. With the lawyers in a remarkably agreeable mood, scheduling posed few problems. A pretrial conference was set for March 20, two weeks before the trial.

The meeting was adjourned.

The meeting reconvened fifteen minutes later in Judge Atlee's office down the hall. Lawyers only, no clients, paralegals, clerks, or anyone else who couldn't be trusted. Just the lawyers and the judge, who'd taken off his robe and was puffing away on his pipe.

When they were seated, he said, "Gentlemen, for the next few minutes or so, we will at least have a discussion about settling this matter. I have no reservations about going forward with the trial; indeed, in many ways, I'm looking forward to it. Jury trials are rare for me, and seldom am I dealt facts as intriguing as those presented here. Nonetheless, I would be remiss in my role as the impartial referee not to explore ways to arrive at an outcome that will give all sides something, though less than what they would like. There's a lot of money on the line here, gentlemen, surely there's a way to slice the pie and make everyone happy." A heavy pause as he sucked hard on the pipe stem. "May I make the first proposal?"

As if he needed approval. All lawyers nodded yes, though cautiously.

"Very well. Take the two smaller bequests of 5 percent each: pay the church in full; put Ancil's in a trust until we figure what to do at a later date. Take the remaining 90 percent and split it three ways: one-third to Lettie Lang; one-third to Herschel Hubbard; one-third to Ramona Hubbard Dafoe. If we assume a tax bite of 50 percent, then each of the three will walk away with something in the neighborhood of three point six million. Far less than what each wants, but far more than each will get if the other side wins. What do you think?"

"I'm sure the church will take it," Jake said.

"It kinda leaves us high and dry, Your Honor," said Zack Zeitler, the attorney for Herschel's children.

"Same here," said Joe Bradley Hunt, the attorney for Ramona's kids.

"Of course," Judge Atlee said. "But it's safe to assume the children will get no small benefit from such a settlement. Their parents get a windfall; surely it will trickle down. Perhaps, you could stipulate that a portion be held in trust for the kids. Just an idea."

"Perhaps," Zeitler said, cutting his eyes around at the other attorneys as if his throat was in danger.

"Interesting," Wade Lanier mumbled. "I think my folks would consider it."

"Same here," said Stillman Rush.

His Honor chewed on his battered pipe stem and looked at Jake, who at the moment was stewing because of the ambush. He had not been forewarned of this impromptu settlement conference, and he certainly had no clue that his old pal was planning to throw some numbers on the table. Judge Atlee said, "Jake?"

Jake said, "You all have copies of the letter Seth Hubbard wrote to me when he mailed along his last will and testament. His instructions to me are rather explicit. His wishes and desires regarding his two adult children could not be clearer. I suggest you all read the letter again, and the will. I represent the estate, and I have my marching orders. My job is to uphold Mr. Hubbard's will and see to it that his children get nothing. I have no choice. I will not be a part of any compromise or settlement."

"Should you discuss this with your client?" Stillman said.

"My client is the estate, which is represented by Mr. Quince Lundy, the administrator."

"I'm talking about Lettie Lang."

"And I don't represent Lettie Lang. We have the same interests—the validation of the handwritten will—but I'm not her lawyer. I've made that clear to everyone, especially to her. As an interested party she has the right to hire a lawyer, which she tried once but he wound up in jail."

"I kinda miss ol' Booker," Wade Lanier said, and again got a few laughs.

Jake pressed on. "My point is that I'm not her lawyer."

Stillman said, "Sure, Jake, technically, but right now you have more influence with her than anyone else. Hell, her daughter is your paralegal, or secretary, or whatever."

"I have quite a staff."

Wade Lanier said, "You can't tell us, Jake, that if you went to Lettie and told her she could walk away with over three million bucks in two months, hell, two weeks, she wouldn't grab the deal and run."

"I don't know what she would do. She's a proud woman who feels scorned by the community. She wants her day in court."

"Three million bucks might ease some of the scorn," Lanier said.

"Perhaps, but I will not be a part of a compromise. If the court wishes, I will resign as the attorney for the estate, but as long as I'm here I'm not authorized to settle."

Judge Atlee relit his pipe with a match and blew some more smoke. He leaned forward on his elbows and said, "Gentlemen, I think he's right. If this will is proven to be valid, that is, if the jury believes Mr. Hubbard was of sound mind and not unduly influenced, then we have no choice but to follow the terms of the will. It is explicit. The adult children get nothing."

Maybe, Wade Lanier thought to himself, but you don't know what I know. You haven't seen the Irene Pickering will. You don't know that Ms. Lettie Lang has a history of worming her way into the private matters of her employers. And when the jury hears and sees this, the adult children of Seth Hubbard will do quite well.

Jake's principled defense of his dead client's last will, as well as his somewhat cocky belief that the trial should be held in Clanton, in *his* courtroom, was severely shaken by a tragedy that occurred later that night in an ice storm near the town of Lake Village, in the southern part of Ford County. Two brothers, Kyle and Bo Roston, were driving home after a high school basketball game. Kyle was Clanton High's senior point guard. Bo was a sophomore substitute. An eyewitness in a car behind them said the driver, Kyle, was proceeding with caution, not in a hurry, and handling the road conditions with skill. Another vehicle topped a hill at a high rate of speed and began sliding. The witness watched in horror as a crash became inevitable. He estimated Kyle was driving about forty miles per hour; the other vehicle, an old pickup, much faster than that. The head-on collision sent the

Rostons' small Toyota flipping through the air and into a ditch. The pickup spun wildly into a field as debris littered the road. The witness was able to stop in time and give assistance.

Kyle died at the scene. Bo was extracted by rescue personnel and taken to the hospital in Clanton where he immediately went into surgery. The trauma to his head was severe and he was barely alive. The other driver was also hospitalized but his injuries were not serious. His blood alcohol content was twice the legal limit. A deputy was parked outside his room.

The other driver was Simeon Lang.

Ozzie called Jake just after midnight and awakened him from a deep sleep. Fifteen minutes later, Ozzie stopped in front of the house and Jake hustled outside and into the sheriff's car. The ice was worse and the streets were slick, and as they crept through town Ozzie gave an update. The second boy was still in surgery but things looked grim. As far as Ozzie could tell at that point, Simeon had not been drinking in a local honky-tonk. According to Lettie, who was already at the hospital, he had not been home in over a week. She thought he was returning from a long haul, though he was not carrying cash or a paycheck. He had a broken nose but was otherwise unhurt.

"The drunks always walk away from their wrecks," Ozzie said.

They found Lettie and Portia hiding at the end of a long hallway, not far from Simeon's room. Both were crying, distraught, almost inconsolable. Jake sat with them while Ozzie left to check on other matters. After a few minutes with little conversation, Lettie walked away to find a restroom. As soon as she was gone, Portia said, "Ten years ago I was fourteen and in the ninth grade, and I begged her to leave him. He was hitting her back then. I saw it. I said, 'Please Momma, let's get away from him, go somewhere else.' I think maybe she tried but she's always been afraid of him. Now look what he's done. What'll happen to him, Jake?" She raked tears off her cheeks with the back of her hand.

Barely above a whisper, Jake said, "Nothing good. Assuming everything is his fault, and that he was drunk, he's looking at vehicular homicide. One count, as of now."

"What's it carry?"

"Five to twenty-five. The judge has a lot of discretion."

"And he can't get out of it?"

"No. I see no way."

"Hallelujah. He'll finally be gone for a long time." She cupped both hands over her mouth and nose and sobbed harder. "Those poor boys," she kept saying.

The crowd continued to grow around the waiting area on the hospital's main wing. Ozzie spoke to Jeff and Evelyn Roston, the parents, who were too stunned to say much. He talked to one of the boys' uncles and explained that Simeon Lang was in custody and would be moved to the jail within hours. Yes, he was drunk, still is. I'm very sorry.

"You better get him outta here," the uncle said, nodding to a group of men nearby. Angry, distraught men, rural types raised around guns and rifles and upset enough to do something drastic. Others joined them. The Rostons grew soybeans and chickens and were active in their country church. They had many relatives and friends, and they had never voted for Ozzie.

Every deputy on the payroll was at the hospital by 2:00 a.m. At three, they sneaked Simeon out of the hospital and took him to jail. Ozzie informed the uncle.

Lettie and Portia used the same side door and left the hospital. Jake accompanied them to their car. He returned to the main wing, avoided the waiting area, and found Ozzie chatting with two of his men. Dumas Lee approached them, camera around his neck, and they immediately went silent.

Dumas said, "Say, Jake, you got a minute?"

Jake hesitated, looked at Ozzie, who said, "No comment whatsoever," then asked Dumas, "What's on your mind?"

"Just a couple of questions."

They walked away, side by side, down a long corridor. Dumas asked, "Can you confirm it's Simeon Lang?"

It was senseless to deny it, so Jake said, "Yes."

"And you're his lawyer?"

"I am not."

"Okay, but he's had a drunk driving charge pending in city court for four months. Your name's on the docket as his lawyer."

Careful, Jake warned himself. He breathed deeply and felt a thick knot in his stomach. "I did that as a favor," he said.

"I don't care why you did it. Your name's on the docket as his lawyer."

"I'm not his lawyer, okay? Never have been. I can't represent the estate of Seth Hubbard and also represent Simeon Lang, the husband of one of the beneficiaries."

"Then why did you show up in court on October 19 to request a postponement of his drunk driving case?"

"It was a favor. I'm not his lawyer, okay Dumas?"

"Why has the case been postponed for four months?"

"I'm not the judge."

"I'll talk to him later," Dumas fired back.

"You do that. No further comment." Jake abruptly turned around and walked away. Dumas followed and kept talking, saying, "Look, Jake, you'd better talk to me because this is gonna look bad."

Jake turned around again and they squared off in the center of the corridor. Jake caught himself, took a deep breath, and said, "Don't draw any conclusions, Dumas. I haven't touched the DUI case in four months because I'm not his lawyer. If you will recall, at the time he was represented by those clowns from Memphis. Not by me. So please be careful here."

Dumas was scribbling furiously. Jake wanted to punch him. Everything was suddenly forgotten by screams from the other end of the building.

Bo Roston was pronounced dead at 4:15 a.m.

29

Jake and Carla sat at the kitchen table and waited for the coffee to brew. It was not yet 5:00 a.m. on Wednesday, February 22, a day that would undoubtedly be one of the saddest and darkest in the county's history. Two teenagers—bright kids, strong students, athletes, church members, popular boys from a good family—slaughtered on an icy road by a drunk. The horrible news was spreading by the minute. The cafés would be packed as the early risers hurried in for the latest word. The churches would open for prayer. Clanton High School would be the worst place to be. Those poor kids.

Carla poured coffee and they spoke softly, in hushed tones so Hanna wouldn't be awakened. Jake was saying, "I never opened a file. Ozzie called me on Monday, told me Simeon was arrested on Saturday morning and was due in court on Wednesday. When he sobered up, Ozzie drove him home and along the way told him to get rid of the Memphis lawyers. I thanked Ozzie and we agreed to meet later. He called back and asked if I would show up in court Wednesday to get the case continued. Ozzie thought he could use the DUI to pressure Simeon to get in line. I went to court that Wednesday, did the paperwork, asked for a continuance, got one, and forgot about it, for the most part. At the time, Simeon was still represented by Booker Sistrunk, and I told Simeon in court that I would not help him with the DUI. I didn't like the guy; in fact, I despised him."

"Did you see a conflict?" Carla asked.

"I thought about it. In fact, I even mentioned it to Ozzie. The truth was, there was no conflict. I'm the attorney for the estate.

Simeon is not an interested party in the estate. His wife is, but he's not."

"That's not real clear, Jake."

"No, it's not, and I should not have gotten involved. It was a huge mistake. I didn't trust my instincts."

"But no one can blame you for Simeon's drunk driving."

"Sure they can. If the case had been handled properly, he would have been convicted before now and his license pulled. He would not have been driving last night, in theory anyway. The truth is half the blacks and rednecks in this county do not have valid licenses."

"It's only four months, Jake. These cases drag on for longer, don't they?"

"Sometimes."

"What was that guy's name, the roofer? You did a DUI for his son and the case lasted a year."

"Chuck Bennett, but I didn't want the boy in jail until they finished with our roof."

"My point is that these cases can drag on."

"Sure, but there's always finger-pointing after a tragedy, the blame game. And since I'm in the Lang camp, I'll get my share. It's always easy to blame the lawyers. Ozzie'll get hammered, too. He'll be seen as the black sheriff trying to protect one of his own, and now two white kids are dead. It could be brutal."

"Maybe not, Jake."

"I'm not optimistic."

"How will it affect the will contest?"

Jake slowly sipped his coffee and stared through a window into the blackness of his backyard. Softly, he said, "It's devastating. Simeon Lang will be the most reviled person in this county for months to come. He'll have his day in court, then get sent away to prison. Over time, he'll be forgotten by most folks. But our trial is only six weeks away. The Lang name is toxic. Imagine trying to pick a jury with that baggage." He took another sip, then rubbed his eyes. "Lettie has no choice but to file for divorce, and quickly. She has to cut all ties to Simeon."

"Will she?"

"Why not? He'll spend the next twenty or thirty years in Parchman, where he belongs."

"I'm sure the Rostons will be pleased with that."

"Those poor people."

"Are you seeing her today, Lettie?"

"I'm sure I will. I'll call Harry Rex first thing this morning and try to arrange a meeting. He'll know what to do."

"Will this make the *Times*?"

"No, the *Times* will be on the street in an hour. I'm sure Dumas will give it the entire front page next week, with photos of the wrecked vehicles, as much gore as possible. And he'd love to grind me up too."

"What's the worst he can say about you, Jake?"

"Well, first, he can label me as Simeon's lawyer. Then he can slant and twist and imply that I've somehow stalled the October DUI case, and that if I had not done so, then Simeon's driver's license would have been yanked by the court and he wouldn't be driving. Thus, the Roston boys wouldn't be dead."

"He can't do that. That's assuming far too much."

"He can and he will."

"Then talk to him. Damage control here, Jake. Today is Wednesday, so the funerals will probably be over the weekend. Wait until Monday, and file the divorce. What do you call that restraining thing?"

"TRO—temporary restraining order."

"That's it. Get the judge to sign one of those so Simeon can't get near Lettie. Sure he's in jail, but if she wants a TRO it makes her look good. A clean break, she's running from the guy. In the meantime, talk to Dumas and make sure he gets the facts straight. Do some research and show him that some DUI cases drag on for more than four months. You never opened a file and you certainly weren't paid a dime. See if you can convince Ozzie to take some heat. If I recall correctly, he got about 70 percent of the vote the last time he ran. He's bulletproof. Plus, he wants

Lettie to win the will contest. If you're getting hit with baggage, get Ozzie to shoulder some. He can handle it."

Jake was nodding along, even smiling. Go girl!

She said, "Look, dear, right now you're shell-shocked and you're scared. Shake it off. You've done nothing wrong, so don't get blamed for anything. Control the damage, then control the spin."

"Can I hire you? My office needs some help."

"You can't afford me. I'm a schoolteacher."

Hanna was coughing. Carla went to check on her.

The real damage control began about an hour later when Jake stormed into the Coffee Shop, ready to convince one and all that he was not the lawyer for Simeon Lang and never had been. So many rumors began there, over eggs and bacon. In the shower, Jake decided to go straight to the source.

Marshall Prather was there in uniform behind a stack of pancakes, waiting, it seemed. He'd been up all night too and looked as bleary-eyed as Jake. During the lull that was caused by Jake's entry, Marshall said, "Hey Jake, saw you at the hospital a few hours ago." This was a deliberate effort to start the spin because Ozzie was also controlling damage.

"Yeah, just awful," Jake said somberly. At full volume he asked, "Did ya'll take Lang to jail?"

"Yep. He's still sobering up."

"You his lawyer, Jake?" asked Ken Nugent from three tables over. Nugent drove the Pepsi truck and spent his days hauling cases of beverages into country stores. Dell had once said, in his absence, that no one spread more gossip than Nugent.

"Never have been," Jake said. "I don't represent him, nor do I represent his wife."

"What the hell you doin' in the case then?" Nugent fired back.

Dell poured coffee into Jake's cup and bumped him with her rear end, part of the routine. "Mornin' sweetie," she whispered. Jake smiled at her, then looked back at Nugent. Things went mute as all other conversations stopped. Jake said, "Under the law, I actually represent Mr. Seth Hubbard, who's no longer with us, of course, but just before he died he selected me as the attorney for his estate. My job is to follow his wishes, present his last will, and protect his estate. My contract of representation is with the administrator of the estate, and no one else. Not Lettie Lang, and certainly not her husband. Frankly, I can't stand the guy. Don't forget he hired those Memphis clowns who tried to steal the case."

Dell, always loyal, piped in, "That's what I tried to tell 'em." She placed Jake's toast and grits in front of him.

"So who's his lawyer?" Nugent asked, ignoring her.

"I have no idea. Probably one appointed by the court. I doubt if he can afford his own."

"What will he get, Jake?" asked Roy Kern, a plumber who'd worked on Jake's previous home.

"A lot. Two counts of vehicular homicide at five to twenty-five a pop. Don't know how it'll go down, but Judge Noose is tough in these cases. I wouldn't be surprised if he got twenty or thirty years."

"Why not the death penalty?" asked Nugent.

"It's not a death case because—"

"The hell it ain't. You got two dead kids."

"There was no deliberate effort to kill, nothing premeditated. A death penalty case requires murder plus something else: murder plus rape; murder plus robbery; murder plus kidnapping. This could never be a death case."

This was not well received by the crowd. When stirred up, the gang at the Coffee Shop could resemble the beginnings of a lynch mob, but it always settled down after breakfast. Jake sprinkled Tabasco on his grits and began buttering his toast.

Nugent asked, "Can the Rostons get any of the money?"

The money? As if Seth's estate were now available and thus vulnerable.

Jake laid down his fork and looked at Nugent. He reminded himself that these were his people, his clients and friends, and they just needed reassuring. They did not understand the ins and outs of the law and of probate, and they were concerned that an injustice might be in the works. "No," Jake said pleasantly, "there's no way. It will be months, probably years before Mr. Hubbard's money is finally disbursed, and as of right now we really don't know who'll get it. The trial will help settle things, but its verdict will certainly be appealed. And even if Lettie Lang eventually gets all the money, or 90 percent of it, her husband doesn't get a dime. He'll be locked away anyway. The Rostons will not have the right to make a claim against Lettie."

He took a bite of toast and chewed quickly. He wanted to control the spin and not waste time with his mouth full.

"He won't get out on bond, will he Jake?" asked Bill West.

"I doubt it. A bond will be set, but it'll probably be too high. My guess is he'll stay in jail until he either pleads under an agreement or goes to trial."

"What kinda defense could he use?"

Jake shook his head as if there could be no defense. "He was drunk and there's an eyewitness, right Marshall?"

"Yep. Guy saw it all."

Jake continued, "I see a plea bargain and a long sentence."

"Ain't he got a boy in prison?" asked Nugent.

"He does. Marvis."

"Maybe he can bunk with his boy, join the same gang, have all sorts of fun at Parchman," Nugent said and got some laughs. Jake laughed too, then attacked his breakfast. He was relieved the conversation had moved away from any connection he might have to Simeon Lang.

They would leave the Coffee Shop and go to their jobs, where all day long they would talk about nothing but the Roston tragedy, and they would have the inside scoop because they'd had breakfast with Jake, the man in the middle. They would assure their co-workers and listeners that their pal Jake was not the lawyer for Simeon Lang, the most hated man in Ford County. They would assuage their fears and promise them that Lang was headed to prison for a long time.

Jake had told them so.

★   ★   ★

Bright, early morning sunlight streamed through the wooden blinds and fell into neat white rows across the long conference room table. Somewhere in the background, a phone rang constantly, but no one had any interest in answering it. The front door was locked, and every fifteen minutes or so there was a knock. The tense discussions rose, then ebbed and waned and finally ceased, though there was so much more to say.

Harry Rex had walked them through the strategies of a divorce filing. File now, file loudly, file loaded with as many sordid allegations as possible to make Mr. Lang appear to be the creep he really was. Allege adultery, habitual cruel and inhuman treatment, desertion, drunkenness, abuse, nonsupport, throw in everything because the marriage is over whether Lettie would admit it or not. Pound him because he cannot respond from jail, and why would he bother anyway? Do it Monday and make sure Dumas Lee and every other reporter with even a passing interest gets a copy of the filing. Include a request for a restraining order to keep the lout off the property and away from Lettie and the kids and grandkids for the rest of their lives. It's about ending a bad marriage, but it's also about posturing for the public. Harry Rex agreed to handle the case.

Portia had told them the first threatening phone call came just after 5:00 a.m. Phedra took it, and after a few seconds calmly hung up. "He called me a 'nigger,'" she said, stunned. "Said we'll pay for killin' those boys." They panicked and locked the doors. Portia found a handgun in a closet and loaded it. They turned off the lights and huddled together in the den, watching the street. Then the phone rang again. And again. They prayed for sunrise. She said her mother would sign the divorce papers, but once she does, look out for the Langs. Simeon's brothers and cousins were notorious lowlifes—same gene pool—and they would cause trouble. They've been pestering Lettie for money anyway, and if they think they're getting cut out they'll do something stupid.

Lucien had had a rough night, but he was there nonetheless and thinking as clearly as ever. He quickly took the position that the trial over the will must not be held in Ford County. Jake had no choice but to request a change of venue, which Atlee would probably deny, but at the very least it would give them a strong argument on appeal. Lucien had never been excited about Jake's chances of winning before a jury, and he had long been convinced the pool had been contaminated by Booker Sistrunk. Lettie's ill-advised decision to move to town, and into a home once owned by a slightly prominent white family, had not helped her standing in the community. There was already resentment and plenty of suspicion. She was not working and had not worked since Hubbard died. And now this. Now she had the most hated name in the county. Filing for divorce was not even an option—it had to be done. But, the divorce could not possibly be finished by the time the trial started on April 3. Her name was Lang in the will; it was Lang now; and it would be Lang during the trial. Put him, Lucien, in Wade Lanier's shoes, and he would have the jury loathing every Lang who ever lived.

"Sorry, Portia," Lucien said. "No offense. That's just the way it would be." She understood, or at least tried to. She was too exhausted to say much. She had left her mother and sisters wrapped in their bathrobes, huddled by the fireplace, with the gun on the mantel, wondering whether they should send the children to school and what they should tell them. Kirk, a sophomore at Clanton High, knew the Roston boys and was swearing he would never return to the school. They were such nice boys. And he hated his father. His life was over. He wanted to get away, like Portia, join the Army and never come back.

Jake and Harry Rex had discussed ways to postpone the trial. Drag it out, burn some clock, give Harry Rex enough time to get the divorce final, give the system enough time to dispose of Simeon and ship him away, and give the county some distance between the horror of the moment, the two burials, and the fight over the estate of Seth Hubbard. Where would they all be in six months? Lettie would be divorced; she could even adopt her old name. Lettie Tayber. It sounded much better, though Portia reminded herself she would still be stuck with Lang. Simeon would be gone. Sistrunk would be all but forgotten. Surely, things would be more conducive to a fair trial in six months. His opponents would object vociferously, and with such momentum on their side, why not?

Jake was slightly optimistic he could have a chat with Judge Atlee, perhaps another late Friday afternoon meeting on the porch with whiskey sours, and after the edge was knocked off he could broach the notion of a delay or change of venue. It was worth a try. The only downside was the risk of angering the judge by such an overt attempt at earwigging, and what would the judge do other than to tell Jake to shut up? He wouldn't do that, not after a couple of whiskey sours. He might not like the conversation, but he would never chastise Jake. A slight scolding maybe, but nothing close to permanent damage.

Let some time pass, Jake said. Let the rage and horror and sadness lose some of their sting, then die down. They would file the divorce on Monday, and in a week or so Jake would approach Judge Atlee.

Quince Lundy arrived for one of two weekly visits. He found them in the conference room, gathered glumly around the table, quiet, subdued, almost mournful as they stared at the walls and looked at a bleak future. He had heard the news on the Clanton radio station as he drove over from Smithfield. He wanted to ask what the tragedy meant for the trial, but after a few moments in the conference room he suspected the trial was in serious trouble.

Willie Hastings was one of four black deputies on Ozzie's staff. His cousin was Gwen Hailey, wife of Carl Lee, mother of Tonya, who was now thirteen years old and doing well. He knocked on the front door of the Sappington house and waited as he heard feet shuffling hurriedly inside. Finally, the door cracked and Lettie peeked through it.

Willie said, "Mornin' Miss Lang. Sheriff Walls sent me over."

The door opened wider and she managed a smile. "That you, Willie?" she said. "Would you like to come in?"

He entered and found the children in the den watching television, obviously skipping school. He followed Lettie to the kitchen where Phedra fixed him a cup of coffee. He chatted with the women, made some notes about the threatening calls, noticed the phone was now off the hook, and said he would hang around for a while. He was parked in the driveway and would stay there in case they needed him, and to show a presence. Sheriff Walls sends his regrets. Simeon was in a cell by himself, pretty banged up, and still sleeping off his booze. Hastings did not know the Rostons and had not spoken with them, but he understood they were at home surrounded by family and friends. Lettie handed him a letter she had written during the early morning and asked if he could make sure it was delivered to the Rostons. "Just our way of saying how awful we feel," she said.

Willie promised to have it in their hands before noon.

They topped off his coffee and he went outside. The temperature was still below freezing, but the heater worked well in his patrol car. Throughout the morning, he sipped coffee, watched the street, saw nothing, and tried to stay awake.

An early news show on the Tupelo station ran the story at 7:00 a.m. Stillman Rush was in the shower and missed it, but an associate did not. Phone calls were made; details verified; and an hour later Stillman called Wade Lanier in Jackson with the tragic but also promising news. Lightning had struck. No juror in Ford County would ever have a shot at Simeon Lang, but his wife had just become an easy target.

30

Early Thursday morning Simeon Lang was awakened, fed, handcuffed, and escorted out of his cell and down a hallway to a cramped meeting room where a stranger was waiting. He sat in a folding chair, still handcuffed, and listened as the stranger said, "My name is Arthur Welch and I'm a lawyer from Clarksdale, over in the Delta."

"I know where Clarksdale is," Simeon said. He had a large bandage taped across his nose. His left eye was shut with stitches around the edge.

"Good for you," Welch said. "I'm here to represent you because no one else will take the case. You have a first appearance and bail hearing this morning at nine, and you'll need a lawyer."

"Why are you here?"

"A friend asked me to be here, okay? That's all you need to know. Right now you need a lawyer, and I'm the only sonofabitch willing to stand beside you."

Simeon nodded slightly.

At 8:30, he was transferred to the courthouse and hustled up the rear stairs to the main courtroom, where he entered the temporary domain of the Honorable Percy Bullard, County Court judge. His own courtroom was down the hall, and quite small, so he preferred to use the big room when it was vacant, which was at least half the time. He'd spent most of his sixteen years on the bench handling minor civil disputes and lighter felonies, but occasionally he was called upon to process and speed along a more serious case. With the county in mourning and tensions high, he decided to haul in Lang, rough him up a bit, and let folks know that the wheels of justice were turning.

Word had spread quickly and there were spectators in the courtroom. At 9:00 a.m. sharp, Simeon was led in, and a guiltier defendant had never been seen. His face was a mess. His orange county jail overalls were too big and bloodstained. He was handcuffed behind his back, and the bailiffs took their sweet time freeing him.

Judge Bullard looked at him and said, "*State versus Simeon Lang*. Over here." He pointed to a spot in front of the bench. Simeon shuffled over, glancing around nervously as if he might get shot from behind. Arthur Welch stood beside him while somehow managing to keep his distance.

"You are Simeon Lang?" Judge Bullard asked.

Simeon nodded.

"Speak up!"

"I am."

"Thanks. And you are?"

"Your Honor, my name is Arthur Welch and I practice law over in Clarksdale. I'm here to represent Mr. Lang."

Bullard looked at him as if to say, "What the hell for?" Instead, he asked Simeon, "Mr. Lang, is Mr. Welch your lawyer?"

"He is."

"Okay, now Mr. Lang, you have been charged with two counts of vehicular homicide and one count of driving under the influence. How do you plead?"

"Not guilty."

"No surprise there. I'll set a preliminary hearing in about thirty days. Mr. Welch, you will be notified by my clerk. I assume you'd like to discuss bail."

As if reading from a script, Welch said, "Yes, Your Honor, we would like to request a reasonable bail at this time. Mr. Lang has a wife and family here in the county and has lived here his entire life. He is not a risk to flee and has assured me, and will assure you, that he always shows up in court when required to."

"Thank you. Bail is hereby set at $2 million, one million for each count of vehicular homicide. Anything else, Mr. Welch?"

"No, Your Honor."

"Very well. Mr. Lang you are remanded to the custody of the Ford County sheriff until you make bail or are called for by this court." He tapped his gavel lightly and winked at Welch. Simeon was re-handcuffed and taken from the courtroom. Welch followed him, and outside, under the rear terrace, exactly where the criminal defendants were always photographed when they were newsworthy enough to be photographed, Dumas Lee clicked away and got plenty of shots of Lang and his lawyer. Later, he chatted with Welch, who had little to report but was nonetheless quite willing to talk. He was completely vague on his involvement in a case two hours from home.

Welch had been rolled out of bed at 5:00 that morning with a profane phone call from Harry Rex Vonner, an old roommate from law school. Welch had handled two of Harry Rex's divorces and Harry Rex had handled two of Welch's, and they owed each other so many favors and debts and IOUs that keeping score was impossible. Harry Rex needed him instantly in Clanton, and Welch, cursing for two hours, made the drive. He had no plans to represent Simeon Lang beyond the indictment and would punt the case in a month or so.

As Harry Rex explained, in some of the most colorful and abusive language imaginable, it was important for the local folks to see and realize that Simeon Lang was not represented by Jake Brigance, but rather by some scumbag they'd never heard of.

Welch understood perfectly. It was another clear example of what was never taught in law school.

It was early on Friday afternoon, the weather was cold and damp, and Jake was suffering through the weekly ritual of trying to tie up some of the week's loose ends so they wouldn't grow and fester and ruin his Monday. Among his many unwritten but nonetheless serious rules was one that required him to return every phone call by noon Friday. He preferred to avoid most of his phone calls, but that was not possible. Returning them was easy to put off. They often slid from one workday to the next, but he was determined not to drag them through the weekend.

Another rule forbade him to take worthless cases that would pay little or nothing and turn his obnoxious clients into people he could choke. But, like every other lawyer, he routinely said yes to some deadbeat whose mother taught Jake in the fourth grade, or whose uncle knew his father, or the broke widow from church who couldn't afford a lawyer but couldn't live without one. Invariably, these matters turned into "fish files," the ones that grew fouler the longer they sat in a corner, untouched. Every lawyer had them. Every lawyer hated them. Every lawyer swore he would never take another; you could almost smell them the first time the client walked in the door.

Freedom for Jake would be an office free from fish files, and he still approached every new year with the determination to say no to the deadbeats. Years ago, Lucien had said repeatedly, "It's not the cases you take that make you, it's the cases you don't take." Just say no. Nonetheless, his special drawer for fish files was depressingly full, and every Friday afternoon he stared at them and cursed himself.

Without knocking, Portia walked into his office, obviously upset. She was patting her chest as if she couldn't breathe. "There's a man here," she said, almost in a whisper because she couldn't speak any louder.

"Are you okay?" he asked, once again tossing aside a fish file.

She shook her head rapidly. "No. It's Mr. Roston. The boys' father."

"What?" Jake said as he bolted to his feet.

She kept patting her chest. "He wants to see you."

"Why?"

"Please, Jake, don't tell him who I am." They stared at each other for a second, neither with a clue.

"Okay, okay. Put him in the conference room. I'll be down in a minute."

Jeff Roston was not much older than Jake, but under the circumstances he was a very old man. He sat with his hands together and his shoulders sagging, as if burdened by an enormous weight. He wore heavily starched khakis and a navy blazer, and looked more like a casual preppy than a man who grew soybeans. He also wore the face of a father in the midst of an unspeakable nightmare. He rose and they shook hands and Jake said, "I'm terribly sorry, Mr. Roston."

"Thank you. Let's go with Jeff and Jake, okay?"

"Sure." Jake sat beside him along one side of the table and they faced each other. After an awkward pause, Jake said, "I can't imagine what you're going through."

"No, you can't," he said softly and slowly, each word laden with grief. "I can't either. I think we're just sort of sleepwalking, you know, just going through the motions, trying to survive this hour so we can deal with the next one. We're praying for time. Praying for the days to turn into weeks and then months, and then maybe one day years from now the nightmare will be over and we can manage the pain and the sorrow. But at the same time we know that'll never happen. You're not supposed to bury your kids, Jake. It's just not the natural course of things."

Jake nodded along, unable to add anything thoughtful or intelligent or helpful. What do you say to a father whose two sons were now lying in caskets waiting for their funeral? "I can't begin to comprehend," Jake said. His initial reaction was "What does he want?"—and now, minutes later, Jake was still wondering.

"The service is tomorrow," Jake said after a long heavy pause.

"That's right. Another nightmare." Jeff's eyes were red and weary and proof he had not slept in days. He could not maintain a direct stare, but chose instead to look down at his knees. He gently tapped all ten fingers together as if in deep meditation. He finally said, "We received a very nice note from Lettie Lang. It was hand delivered by Sheriff Walls, who, I must say, has been wonderful. He said the two of you are friends." Jake nodded, listened, offered nothing. Jeff continued, "The note was heartfelt and conveyed the family's sense of grief and guilt. It meant a lot to Evelyn and me. We could tell that Lettie is a fine Christian lady who's horrified at what her husband did. Could you please thank her for us?"

"Of course."

He again stared at his knees, tapped his fingertips, breathed slowly as if even that was painful, then he said, "I want you to tell them something else, Jake, if you don't mind, something I'd like for you to pass along to Lettie and her family, even to her husband."

Sure. Anything. What would Jake not do for such a grief-stricken father?

"Are you a Christian, Jake?"

"I am. Sometimes more of one than others, but I'm trying."

"I thought so. In the sixth chapter of the Gospel of Luke, Jesus teaches the importance of forgiveness. He knows we're human and our natural tendency is to seek revenge, to strike back, to condemn those who hurt us, but this is wrong. We're supposed to forgive, always. So I'd like for you to tell Lettie and her family, and especially her husband, that Evelyn and I forgive Simeon for what he did. We've prayed about this. We've spent time with our minister. And we cannot allow ourselves to live the rest of our days filled with hatred and ill will. We forgive him, Jake. Can you tell them?"

Jake was too stunned to respond. He was aware that his jaw had dropped slightly, that his mouth was open, and that he was looking at Jeff Roston in disbelief, but for a few seconds he couldn't adjust. How could you possibly, humanly forgive a drunk who slaughtered your two sons less than seventy-two hours earlier? He thought of Hanna, and the almost incomprehensible visual of her in a coffin. He would scream for bloody revenge.

Finally, he managed to nod. Yes, I will tell them.

Roston said, "When we bury Kyle and Bo tomorrow, when we say good-bye, we will do so with complete love and forgiveness. There's no room for hatred, Jake."

Jake swallowed hard and said, "That black girl out there is Lettie's daughter. Simeon's daughter. She works for me. Why don't you tell her?"

Without a word, Jeff Roston rose and walked to the door. He opened it, and with Jake following he stepped into the reception area and looked at Portia. "So you're Simeon Lang's daughter," he said, and she almost flinched. Slowly, she stood and faced him and said, "Yes sir."

"Your mother sent me a very nice note. Please thank her."

"I will, yes, thanks," she said nervously.

"And will you tell your father that my wife, Evelyn, and I forgive him for what happened?"

Portia cupped her right hand over her mouth as her eyes suddenly moistened. Roston took a step closer and gently hugged her. Then he abruptly stepped back, said again, "We forgive him," and walked out the front door without another word.

They stared at the door long after he left. They were speechless, overwhelmed. Finally, Jake said, "Let's lock up and go home."

The effort to validate the handwritten will of Seth Hubbard continued to unravel late Sunday morning, though Jake and its proponents had no way of knowing it. Randall Clapp was sniffing around the town of Dillwyn, in extreme south Georgia, some six miles from the Florida line, when he finally found a black woman he'd been tracking for a week. Her name was Julina Kidd, age thirty-nine, a divorced mother of two.

Five years earlier, Julina worked in a large furniture factory near Thomasville, Georgia. She was a clerk in payroll, earned $15,000 a year, and was surprised to hear one day that the company had been bought by a faceless corporation with an Alabama domicile. Not long afterward, the new owner, a Mr. Hubbard, showed up and said hello.

One month later, Julina was fired. One week after that she filed a sexual harassment complaint with Equal Employment. The complaint was dismissed three weeks after it was filed. Her lawyer in Valdosta would not discuss the case with Clapp, said he'd lost contact with Julina, and had no idea where she was.

When Clapp found her she was living in subsidized housing with her two teenagers and a younger sister, and she was working part-time for an oil jobber. Initially, she had little interest in talking to an unknown white man. Clapp, though, did this for a living and was adept at extracting information. He offered her $200 in cash, plus lunch, for one hour of her time and direct answers to his questions. They met at a truck stop and ordered the special, baked chicken. Clapp, a simmering racist who would never be tempted to chase a black woman, struggled to control his thoughts. This one was a knockout—beautiful dark skin with a touch of cream, hazel eyes that penetrated to the core, high African cheekbones, perfect teeth that revealed an easy, seductive smile. She was reserved and her eyebrows were perpetually arched, as if she suspected every word he uttered.

He didn't tell her much, not at first anyway. He said he was involved in some high-powered litigation with Seth Hubbard on the other side, and he knew they had a history. Yes, he was digging for dirt.

She had it. Seth had come on to her like an eighteen-year-old sailor on shore leave. At the time, she was thirty-four and in the late stages of a bad divorce. She was fragile and frightened about her future. She had no interest in a sixty-six-year-old white man who smelled like an ashtray, regardless of how many companies he owned. But he was persistent and spent a lot of his time at the Thomasville factory. He gave her a substantial raise and moved her to a desk near his office. He fired the old secretary and appointed Julina as his "executive assistant." She could not type.

He owned two furniture factories in Mexico and needed to visit them. He arranged for Julina to obtain a passport and asked her if she wanted to accompany him. She took it more as a demand than an invitation. But she had never left the country and was mildly intrigued by the notion of seeing a bit of the world, even though she knew a compromise would be involved.

"I doubt if Seth was the first white man to chase you," Clapp said.

She smiled slightly, nodded her head, and said, "No. It does happen." Again, Clapp tried to control his thoughts. Why was she still single? And living in a subsidized apartment? Any woman, black or white, with her looks and figure could parlay them into a much better life.

Her first trip on an airplane was to Mexico City. They checked into a luxury hotel—two adjoining rooms. The dreaded knock on her door came that night, and she opened it. Afterward, lying in bed with him, she was disgusted by what she had done. Sex for money. At the moment, she was nothing but a prostitute. She bit her tongue, though, and as soon as he disappeared the next day she took a cab to the airport. When he returned a week later, she was fired on the spot and escorted out of the office by an armed guard. She hired a lawyer who slapped a sexual harassment claim on Seth, whose own lawyer was horrified by the facts. They quickly capitulated and wanted to settle. After some haggling, Seth agreed to a lump sum payment of $125,000 in a confidential deal. Her lawyer kept $25,000, and she had been living off the rest. She wasn't supposed to reveal that to anyone, but what the hell. It had been five years.

"Don't worry, Seth's dead," Clapp said, then told her the rest of the story. She listened as she chewed the elastic chicken and washed it down with sugared iced tea. She had no feelings for Seth and did not pretend to. She had practically forgotten about the old man.

"Did he ever say anything about preferring black women?"

"He said he didn't discriminate," she said, slower now. "He said I wasn't the first black one."

"When did he say these things?"

"Pillow talk, you know? I'm not getting involved in a lawsuit."

"Didn't say you were," Clapp tried to reassure her, but she was even more careful. Clapp knew he had once again stumbled onto something huge but played it cool. "But I'm sure the lawyers I work for would be willing to pay for your testimony."

"Is that legal?"

"Of course it's legal. Lawyers pay for testimony all the time. Every expert charges a fortune. Plus they fly you up there and cover your expenses."

"How much?"

"Don't know but we can talk about it later. Can I ask you something that's, well, rather delicate?"

"Oh why not? What have we not discussed?"

"When you were with Seth, how was he, know what I mean? He was sixty-six then, and he hired this black housekeeper a couple of years later. This was long before he got sick. The old boy was getting on in years, but sounds like he was fairly frisky, you know?"

"He was all right. I mean, for a man his age he was pretty good." She said this as though she'd had many, and of all ages. "I got the impression he just wanted to hole up in the room and screw for a week. That's kind of impressive for an old guy, black or white."

Wade Lanier was having a beer in the men's grill at the country club when Clapp tracked him down. He teed off every Sunday morning at precisely 7:45 with the same three pals, played eighteen holes, usually won more money than he lost, then drank beer for a couple of hours over poker. He quickly forgot about the cards and the beer and made Clapp repeat every word of his conversation with Julina Kidd.

Most of what she said would not be admissible in court; however, the fact that she could take the stand, let the jury absorb her ethnicity, and chat about her claim for sexual harassment at the hands of Seth Hubbard would sway any white jury to believe the old guy and Lettie were probably doing business. They would believe that Lettie had gotten as close as humanly possible, and she had influenced him. She had used her body to work her way into his will. Lanier couldn't prove it by a preponderance of evidence, but he could certainly imply it in a powerful way.

He left the country club and drove to his office.

Early Monday morning, Ian and Ramona Dafoe drove three hours from Jackson to Memphis and had a late breakfast with Herschel. Their relationship had deteriorated and it was time to patch things up, or that's what Ramona said anyway. They were on the same side; it was foolish for them to bicker and distrust one another. They met at a pancake house, and, after the usual efforts at reconciliation, Ian launched into a strong-armed plea for Herschel to ditch Stillman Rush and his firm. His lawyer, Wade Lanier, was far more experienced, and, frankly, was worried that Rush would be a hindrance at trial. He was a pretty boy, too showy, cocky, and likely to alienate the jury. Lanier had watched him closely now for over four months and did not like what he saw. There was a big ego and not much talent. Trials can be won or lost by the arrogance of a lawyer, and Wade Lanier was worried sick. He was even threatening to bail out.

And there was more. As evidence of the inequality of their lawyers, Ian revealed the story of the other will and its attempted bequest of $50,000 to Lettie. He did not name names because he didn't want Stillman Rush to screw up things. Herschel was stunned, but also thrilled. But wait—it gets better. Now Wade Lanier had found a black woman who sued Seth for sexual harassment.

Look at what my lawyer is doing, and compare it to yours. Your boy is not in the game, Herschel. Lanier understands guerrilla warfare; your lawyer is a Boy Scout. Let's join forces here. Lanier even has a deal to offer: if we come together, get rid of Rush, and allow Lanier to represent both of us, he'll cut his fee to 25 percent of any settlement. He has a strategy to force a settlement, especially in light of what his chief investigator is digging up. He'll pick the right moment and spring it all on Jake Brigance, who'll crack under the pressure. We can have the money within a few months!

Herschel held his ground for a while, but eventually agreed to drive to Jackson and meet with Lanier in secret.

Simeon Lang was finishing Monday's dinner of pork and beans from a can and four slices of stale white bread when the jailer appeared and stuck a package through the bars. "Happy reading," he said and walked away. It was from the law offices of Harry Rex Vonner.

Inside was a letter from the lawyer, addressed to Simeon, care of the Ford County jail, and the letter tersely announced to Simeon that what followed was a Complaint for Divorce. He had thirty days to respond.

He read it slowly. What was the hurry? Habitual cruel and inhuman treatment; adultery; desertion; physical abuse. Page after page of allegations, some of them wild, some of them true.

What difference did it make? He'd killed two boys and was headed to Parchman for a long time. His life was over. Lettie needed someone else. She hadn't been to see him since they locked him up, and he doubted she would ever visit. Not here, not in Parchman. Portia had stopped by to say hello but didn't hang around too long.

"What're you reading?" asked Denny from the top bunk. Denny was his new cell mate who'd been caught driving a stolen car. Simeon was already tired of him. He preferred living alone, though at times it was almost pleasant having someone to talk to.

"My wife just filed for divorce," he said.

"Lucky you. I've had two of them already. They get kinda crazy when you're in jail."

"If you say so. You ever had a restrainin' order?"

"No, but my brother did. Bitch convinced a judge he was dangerous, which he was, and a judge told him to stay away from the house and keep his distance in public. Didn't bother him. Killed her anyway."

"Your brother killed his wife?"

"Yep, but she had it coming. It was justifiable homicide, but the jury didn't exactly see it that way. Found him guilty of second-degree."

"Where is he?"

"Angola, Louisiana, twenty years. That's about what you'll get, accordin' to my lawyer."

"Your lawyer?"

"Yeah, I asked him this afternoon when I saw him. He knows about your case, said the whole town is talkin' about it, said folks are really upset. Said your wife's about to get rich from this big will contest but your ass'll be locked away for the next twenty years. By the time you get out all the money'll be gone, what with all the new friends she's got. That true?"

"Ask your lawyer."

"How'd your wife get herself into that old man's will like that? Said he left behind twenty million bucks or so, that true?"

"Ask your lawyer."

"I'll do that. Didn't mean to piss you off or anything."

"I ain't pissed. Just don't want to talk about it, okay?"

"You got it, man." Denny picked up his paperback and started reading.

Simeon stretched out on the bottom bunk and went back to page one. In twenty years he would be sixty-six. Lettie would have another husband and a much better life. She would have the children and grandchildren and probably great-grandchildren, and he would have nothing.

He wouldn't fight the divorce. She could have it all.

Maybe he could see Marvis in prison.

32

Eight days after the Roston tragedy, and just as it was beginning to wind down and folks were discussing other matters, it bolted back onto center stage in the weekly edition of *The Ford County Times*. On the front page, under a bold headline—COUNTY MOURNS LOSS OF ROSTON BROTHERS—were large class photos of Kyle and Bo. Below that and beneath the fold were photos of their wrecked car, their coffins being carried out of their church, and their classmates holding candles at a vigil outside Clanton High School. Dumas Lee had missed little. His stories were long and detailed.

On page two was a large photo of Simeon Lang, his face ominously bandaged, leaving the courthouse in handcuffs the previous Thursday with his attorney of record, Mr. Arthur Welch of Clarksdale. The story that accompanied the photo made no mention of Jake Brigance, primarily because Jake had threatened Dumas and the newspaper with a libel suit if it even remotely implied that he represented Simeon. There was mention of the old but still pending DUI charge from the previous October, but Dumas did not pursue it or imply that it had been improperly handled. He was terrified of litigation and usually backed down quickly. The two obituaries were lengthy and heartbreaking. There was a story from the high school with glowing comments from classmates and teachers. There was one from the accident scene with Ozzie providing the details. The eyewitness had a lot to say and got his photo in the newspaper. The parents were silent. An uncle asked that their privacy be respected.

Jake had read every word by 7:00 a.m., and felt exhausted. He skipped the Coffee Shop because he was tired of the endless prattling about the tragedy. He kissed Carla good-bye at 7:30 and went to the office, hoping for a return to his normal routine. His goal was to spend most of the day working on cases other than Hubbard. He had a handful of clients in real need of some attention.

Just after 8:00, Stillman Rush called with the news that he had just been fired by Herschel Hubbard. Jake listened thoughtfully. On the one hand he was delighted to see Stillman hit the back door because he really didn't care for the guy, but on the other hand he was bothered by Wade Lanier's powers of manipulation. In his only other major trial, that of Carl Lee Hailey, Jake had gone toe-to-toe with Rufus Buckley, then an accomplished district attorney. And while Buckley was quite skilled in the courtroom and smooth on his feet, he was not overly bright, not a crafty manipulator or a clever schemer. Not at all like Wade Lanier, who seemed to be always one step ahead. Jake was convinced Lanier would do anything, lie, cheat, steal, cover up, whatever it took to win at trial, and he had the experience, quick wit, and bag of tricks to do so. Jake wanted Stillman in the courtroom, bungling things and strutting in front of the jury.

Jake sounded sufficiently sad to say good-bye, but forgot about the call within the hour.

Portia needed reassuring. They had fallen into the habit of having a morning coffee around 8:30, always in Jake's office. The family had received four threatening calls in the days after the accident, but now the calls seemed to have stopped. A deputy still hung around the house, sitting in the driveway, checking the rear door at night, and the family was feeling safer. The Rostons had handled themselves with such grace and courage that the raw feelings had been contained, at least for now.

However, if Simeon decided he wanted a trial, then the entire nightmare would be replayed. Portia, Lettie, and the rest of the family were worried about the spectacle of a trial, of having to face the Roston family in court. Jake doubted that would ever happen, and if it did it would be at least a year away.

For three months, he had been prodding Lettie to get a job, any job. It would be important at trial for the jurors to know she was working and trying to support her family, not retired at forty-seven and expecting the windfall. But no white home-maker would hire her as a housekeeper, not with her baggage and controversies. She was too old for the fast-food joints; too black for anyone's office staff.

"Momma got a job," Portia said proudly.

"Excellent. Where?"

"The Methodist church. She'll clean their preschool three days a week. Minimum wage but that's all she can find right now."

"Is she happy?"

"She filed for divorce two days ago, Jake, and her last name is pretty toxic around here. She has a son in prison, a houseful of deadbeat relatives, a twenty-one-year-old daughter with two unwanted kids. Life's pretty tough for my mom. A job that pays three and a half bucks an hour is not likely to bring much happiness."

"Sorry I asked."

They were on his balcony, outside where the air was brisk but not too cold. Jake had a million things on his mind, and he'd already had a gallon of coffee.

"You remember Charley Pardue, my so-called cousin from Chicago?" she asked. "Met him at Claude's a couple of months ago."

"Sure. You called him a shyster who wants money for a new funeral home."

"Yep, we've been talking on the phone, and he's found a rela-tive over near Birmingham. An old guy in a nursing home, last name of Rinds. He thinks this guy could be the link."

"But Pardue is after money, right?"

"They're all after money. Anyway, I'm thinking about driving over this Saturday to find the old guy and ask him some questions."

"Is he a Rinds?"

"Yes, Boaz Rinds."

"Okay. Have you told Lucien?"

"I have, and he thinks it's worth the effort."

"Saturday is your day off. I'm not in charge."

"Just wanted you to know. And there's something else, Jake. Lucien told me the county keeps some of the ancient court-house records at Burley, the old black school."

"Yes, that's true. I went there once, looking for an old file, didn't find it. The county stores a lot of junk there."

"How far back do the records go?"

Jake thought for a moment. His phone rang in the distance. Finally, he said, "The land records are still in the courthouse because they get used. But a lot of stuff is basically worthless— marriage and divorce records, birth and death records, lawsuits, judgments, and so on. Most of it should be tossed out but no one wants to destroy court documents, not even from a hundred years ago. I heard once there are trial transcripts dating back to before the Civil War, all handwritten. Interesting, but of little value today. Too bad the fire didn't destroy it all."

"When was the fire?"

"Every courthouse burns at one time or another. Ours was severely damaged in 1948. A lot of records were lost."

"Can I dig through the old files?"

"Why? It's a waste."

"Because I love the legal history, Jake. I've spent hours in the courthouse reading old court files and land records. You can learn a ton about a place and its people. Did you know that in 1915 they hung a man in front of the courthouse one month after his trial? He robbed Security Bank, shot a man but didn't really hurt him, made off with $200, then got caught. They tried him on the spot, then strung him up."

"That's pretty efficient. I guess they didn't worry about over-crowded prisons."

"Or congested dockets. Anyway, I'm fascinated with this stuff. I've read an old will from 1847 where some white guy gave away his slaves; talked about how much he loved and treasured them, then gave them away like horses and cows."

"Sounds depressing. You'll never find a Brigance who owned a slave. We were lucky to have a cow."

"Anyway, I need written permission from a member of the bar to get into the old files. County rule."

"Done. Just do it after hours. You still digging for your roots?"

"Sure. I'm looking everywhere. The Rindses abruptly left this county in 1930 without a trace, without a clue, and I want to know why."

Lunch in the rear of Bates Grocery was a selection of four vegetables chosen at random from a collection of ten pots and skillets simmering on a large gas stove. Mrs. Bates herself pointed, dipped, served, and commented as she loaded the plates and handed them over while Mr. Bates punched the cash register and collected $3.50, iced tea included, with corn bread. Jake and Harry Rex made the drive out once a month when they needed to eat and talk without being overheard. It was a rural crowd, farmers and farmworkers with a pulpwood cutter sometimes thrown in for balance. All white. Blacks would be served without incident but that had yet to happen. Blacks shopped up front in the grocery; in fact, Tonya Hailey had bought a sack of groceries there and was walking the mile back to her home when she was abducted three years earlier.

The two lawyers huddled around a small table as far away as possible from the others. The table rocked and the ancient floor squeaked, and just above them a rickety fan spun unevenly, though it was still wintertime and the entire building was drafty. In another corner a potbellied stove radiated a thick, pungent heat that kept the narrow room comfortable. After a few bites, Harry Rex said, "Dumas did a good job, for him anyway. That boy loves a good car wreck as much as any lawyer."

"I had to threaten him, but, yes, he did us no harm. No more than was already done. Thanks for hauling in Arthur Welch for a cameo."

"He's an idiot, but my kind of idiot. The stories we could tell.

We once spent two nights in a county jail when we were supposed to be in law school. Almost got kicked out."

Jake knew better than to take the plunge but couldn't help himself. "Why were you in jail?"

Harry Rex shoveled in a load of collard greens and began, "Well, we'd been to New Orleans for a long weekend, and we were trying to get back to Ole Miss. I was driving, drinking, and somewhere down in Pike County we got lost. Saw blue lights, and I said, 'Shit, Welch, you gotta take the wheel. Here come the cops and I'm drunk.' Welch said, 'I'm drunk too big ass, you're on your own.' But we were in his car and I knew for a fact he was not as drunk as I was. I said, 'Hey Welch, you ain't had but a coupla beers. I'm stopping this thing right now and you get your ass over here.' The blue lights were getting closer. He said, 'No way. I been drunk since Friday. Plus, I already got one DUI and my old man'll kill me if I get another.' I hit the brakes and slid to a stop on the shoulder. The blue lights were right behind us. I grabbed Welch, who was quite a bit smaller back then, and tried to pull him over to the driver's side, and this really pissed him off. He fought back. He grabbed his door handle and stuck his feet into the floorboard and I couldn't budge him. I was really mad by now so I back-handed him, slapped the shit out of him right across the nose and this jolted him so bad he let go for a second. I grabbed his hair and yanked him over, but the car had a stick shift in the console and he got all caught up in it. We were both tangled up and mad as hell, cussing and clawing like a couple of cats. I had him in a death grip when the trooper said through the window, ''Scuse me fellas.'

"We froze. At the station, the trooper talked to both of us and declared us to be equally drunk. This was before Breathalyzers and such, back in the good old days." He gulped some tea, then attacked a small heap of fried okra.

"So what happened?" Jake finally asked.

"I wouldn't call my dad and Welch wouldn't call his. A lawyer was visiting a client in jail and heard about the two drunk Ole

Miss law students in a cell back there, sobering up and missing classes. He went to the judge, pulled some strings, and got us out. The dean was waiting on us at school, threatened to kill us or at least disbar us before we even graduated. With time we got it all dismissed. The dean knew I would be too valuable an addition to the state bar to give up on."

"Of course."

"Needless to say, Welch and I go way back. A lot of skeletons. He'll take care of Simeon until the will contest is over, then get rid of him. Dude's going down anyway, not much anybody can do for him."

"How much damage to our case?"

Lucien, the pessimist, was convinced the damage was irreparable, but Jake wasn't so sure. Harry Rex swiped his face with a cheap paper napkin and said, "You know how trials go, Jake. Once they start, the judge and lawyers and witnesses and jurors are all locked in the same room, all within spitting distance of each other. They hear everything, see everything, even feel everything. They tend to forget what's on the outside, what happened last week, last year. They're consumed with what's happening before their eyes, and with the decisions they'll have to make. My hunch is that they won't be thinking about Simeon Lang and the Roston boys. Lettie certainly had nothing to do with that tragedy. She's doing her best to get rid of Simeon, who's about to leave the county for a long time." A swig of tea, a bite of corn bread. "Right now it looks worrisome, but in a month or so it will be less so. I believe the jury will be so riveted by Seth Hubbard's will they won't spend much time thinking about a car wreck."

"I don't think they'll forget that easily. Wade Lanier will be there to remind them."

"You still plan to lobby Atlee for a change of venue?"

"That's the plan. We're meeting this Friday on his front porch, at my request."

"That's a bad sign. If he wants you to come over, fine. But if you have to ask, then it probably won't go so well."

"I don't know. I saw him at church Sunday and he asked how I was handling the situation. He seemed genuinely concerned and even willing to talk about the case after the sermon. Very unusual."

"Let me tell you something, Jake, about Atlee. I know you're close to him, or as close as any lawyer can get, but there's a darker side there. He's from the old school, the old South, old family ties and traditions. I'd bet that deep inside he's appalled at the notion of a white man taking the family money and leaving it to a black woman. We may one day understand why Seth Hubbard did what he did, or we may not, but regardless of why, Reuben Atlee doesn't like it at all. He's got what he's got because his ancestors passed it down. His family owned slaves, Jake."

"A thousand years ago. So did Lucien's."

"Yes, but Lucien's crazy. He wandered off the reservation a long time ago. He doesn't count. Atlee does, and don't expect him to do you any favors. He'll run a fair trial, but I'll bet his heart is with the other side."

"All we can ask for is a fair trial."

"Sure, but a fair trial in another county sounds better right now than a fair trial here."

Jake took a drink and spoke to a gentleman who passed by. He leaned in lower and said, "I still have to file a motion to change venue. It gives us something to argue on appeal."

"Oh sure. File it. But Atlee is not moving the case."

"Why are you so sure?"

"Because he's an old man in bad health and he doesn't want to drive a hundred miles every day. He's still the presiding judge, Jake, regardless of where the trial takes place. Atlee's lazy, like most judges, and he wants this spectacle of a case right here in his courtroom."

"So do I, to be perfectly honest."

"His days are filled with no-fault divorces and who gets the pots and pans. Like any other judge, he wants this case and he wants it at home. We can pick a jury here, Jake. I'm confident."

"We?"

"Of course. You can't do it by yourself. We proved that during the Hailey trial. You're okay in the courtroom but it's my brains that won the case."

"Gee, I didn't remember it that way."

"Just trust me, Jake. You want some banana pudding?"

"Sure, why not?"

Harry Rex lumbered over to the counter and paid for two hefty servings of dessert, in paper cups. The floor shook as he waddled back to their table and sat violently into his chair. With a mouth full, he said, "Willie Traynor called last night. Wants to know what you're thinking about that house."

"Judge Atlee told me not to buy it, not now anyway."

"Beg your pardon?"

"You heard me."

"Didn't know His Honor was in the real estate business."

"He thinks it might look bad, thinks the gossip will be that I'm clipping the estate for a chunk of money so I'm suddenly in the market for a fine old home."

"Tell Atlee to kiss your ass. Since when is he in charge of your personal affairs?"

"Oh he's very much in charge. He's approving my legal fees these days."

"Bullshit. Look, Jake, tell that old fart to take a hike, to mind his own business. You're gonna screw around and lose this house and then for the rest of your life, and dear Carla's too, ya'll will kick yourselves for not buying it."

"We cannot afford it."

"You cannot afford not to buy it. They don't build 'em like that anymore, Jake. Plus, Willie wants you to have it."

"Then tell him to cut the price."

"It's already below market."

"Not enough."

"Look, Jake, here's the deal. Willie needs the money. I don't know what he's up to, but evidently he's stretched pretty thin. He'll cut it from two fifty to two twenty-five. It's a steal, Jake. Hell I'd buy it if my wife would move."

"Get another wife."

"I'm thinking about it. Look, dumbass, here's what I'll do for you. You got your arson case so screwed up it'll never get settled. Why, because your client is yourself and they taught us in law school that a lawyer who represents himself has a fool for a client, right?"

"Something like that."

"So, I'll take the case at no charge and get it settled. Who's the insurance company?"

"Land Fire and Casualty."

"Crooked sonofabitches! Why'd you buy a policy from them?"

"Is that really helpful at this point?"

"No. What was their last offer?"

"It's a replacement value policy, for one fifty. Since we paid only forty thousand for the house, Land is claiming it was worth a hundred grand when it burned. I kept the receipts, invoices, contractors' bills, everything, and I can prove we put another fifty into the house. This was over a three-year period. That, plus market appreciation, and I'm claiming the house was worth a hundred and fifty when it burned. They won't budge. And they totally discount the sweat Carla and I poured into the house."

"And that pisses you off?"

"Damned right it does."

"See! You're too emotionally attached to the case to do any good. You have a fool for a client."

"Thanks."

"Don't mention it. How much is the mortgage?"

"Mortgages, plural. I refinanced it when the renovation was complete. The first mortgage is eighty thousand, the second is just under fifteen."

"So Land is offering you just enough to pay off both mortgages."

"Basically, yes, and we'd walk away with nothing."

"Okay, I'll make some phone calls."

"What kinda phone calls?"

"Settlement calls, Jake. It's the art of negotiation, and you got a lot to learn. I'll have them crooks on the run by five o'clock this afternoon. We'll settle the case, walk away with some cash, for you, nothing for me, then we'll put together a deal with Willie for the Hocutt House, and in the meantime you'll tell the Honorable Reuben Atlee to kiss your ass."

"I will?"

"Damned right you will."

33

Instead, Jake uttered not a single word that could have been considered even remotely disrespectful. They gathered on the porch on a windy but warm March afternoon and spent the first half hour talking about Judge Atlee's two sons. Ray was a law professor at the University of Virginia and had managed to live a peaceful, productive life, so far. Forrest, the younger, had not. Both had been shipped back east for boarding school, and thus were not well known in Clanton. Forrest was battling addictions and this weighed heavy on his father, who knocked back two whiskey sours in the first twenty minutes.

Jake paced himself. When the timing was right, he said, "I think our jury pool is contaminated, Judge. The Lang name is toxic around here and I don't think Lettie can get a fair trial."

"That convict should've had his license yanked anyway, Jake. I hear you and Ozzie were stalling his DUI. I don't like that at all."

Jake felt stung and took a deep breath. As a Chancellor, Reuben Atlee had absolutely no jurisdiction over drunk driving cases in the county, though, as always, he assumed they were his business.

Jake said, "That's not true, Judge, but even if Simeon Lang had no license he would've been driving anyway. A valid license is not important to those people. Ozzie set up a roadblock three months ago on a Friday night. Sixty percent of the blacks had no driver's license and 40 percent of the whites."

"I fail to see the relevance," Judge Atlee replied, and Jake was not about to enlighten him. "He was caught driving drunk in

October. If his case had been processed in an orderly manner through the courts, he would not have had a driver's license. There's a reasonable chance to believe he would not have been driving on Tuesday night of last week."

"I'm not his lawyer, Judge. Not now, not then."

Both rattled their ice cubes and let the moment pass. Judge Atlee took a sip and said, "File your motion to change venue if you wish. I can't stop you."

"I'd like for the motion to be taken seriously. I get the impression you made up your mind some time ago. Things have changed."

"I take everything seriously. We'll learn a lot when we start picking a jury. If it appears as though folks know too much about the case, then I'll call time-out and we'll deal with it. I thought I had explained this already."

"You have, yes sir."

"What happened to our pal Stillman Rush? He sent over a fax Monday and informed me he was no longer counsel of record for Herschel Hubbard."

"He got fired. Wade Lanier has been maneuvering for months, trying to consolidate the contestants into his camp. Looks like he scored big."

"Not much of a loss. Just one less lawyer to deal with. I found Stillman less than impressive."

Jake bit his tongue and managed to say nothing. If His Honor wanted to trash another lawyer, Jake was certainly willing to participate. But he had a hunch that nothing else would be said, not by the old guy.

"Have you met this fella Arthur Welch, from Clarksdale?" Judge Atlee asked.

"No sir. I just know he's a friend of Harry Rex's."

"We spoke by phone this morning and he says he'll represent Mr. Lang in the divorce also, though there won't be much to do. He says his client will agree to waive everything and get it over with. Not that it matters. With his bail, and the charges, he won't be getting out anytime soon."

Jake nodded in agreement. Arthur Welch was doing exactly what Harry Rex told him to do, and Harry Rex was briefing Jake on all of it.

"Thanks for granting the restraining order," Jake said. "That certainly read well in the newspaper."

"It seems rather foolish to tell a man who's in jail and locked up for a while that he can't get near his wife and family, but not everything I do makes sense."

True, Jake thought, but said nothing. They watched the grass bend with the wind and the leaves scatter. Judge Atlee sipped his drink and thought about what he'd just said. Changing the subject, he asked, "Any news on Ancil Hubbard?"

"Nothing, really. We've spent $30,000 so far and still don't know if he's alive. The pros suspect he is, though, primarily because they can find no evidence that he's ever died. But they're digging."

"Stay after it. I'm still cautious about proceeding to trial without something definite."

"We really should delay it for a few months, Judge, while we finish the search."

"And while the people around here get over the Roston tragedy."

"That too."

"Bring it up when we meet on March 20. I'll consider it then."

Jake took a deep breath and said, "Judge, I need to hire a jury consultant for the trial."

"What's a jury consultant?"

Jake was not surprised by the question. Jury consultants did not exist back in the judge's heyday as a lawyer, nor did His Honor pay attention to trends. Jake said, "An expert who does several things. First, he will study the demographics of the county and analyze this in light of the case to compose the model juror. He will then do a telephone survey using generic names but similar facts to gauge the public's reaction. Once we get the names in the pool, he'll do background research on all of the prospective jurors, at a safe distance of course. When the selection process begins, he'll actually be in the courtroom to observe the pool. These guys are quite good at reading body language and such. And once the trial starts he'll be in the courtroom every day reading the jurors. He'll know which witnesses are believed, which are not believed, and which way the jury is leaning."

"That's a lot. How much does he cost?"

Jake gritted his teeth and said, "Fifty thousand dollars."

"The answer is no."

"Sir?"

"No. I will not authorize the expenditure of that kind of money from the estate. Sounds like a waste to me."

"It's pretty standard these days in big jury trials, Judge."

"I find such a fee unconscionable. It's the lawyer's job to pick the jury, Jake, not some fancy consultant's. Back in my day, I relished the challenge of reading the minds and body language of prospective jurors and picking just the right ones. I had a real talent for it, Jake, if I do say so myself."

Yes sir. Like the case of the One-Eyed Preacher.

Back in his day, some thirty years earlier, young Reuben Atlee was hired by the First United Methodist Church of Clanton to defend it in a lawsuit brought by a Pentecostal evangelist who was in town whipping up the devotees in the annual Fall Revival. Part of his routine was to visit other mainstream churches in town and exorcise evil spirits on their front steps. He and a handful of his rabid followers claimed that these older, more sedate congregations were corrupting the Word of God and placating backsliders and otherwise serving as havens for alleged Christians who were lukewarm at best. God had ordered him to call out these heretics on their own turf, and so each afternoon during Revival Week! he and his little gang huddled at the various churches for prayers and rants. For the most part, they were ignored by the Methodists, Presbyterians, Baptists, and Episcopalians. At the Methodist church, the evangelist, while praying at full throttle and with his eyes fiercely closed, lost his balance and fell down eight marble steps. He was grievously wounded and suffered brain damage. He lost his right eye. A year later (1957) he filed suit, claiming negligence on the part of the church. He wanted $50,000.

Reuben Atlee was incensed over the lawsuit and eagerly took on the defense of the church, and for no fee. He was a man of faith and considered it his Christian duty to defend a legitimate house of worship from such a worthless claim. During jury selection, he famously and arrogantly told the judge, "Give me the first twelve."

The lawyer for the preacher wisely acceded, and the first twelve were sworn in and seated in the jury box. The lawyer proved the church's front steps were in bad repair and had been neglected for years. There had been complaints, and so on. Reuben Atlee stomped around the courtroom, full of arrogance and bluster and indignation that the lawsuit had even been filed. After two days, the jury gave the preacher $40,000, a record for Ford County. It was a nasty rebuke to lawyer Atlee and he was ridiculed for years, until he got himself elected Chancellor.

Later, it was learned that five of the first twelve jurors were also Pentecostals, a notoriously clannish and sensitive bunch. A cursory probing by any lawyer would have revealed this. Thirty years on, "Give me the first twelve" was often mumbled in jest by lawyers as they surveyed the pool of prospects sitting expectantly in the main courtroom.

The One-Eyed Preacher was later elected to the state senate, brain damage and all.

Jake said, "I'm sure Wade Lanier will have a jury consultant. He uses them all the time. I'm just trying to level the playing field. That's all."

"Did you use one in the Hailey trial?" Judge Atlee asked.

"No sir. I got paid $900 for that trial, Judge. By the time it was over I couldn't afford my telephone bill."

"And you won anyway. I'm getting concerned over the costs of this administration and litigation."

"The estate's worth twenty-four million, Judge. We haven't spent 1 percent of that."

"Yes, but at the rate you're going it won't be long."

"I'm not exactly padding the file."

"I'm not questioning your fees, Jake. But we've paid accountants, appraisers, Quince Lundy, you, investigators, court reporters, and now we're paying experts to testify at trial. I realize we're doing this because Seth Hubbard was foolish enough to make such a will, and he knew there would be a nasty fight over it, but, nonetheless, we have a duty to protect his estate." He made it sound as though the money was coming out of his own pocket. His tone was clearly unsympathetic, and Jake was reminded of Harry Rex's warnings.

He took a deep breath and let it pass. With two strikes—no change of venue, no jury consultant—Jake decided to leave things alone; he would try again another day. Not that it mattered. Judge Atlee was suddenly snoring.

Boaz Rinds lived in a sad, run-down nursing home on the edge of the north-south highway leading to and from the small town of Pell City, Alabama. After a four-hour drive, with some detours, wrong turns and dead ends, Portia and Lettie found the place just after lunch on a Saturday. Talking to distant kinfolk in Chicago, Charley Pardue had been able to track down Boaz. Charley was working hard to keep in touch with his newest and favorite cousin. The profit outlook for the funeral home was looking stronger each week, and it would soon be time to strike.

Boaz was in poor health and could barely hear. He was in a wheelchair but unable to maneuver it himself. They rolled him outside onto a concrete deck and left him there for the two ladies to interrogate. Boaz was just happy to have a visitor. There appeared to be no others on that Saturday. He said he was born "around" 1920 to Rebecca and Monroe Rinds, somewhere near Tupelo. That would mean he was around sixty-eight years old, which they found shocking. He looked much older, with snow-white hair and layers of wrinkles around his glassy eyes. He said he had a bad heart and had once smoked heavily.

Portia explained that she and her mother were trying to put together their family tree and there was a chance they might be related to him. This made him smile, a jagged one with missing teeth. Portia knew there was no birth record of a Boaz Rinds in Ford County, but by then she knew perfectly well how spotty the record keeping had been. He said he had two sons, both dead, and his wife had died years earlier. If he had grandkids he didn't know it. No one ever came to visit him. From the looks of the place, Boaz was not the only resident who'd been abandoned.

He spoke slowly, stopping occasionally to scratch his forehead while he tried to remember. After ten minutes, it was obvious he was suffering from some type of dementia. He'd had a harsh, almost brutal life. His parents were farmworkers who drifted throughout Mississippi and Alabama, dragging their large family—seven kids—from one cotton field to the next. He remembered picking cotton when he was five years old. He never went to school, and the family never stayed in one place. They lived in shacks and tents and hunger was not uncommon. His father died young and was buried behind a black church near Selma. His mother took up with a man who beat the kids. Boaz and a brother ran away and never went back.

Portia took notes as Lettie prodded with soft questions. Boaz loved the attention. An orderly brought them iced tea. He could not remember the names of his grandparents and did not remember anything about them. He thought they lived in Mississippi. Lettie asked about several names, all in the Rinds family. Boaz would grin, nod, then admit he didn't know the person. But when she said "Sylvester Rinds," he kept nodding, and nodding, and finally he said, "He was my uncle. Sylvester Rinds. He and my daddy were cousins."

Sylvester was born in 1898 and died in 1930. He owned the eighty acres that was deeded by his wife to Cleon Hubbard, father of Seth.

If Monroe Rinds, father of Boaz, was a cousin to Sylvester, then he wasn't really an uncle of Boaz's. However, in light of the meandering nature of the Rinds tree, they were not about to correct him. They were too thrilled to get this information. Lettie had come to believe her birth mother was Lois Rinds, the daughter of Sylvester, and she was anxious to prove it. She asked, "Sylvester owned some land, didn't he?"

The usual nod, then a smile. "Seem like he did. Believe so."

"Did you and your family ever live on his land?"

He scratched his forehead. "Believe so. Yes, when I was a little boy. I remember it now, pickin' cotton on my uncle's land. Remember now. And there was a fight over payin' us for the cotton." He rubbed his lips and mumbled something.

"So there was a disagreement, and what happened?" Lettie asked gently.

"We left there and went to another farm, don't know where. We worked so many."

"Do you remember if Sylvester had any children?"

"Ever'body had kids."

"Do you remember any of Sylvester's?"

Boaz scratched and thought so hard he eventually nodded off. When they realized he was napping, Lettie gently shook his arm and said, "Boaz, do you remember any of Sylvester's kids?"

"Push me over there, in the sun," he said, pointing to a spot on the deck that wasn't shaded. They rolled him over and rearranged their lawn chairs. He sat as straight as possible, looked up at the sun, and closed his eyes. They waited. Finally, he said, "Don't know 'bout that. Benson."

"Who was Benson?"

"The man who beat us."

"Do you remember a little girl named Lois? Lois Rinds?"

He jerked his head toward Lettie and said, quickly and clearly, "I do. Now I remember her. She was Sylvester's little girl, and they owned the land. Lois. Little Lois. It won't common, you know, for colored folk to own land, but I remember now. At first it was good, then they had a fight."

Lettie said, "I think Lois was my mother."

"You don't know?"

"No, I don't. She died when I was three and somebody else adopted me. But I'm a Rinds."

"Me too. Always have been," he said, and they laughed. Then he looked sad and said, "Not much of a family now. Ever'body's so scattered."

"What happened to Sylvester?" Lettie asked.

He grimaced and shifted weight as if in great pain. He breathed heavily for a few minutes and seemed to forget the question. He looked at the two women as if he'd never seen them before, and wiped his nose on a sleeve. Then he returned to the moment and said, "We left. Don't know. Heard later that somethin' bad happened."

"Any idea what?" Portia's pen was not moving.

"They killed him."

"Who killed him?"

"White men."

"Why did they kill him?"

Another drifting away as if the question had not been heard. Then, "Don't know. We were gone. I remember Lois now. A sweet little girl. Benson was the man who beat us."

Portia was wondering if they could believe anything at this point. His eyes were closed and his ears were twitching as if gripped by a seizure. He repeated, "Benson, Benson."

"And Benson married your mother?" Lettie asked gently.

"All we heard was some white men got him."

34

Jake was in the middle of a fairly productive morning when he heard the unmistakable sound of Harry Rex's size 13s clomping up his already battered wooden staircase. He took a deep breath, waited, then watched as the door burst open without the slightest trace of a polite knock. "Good morning, Harry Rex," he said.

"You ever heard of the Whiteside clan from over by the lake?" he asked, huffing as he fell into a chair.

"Distantly. Why do—"

"Craziest bunch of lunatics I've ever run across. Last weekend Mr. Whiteside caught his wife in bed with one of their sons-in-law, so that makes two divorces all of a sudden. Before that, one of their daughters had filed and I got that one. So now I got—"

"Harry Rex, please, I really don't care." Jake knew the stories could go on forever.

"Well, excuse me. I'm here because they're all in my office right now, kicking and scratching, and we just had to call the law. I'm so sick of my clients, all of them." He wiped his forehead with a sleeve. "You got a Bud Light?"

"No. I have some coffee."

"The last thing I need. I talked to the insurance company this morning and they're offering one thirty-five. Take it, okay? Now."

Jake thought he was joking and almost laughed. The insurance company had been stuck on $100,000 for two years. "You're serious?"

"Yes, I'm serious dear client. Take the money. My secretary is typing the settlement agreement now. She'll bring it over by noon. Take it and get Carla to sign it and hustle the damned thing back to my office. Okay?"

"Okay. How'd you do it?"

"Jake, my boy, here's where you screwed up. You filed the case in Circuit Court and demanded a jury because after the Hailey trial you let your ego get carried away and you figured any insurance company would be terrified of facing you, the great Jake Brigance, in front of a jury in Ford County. I saw it. Others saw it. You sued for punitive damages and you figured you'd get a big verdict, make some real money, and knock a home run on the civil side. I know you and I know that's what you were thinking, deny it or not. When the insurance company didn't blink, the two sides settled into the trenches, things got personal, and the years went by. The case needed a fresh set of eyes, and it also needed someone like me who knows how insurance companies think. Plus, I told them I'd non-suit the case in Circuit Court, dismiss it, and then refile in Chancery Court where I pretty much control the docket and everything else. The idea of facing me in Chancery Court, in this county, is not something other lawyers like to think about. So we pushed and shoved and bitched a little, and I finally got 'em up to one thirty-five. You'll clear about forty, no fee for me because that was the deal, and you're back on your feet. I'll call Willie and tell him you and Carla will pay two twenty-five for the Hocutt place."

"Not so fast, Harry Rex. I'm hardly rich with forty grand in my pocket."

"Don't bullshit me, Jake. You're clipping the estate for thirty thousand a month."

"Not quite, and the rest of my practice is disappearing in the process. It'll take me a year to get over this case. Same as Hailey."

"But at least you're getting paid on this one."

"I am, and I appreciate you using your amazing skills to settle my fire claim. Thank you, Harry Rex. I'll get the paperwork signed by this afternoon. And, I'd feel better if you would take a fee. A modest one."

"Not for a friend, Jake, and not a modest one. If it were a fat fee I'd say screw the friendship. Besides, I can't take any more income this quarter. Money's piling up so fast I can't stuff any more in the mattress. I don't want the IRS becoming alarmed and sending in their goons again. It's on me. What do I tell Willie?"

"Tell him to keep cutting the price."

"He's in town this weekend, throwing another gin-and-tonic party Saturday afternoon. He told me to invite you and Carla. Ya'll in?"

"I'll have to ask the boss."

Harry Rex climbed to his feet and began stomping away. "See you Saturday."

"Sure, and thanks again, Harry Rex."

"Don't mention it." He slammed the door, and Jake chuckled to himself. What a relief to have the lawsuit settled. He could close a rather thick and depressing fish file, pay off the two mortgages, get the banks off his back, and pocket some cash. He and Carla could never replace their home, but wasn't that the case in every major fire claim? They weren't the only ones who'd lost everything in a disaster. Finally, they could move on and put the past behind them.

Five minutes later, Portia knocked on the door. She had something to show Jake, but they would need to take a short drive.

At noon, they left the office and crossed the tracks and drove through Lowtown, the colored section. Beyond it, at the far eastern edge of Clanton, was Burley, the old black elementary and middle school that had been abandoned in 1969 with desegregation. Not long afterward, it had been reclaimed by the county, spruced up, and put to good use as a facility for storage and maintenance. The school was a complex of four large, barnlike buildings of white wood and tin roofs. The parking lot was filled with the vehicles of county employees. Behind the school was a large maintenance shed with gravel trucks and machinery scattered around it. East, the black high school, was across the street.

Jake had known many blacks who'd gone to school at Burley, and while they were always grateful for an integrated system, there was usually a twinge of nostalgia for the old place and the old ways. They got the leftovers, the worn-out desks, books, chalkboards, typewriters, file cabinets, athletic gear, band instruments, everything. Nothing was new, it was all discarded from the white schools in Ford County. The white teachers earned less than those in any other state, and the black teachers earned only a fraction of that. Combined, there wasn't enough money for a single good school system, but for decades the county, like all the rest, tried to maintain two. Separate but equal was a cruel farce. But in spite of its sizable disadvantages, Burley was a place of pride for those lucky enough to study there. The teachers were tough and dedicated. The odds were against them, so their successes were even sweeter. Occasionally, an alum made it through college, and he or she became a model for the younger generations.

"You say you've been here," Portia said as they walked up the steps to what was once the administration building.

"Yes, once, during my rookie year with Lucien. He sent me on a goose chase to find some ancient court records. I struck out."

They climbed the stairs to the second floor. Portia knew exactly where to go and Jake followed along. The classrooms were now packed with recycled Army file cabinets filled with old tax records and property assessments. Nothing but junk, Jake thought to himself as he read the index placards on the doors. One room held car registration records, another archived ancient editions of the local newspapers. And so on. What a waste of space and manpower.

Portia flipped on the light to a dark, windowless room, also lined with file cabinets. From a shelf she carefully lifted a heavy tome and placed it gently on a table. It was bound in dark green leather, cracked now after decades of aging and neglect. In the

center was one word: "Docket." She said, "This is a docket book
from the 1920s, specifically August of 1927 through October of
1928." She opened it slowly and with great care began turning
the yellow and fragile, almost flaky pages. "Chancery Court,"
she said, much like a curator in command of her subject matter.

"How much time have you spent here?" Jake asked.

"I don't know. Hours. I'm fascinated by this stuff, Jake. The
history of the county is right here in the history of its legal system."
She turned more pages, then stopped. "Here it is. June of 1928,
sixty years ago." Jake leaned down for a closer look. All entries
were by hand and the ink had faded significantly. With an index
finger she went down one column and said, "On June 4, 1928."
She moved to the right, to the next column. "The plaintiff, a man
named Cleon Hubbard, filed a lawsuit against the defendant."
She moved to the next column. "A man named Sylvester Rinds."
She moved to the next column. "The lawsuit was described
simply as a property dispute. Next column shows the attorney.
Cleon Hubbard was represented by Robert E. Lee Wilbanks."

"That's Lucien's grandfather," Jake said. Both were hunched
over the docket book, shoulder to shoulder. She said, "And the
defendant was represented by Lamar Thisdale."

"An old guy, dead for thirty years. You still see his name on
wills and deeds. Where's the file?" Jake asked, taking a step back.
She stood straight and said, "I can't find it." She waved an arm
around the room. "If it exists, it should be in here, but I've
looked everywhere. There are gaps in everything and I guess it's
because of the courthouse burning down."

Jake leaned on a file cabinet and pondered things. "So, they
were fighting over some land in 1928."

"Yes, and it's safe to say it's the eighty acres Seth owned when
he died. We know from Lucien's research that Sylvester owned
no other land at that time. Cleon Hubbard took title to the property in 1930 and it's been in the Hubbard family ever since."

"And the fact that Sylvester still owned the land in 1930 is
pretty clear evidence he won this lawsuit in 1928. Otherwise,
Cleon Hubbard would have owned it."

"That's what I was going to ask you. You're the lawyer. I'm just the lowly secretary."

"You're becoming a lawyer, Portia. I'm not sure you even need law school. Are you assuming Sylvester was your great-grandfather?"

"Well, my mother is pretty sure these days that he was her grandfather, that his only child was Lois, and that Lois was her mother. That would make the old guy my great-grandfather, not that we're that close or anything."

"Have you told Lucien what his ancestors were up to?"

"No. Should I? I mean, why bother? It's not his fault. He wasn't alive."

"I would do it just to torment him. He'll feel like crap if he knows his people represented old man Hubbard, and lost."

"Come on, Jake. You know how Lucien hates his family and their history."

"Yes, but he loves their assets. I would tell him."

"Do you think the Wilbanks firm has any of its old records?"

Jake grunted and smiled and said, "I doubt if they go back sixty years. There's a pile of junk in the attic, but nothing this old. As a rule, lawyers throw away nothing, but over time the stuff just disappears."

"Can I go through the attic?"

"I don't care. What are you looking for?"

"The file, something with clues. It's pretty clear there was a dispute over the eighty acres, but what was behind it? And what happened in the case? How could a black man win a lawsuit over land in the 1920s in Mississippi? Think about it, Jake. A white landowner hired the biggest law firm in town, one with all the power and connections, to sue some poor black man over a property dispute. And the black man won, or so it appears."

"Maybe he didn't win. Maybe the case was still dragging on when Sylvester died."

"Exactly. That's it, Jake. That's what I have to find out."

"Good luck. I'd tell Lucien everything and enlist his help. He'll cuss his ancestors, but he does that before breakfast most days anyway. He'll get over it. Believe me, they did far worse."

"Great. I'll tell him, and I'll start digging through the attic this afternoon."

"Be careful. I go up there once a year and only when I have to. I seriously doubt you'll find anything."

"We'll see."

Lucien took it well. He offered a few of his usual vile condemnations of his heritage but seemed placated by the fact that his grandfather had lost the case against Sylvester Rinds. Without invitation, he launched into history and explained to Portia, and at times throughout the afternoon to Jake as well, that Robert E. Lee Wilbanks had been born during Reconstruction and had spent most of his life laboring under the belief that slavery would one day return. The family managed to keep the carpetbaggers away from its land, and Robert, to his credit, built a dynasty that included banks, railroads, politics, and the law. He'd been a harsh, unpleasant man, and as a child Lucien had feared him. But give the devil his due. The fine home Lucien now owned had been built by dear old grandpa and properly handed down.

After hours, they climbed to the attic and slid further into history. Jake hung around for a while, but soon realized it was a waste of time. The files went back to 1965, the year Lucien inherited the law firm after his father and uncle were killed in a plane crash. Someone, probably Ethel Twitty, the legendary secretary, had cleaned house and purged the old records.

35

Two weeks before the scheduled start of the war, the lawyers and their staffs met in the main courtroom for a pretrial conference. Such gatherings were unheard-of back in the old days, but the more modern rules of engagement called for them and even provided an acronym, the PTC. Lawyers like Wade Lanier who fought on the civil side were well versed in the strategies and nuances of the PTC. Jake less so. Reuben Atlee had never presided over one, though he would not admit this. For him and his Chancery Court, a major trial was a nasty divorce with money on the line. These were rare, and he handled them the same way he had for thirty years, modern rules be damned.

Critics of the new rules of discovery and procedure whined that the PTC was nothing more than a rehearsal for the trial, and thus it required the lawyers to prepare twice. It was time-consuming, expensive, burdensome, and also restrictive. A document, an issue, or a witness not properly covered in the PTC could not be considered at trial. Old lawyers like Lucien who reveled in dirty tricks and ambushes hated the new rules because they were designed to promote fairness and transparency. "Trials are not about fairness, Jake, trials are about winning," he'd said a thousand times.

Judge Atlee wasn't too keen on them either, though he was duty-bound to follow them. At ten o'clock Monday morning, March 20, he shooed away the handful of spectators and told the bailiff to lock the door. This was not a public hearing.

As the lawyers were getting situated, Lester Chilcott, Lanier's co-counsel, walked over to Jake's table and laid down some paperwork. "Updated discovery," he said, as if everything were routine. As Jake flipped through it, Judge Atlee called them to order and began scanning faces to make sure all lawyers were present. "Still missing Mr. Stillman Rush," he mumbled into his microphone.

Jake's surprise quickly turned to anger. In a section where all potential witnesses were listed, Lanier had included the names of forty-five people. Their addresses were scattered throughout the Southeast, with four in Mexico. Jake recognized only a handful; a few he had actually deposed during discovery. A "document dump" was a common dirty trick, one perfected by corporations and insurance companies, in which they and their lawyers hid discoverable documents until the last possible moment. They then dumped several thousand pages of documents on the opposing lawyer just before the trial, knowing he and his staff could not possibly dig through them in time. Some judges were angered by document dumps; others let them slide. Wade Lanier had just pulled off a "witness dump," a close cousin. Withhold the names of many of the potential witnesses until the last moment, then hand them over along with a bunch of surplus names to bewilder the opponent.

The opponent seethed, but suddenly had more pressing matters. Judge Atlee said, "Now, Mr. Brigance, you have two motions pending. One to change venue, the other for a continuance. I've read your briefs, and the responses from the contestants, and I'm assuming you have nothing more to add to these motions."

Jake rose and wisely said, "No sir."

"Just keep your seats, gentlemen. This is a pretrial conference, not a formal hearing. Now, is it also safe to assume there has been no progress in the search for Ancil Hubbard?"

"Yes sir, that's safe to assume, though with more time we may make some progress."

Wade Lanier stood and said, "Your Honor, please, I'd like to respond. The presence or absence of Ancil Hubbard is of no importance here. The issues have been boiled down to what we expected, to those always in play in a will contest; to wit, testamentary capacity and undue influence. Ancil, if he's alive, did not see his brother Seth for decades prior to Seth's suicide. Ancil can't possibly testify to how or what his brother was thinking. So let's proceed as planned. If the jury finds in favor of the handwritten will, then Mr. Brigance and the estate will have plenty of time to keep searching for Ancil and hopefully give him his 5 percent. But if the jury rejects the handwritten will, then Ancil himself becomes irrelevant because he's not mentioned in the prior will. Let's move on, Judge. You set the trial date of April 3 many months ago, and there's no good reason not to go on as planned."

Lanier was not flashy, but he was down-to-earth, even homey, and persuasive. Jake had already learned the man could argue effortlessly off-the-cuff and convince anybody of just about anything.

"I agree," Judge Atlee said gruffly. "We will proceed as planned on April 3. Here, in this courtroom. Please sit down, Mr. Lanier."

Jake took notes and waited for the next argument. Judge Atlee looked at his notes, adjusted the reading glasses far down his nose, and said, "I count six lawyers sitting over here on the contestants' side of the courtroom. Mr. Lanier is the chief counsel for the children of Seth Hubbard—Ramona Dafoe and Herschel Hubbard. Mr. Zeitler is the chief counsel for the two children of Herschel Hubbard. Mr. Hunt is the chief counsel for the two children of Ramona Dafoe. The rest of you guys are associates." He removed his glasses and stuck a stem in his mouth. A lecture was coming. "Now gentlemen, when we get to trial, I have no intention of tolerating a lot of excessive and unnecessary chatter from six lawyers. In fact, no one except lawyers Lanier, Zeitler, and Hunt will be allowed to speak in court on behalf of the contestants. God knows that should be enough. And, I'm not going to subject the jury to three different opening statements, three different closing arguments, and three different examinations of witnesses. If there is an objection, I do not want three or four of you jumping up and waving

your arms and yelling, 'Objection!' 'Objection!' Do you follow
me?"

Of course they did. He was speaking slowly, clearly, and with
his usual heavy authority. He continued, "I suggest that Mr.
Lanier take the lead for the contestants and handle the bulk of
the trial. He certainly has more trial experience, not to mention
the clients with the greatest interests. Divide the work any way
you want—I wouldn't dare give advice," he said gravely, advis-
ing. "I'm not trying to muzzle anyone. You have the right to
advocate for your client or clients. Each of you may call your
own witnesses and cross-examine those called by the proponents. But the first time you start repeating what's already been
said, as lawyers have a natural inclination to do, you can expect
swift intervention from up here. I will not tolerate it. Are we on
the same page?"

They certainly were, for the moment anyway.

He jammed the reading glasses back onto his nose and looked
at his notes. "Let's talk about exhibits," he said. They spent an
hour discussing the documents that would be admitted into
evidence and shown to the jury. At Judge Atlee's heavy-handed
insistence, the handwriting was stipulated to be that of Henry
Seth Hubbard. Arguing otherwise would be a waste of time. The
cause of death was stipulated. Four large color photos were
approved. They showed Seth hanging from the tree and elimi-
nated any doubt as to how he died.

Then Judge Atlee said, "Now, let's review the witnesses. I see
that Mr. Lanier has added quite a few."

Jake had been waiting impatiently for over an hour. He tried
to keep his cool, but it was difficult. He said, "Your Honor, I'm
going to object to a lot of these witnesses being allowed to testify
at trial. If you'll look on page six, beginning there and running
for a while, you see the names of forty-five potential witnesses.
Looking at their addresses, I'm assuming these people worked
in Mr. Hubbard's various factories and plants. I don't know
because I've never seen these names before. I've checked the
latest updated responses to interrogatories, and of the forty-five,

only fifteen or sixteen have ever been mentioned by the contestants before today. Under the rules, I was entitled to have these
names months ago. It's called a witness dump, Your Honor.
Dump a pile of witnesses on the table two weeks before the trial,
and there's no way I can possibly talk to them all and find out
what their testimony might be. Forget depositions—it would
take another six months. This is a clear violation of the rules,
and it's underhanded."

Judge Atlee scowled at the other table and said, "Mr. Lanier?"

Lanier stood and said, "May I stretch my legs, Your Honor? I
have a bad knee."

"Whatever."

Lanier began pacing in front of his table, limping slightly.
Probably a courtroom trick of some variety, Jake thought.

"Your Honor, this is not underhanded and I resent the accu-
sation. Discovery is always a work in progress. New names are
always popping up. Reluctant witnesses sometimes come
forward at the last minute. One witness remembers another one,
or another one, or he remembers something else that happened.
We've had investigators digging and digging for five months
now, nonstop, and, frankly, we've outworked the other side.
We've found more witnesses, and we're still looking for more.
Mr. Brigance has two weeks to call or go see any witness on my
list. Two weeks. No, it's not a lot of time, but is there ever enough
time? We know there is not. This is the way high-powered litigation goes, Your Honor. Both sides scramble until the very last
moment." Pacing, limping, arguing quite effectively, Lanier
inspired grudging admiration, though at the same time Jake
wanted to throw a hatchet at him. Lanier did not play by the
rules but he was quite adept at legitimizing his cheating.

For Wade Lanier, it was a crucial moment. Buried in the list
of forty-five was the name Julina Kidd, the only black woman
Randall Clapp had found so far who was willing to testify and
admit she'd slept with Seth. For $5,000 plus expenses, she had
agreed to travel to Clanton and testify. She had also agreed to
ignore phone calls or any contact from any other lawyer, namely

one Jake Brigance, who might show up desperately sniffing around for clues.

Not buried in the list was Fritz Pickering; his name had not been mentioned, nor would it be until a critical moment in the trial.

Judge Atlee asked Jake, "How many depositions have you taken?"

Jake replied, "Together, we've taken thirty depositions."

"Sounds like a lot to me. And they're not cheap. Mr. Lanier, surely you don't plan to call forty-five witnesses."

"Of course not, Your Honor, but the rules require us to list all potential witnesses. I may not know until we're in the middle of the trial who I need next on the stand. This is the flexibility the rules contemplate."

"I understand that. Mr. Brigance, how many witnesses do you plan to call?"

"Approximately fifteen, Your Honor."

"Well, I can tell you fellas right now I'm not going to subject the jury, or myself, to the testimony of sixty witnesses. At the same time, I'm not inclined to restrict who you may or may not call at trial. Just make sure all witnesses are disclosed to the other side. Mr. Brigance, you have all the names and you have two weeks to dig."

Jake shook his head in frustration. The old Chancellor couldn't help but revert to his old ways. Jake asked, "Then would it be possible to require the attorneys to submit a brief overview of what each witness might say on the stand? This seems only fair, Your Honor."

"Mr. Lanier?"

"I'm not sure how fair it is, Your Honor. Just because we've hustled our butts off and found a bunch of witnesses Mr. Brigance has never heard of doesn't mean we should be required to tell him what they might say. Let him do the work." The tone was condescending, almost insulting, and for a split second Jake felt like a slacker.

"I agree," Judge Atlee said. Lanier shot Jake a look of contemptuous victory as he walked by him and sat down again.

The PTC dragged on as they discussed the expert witnesses and what they might say. Jake was irritated at Judge Atlee and did not try to hide his feelings. The highlight of the meeting was the distribution of the jury list, and the judge saved it for last. It was almost noon when a clerk distributed it. "There are ninety-seven names," Atlee said, "and they've been screened for everything but age. As you know, some folks over the age of sixty-five do not want to be exempted from service, so I'll let you gentlemen handle that during selection."

The lawyers scanned the names, looking for friendly ones, sympathetic ones, smart folks who would instantly side with them and bring back the right verdict. Atlee went on, "Now, and listen to me, I will not tolerate contact with these people. As I understand the nature of big lawsuits these days, it's not unusual for the attorneys to investigate the jury pool as thoroughly as possible. Go right ahead. But do not contact them, or follow them, or frighten them, or in any way harass them. I will deal harshly with anyone who does. Keep these lists close. I do not want the entire county knowing who's in the pool."

Wade Lanier asked, "In what order will they be seated for selection, Your Honor?"

"Entirely at random."

The lawyers were silent as they rapidly read through the names. Jake had a distinct advantage because it was home turf. Every time he looked at a jury list, though, he was astonished at how few names he recognized. A former client here, a church member there. A high school buddy from Karaway. His mother's first cousin. A quick review yielded maybe twenty hits out of ninety-seven. Harry Rex would know even more. Ozzie would know all the black ones and many of the whites. Lucien would boast about how many he knew, but in reality he'd been sitting on the front porch for too long.

Wade Lanier and Lester Chilcott, from Jackson, recognized no one, but they would have plenty of help. They were chumming up with the Sullivan firm, at nine lawyers still the biggest in the county, and there would be a lot of advice.

At 12:30, Judge Atlee was tired and dismissed everyone. Jake hurried out of the courtroom, wondering if the old man was physically up to a grueling trial. He was also worried about which rules would control the trial. It was obvious the official rules, the new ones on the books, would not be strictly adhered to.

Regardless of the rules, Jake, and every other lawyer in the state, knew the Supreme Court of Mississippi was famous for deferring to the wisdom of local Chancellors. They were there, in the heat of the battle. They saw the faces, heard the testimony, felt the tension. Who are we, the Supreme Court had asked itself over the decades, to sit here far removed and dispassionately substitute our judgment for Chancellor So-and-So?

As always, the trial would be governed by Reuben's Rules.

Whatever they happened to be at any particular moment.

Wade Lanier and Lester Chilcott walked straight to the offices of the Sullivan firm and made their way to a conference room on the second floor. A platter of sandwiches was waiting, as was a feisty little man with a crisp Upper Midwest accent. He was Myron Pankey, a former lawyer who'd found a niche in the relatively new field of jury consultation, an area of expertise now nudging itself into many major trials. For a handsome fee, Pankey and his staff would work all sorts of miracles and deliver the perfect jury, or at least the best available. A phone survey had already been done. Two hundred registered voters in counties adjoining Ford County had been interviewed. Fifty percent said a person should be able to leave his or her estate to anyone, even at the expense of his or her own family. But 90 percent would be suspicious of a handwritten will that left everything to the last caregiver. The data had piled up and was still being analyzed at Pankey's home office in Cleveland. Race was not a factor in any part of the survey.

Based on the preliminary numbers, Wade Lanier was optimistic. He ate a sandwich while standing and talking and sipping a Diet Coke through a straw. Copies of the jury lists were made and scattered across the conference table. Each of the nine members of the Sullivan firm was given a copy and asked to review the names as soon as possible, though all were swamped as usual and just couldn't see how they could add five more minutes of work to their overloaded schedules.

A greatly enlarged road map of Ford County was mounted along one wall. A former Clanton cop named Sonny Nance was already sticking numbered pins onto streets and roads where the jurors lived. Nance was from Clanton, married to a woman from Karaway, and said he knew everyone. He'd been hired by Myron Pankey to showcase this knowledge. At 1:30, four more new employees arrived and received their instructions. Lanier was blunt but precise. He wanted color photos of each home, each neighborhood, each vehicle if possible. If there were stickers on the bumpers, take photos. But do not, under any circumstances, take the risk of getting caught. Pose as survey takers, bill collectors, insurance runners delivering checks, door-to-door proselytizers, whatever might be believable, but talk to the neighbors and learn what you can without being suspicious. Do not, under any circumstances, have direct contact with any potential juror. Find out where these people work, worship, and send their kids to school. We have the basics—name, age, sex, race, address, voting precinct—and nothing else. So there are a lot of blanks to be filled in.

Lanier said, "You cannot get caught. If your activity arouses suspicion, then immediately disappear. If you are confronted, give them a bogus name and report back here. Even if you think you might be spotted, leave, disappear, and eventually call in. Questions?"

None of the four were from Ford County, so the chances of being recognized were zero. Two were former cops, two were part-time investigators; they knew how to work the streets. "How much time do we have?" one asked.

"The trial starts two weeks from today. Check in every other day and give us the info you've collected. Friday of next week is the deadline."

"Let's go," one said.

"And don't get caught."

Jake's expert trial consultant was also his secretary/paralegal. Since Judge Atlee was now administering the estate as if all funds came directly from his own tight pocket, a real consultant was out of the question. Portia would be in charge of gathering the data, or rather, keeping up with all of it. At 4:30 Monday afternoon, she, Jake, Lucien, and Harry Rex gathered in a workroom on the second floor, next to her old office. Present also was Nick Norton, a lawyer from across the square who had represented Marvis Lang two years earlier.

They went through all ninety-seven names.

36

From their looks and accents it was obvious to Lonny they were a bunch of Russians, and after watching them drink straight vodka for an hour, he was certain. Crude, crass, loud, and looking for trouble. They would pick a night when only one bouncer was on duty. The owner of the bar had threatened to post a sign barring all Russians, but of course he could not. Lonny figured they were crewing a cargo ship, probably one hauling grain from Canada.

He called the other bouncer at home but got no answer. The owner wasn't there and, at the moment, Lonny was in charge. More vodka was ordered. Lonny thought about cutting it with water, but these guys would know it immediately. When one slapped a waitress on her shapely rear end, events spiraled out of control, and quickly. The lone bouncer, a man who had never shied away from violence, barked at the offending Russian, who barked back in another language while rising angrily. He threw a wild punch, which missed, and then took one that didn't. From across the room, a gang of patriotic bikers hurled beer bottles at the Russians, all of whom were springing into action. Lonny said, "Oh shit!" and thought about leaving through the kitchen, but he'd seen it all before, many times. His bar had a tough reputation, which was one reason it paid so well, and in cash.

When another waitress was knocked down, he ducked around the bar to help her. The melee raged on just a few feet away, and as he reached to grab her a blunt object of some variety struck him in the back of his head. He fell comatose, blood pouring from his wound and draining into his long gray ponytail. At sixty-six, Lonny was simply too old to even watch such a brawl.

For two days he lay unconscious in a Juneau hospital. The owner of the bar reluctantly came forward and admitted he had no paperwork on the man. Just a name—Lonny Clark. A detective was hanging around, and when it became apparent he might never wake up, a plan was hatched. The owner told them which flophouse Lonny called home, and the cops broke in. Along with almost nothing in the way of assets, they found thirty kilos of cocaine wrapped neatly in foil and seemingly untouched. Under the mattress, they also found a small plastic binder with a zipper. Inside was about $2,000 in cash; an Alaska driver's license that turned out to be fake, name of Harry Mendoza; a passport, also fake, for Albert Johnson; another fake passport for Charles Noland; a stolen Wisconsin driver's license for Wilson Steglitz, expired; and a yellowed naval discharge summary for one Ancil F. Hubbard, dated May 1955. The binder consisted of Lonny's worldly assets, discounting of course the cocaine, which had a street value of roughly $1.5 million.

It took the police several days to verify records and such, and by then Lonny was awake and feeling better. The police decided not to approach him about the coke until he was ready to be discharged. They kept an officer in street clothes outside his room. Since the only legitimate names in his arsenal appeared to be Ancil F. Hubbard and Wilson Steglitz, they entered them into the national crime computer system to see what, if anything, might turn up. The detective began chatting with Lonny, stopping by and bringing him milk shakes, but there was no mention of the drugs. After a few visits, the detective said they could find no records of a man named Lonny Clark. Birth place and date, Social Security number, state of residence? Anything, Lonny?

Lonny, who'd spent a lifetime running and ducking, grew suspicious and less talkative. The detective asked, "You ever know a man by the name of Harry Mendoza?"

Oh really? From where and when? How? Under what circumstances? Nothing.

What about Albert Johnson, or Charles Noland? Lonny said maybe he'd met those men long ago but wasn't sure. His memory was foggy, coming and going. He had, after all, a cracked skull and a bruised brain, and, well, he couldn't remember much before the fight. Why all the questions?

By then Lonny knew they had been in his room, but he wasn't sure if they had found the cocaine. There was an excellent chance the man who owned it went to the flophouse not long after the fight and removed it himself. Lonny was not a dealer; he was just doing a friend a favor, one for which he was to be paid nicely. So, the question was whether the cops had found the cocaine. If so, Lonny was in some serious trouble. The less he said the better. As he had learned decades earlier, when the cops start asking serious questions, deny, deny, deny.

Jake was at his desk when Portia rang through and said, "It's Albert Murray." Jake grabbed the phone and said hello.

Murray ran a firm out of D.C. and specialized in locating missing persons, both nationally and internationally. So far, the estate of Seth Hubbard had paid the firm $42,000 to find a long-lost brother and had almost nothing to show for it. Its results had been thoroughly unimpressive, though its billing procedures rivaled those of any big-city law firm.

Murray, always skeptical, began with "We have a soft hit on Ancil Hubbard, but don't get excited." He relayed the facts as he knew them—an assumed name of Lonny, a bar brawl in Juneau, a cracked skull, lots of cocaine, and fake papers.

"He's sixty-six years old and dealing drugs?" Jake asked.

"There's no mandatory retirement age for drug dealers."

"Thanks."

"Anyway," Murray continued, "this guy is pretty crafty and won't admit to anything."

"How bad is he hurt?"

"He's been in the hospital for a week. He'll go from there to the jail, so his doctors are in no hurry. A cracked skull is a cracked skull."

"If you say so."

"The locals there are curious about the discharge paperwork from the Navy. It appears to be authentic and it doesn't really fit. A fake driver's license and a fake passport might take you places, but a discharge that's thirty years old? Why would a con man like this need it? Of course it could be stolen."

"So we're back to the same old question," Jake said. "How do we verify him if we find him?"

"You got it."

There were no helpful photos of Ancil Hubbard. In a box in Seth's closet they had found several dozen family photos, mainly of Ramona, Herschel, and Seth's first wife. There were none from Seth's childhood; not a single photo of his parents or younger brother. Some school records tracked Ancil through the ninth grade, and his grainy, smiling face appeared in a group photo taken at the Palmyra junior high school in 1934. That photo had been enlarged, along with several of Seth as an adult. Since Ancil had not been seen in Ford County in fifty years, there was not a single person who could offer an opinion as to whether he favored his older brother as a child, or looked completely different.

"Do you have someone in Juneau?" Jake asked.

"No, not yet. I've talked to the police twice. I can have a man there within twenty-four hours."

"What's he gonna do when he gets there? If Lonny Clark is not talking to the locals, why would he talk to a complete stranger?"

"I doubt if he would."

"Let me think about it."

Jake hung up and thought about nothing else for an hour. It was the first lead in months, and such a weak one at that. The trial started in four days, and there was no way he could race off to Alaska and somehow verify the identity of a man who did not want to be identified; indeed, one who'd apparently spent the past thirty years changing identities.

He walked downstairs and found Lucien in the conference room studying index cards with the jurors' names in bold letters.

They were arranged neatly on the long table, alphabetized, all ninety-seven of them. They were rated on a scale of 1 to 10, with 10 being the most attractive. Many of them had not yet been rated because nothing was known of the jurors.

Jake replayed the conversation with Albert Murray. Lucien's first response was, "We're not telling Judge Atlee, not yet anyway. I know what you're thinking—if Ancil's alive and we might know where he is, then let's scream for a continuance and buy some more time. That's a bad idea, Jake."

"I wasn't thinking about that."

"There's a good chance the old boy might be locked up for the rest of his life. He couldn't show up for a trial if he wanted to."

"No, Lucien, I'm more concerned with verification. There's no way to do it unless we go talk to him. Keep in mind he has a chunk of money on the line here. He might be more cooperative than we think."

Lucien took a deep breath and began pacing around the table. Portia was too inexperienced, and she was also a young black female, not the type to pry secrets out of an old white man who was running from something, or everything. That left him, the only available member of the firm. He walked to the door and said, "I'll go. Get me all the information you can."

"Are you sure, Lucien?"

There was no response as he closed the front door behind himself. Jake's only thought was, I hope he can stay sober.

Ozzie stopped by late Thursday afternoon for a quick visit. Harry Rex and Portia were in the war room poring over juror names and addresses. Jake was upstairs at his desk, on the phone, wasting time trying to track down a few more of Wade Lanier's forty-five witnesses. So far the task had been frustrating.

"Wanna beer?" Harry Rex asked the sheriff. A fresh Bud Light sat nearby.

"I'm on duty and I don't drink," Ozzie replied. "I hope you're not driving. I'd hate to see you busted for a DUI."

"I'd just hire Jake to postpone it forever. You got some names?"

Ozzie handed him a sheet of paper and said, "A few. That Oscar Peltz guy we were talkin' about yesterday, from down near Lake Village, well, he goes to the same church with the Roston family." Portia picked up the card with "OSCAR PELTZ" written in a black marker across the top.

"I'd stay away from him," Ozzie said.

Harry Rex looked at his notes and said, "We had him as a five anyway, not too attractive."

"Mr. Raymond Griffis, lives down from Parker's Country Store, south of here. What do you have on him?"

Portia picked up another card and said, "White male, age forty-one, works for a fencing contractor." Harry Rex added, "Divorced, remarried, father died in a car wreck about five years ago."

Ozzie said, "Stay away from him. I got a source says his brother was involved with the Klan three years ago during the Hailey trial. Don't think the brother ever joined up, but he was a bit too close. They might be presentable on the surface, but could be a rough bunch."

"I had him as a four," Harry Rex said. "I thought you were going after all the black folks."

"That's a waste of time. All black folks get automatic tens in this trial."

"How many are on the list, Portia?"

"Twenty-one, out of ninety-seven."

"We'll take 'em."

"Where's Lucien?" Ozzie asked.

"Jake ran him off. Any luck with Pernell Phillips? You thought Moss Junior might know him."

"He's Moss Junior's wife's third cousin, but they try to avoid family gatherings. Backwater Baptists. He wouldn't get too many points from me."

"Portia?"

"Let's give him a three," she said, with the authority of a veteran jury consultant.

"That's the problem with this damn pool," Harry Rex said. "Far too many threes and fours, not enough eights and nines. We're gonna get clobbered."

"Where's Jake?" Ozzie asked.

"Upstairs, fighting the phone."

Lucien drove to Memphis, flew to Chicago, and from there flew all night to Seattle. He drank on the flight but went to sleep before being excessive. He killed six hours in the Seattle airport, then caught a two-hour flight to Juneau on Alaska Air. He checked into a hotel downtown, called Jake, slept three hours, showered, even shaved, and dressed himself in an old black suit that hadn't been worn in a decade. With the white shirt and paisley tie, he could pass himself off as a lawyer, which was exactly what he planned to do. With a battered briefcase in hand, he walked to the hospital. Twenty-two hours after leaving Clanton, he said hello to the detective and got the latest scoop over coffee.

The update revealed little. An infection was causing his brain to swell and Lonny was not in the mood to talk. His doctors wanted things quiet and the detective had not spoken to him that day. He showed Lucien the fake paperwork they found in the flophouse, along with the naval discharge. Lucien showed the detective two enlarged photos of Seth Hubbard. Maybe there was a vague resemblance, maybe not. It was a long shot. The detective called the owner of the bar and insisted he come to the hospital. Since he knew Lonny well, he could look at the photos. He did, and saw nothing.

After the owner left, and with little else to do, Lucien explained to the detective the purpose of his visit. They had been looking for Ancil for six months, but it had been a cold trail. His brother, the one in the photos, had left him some money in a will. Not a fortune, but certainly enough to scramble Lucien from Mississippi to Alaska overnight.

The detective had little interest in a lawsuit so far away. He was more concerned with the cocaine. No, he did not believe

Lonny Clark was a drug dealer. They were about to crack a syndicate out of Vancouver, and they had a couple of informants. The buzz was that Lonny was simply hiding the stuff for a fee. Sure, he would serve some time, but time measured in months and not years. And no, he would not be allowed to travel back to Mississippi for any reason, if in fact his name was really Ancil Hubbard.

After the detective left, Lucien roamed around the hospital to familiarize himself with the maze of corridors and annexes and split-levels. He found Lonny's room on the third floor and saw a man standing nearby, flipping through a magazine, trying to stay awake. He assumed he was an officer.

After dark, he returned to his hotel, called Jake for the update, and went to the bar.

It was either his fifth or sixth night in this damp, dark room with windows that never opened and somehow blocked out all light during the day. The nurses came and went, sometimes tapping softly on the door as they pushed it open, and other times appearing at his bedside without making a sound to warn him. He had tubes in both arms and monitors above his head. He'd been told he wouldn't die, but after five or six days and nights with virtually no food but plenty of meds and too many doctors and nurses, he wouldn't mind a prolonged blackout. His head pounded in pain and his lower back was cramping from the inactivity, and at times he wanted to rip off all the tubes and wires and bolt from the room. A digital clock gave the time as 11:10.

Could he leave? Was he free to walk out of the hospital? Or were the goons waiting just outside his door to take him away? No one would tell him. He had asked several of the friendlier nurses if someone was waiting, but all responses had been vague. Many things were vague. At times the television screen was clear, and then it would blur. There was a constant ringing in his ears that made him mumble. The doctors denied this. The nurses just gave him another pill. There were shadows at all hours of the night, observers sneaking into his room. Maybe they were students looking at real patients; maybe they were just shadows that did not really exist. They changed his meds frequently to see how he would react. Try this one for the pain. This one for the blurred vision. This one for the shadows. This one is a blood thinner. This is an antibiotic. Dozens and dozens of pills, and at all hours of the day and night.

He dozed off again, and when he awoke it was 11:17. The room was pitch-black, the only light a red haze cast off from a monitor above his head, one he could not see.

The door opened silently, but no light entered from the dark hallway. But it wasn't a nurse. A man, a stranger, walked straight to the side of the bed: gray hair, long hair, a black shirt, an old man he'd never seen before. His eyes were squinted and fierce, and as he leaned down even closer the smell of whiskey almost slapped Lonny in the face.

He said, "Ancil, what happened to Sylvester Rinds?"

Lonny's heart froze as he stared in horror at the stranger, who gently placed a hand on his shoulder. The whiskey smell grew stronger. He repeated, "Ancil, what happened to Sylvester Rinds?"

Lonny tried to speak but words failed him. He blinked his eyes to refocus, but he was seeing clearly enough. The words were clear too, and the accent was unmistakable. The stranger was from the Deep South.

"What?" Lonny managed to whisper, almost in a gasp.

"What happened to Sylvester Rinds?" the stranger repeated, his laser-like eyes glowing down at Lonny.

There was a button on the bedstead that summoned a nurse. Lonny quickly punched it. The stranger withdrew, became a shadow again, then vanished from the room.

A nurse eventually arrived. She was one of his least favorites and didn't like to be bothered. Lonny wanted to talk, to tell her about the stranger, but this gal was not a listener. She asked what he wanted, and he said he couldn't go to sleep. She promised to check back later, the same promise as always.

He lay in the dark, frightened. Was he frightened because he'd been called by his real name? Because his past had caught up with him? Or was he frightened because he wasn't sure he'd actually seen and heard the stranger? Was he finally losing his mind? Was the brain damage becoming permanent?

He faded away, drifting in and out of blackness, sleeping for only a moment or two before thinking of Sylvester.

37

Jake walked into the Coffee Shop at five minutes after seven on Saturday morning, and, as usual, the conversation lagged for a few seconds as he found a seat and swapped a few insults. The trial started in two days, and, according to Dell, the early morning chatter was dominated by rumors and endless opinions about the case. The subject was changed the moment Jake walked in each morning, and as soon as he left it was as if someone flipped a switch and Seth's will was again front and center. Though her customers were all white, they seemed to be divided into several camps. There were strong opinions that a man in his right mind should be able to give away his property as he pleased, regardless of his family. Others argued he wasn't in his right mind. Lettie had her share of detractors. She was widely believed to be a loose woman who took advantage of poor old Seth.

Jake stopped by at least once a week when the café was empty and got the lowdown from Dell. Of particular interest was a regular named Tug Whitehurst, a state meat inspector. His brother was on the jury list, though she was certain Tug had not mentioned this. He wasn't much of a talker, but during one conversation he did side with Kerry Hull when Hull declared it was no one's business how he left his estate. Hull was notoriously broke and in debt and everyone knew his estate would be a disaster, but this was allowed to pass without comment. At any rate, Dell thought Tug Whitehurst would be okay with Jake, but who knew about his brother?

At this point in the case, Jake was desperate for any information about the chosen ninety-seven.

He sat at a table with a couple of farmers and waited on his grits and toast. Bass fishing dominated the conversation, so Jake had little to offer. For at least the last three years, a great debate had raged in certain circles over whether the large-mouth bass population in Lake Chatulla was declining or increasing. Opinions were strong and loud and there appeared to be no room for compromise. Experts were plentiful. Just as the tide shifted in favor of a dwindling population, someone would land a trophy and the debate would fire up again. Jake was weary of the topic but now thankful for it nonetheless; it kept attention away from the Hubbard case.

As he was eating, Andy Furr asked, "Say, Jake, is the trial still a go for Monday?"

"It is."

"So no chance of a postponement or anything like that?"

"I don't see one. The prospective jurors will be there at nine and we should get started soon after. You coming?"

"Naw, gotta work. Ya'll expectin' a crowd?"

"You never know. Civil trials tend to be fairly dull. We may start off with some spectators, but I suspect they'll disappear quickly."

Dell topped off his coffee and said, "The place'll be packed and you know it. We haven't had this much excitement since the Hailey trial."

"Oh, I forgot about that one," Jake said and got a few laughs.

Bill West said he'd heard the FBI had just raided the offices of two supervisors down in Polk County, a notoriously corrupt place, and this ignited a round of condemnation from almost everyone but Jake and Dell. It also changed the subject, and for that Jake was grateful. At that moment, facing a long weekend at the office, all he wanted was breakfast.

Portia arrived around 9:00, and they had a coffee together on the balcony as the town came to life around them. She reported that she'd had an early breakfast with Lettie, who was nervous, even fragile, and terrified of the trial. Lettie was exhausted from the strain of living in a house packed with relatives, and of trying to work part-time, and of trying to ignore the fact that her husband was in jail for killing two boys. Add a pending divorce and a gut-wrenching will contest, and Lettie was understandably a wreck.

Portia admitted she was exhausted too. She was working long hours at the office and sleeping little. Jake was sympathetic, but only to a point. Litigation often required eighteen-hour days and lost weekends, and if Portia was serious about becoming a lawyer she needed a good dose of the pressure. In the past two weeks, they had pushed each other into memorizing all ninety-seven names on the jury list. If Jake said "R," then Portia responded, "Six. Rady, Rakestraw, Reece, Riley, Robbins, and Robard." If Portia said "W," then Jake responded, "Three. Wampler, Whitehurst, Whitten." Back and forth, the mental contests raged throughout each day.

Jury selection in Mississippi was normally a one-day ordeal, at most. Jake was continually fascinated by trials in other states where it took two weeks or a month to pick a jury. He could not fathom such a system; neither could Mississippi judges. They were dead serious about selecting fair and impartial panels; they just didn't waste time.

Speed would be crucial. Quick decisions would be required. The lawyers on both sides would not have much time to think about names or to look them up in some batch of research. It was imperative that they know the names and quickly put them with faces. Jake was determined to know every single juror, and their ages, addresses, jobs, education, churches, as much info as they could gather.

Once the ninety-seven names were filed away, Portia was given the task of wading through the courthouse records. She spent hours in the deed books and land records searching for transactions over the past ten years. She combed the court dockets, looking for plaintiffs and defendants, winners and losers. Of the ninety-seven, sixteen had gone through a divorce in the past ten years. She wasn't sure what that meant in the course of a trial over a will, but she had the knowledge anyway. One gentleman, a Mr. Eli Rady, had filed four lawsuits and lost them all. She checked the lien books and found dozens of claims for unpaid taxes, unpaid supplies, unpaid subcontractors. A few of their prospective jurors owed the county money for property taxes. In the tax assessor's office, she dug through property tax receipts and made a register of which jurors owned what make and model of vehicles. Not surprisingly, there were a lot of pickup trucks.

The work was tedious and often mind-numbing, but she never slowed down, never thought of quitting. After two weeks of living with these people, she was confident she knew them.

After coffee, they grudgingly went back to work. Jake began roughing out an outline for his opening statement. Portia returned to the conference room and to her ninety-seven new friends. At ten, Harry Rex finally rolled in with a sackful of greasy sausage biscuits straight from Claude's. He handed one to Jake, insisted he take it, then slid across an envelope.

"It's a check from your insurance company, Land Fire and Casualty, a bunch of crooked morons, so don't ever buy another policy from them, understand? A hundred and thirty-five thousand bucks. Settlement in full. And not a dime of it siphoned off for attorney's fees, so you owe me big-time, buddy."

"Thanks. Since your fees are so cheap, get busy."

"I'm really tired of this case, Jake. On Monday, I'm gonna help you pick the jury, then I'm outta there. I got my own cases to lose."

"Fair enough. Just be there for the selection." Jake knew Harry Rex would in fact miss little of the actual courtroom testimony, then he would park himself in the downstairs conference room each evening as they ate pizza and sandwiches and argued about what went wrong and what might happen the following day. He would second-guess every move Jake made; excoriate Wade Lanier with scathing criticism; curse the negative rulings made by Judge Atlee; offer unsolicited advice at every turn; maintain the constant gloom of losing an unwinnable case; and at times be so unbearable Jake would want to throw something at him. But he was seldom wrong. He knew the law and its intricacies. He read people like others read magazines. Without being obvious, he watched the jurors as they watched Jake. And his advice would be invaluable.

Despite Seth Hubbard's rather explicit command that no other lawyer in Ford County profit from his estate, Jake was determined to find a way to channel some fees to Harry Rex. Seth wanted his last-minute, handwritten will to survive all challenges, and whether he liked it or not, Harry Rex Vonner was crucial to the effort.

The phone on Jake's desk started a muted ringing. He ignored it. Harry Rex said, "Why have ya'll stopped answering the phones around here? I've called ten times this week and nobody answered."

"Portia's been in the courthouse. I've been busy. Lucien doesn't answer the phone."

"Think of all the car wrecks and divorces and shoplifting cases you're missing. All the human misery out there trying like hell to get through."

"I'd say we're tied up right now."

"Any word from Lucien?"

"Nothing this morning, but then it's only six in Alaska. I doubt if he's up and about yet."

"He's probably just now getting in. You're an idiot, Jake, for sending Lucien on a road trip. Hell, he gets drunk between here and his house. Put him on the road, in airport lounges, hotel bars, you name it, and he'll kill himself."

"He's cutting back. He plans to study for the bar and get reinstated."

"Cutting back for that old goat means stopping at midnight."

"When did you get so clean and sober, Harry Rex? You've been drinking Bud Light for breakfast."

"I know how to pace myself. I'm a professional. Lucien's just a drunk, that's all."

"Are you going to perfect those jury instructions or just sit here and bad-mouth Lucien all morning?"

Harry Rex stood and began lumbering away. "Later. You got a cold Bud Light?"

"No." When he was gone, Jake opened the envelope and studied the check from the insurance company. On the one hand, he was sad because the check represented the end of their first home. Sure it went up in flames more than three years earlier, but the lawsuit against the insurance company gave Carla and him hope that it might be rebuilt. That was still possible, but unlikely. On the other hand, the check meant cash in the bank; not much by any means, but after paying off the two mortgages they would net close to $40,000. It wasn't exactly unrestricted, but it did take some pressure off.

He called Carla and said a small celebration was in order. Find a babysitter.

Lucien sounded normal on the phone, though normal for him meant the usual scratchy voice and the pained delivery of a drunk trying to shake off cobwebs. He said their man Lonny Clark had a rough night; the infection would not subside; the doctors were more concerned than the day before; and, most important, he was not receiving visitors.

"What are your plans?" Jake asked.

"Hang around for a while, maybe take a road trip. You ever been out here, Jake? Pretty spectacular, with mountains on three sides and the Pacific right here at the door. The town's not a big place and not that pretty, but, man, what scenery. I like it. I think I'll get out and explore."

"Do you think it's him, Lucien?"

"I know less than I did when I left Clanton. Still a mystery. The cops don't care who he is or what's happening back there; they've got a drug ring to break up. I like it here, Jake. I might stay awhile. I'm in no hurry to get back. You don't need me in that courtroom."

Jake certainly agreed but said nothing.

Lucien continued, "It's cool and there's no humidity. Imagine that, Jake, a place with no humidity. I like it here. I'll keep an eye on Lonny and chat with him when they let me."

"Are you sober, Lucien?"

"I'm always sober in the morning. It's ten at night when I run into trouble."

"Keep in touch."

"You got it, Jake. Don't worry."

They dropped off Hanna at Jake's parents in Karaway and drove an hour to Oxford, where they drove through the Ole Miss campus and soaked in the sights and memories of another lifetime. It was a warm, clear spring day, and the students were out in shorts and bare feet. They slung Frisbees across The Grove, sneaked beer from coolers, and soaked up the sun as it was disappearing. Jake was thirty-five, Carla thirty-one, and their college days seemed so recent, yet so long ago.

A walk through campus always triggered a wave of nostalgia. And disbelief. Were they really in their thirties? It seemed like they were students just last month. Jake avoided walking near the law school—that nightmare was not distant enough. At dusk they drove to the Oxford square and parked by the courthouse. They browsed for an hour in the bookstore, had a coffee on the balcony upstairs, then went to dinner at the Downtown Grill, the most expensive restaurant within eighty miles. With money to burn, Jake ordered a bottle of Bordeaux—sixty bucks.

Returning, at almost midnight, they took their customary turns and slowly drove by the Hocutt House. Some of its lights were on, and the grand old place beckoned them. Parked in the driveway was Willie Traynor's Spitfire with Tennessee plates. Still a bit loose from the wine, Jake said, "Let's check on Willie."

"No, Jake! It's too late," Carla protested.

"Come on. Willie won't care." He'd stopped the Saab and was shifting into reverse.

"Jake, this is so rude."

"For anyone else, yes, but not for Willie. Plus he wants us to buy this place." Jake parked behind the Spitfire.

"What if he has company?"

"Now he has more. Let's go."

Carla reluctantly got out. They paused for a second on the narrow sidewalk and took in the sweeping front porch. The air was rife with the fragrant aromas of tree peonies and irises. Pink and white azaleas burst forth from the flower beds.

"I say we buy it," Jake said.

"We can't afford it," she replied.

"No, but the bank can."

They stepped onto the porch, rang the bell, and heard Billie Holiday in the background. Willie eventually came to the door, in jeans and a T-shirt, and pulled it open with a big smile. "Well, well," he said, "if it's not the new owners."

"We were just in the neighborhood and wanted a drink," Jake said.

"I hope we're not intruding," Carla said, somewhat embarrassed.

"Not at all. Come in, come in," Willie insisted as he waved them in. They went to the front parlor where he had a bottle of white wine on ice. It was almost empty, and he quickly grabbed another and uncorked it. As he did so he explained that he was in town to cover the trial. His latest venture was the launch of a monthly magazine devoted to southern culture, and its inaugural issue would have an in-depth story about Seth Hubbard and the fortune he'd left to his black housekeeper. Willie had not mentioned this before.

Jake was thrilled at the idea of some publicity outside Ford County. The Hailey trial had given him a dose of notoriety, and it was intoxicating. "Who's on the cover?" he asked, joking.

"Probably not you," Willie said as he handed over two glasses filled to the top. "Cheers."

They talked about the trial for a moment or two, but all three were having other thoughts. Finally, Willie broke the ice by saying, "Here's what I propose. Let's shake hands tonight on the house, a verbal contract, just the three of us."

"Verbal contracts for real estate are not enforceable," Jake said.

"Don't you just hate lawyers?" Willie said to Carla.

"Most of them."

Willie said, "It's enforceable if we say it's enforceable. Let's shake hands tonight on a secret deal, then after the trial we'll find a real lawyer who can draft a proper contract. You guys go to the bank and line up a mortgage, and we'll close in ninety days."

Jake looked at Carla who looked right back. For a moment they froze, as if the idea was entirely new. In reality, they had discussed the Hocutt House until they were weary of it.

"What if we can't qualify for a mortgage?" Carla asked.

"Don't be ridiculous. Any bank in town will loan you the money."

"I doubt it," Jake said. "There are five in town and I've sued three of them."

"Look, this place is a bargain at two fifty and the banks know it."

"I thought it was two twenty-five," Jake said, glancing at Carla.

Willie took a sip of his wine, smacked his lips with satisfaction, and said, "Well, yes, it was, briefly, but you didn't take the bait at that price. Frankly, the house is worth at least $400,000. In Memphis—"

"We've had that conversation, Willie. This is not midtown Memphis."

"No, it's not, but two fifty is a more reasonable price. So, it's two fifty."

Jake said, "That's a strange way to sell, Willie. If you don't get your price, you keep raising it?"

"I'm not raising it again, Jake, unless some doctor comes along. It's two fifty. That's fair. You guys know it. Now let's shake hands."

Jake and Carla stared at each other for a moment, then she slowly reached over and shook Willie's hand. "Atta girl," Jake said. The deal was closed.

★   ★   ★

The only sound was the faint hum of a monitor, somewhere above and behind him. The only light was the red glow of digital numbers that recorded his vitals. His lower back was cramping and Lonny tried to shift slightly. An IV drip kept the clear but potent meds in his blood, and for the most part kept the pain away. In and out, in and out, he came and went, barely awake for a few moments, then dead again. He'd lost track of the days and hours. They had turned off his television and taken away his remote. The meds were so strong that not even the worrisome nurses could awaken him at all hours of the night, though they tried.

When awake, he could feel movement in the room—orderlies, housekeepers, doctors, lots of doctors. He occasionally heard them speak in low, grave voices, and Lonny had already decided he was dying. An infection he couldn't pronounce or remember was now in control, and the doctors were struggling. In and out.

A stranger appeared without a sound and touched the guardrail. "Ancil," he said in a low but strong voice. "Ancil, are you there?"

Lonny's eyes opened wide at the sound of his name. It was an old man with long gray hair and a black T-shirt. It was the same face, back again. "Ancil, can you hear me?"

Lonny did not move a muscle.

"Your name's not Lonny, we know that. It's Ancil, Ancil Hubbard, brother of Seth. Ancil, what happened to Sylvester Rinds?"

Though terrified, Lonny remained frozen. He smelled whiskey and remembered it from the night before.

"What happened to Sylvester Rinds? You were eight years old, Ancil. What happened to Sylvester Rinds?"

Lonny closed his eyes and breathed deeply. For a second he was gone, then he jerked his hands and opened his eyes. The stranger was gone.

He called the nurse.

38

Before his wife died, Judge and Mrs. Atlee once went eight consecutive years without missing Sunday worship at the First Presbyterian Church. Fifty-two Sundays in a row, for eight years. A flu virus halted the streak. Then she passed on, and the judge lost some focus and actually missed once or twice a year. But not often. He was such a presence in the church that his absence was always noted. He wasn't there the Sunday before the trial began, and when Jake realized it he allowed his mind to wander during the sermon. Could the old guy be sick? If so, might the trial be postponed? How would this affect his strategy? A dozen questions and no answers.

After church, Jake and his girls returned to the Hocutt House where Willie was preparing a brunch on the back porch. He insisted on hosting the new owners, claiming he wanted to meet Hanna and show her around. All top secret of course. Jake and Carla would have preferred to keep their daughter out of it for the moment, but they could hardly suppress their excitement. Hanna promised to keep this rather significant secret. After a tour, which included Hanna's tentative selection of her new bedroom, they settled around a plank farm table on the porch and had French toast and scrambled eggs.

Willie moved the conversation away from the house and to the trial. Fluidly, he became a journalist again, probing and nibbling around the edges of sensitive material. Twice Carla shot warning glances at Jake, who realized what was happening. When Willie asked if they could expect any evidence that Seth Hubbard had been intimate with Lettie Lang, Jake politely said he couldn't answer that question. The brunch became a little awkward as Jake grew quieter while his host kept chatting on about rumors he was chasing. Was it true Lettie had offered to split the money and settle the case? Jake replied firmly that he could not comment. There was so much gossip. When Willie pursued another question about "intimacy," Carla said, "Please, Willie, there's a seven-year-old present."

"Yes, sorry."

Hanna was not missing a word.

After an hour, Jake looked at his watch and said he had to get to the office. It would be a long afternoon and night. Willie poured some more coffee as they thanked him and placed their napkins on the table. It took fifteen minutes to gracefully say good-bye. As they drove away, Hanna stared at the house through the car's rear window and said, "I like our new house. When can we move in?"

"Soon, honey," Carla said.

"Where's Mr. Willie going to live?"

"Oh, he has several houses," Jake said. "Don't worry about him."

"He's such a nice man."

"Yes, he is," Carla said.

Lucien followed the detective into the room where Lonny sat waiting expectantly with a stout nurse at his side, sentry-like. She was not smiling and seemed irritated by this intrusion. One of the doctors had reluctantly acceded to the request for a few questions. Lonny's condition had improved overnight and he was feeling better, but his team was still protective. They didn't like lawyers anyway.

"This is the guy I told you about, Lonny," the detective said, without the slightest attempt at an introduction. Lucien, in his black suit, stood down by Lonny's feet and offered a phony smile. "Mr. Clark, my name is Lucien Wilbanks, and I work for a lawyer in Clanton, Mississippi," he said.

Lonny had seen the face before, hadn't he? In the middle of the night, the face had appeared and disappeared like a ghost.

"A pleasure," Lonny said, as if still groggy, though his mind had not been this clear since before the blow to his skull.

Lucien said, "We're involved in some litigation that makes it imperative that we locate a man named Ancil Hubbard. Mr. Hubbard was born in Ford County, Mississippi, on August 1, 1922. His father was Cleon Hubbard, his mother was Sarah Belle Hubbard, and he had one brother, Seth, who was five years older. We've been searching high and low for Ancil Hubbard, and it's come to our attention that there's a chance you might know him or perhaps your paths have crossed in recent years."

Lonny said, "You've come all the way from Mississippi?"

"Sure, but it's no big deal. We have airplanes down there too. And we've covered the continent looking for Ancil."

"What kind of litigation?" Lonny asked, with the same disdain most people heap onto the unsavory subject.

"Some pretty complicated stuff. Seth Hubbard died suddenly about six months ago and he left behind a mess. A lot of business interests and not much in the way of estate planning. Our job as lawyers is to first try and round up the family, which in the case of the Hubbards is quite a task. We have reason to believe you might know something about Ancil Hubbard. Is this right?"

Lonny closed his eyes as a wave of pain rolled through his head. He reopened them, looked at the ceiling, and said softly, "That name doesn't ring a bell, sorry."

As if he was either expecting this or not hearing it, Lucien went on, "Can you think of anyone in your past who might have known Ancil Hubbard, or mentioned his name? Help me here, Mr. Clark. Think back. It looks like you've moved around a lot, so you've known many people in many places. I know you got a sore head and all, but take your time, think real hard about this."

Again, he said, "That name does not ring a bell."

The nurse glared at Lucien and seemed ready to pounce. He did not acknowledge her presence. He carefully sat his battered leather briefcase on the foot of the bed so Lonny could see it. It probably contained something important. Lucien said, "Have you ever been to Mississippi, Mr. Clark?"

"No."

"Are you sure?"

"Sure I'm sure."

"Well, hey, that's a real surprise, because we thought you were born there. We've paid a lot of money to some high-priced investigators who've been tracking Ancil Hubbard. When your name popped up, they took off after you and found several Lonny Clarks. One of them was born in Mississippi sixty-six years ago. You are sixty-six years old, aren't you, Mr. Clark?"

Lonny stared at him, overwhelmed and uncertain. Slowly, he said, "I am."

"So what's your connection to Ancil Hubbard?"

The nurse said, "He said he didn't know him."

Lucien snapped at her: "And I'm not talking to you! This is an important legal matter, a big case involving dozens of lawyers, several courts, and a pile of money, and if I need you to stick your nose into the middle of it, then I'll let you know. Until then, please butt out." Her cheeks blushed crimson as she gasped for breath.

Lonny despised that particular nurse and said to her, "Don't speak for me, okay? I can take care of myself." The nurse, completely chastised, took a step back from the bed. Lucien and Lonny, now joined in their contempt for the nurse, looked at each other carefully. Lonny said, "I'll have to sleep on it. My memory is coming and going these days, and they got me so doped up, you know?"

"I'll be happy to wait," Lucien said. "It's very important that we find Ancil Hubbard." He pulled a business card from a pocket and handed it to Lonny. "This is my boss, Jake Brigance. You can call him and check me out. He's the lead lawyer in the case."

"And you're a lawyer too?" Lonny asked.

"I am. I just ran out of cards. I'm staying at the Glacier Inn on Third Street."

Late in the afternoon, Herschel Hubbard unlocked the door to his father's house and stepped inside. It had been empty now, for how long? He paused and did the math. His father had killed himself on October 2, a Sunday. Today was April 2, a Sunday. To his knowledge, the house had not been cleaned since the day Lettie was fired, the day after the funeral. A thick layer of dust covered the television console and bookcases. The smell was of stale tobacco and stagnant air. He flipped a switch and the lights came on. He'd been told that Quince Lundy, the administrator, was in charge of paying the utility bills. The kitchen counters were spotless; the refrigerator empty. A faucet dripped slowly into a brown stain in the porcelain sink. He made his way to the rear of the house, and in the room he'd once called his own he slapped the bedspread to stir the dust, then he stretched out on the bed and gazed at the ceiling.

In six months, he'd gone through the fortune several times, spending as he pleased but also doubling and tripling it with shrewd investments. At times he felt like a millionaire; at others he was consumed with the awful emptiness of seeing the riches slip away and being left with nothing. Why did the old man do it? Herschel was willing to accept and shoulder more than his share of responsibility for their fractious relationship, but he could not begin to comprehend getting cut out completely. He could have loved Seth more, but then Seth gave little love in return. He could have spent more time here, in the house, but then Seth didn't want him around. Where had they gone wrong? How young was Herschel when he realized his father was cold and distant? A child can't chase a father who has no time for him.

But Herschel had never fought his father, had never embarrassed him with open rebellion or worse—addictions, arrests, a life of crime. He parted with Seth when he was eighteen and left home to become a man. If he neglected Seth as an adult, it was because Seth had neglected him as a little boy. A child is not born with the tendency to neglect; it has to be acquired. Herschel learned from a master.

Would the money have changed things? If Herschel had known the extent of his father's wealth, what would he have done differently? One hell of a lot, he was finally admitting to himself. Initially, he had taken the high road and said, at least to his mother, that he wouldn't have changed a thing. No sir. If Seth wanted no part of his only son, then the son would certainly allow him to have it that way. Now, though, as time passed and his own unhappy world was growing darker, Herschel knew he would have been here, in the house, taking care of his dear old dad. He would have shown an enthusiastic burst of interest in lumber and furniture. He would have begged Seth to teach him the business and possibly groom him as a successor. He would have swallowed hard and returned to Ford County, renting a place somewhere nearby. And, he definitely would have kept an eye on Lettie Lang.

Getting shut out of such a large inheritance was so humiliating. His friends had whispered behind his back. His enemies had reveled in his misfortune. His ex-wife loathed him almost as much as she despised Seth, and she had gleefully spread the awful but true gossip around Memphis. Even though her children also got the ax, she couldn't stop herself from piling on poor Herschel. For six months he had found it difficult to run his business and concentrate on his affairs. The bills and debts were adding up; his mother was becoming less sympathetic and helpful. On two occasions she had asked him to leave her home and find another place to live. He wanted to, but he couldn't afford it.

His fate now lay in the hands of a crafty lawyer named Wade Lanier, a cranky old judge named Reuben Atlee, and a haphazard gang of accidental jurors in rural Mississippi. At times he was confident. Justice would prevail; right over wrong and all that. It was simply wrong for a housekeeper, whatever her skin color, to appear in the final years of a long life and manipulate things in such a fiendish manner. Fairness was on their side. At other times, though, he could still feel the unspeakable pain of having it slip away. If it could happen once, it could certainly happen again.

The walls inched closer and the musty air grew thicker. It had been a joyless home with two parents who despised each other. He cursed them for a while, both of them equally, then concentrated more on Seth. Why have children if you don't want them? But he had wrestled with these questions for years and there were no answers. Let it go.

Enough. He locked the house, left it, and drove to Clanton, where he was expected around 6:00 p.m. Ian and Ramona were already there, in the large conference room on the second floor of the Sullivan firm. Their ace jury consultant, Myron Pankey, was going on about their meticulous research when Herschel arrived. Cursory greetings and introductions were made. Pankey had two staffers with him, two attractive young ladies preoccupied with note-taking.

Wade Lanier and Lester Chilcott sat at the center on one side of the table, flanked by paralegals. Pankey was saying, "Our phone survey also revealed that when given the additional facts that the will was written by a wealthy man, age seventy, and the caregiver was an attractive woman much younger, over half of those surveyed asked if sex was involved. We never mentioned sex, but it's often the automatic response. What was really going on? Race was never mentioned, but of the black respondents almost 80 percent were suspicious of sexual activity. Of the white, 55 percent."

"So the issue is very much in the air, though unspoken," Lanier said.

Didn't we know this six months ago? Herschel asked himself as he doodled on a legal pad. So far, they had paid Pankey two-thirds of his $75,000 fee. The money was now being fronted by Wade Lanier's law firm, which was paying all the litigation expenses. Ian had chipped in $20,000; Herschel nothing. If there was a recovery, there would also be a war dividing it.

Pankey passed out thick booklets for their reading pleasure, though the lawyers had already spent hours with the material. Beginning with Ambrose and ending with Young, there was a one- or two-page summary of each juror. Many included photos of homes and automobiles, and a few had actual photos of the jurors. These were taken from church and club directories, high school yearbooks, and a few candid shots handed over on the sly by friends.

Pankey was saying, "Our perfect juror is a Caucasian over the age of fifty. The younger people went to integrated schools and tend to be more tolerant on race, and obviously we are not looking for tolerance. Sadly for us, the more racist the better. White women are slightly preferable over white men, and this is because they tend to show more jealousy toward another woman who has managed to manipulate the will. A man might excuse another man for fooling around with his housekeeper, but a woman is not so understanding."

Seventy-five thousand for this? Herschel doodled to himself. Isn't this fairly obvious? He shot a bored look at his sister, who was looking old and tired. Things were not going well with Ian, and the Hubbard siblings had spoken on the phone more in the past three months than in the past ten years. Ian's deals were not paying off, and the strained marriage was continuing to crack. Ian spent most of his time on the Gulf Coast where he and some partners were renovating a mall. This was fine with her; she didn't want him at home. She talked openly of divorce, to Herschel anyway. But if they lost this case, she might be stuck. We're not going to lose, Herschel kept reassuring her.

They slogged through the research until 7:30, when Wade Lanier said he'd had enough. They drove to a fish shack overlooking Lake Chatulla, and enjoyed a long meal, just the lawyers and their clients. After a few drinks their nerves were settled, and they managed to relax. Like most trial lawyers, Wade Lanier was a gifted storyteller and he regaled them with hilarious tales from his courtroom brawls. More than once, he said, "We're gonna win, folks. Just trust me."

Lucien was in his hotel room, a Jack on the rocks on his nightstand, his nose stuck deep into another impenetrable Faulkner novel, when the phone rang. A weak voice on the other end said, "Is this Mr. Wilbanks?"

"It is," Lucien said, gently closing the book and swinging his feet to the floor.

"This is Lonny Clark, Mr. Wilbanks."

"Please call me Lucien, and I'll call you Lonny, okay?"

"Okay."

"How are you feeling tonight, Lonny?"

"Better, much better. You came to my room last night, didn't you, Lucien? I know you did. I thought I was dreaming last night when a stranger appeared in my room and said something to me, but then when I met you today I recognized you and I recalled your voice."

"I'm afraid you were indeed dreaming, Lonny."

"No, I wasn't. Because you came the night before too. Friday night and Saturday night, it was you. I know it was."

"No one can get in your room, Lonny. There's a cop at the door, around the clock I'm told."

Lonny paused as if he didn't know this; or if he did, then how could a stranger sneak into his room? Finally he said, "The stranger said something about Sylvester Rinds. Do you know Sylvester Rinds, Lucien?"

"Where is he from?" Lucien asked, casually taking a sip.

"I'm asking you, Lucien. Do you know Sylvester Rinds?"

"I've lived in Ford County all my life, Lonny. I know everyone, black and white. But something tells me Sylvester Rinds died before I was born. Did you know him?"

"I don't know. It's all so muddled now. And so long ago . . ." His voice faded as if he'd dropped the phone.

Keep him talking, Lucien said to himself. "I'm much more interested in Ancil Hubbard," he said. "Any luck with that name, Lonny?"

Weakly, he said, "I might be onto something. Can you stop by tomorrow?"

"Of course. What time?"

"Come early. I'm not as tired in the mornings."

"What time will the doctors be finished with their rounds?"

"I don't know. Nine or so."

"I'll be there at nine thirty, Lonny."

39

Nevin Dark parked his truck facing the courthouse and checked his watch. He was early, but that was the plan. He had never before been summoned for jury duty, and he could grudgingly admit to being somewhat excited. He farmed two hundred acres west of Karaway and rarely made it to Clanton; indeed, he could not remember his last trip to the county seat. For the occasion he wore his newest pair of starched khakis and a leather flight jacket handed down by his father, who'd flown in World War II. His wife had firmly pressed his cotton shirt with buttons on the collar. Nevin was rarely this dressed up. He paused and gazed around the courthouse, looking for others who might be holding a summons.

Of the case, he knew little. His wife's brother, a blowhard, had said he thought the trial was over a will that was handwritten, but beyond that the details were scarce. Neither Nevin nor his wife subscribed to the local newspapers. They had not been to church in ten years, so that rich source of gossip had passed them by. The summons said nothing about the type of jury service facing him. Nevin had never heard of Seth Hubbard, nor Lettie Lang. He would recognize the name of Jake Brigance, but only because Jake was from Karaway and the Hailey trial had been so notorious.

In short, Nevin was a model juror: reasonably smart, fair-minded, and uninformed. The summons was folded in his coat pocket. He walked around the square to kill a few minutes, then wandered over to the courthouse where things were getting busy. He climbed the stairs and joined the crowd milling around the large oak doors of the main courtroom. Two deputies in uniform were holding clipboards. Nevin was eventually processed through, and as he entered the courtroom a clerk smiled and pointed to a seat on the left side. He sat down next to an attractive lady in a short skirt, and within two minutes she informed Nevin that she taught school with Carla Brigance and would probably not make the cut. When he confessed he knew nothing about the case, she found it hard to believe. All the jurors were whispering away as they watched the lawyers move about with their important airs. The bench was empty. Half a dozen clerks moved papers here and there, doing little really but trying to justify their presence in the biggest will contest in the history of Ford County. Some of the lawyers had no connections at all, no reason to be there, but a courtroom filled with prospective jurors always attracted a few of the courthouse regulars.

For example, a lawyer named Chuck Rhea had no clients, no office, and no money. He occasionally checked land titles; thus, he was always in the courthouse, killing enormous amounts of time, sipping free coffee from whatever office had the freshest pot, flirting with the clerks who knew him well, gossiping with every lawyer who came within earshot, and in general just being there. Chuck rarely missed a trial. Since he had none of his own, he watched all the others. On this day he was wearing his darkest suit and his wing tips fairly gleamed with fresh polish. He spoke to Jake and Harry Rex—men who knew him all too well—and also to the out-of-town lawyers, who by then knew that Chuck was just another fixture. Every courthouse had them.

A gentleman to Nevin's left struck up a conversation. He said he owned a fence company in Clanton and had once put up some chain link for Harry Rex Vonner's hunting dogs. He pointed and said, "That fat one over there in the bad suit. That's Harry Rex Vonner. Meanest divorce lawyer in the county."

"Is he working with Jake Brigance?" Nevin asked, completely clueless.

"Looks like it."

"Who are those other lawyers?"

"Who knows? There are so many lawyers around here these days. The square is full of them."

A bailiff came to life and yelled, "All rise for the court. The Chancery Court of the Twenty-Fifth Judicial District of Mississippi, the Honorable Reuben V. Atlee presiding." Judge Atlee appeared from the rear and assumed the bench while the crowd jumped to its feet.

"Please be seated," he said. The crowd made a noisy retreat back onto the benches. He said hello and good morning and thanked the prospective jurors for being there, as if they had a choice. He explained that the first order of business was the selection of the jury, twelve jurors plus two alternates, and he figured that might take most of the day. At times things would move slowly, as they often do in court, and he asked for their patience. A clerk had written each of their names on a small piece of paper and put them in a plastic bin. He would pull them out at random, and that's how the jurors would initially be seated. Once the first fifty were in place, the rest would be excused for the day, and maybe called back tomorrow if needed.

The courtroom had two sections, right and left of a center aisle, and each section had ten long benches that held about ten people each. Since the courtroom was at full capacity, Judge Atlee asked the rest of the spectators to please rise and clear out the first four rows to his left. This took a few minutes as people shuffled and stumbled and shoved about, uncertain where to go. Most stood along the walls. He reached into the plastic bin, extracted a name, and called out, "Mr. Nevin Dark."

Nevin's heart skipped a beat, but he stood and said, "Yes sir."

"Good morning, Mr. Dark. Would you please sit over here on the first row, far to the left, and we'll refer to you as Juror Number One for the time being."

"Certainly."

As Nevin walked down the aisle, he noticed the lawyers staring at him as if he'd just shot someone. He took his seat on the empty front row; the lawyers continued to stare. All of them.

Nevin Dark. White male, age fifty-three, farmer, one wife, two adult children, no church affiliation, no civic clubs, no college degree, no criminal record. Jake rated him as a seven. He and Portia looked at their notes. Harry Rex, who was standing in a corner by the jury box, studied his notes. Their model juror was a black male or female of any age, but there weren't many in the crowd. At the contestants' table, Wade Lanier and Lester Chilcott compared their research. Their model juror was a white female, age forty-five or older, someone raised in the deeply segregated old South and not the least bit tolerant of blacks. They liked Nevin Dark, though they knew nothing more about him than Jake did.

Number Two was Tracy McMillen, a secretary, white female, age thirty-one. Judge Atlee took his time unfolding the scraps of paper, studying the names, trying to pronounce them perfectly, allowing each to assume a new position. When the first row was filled, they moved to the second with Juror Number Eleven, one Sherry Benton, the first black to be called forth.

It took an hour to seat the first fifty. When they were in place, Judge Atlee excused the others and said they should remain on standby until further notice. Some of them left, but most stayed where they were and became part of the audience.

"Let's recess for fifteen minutes," the judge said, tapping his gavel as he lifted his cumbersome frame and waddled off the bench, black robe flowing behind. The lawyers gathered into frantic groups, all chattering at once. Jake, Portia, and Harry Rex went straight to the jury deliberation room, which was empty at the moment. As soon as Jake shut the door, Harry Rex said, "We're screwed, you know that? A bad draw. Terrible, terrible."

"Hang on," Jake said, tossing his legal pad onto the table and cracking his knuckles.

Portia said, "We have eleven blacks out of fifty. Unfortunately, four of them are on the back row. Once again, we're stuck on the back row."

"Are you trying to be funny?" Harry Rex barked at her.

"Well, yes, I thought it was rather clever."

Jake said, "Knock it off, okay? I doubt if we make it past number forty."

"So do I," replied Harry Rex. "And just for the record, I sued numbers seven, eighteen, thirty-one, thirty-six, and forty-seven, for divorce. They don't know I'm working for you, Mr. Brigance, and once again I'm not sure why I am working for you because I'm damned sure not getting paid. It's Monday morning, my office is filled with divorcing spouses, some of them carrying guns, and here I am hanging around the courtroom like Chuck Rhea and not getting paid."

"Would you please shut up?" Jake growled.

"If you insist."

"It's not hopeless," Jake said. "It's not a good draw, but not completely hopeless."

"I'll bet Lanier and his boys are smiling right now."

Portia said, "I don't understand you guys. Why is it always black versus white? I looked at those people, those faces, and I didn't see a bunch of hard-core racists who'll burn the will and give everything to the other side. I saw some reasonable people out there."

"And some unreasonable ones," Harry Rex said.

"I agree with Portia, but we're a long way from the final twelve. Let's save the bickering for later."

After the recess, the lawyers were allowed to move their chairs around to the other sides of their tables so they could stare at the panel while the panel stared right back. Judge Atlee assumed the bench without the ritual of "Please rise for the court" and began with a concise statement of the case. He said he expected the trial to last three or four days and that he certainly planned to be finished by Friday afternoon. He introduced the lawyers, all of them, but not the paralegals. Jake was alone, facing an army.

Judge Atlee explained that he would cover a few areas that had to be discussed, then he would allow the attorneys to question and probe. He began with health—anyone sick, facing treatment, or unable to sit and listen for long periods of time? One lady stood and said her husband was in the hospital in Tupelo and she needed to be there. "You are excused," Judge Atlee said with great compassion, and she hustled out of the courtroom. Number twenty-nine, gone. Number forty had a herniated disk that had flared up over the weekend and he claimed to be in considerable pain. He was taking painkillers that made him quite drowsy. "You are excused," Judge Atlee said.

He seemed perfectly willing to excuse anyone with a legitimate concern, but this proved not to be the case. When he asked about conflicts with work, a gentleman wearing a coat and a tie stood and said he simply could not be away from the office. He was a district manager for a company that made steel buildings, and was clearly an executive taken with his own importance. He even hinted he might lose his job. Judge Atlee's lecture on civic responsibility lasted five minutes and scorched the gentleman. He ended with "If you lose your job, Mr. Crawford, let me know. I'll subpoena your boss, put him on the stand here, and, well, he'll have a bad day."

Mr. Crawford sat down, thoroughly chastised and humiliated. There were no more efforts to skip jury duty on account of work. Judge Atlee then moved to the next issue on his checklist—prior jury service. Several said they had served before, three in state court and two in federal. Nothing about those experiences would alter their ability to deliberate in the case at hand.

Nine people claimed to know Jake Brigance. Four were former clients and they were excused. Two ladies attended the same church but felt as though that fact would not influence their judgment. They were not excused. A distant relative was. Carla's schoolteacher friend said she knew Jake well and was too close for any objectivity. She was excused. The last was a high school pal from Karaway who admitted he hadn't seen Jake in ten years. He was left on the panel, to be dealt with later.

Each lawyer was introduced again, with the same questions. No one knew Wade Lanier, Lester Chilcott, Zack Zeitler, or Joe Bradley Hunt, but then they were out-of-town lawyers.

Judge Atlee said, "Now, moving along, the last will and testament in question was written by a man named Seth Hubbard, now deceased, of course. Did any of you know him personally?" Two hands were timidly lifted. A man stood and said he had grown up in the Palmyra area of the county and had known Seth when they were quite a bit younger.

"How old are you, sir?" Judge Atlee asked.

"Sixty-nine."

"You know you can claim an exemption from service if you're above the age of sixty-five, right?"

"Yes sir, but I don't have to, do I?"

"Oh no. If you want to serve, that's admirable. Thank you."

A woman stood and said she had once worked at a lumber yard owned by Seth Hubbard, but it would not be a problem. Judge Atlee gave the names of Seth's two wives and asked if anyone knew them. A woman said her older sister had been friends with the first wife, but that had been a long time ago. Herschel Hubbard and Ramona Hubbard Dafoe were asked to stand. They smiled awkwardly at the judge and the jurors, then sat down. Methodically, Judge Atlee asked the panel if anyone knew them. A few hands went up, all belonging to old classmates from Clanton High. Judge Atlee asked each one a series of questions. All claimed to know little about the case and to be unaffected by what little knowledge they possessed.

Tedium set in as Judge Atlee went through page after page of questions. By noon, twelve of the fifty had been dismissed, all of them white. Of the thirty-eight remaining, eleven were black, not a single one of whom had lifted a hand.

During the lunch recess, the lawyers met in tense groups and debated who was acceptable and who had to be cut. They ignored their cold sandwiches while they argued over body language and facial expressions. In Jake's office, the mood was lighter because the panel was darker. In the main conference room over at the Sullivan firm, the mood was heavier because the blacks were sandbagging. Of the eleven remaining, not one admitted to knowing Lettie Lang. Impossible in such a small county! There was obviously a conspiracy of some nature at work. Their expert consultant, Myron Pankey, had watched several of them closely during the questioning and had no doubt that they were trying their best to get on the jury. But Myron was from Cleveland and knew little about southern blacks.

Wade Lanier, though, was unimpressed. He'd tried more cases in Mississippi than the rest of the lawyers combined, and he was not concerned about the remaining thirty-eight members of the pool. In almost every trial, he hired consultants to dig into the backgrounds of the jurors, but once he saw them in the flesh he knew he could read them. And though he did not say so, he liked what he had seen that morning.

Lanier still had two great secrets up his sleeve—the handwritten will of Irene Pickering, and the testimony of Julina Kidd. To his knowledge, Jake had no idea what was coming. If Lanier managed to successfully detonate these two bombs in open court, he might just walk away with a unanimous verdict. After considerable negotiating, Fritz Pickering had agreed to testify for $7,500. Julina Kidd had jumped at the offer of only $5,000. Neither Fritz nor Julina had spoken to anyone on the other side, so Lanier was confident his ambushes would work.

So far, his firm had either spent or committed to spending just over $85,000 in litigation expenses, moneys the clients were ultimately responsible for. The cost of the case was rarely discussed, though it was always in their thoughts. While the clients were troubled by rising expenses, Wade Lanier understood the economic realities of big-time litigation. Two years earlier, his firm had spent $200,000 on a product liability case, and lost.

You roll the dice and sometimes you lose. Wade Lanier, though, was not contemplating a loss in the Seth Hubbard case.

Nevin Dark settled into a booth at the Coffee Shop with three of his new friends and ordered iced tea from Dell. All four wore white lapel buttons with the word "Juror" in bold blue letters, as if they were now officially off-limits and beyond approach. Dell had seen the same buttons a hundred times, and knew she should listen hard but ask no questions and offer no opinions.

The thirty-eight remaining jurors had been warned by Judge Atlee not to discuss the case. Since none of the four at Nevin's table had ever met, they chatted about themselves for a few minutes while looking over the menus. Fran Decker was a retired schoolteacher from Lake Village, ten miles south of Clanton. Charles Ozier sold farm tractors for a company out of Tupelo and lived near the lake. Debbie Lacker lived in downtown Palmyra, population 350, but had never met Seth Hubbard. Since they couldn't talk about the case, they talked about the judge, the courtroom, and the lawyers. Dell listened hard but gleaned nothing from their lunch conversation, at least nothing she could report to Jake in the event he stopped by later for the gossip.

At 1:15, they paid their separate checks and returned to the courtroom. At 1:30, when all thirty-eight were accounted for, Judge Atlee appeared from the rear and said, "Good afternoon." He went on to explain that he would now continue with the selection of the jury, and he planned to do so in a manner that was somewhat unusual. Each juror would be asked to step into his chambers to be quizzed by the lawyers in private.

Jake had made this request because he assumed the jurors, as a group, knew more about the case than they were willing to admit. By grilling them in private, he was confident he could elicit more thorough responses. Wade Lanier did not object.

Judge Atlee said, "Mr. Nevin Dark, would you join us in my chambers, please?"

A bailiff showed him the way, and Nevin nervously walked past the bench, through a door, down a short hallway, and into a rather small room where everyone was waiting. A court reporter sat ready to transcribe every word. Judge Atlee occupied one end of the table and the lawyers crowded around the rest of it.

"Please remember that you're under oath, Mr. Dark," Judge Atlee said.

"Of course."

Jake Brigance flashed him an earnest smile and said, "Some of these questions might be kind of personal, Mr. Dark, and if you don't want to answer them, that's fine. Do you understand?"

"I do."

"Do you currently have a last will and testament?"

"I do."

"Who prepared it?"

"Barney Suggs, a lawyer in Karaway."

"And your wife?"

"Yes, we signed them at the same time, in Mr. Suggs's office, about three years ago."

Without asking the specifics of their wills, Jake nibbled around the edges of the will-making process. What prompted them to prepare their wills? Do their children know what's in the wills? How often have they changed their wills? Did they name each other as executor of their wills? Have they ever inherited anything from another will? Did he, Nevin Dark, believe a person should have the right to leave his property to anyone? To a non–family member? To charity? To a friend or employee? To cut out family members who may have fallen out of favor? Had either Mr. Dark or his wife ever considered changing their wills to exclude a person currently named as a beneficiary?

And so on. When Jake finished, Wade Lanier asked a series of questions about drugs and painkillers. Nevin Dark said he'd used them only sparingly, but his wife was a breast cancer survivor and at one time had relied on some strong medications for pain. He could not remember their names. Lanier showed genuine concern for this woman he'd never met, and poked and prodded enough to convey the message that strong painkillers taken by very sick people often cause a lapse in ra- tional thinking. The seed was skillfully planted.

Judge Atlee was watching the clock, and after ten minutes he called time. Nevin returned to the courtroom, where everyone stared at him. Juror Number Two, Tracy McMillen, was waiting in a chair by the bench, and was quickly led to the back room, where she faced the same questioning.

Boredom hit hard and many of the spectators left. Some of the jurors napped while others read and reread newspapers and magazines. Bailiffs yawned and gazed from the large plate-glass windows overlooking the courthouse lawn. One prospective juror replaced the next in a steady parade to Judge Atlee's chambers. Most disappeared for the full ten minutes, but a few were finished in less time. When Juror Number Eleven emerged from her interrogation, she passed the benches and headed for the door, excused from service for reasons those sitting in the courtroom would never know.

Lettie and Phedra left for a long break. As they walked down the aisle toward the double doors, they were careful to avoid glancing at the Hubbard clan, bunched together on the back row.

It was almost 6:30 when Juror Number Thirty-eight left chambers and returned to the courtroom. Judge Atlee, showing remarkable energy, rubbed his hands together and said, "Gentlemen, let's finish this job now so we can start fresh with the opening statements in the morning. Agreed?"

Jake said, "Judge, I'd like to renew my motion for a change of venue. Now that we've interviewed the first thirty-eight jurors, it is apparent that, as a whole, this panel knows far too much about this case. Almost every juror was willing to admit he or she had heard something about it. This is quite unusual in a civil case."

"Quite the contrary, Jake," Judge Atlee said. "I thought they answered the questions well. Sure they've heard about the case, but almost all of them claimed to be able to keep an open mind."

"I agree, Judge," Wade Lanier said. "With a few exceptions, I'm impressed with the panel."

"Motion is overruled, Jake."

"No surprise," Jake mumbled, just loud enough to be heard.

"Now, can we pick our jury?"

"I'm ready," Jake said.

"Let's go," replied Wade Lanier.

"Very well. I'm dismissing jurors number three, four, seven, nine, fifteen, eighteen, and twenty-four for cause. Any discussion?"

Slowly, Lanier said, "Yes, Your Honor, why number fifteen?"

"He said he knew the Roston family and was deeply saddened by the deaths of their two sons. I suspect he holds a grudge against anyone with the last name of Lang."

"He said he did not, Your Honor," Lanier argued.

"Of course that's what he said. I just don't believe him. He's excused for cause. Anyone else?"

Jake shook his head no. Lanier was angry but said nothing. Judge Atlee pressed on, "Each side has four peremptory challenges. Mr. Brigance, you must present the first twelve."

Jake nervously scanned his notes, then slowly said, "Okay, we'll take numbers one, two, five, eight, ten, twelve, fourteen, sixteen, seventeen, nineteen, twenty-one, and twenty-two." There was a long pause as everyone in the room looked at their charts and made notes. Finally, Judge Atlee said, "So you struck six, thirteen, twenty, and twenty-three, correct?"

"That's right."

"Are you ready, Mr. Lanier?"

"Just a second, Judge," Lanier said as he huddled with Lester Chilcott. They whispered for a while, obviously in disagreement. Jake listened hard but could not decipher anything. He kept his eyes on his notes, on his chosen twelve, knowing he could not keep them all.

"Gentlemen," Judge Atlee said.

"Yes sir," Lanier said slowly. "We'll strike numbers five, sixteen, twenty-five, and twenty-seven."

The air left the room again as every lawyer and the judge struck names from makeshift charts and moved the higher numbers up the ladder. Judge Atlee said, "So, it looks like our jury will consist of numbers one, two, eight, ten, twelve, fourteen, seventeen, nineteen, twenty-one, twenty-two, twenty-six, and twenty-eight. Does everyone concur?"

The lawyers shook their heads in agreement without taking their eyes from their legal pads. Ten whites, two blacks. Eight women, four men. Half had wills, half did not. Three had college degrees; seven finished high school; two did not. Median age of forty-nine, with two women in their twenties, a pleasant surprise for Jake. Overall he was pleased. On the other side of the table, Wade Lanier was too. The truth was that Judge Atlee did a fine job of eliminating those who might possibly begin deliberations with preconceived notions or prejudices. On paper, it appeared as if the extremists were gone, and the trial was left in the hands of twelve people who appeared to be open-minded.

"Let's pick a couple of alternates," His Honor said.

At 7:00 p.m., the new jurors gathered in the jury room and got themselves organized, according to Judge Atlee's instructions. Because he had been the first one selected, the first name called, the first to be seated, and because he gave every indication of being an amicable type with an easy smile and kind word to all, Mr. Nevin Dark was elected foreman of the jury.

It had been a very long day, but an exciting one. As he drove home, he found himself eager to chat with his wife over a late dinner and tell her everything. Judge Atlee had warned them against discussing the case with each other, but he didn't say a word about spouses.

40

Lucien shuffled the deck and deftly dealt ten cards to Lonny and the same to himself. As usual now, Lonny slowly lifted his cards from the top of the folding table and took forever arranging them in his preferred order. His hands and words were slow, but his mind seemed to be clicking right along. He was up thirty points in this their fifth game of gin rummy; he'd won three of the first four. He was wearing a saggy hospital gown and an IV hung just over his head. A nicer nurse had given him permission to leave his bed and play cards in front of the window, but only after Lonny had raised his voice. He was sick and tired of the hospital and wanted to leave. But then, he really had no place to go. Only the city jail, where the food was even worse and the cops were waiting with questions. In fact, they were waiting just outside his door now. Thirty kilos of cocaine will always create problems. His new pal Lucien, who said he was a lawyer, had guaranteed him the evidence would be tossed on a motion to suppress. The cops had no probable cause to enter Lonny's room at the flophouse. Just because a man gets hurt in a bar fight does not give the police the right to rummage through his locked living quarters. "It's a slam dunk," Lucien had promised. "Any half-assed criminal lawyer gets the coke thrown out. You'll walk."

They had talked about Seth Hubbard, with Lucien throwing in all the facts, gossip, fabrications, speculations, and rumors that had been roaring through Clanton during the past six months. Lonny claimed to be only mildly curious, but he seemed to enjoy listening. Lucien did not mention the handwritten will, nor the black housekeeper. Expansively, he recounted Seth's amazing ten-year run from a man broken by his second nasty divorce to a high-flying risk taker who parlayed his own mort-gaged property into a fortune. He described Seth's zeal for secrecy, his offshore bank accounts and maze of corporations. He told the amazing historical anecdote of Seth's father, Cleon, hiring Lucien's grandfather Robert E. Lee Wilbanks to handle a land dispute in 1928. And they lost!

Lucien talked almost nonstop in an effort to gain Lonny's trust, to convince him there was no harm in telling secrets from the past. If Lucien could open up so completely, then Lonny could too. On two occasions during the morning, Lucien had gently poked into the business of Lonny knowing anything about Ancil, but neither punch had landed. Lonny seemed to have no interest in that subject. They talked and played through-out the morning. By noon, Lonny was fatigued and needed rest. The nurse enjoyed telling Lucien to leave.

He did so but was back two hours later to check on his new friend. Lonny now wanted to play blackjack, at a dime a hand. After half an hour or so, Lucien said, "I called Jake Brigance, the lawyer I work for in Mississippi, and I asked him to check out this Sylvester Rinds guy you mentioned. He found something."

Lonny put his cards down and gave Lucien a curious look. Deliberately, he said, "What?"

"Well, according to the land records in Ford County, Sylvester Rinds owned eighty acres of land in the northeast part of the county, land he had inherited from his father, a man named Solomon Rinds, who was born about the time the Civil War started. Though the records are not clear, there's a good chance the Rinds family came to own the land just after the war, during Reconstruction, when freed slaves were able to obtain land with the help of carpetbaggers and federal gover-nors and other scum that flooded our land back then. It looks as though this eighty acres was in dispute for some time. The Hubbard family owned another eighty acres that adjoined the Rinds property, and evidently they contested this property. The lawsuit I mentioned this morning, the one filed in 1928 by

Cleon Hubbard, was a dispute over the Rinds property. My grandfather, who was the finest lawyer in the county and well connected, lost the case for Cleon. I gotta figure that if my grandfather lost the case then the Rinds family must have had a pretty strong claim to the land. So Sylvester managed to hang on to his property for a few more years, but then he died in 1930. After he died, Cleon Hubbard obtained the land from Sylvester's widow."

Lonny had picked up his cards and he studied them without seeing them. He was listening and recalling images from another lifetime.

"Pretty interesting, huh?" Lucien said.

"It was a long time ago," Lonny said, grimacing as pain rippled through his skull.

Lucien plowed ahead. With nothing to lose, he was not about to relax. "The strangest part of this entire story is that there is no record of Sylvester's death. There's not a single Rinds now living in Ford County, and it appears as though they all left about the time Cleon Hubbard got his hands on the property. They all vanished; most fled to the North, to Chicago, where they found jobs, but this was not uncommon in the Depression. A lot of starving blacks fled the Deep South. According to Mr. Brigance, they found a distant relative over in Alabama, a man named Boaz Rinds, who claims that some white men took Sylvester and killed him."

"What does this have to do with anything?" Lonny asked.

Lucien stood and walked to the window where he gazed at a parking lot below. He debated telling the truth now, telling Lonny about the will and Lettie Lang and her ancestry: that she was almost certainly a Rinds instead of a Tayber; that her people were from Ford County and had once lived on the land owned by Sylvester; that it was highly probable Sylvester was in fact her grandfather.

But he sat back down and said, "Nothing really. Just some old history involving my kinfolks, Seth Hubbard's, and maybe Sylvester Rinds's."

There was a moment of silence in which neither man touched his cards. Neither made eye contact. As Lonny seemed to drift away, Lucien jolted him with "You knew Ancil, didn't you?"

"I did," Lonny said.

"Tell me about him. I need to find him, and quick."

"What do you want to know about him?"

"Is he alive?"

"He is, yes."

"Where is he right now?"

"Don't know."

"When did you last see him?"

A nurse entered chattering away about checking his vitals. He said he was tired, and so she helped him into his bed, arranged his IV, glared at Lucien, then checked Lonny's blood pressure and pulse. "He needs to rest," she said.

Lonny closed his eyes and said, "Don't go. Just turn down the lights."

Lucien pulled a chair close to his bed and sat down. After the nurse left, he said, "Tell me about Ancil."

With his eyes still closed and his voice almost a whisper, Lonny began, "Well, Ancil has always been a man on the run. He left home when he was young and never went back. He hated home, hated his father especially. He fought in the war, got wounded, almost died. A head injury, and most folks think Ancil's always been a bit off upstairs. He loved the sea, said he'd been born so far away from it that it captivated him. He spent years on cargo ships and saw the world, all of it. You can't find a spot on the map that Ancil hasn't seen. Not a mountain, a port, a city, a famous site. Not a bar, a dance club, a whorehouse, you name it, and Ancil's been there. He hung out with rough characters and from time to time fell into bad ways: petty crime, then some not so petty. He had some near misses, once spent a week in a hospital in Sri Lanka with a knife wound. The knife wound was nothing compared with the infection he got in the hospital. He had lots of women, some of whom had lots of children, but Ancil was never one to stay in one place. Last he knew, some of those women were still looking for him, with their children. Others might be looking for him too. Ancil has lived a crazy life and he's always looked over his shoulder."

When he said the word "life," it came out wrong; or, perhaps it came out naturally. The long *i* was much flatter than before, much like the flattened *i*'s so common in north Mississippi. Lucien had deliberately fallen back into a twangier version of speech, in hopes that it might lure old Lonny here into the same habit. Lonny was from Mississippi, and they both knew it.

He closed his eyes and seemed to sleep. Lucien stared at him for a few minutes, waiting. His breathing became heavier as he drifted away. His right hand fell to his side. The monitors showed a normal blood pressure and heartbeat. To stay awake, Lucien paced around the darkened room, waiting for a nurse to appear and shoo him away. He eased next to the bed, squeezed Lonny's right wrist firmly, and said, "Ancil! Ancil! Seth left behind a last will and testament that gives you a million bucks."

The eyes came open and Lucien repeated himself.

The debate had raged for an hour, unabated, and tempers were on edge. In fact, the issue had been hotly discussed for a month with no shortage of opinions. It was almost 10:00 p.m. The conference table was littered with notes, files, books, and the remains of a bad take-out pizza they had devoured for dinner.

Should the jury be told the value of Seth's estate? The only issue at trial was whether the handwritten will was valid. Nothing more, nothing less. Legally, technically, it didn't matter how big or how small the estate was. On one side of the table, the side being occupied by Harry Rex, the strong feeling was that the jury should not be told because if the jurors knew that $24 million was in play and about to be given to Lettie Lang, they would balk. They would naturally take a dim view of such a transfer of wealth outside the family. Such a sum was so unheard-of, so shocking, that it was inconceivable that a lowly black housekeeper should walk away with it. Lucien, while absent, agreed with Harry Rex.

Jake, though, felt otherwise. His first point was that the jurors probably had a hunch that a lot of money was on the table, though virtually all had denied such knowledge during the selection process. Look at the size of the fight. Look at the number of lawyers on deck. Everything about the case and the trial was evidence of big money. His second point was that full disclosure was the best policy. If the jurors felt as though Jake was trying to hide something, he would start the trial with an immediate loss of credibility. Every person in the courtroom wants to know what the brawl is about. Tell them. Lay it out. Withhold nothing. If they concealed the size of the estate, then the size of the estate would become a festering and unspoken issue.

Portia went back and forth. Before the jury was seated, she was leaning in favor of a full disclosure. But after looking at the ten white faces, and only two black ones, she was struggling to believe they had any chance at all. After all the witnesses had testified, after all the lawyers had been silenced, after all the wise words had been uttered by Judge Atlee, could those ten white people reach deep and find the courage to uphold Seth's last will? At the moment, fatigued and weary, she was doubtful.

The phone rang and she answered it. "It's Lucien," she said, handing it to Jake, who said, "Hello."

From Alaska came the report: "Got him, Jake. Our pal here is Ancil Hubbard, one and the same."

Jake exhaled and said, "Well, I guess that's good news, Lucien." He pulled the receiver away and said, "It's Ancil."

"What are you guys doing?" Lucien asked.

"Just prepping for tomorrow. Me, Portia, Harry Rex. You're missing the party."

"Do we have a jury?"

"Yes. Ten whites, two blacks, no real surprises. Tell me about Ancil."

"Pretty sick puppy. His head wound is infected and the doctors are concerned. Tons of meds, antibiotics and painkillers. We played cards all day and talked about everything. He sort of comes and goes. I finally mentioned the will and told him his big brother left him a million bucks. Got his attention and he admitted who he is. Half an hour later he'd forgotten about it."

"Should I tell Judge Atlee?" Harry Rex shook his head, no.

"I don't think so," Lucien said. "The trial has started and it won't be stopped for this. Ancil has nothing to add. He damned sure can't get there, what with a cracked skull and the cocaine thing waiting just outside his door. Poor guy'll probably serve some time eventually. The cops seem determined."

"Did you guys climb the family trees?"

"Yes, quite a bit, but long before he came clean. I laid out the history of the Hubbard and Rinds families, with emphasis on the mystery of Sylvester. But he had little interest. I'll try again tomorrow. I'm thinking about leaving tomorrow afternoon. I really want to see some of the trial. I'm sure you'll have it all screwed up by the time I get there."

"No doubt, Lucien," Jake said, and hung up a moment later. He relayed the conversation to Portia and Harry Rex, who, though intrigued by it, had other matters at hand. The fact that Ancil Hubbard was alive and living in Alaska would mean nothing in the courtroom.

The phone rang again and Jake grabbed it. Willie Traynor said, "Say, Jake, just for your information, there's a guy on the jury who shouldn't be there."

"It's probably too late, but I'm listening."

"He's on the back row, name's Doley, Frank Doley." Jake had seen Willie taking notes throughout the day. "Okay, so what's Frank up to?" Jake asked.

"He has a distant cousin who lives in Memphis. Six or seven years ago, this cousin's fifteen-year-old daughter was snatched by some black punks outside a mall in East Memphis. They kept her in a van for several hours. Terrible things happened. The girl survived but was too messed up to identify anyone. No one was ever arrested. Two years later the girl committed suicide. A real tragedy."

"Why are you telling me this now?"

"I didn't catch the name until an hour ago. I was in Memphis at the time, and I remembered some Doleys from Ford County. You'd better get him bumped, Jake."

"It's not that easy. In fact, it's impossible at this point. He was quizzed by the lawyers and the judge and gave all the right answers." Frank Doley was forty-three years old and owned a roofing company out near the lake. He claimed to know nothing about the Seth Hubbard matter and seemed perfectly open-minded.

Thanks for nothing, Willie.

Willie said, "Sorry, Jake, but it didn't register in court. I would have said something."

"It's okay. I'll deal with it somehow."

"Other than Doley, what do you think of your jury?"

Jake was talking to a journalist, so he played it safe. "A good panel," he said. "Gotta run."

Harry Rex's response was, "I was worried about that guy. Something wasn't right."

To which Jake shot back, "Well, I don't recall you saying anything at the time. It's always easy to call plays on Monday morning."

"Testy, testy."

Portia said, "He seemed eager to serve. I gave him an eight."

Jake said, "Well, we're stuck with him. He gave all the right answers."

"Maybe you didn't ask the right questions," Harry Rex said as he took another swig of Bud Light.

"Thank you so much, Harry Rex. For your own future reference, during the jury selection process lawyers are not normally allowed to ask questions like, 'Say, Mr. Doley, is it true your distant cousin was gang-raped by a bunch of black thugs in Memphis?' and the reason for this prohibition is that the lawyers generally don't know about such horrible crimes."

"I'm going home." Another swig.

"Let's all go home," Portia said. "We're not accomplishing much."

It was almost 10:30 when they turned out the lights. Jake walked around the square to clear his head. At the Sullivan firm, lights were still on. Wade Lanier and his team were still in there, still working.

41

In his defense of Carl Lee Hailey, Jake's opening statement to the jury lasted only fourteen minutes. Rufus Buckley had kicked things off with a one-and-a-half-hour marathon that had put the jury to sleep, and Jake's concise follow-up had been well received and much appreciated. The jury had listened to him and absorbed every word. "Jurors are captives," Lucien always said. "So keep it short."

In the matter of the last will and testament of Henry Seth Hubbard, Jake was aiming for ten minutes. He stepped to the podium, smiled to the fresh and eager faces, and began with "Ladies and gentlemen of the jury, your job is not to give away Seth Hubbard's money. There's a lot of it, and all of it was earned by Seth Hubbard himself. Not by you, not by me, not by any of the lawyers in this courtroom. He took chances, borrowed heavily at times, ignored the advice of his trusted lieutenants, mortgaged his own house and land, made deals that looked bad on paper, borrowed even more, took risks that seemed outrageous, and in the end, when Seth Hubbard was told he was dying of lung cancer, he sold out. He cashed in his chips, paid off the banks, and counted his money. He won. He was right and everybody else was wrong. You can't help but admire Seth Hubbard. I never met the man, but I wish I had.

"How much money? You will hear testimony from Mr. Quince Lundy, the gentleman sitting right here, and the court-appointed administrator of Seth Hubbard's estate, that the estate has a value of approximately $24 million."

Jake was pacing slowly, and when he gave the amount he stopped and looked at some of the faces. Almost every juror smiled. Go, Seth. Attaboy. A couple were obviously shocked. Tracy McMillen, Juror Number Two, looked at Jake with wide eyes. But the moment passed quickly. No one in Ford County could grasp a number like that.

"Now, if you think a man who put together a $24 million fortune in about ten years knows what he's doing with his money, then you're right. Because Seth knew exactly what he was doing. The day before he hung himself he went to his office, locked his door, sat down at his desk, and wrote a new will. A handwritten will, one perfectly legal, nice and legible, easy to understand, not the least bit complicated or confusing. He knew he was going to commit suicide the following day, Sunday, October 2, and he was putting everything in order. He planned it all. He wrote a note to a man named Calvin Boggs, an employee, in which he explained he was taking his own life. You will see the original. He wrote detailed funeral and burial instructions. You will see the originals. And on that same Saturday, presumably at his office while he was writing his will, he wrote a letter to me and gave me specific instructions. Again, you will see the original. He planned it all. After he finished writing, he drove to Clanton, to the main post office, and mailed the letter to me, along with the will. He wanted me to receive the letter on Monday because his funeral was on Tuesday, at 4:00 pm., at the Irish Road Christian Church. Details, folks. Seth took care of the details. He knew exactly what he was doing. He planned it all.

"Now, as I said, it's not your job to give away Seth's money, or to decide who should get what or how much. However, it is your job to determine if Seth knew what he was doing. The legal term is 'testamentary capacity.' To make a valid will, one that is handwritten on the back of a grocery bag or one typed by five secretaries in a big law office and signed before a notary public, one has to have testamentary capacity. It's a legal term that's easy to understand. It means you have to know what you're doing, and, ladies and gentlemen, Seth Hubbard knew exactly what he was doing. He wasn't crazy. He wasn't delusional. He wasn't under the influence of painkillers or other meds. He was as mentally sound and sane as the twelve of you are right now.

"It might be argued that a man planning his own suicide cannot be of sound mind. You gotta be crazy to kill yourself, right? Not always. Not necessarily. As jurors you are expected to rely on your own experiences in life. Perhaps you've known someone, a close friend or even a family member, who came to the end of the road and chose his or her own final exit. Were they out of their minds? Perhaps, but probably not. Seth certainly was not. He knew exactly what he was doing. He'd battled lung cancer for a year, with several rounds of chemo-therapy and radiation, all unsuccessful, and the tumors had finally metastasized to his ribs and spine. He was in terrible pain. At his last visit to his doctor he was given less than a month to live. When you read what he wrote the day before he died, you'll be convinced that Seth Hubbard was in complete control of his life."

As a prop, Jake was holding a legal pad but he wasn't using it. He didn't need it. He walked back and forth before the jurors, making eye contact with every one of them, speaking slowly and clearly as if they were sitting in his den and chatting about their favorite movies. But every word was written somewhere. Every sentence had been rehearsed. Every pause was calculated. The timing, cadence, rhythm—all memorized to near perfection.

Even the busiest of trial lawyers spend only a fraction of their time in front of juries. These moments were rare, and Jake relished them. He was an actor on a stage, in the midst of a monologue he created, speaking words of wisdom to his chosen audience. His pulse was spiking; his stomach was flipping; his knees were weak. But those internal battles were all under control and Jake calmly lectured his new friends.

Five minutes in, and he had not missed a word. Five minutes to go, with the roughest part just ahead.

"Now, ladies and gentlemen, there is an unpleasant part of this story, and that's why we're all here. Seth Hubbard was survived by a son and a daughter and four grandchildren. In his will, he left them nothing. In language that is plain and clear, but also painful to read, Seth specifically excluded his family from inheriting under his will. The obvious question is, Why? It is our natural tendency to ask, 'Why would a man do this?' However, it is not your responsibility to ask that question. Seth did what he did for reasons known only to him. Again, he made the money—it all belonged to him. He could have given every penny to the Red Cross, or to some slick televangelist, or to the Communist Party. That's his business, not yours, not mine, not this court's.

"Instead of leaving his money to his family, Seth left 5 percent to his church, 5 percent to a long-lost brother, and the remaining 90 percent was given to a woman by the name of Lettie Lang. Ms. Lang is sitting right here between me and Mr. Lundy. She worked for Seth Hubbard for three years as his housekeeper, his cook, and sometimes his nurse. Again, the obvious question is, Why? Why did Seth cut out his family and leave almost everything to a woman he'd known for such a short period of time? Believe me, ladies and gentlemen, that is the greatest question I've ever confronted as a lawyer. That question has been asked by me, by the other lawyers, by the Hubbard family, by Lettie Lang herself, by friends and neighbors, and by virtually everyone in this county who's heard the story. Why?

"The truth is that we'll never know. Only Seth knew and he's no longer with us. The truth, folks, is that it's none of our business. We—the lawyers, the judge, you the jurors—are not supposed to concern ourselves with why Seth did what he did. Your job, as I've said, is to decide only one important issue, and that is simply this: At the time Seth wrote his last will, was he thinking clearly and did he know what he was doing?

"He was, and he did. The evidence will be clear and convincing."

Jake paused and picked up a glass of water. He took a quick sip, and as he did so he scanned the crowded courtroom. On the second row, Harry Rex stared at him. He nodded quickly. You're doing fine so far. You have their attention. Wrap it up.

Jake returned to the podium, glanced at his notes, and continued: "Now, with this much money on the line, we can expect things to get somewhat tense over the next few days. The family of Seth Hubbard is contesting the handwritten will, and they are not to be faulted for this. They sincerely believe the money should have been given to them, and they've hired a bunch of good lawyers to attack the handwritten will. They claim that Seth lacked testamentary capacity. They claim his judgment was clouded. They claim he was unduly influenced by Lettie Lang. The term 'undue influence' is a legal term and will be crucial in this case. They will attempt to convince you that Lettie Lang used her position as a caregiver to become intimate with Seth Hubbard. Intimacy can mean many things. She cared for Seth, at times bathed him, changed his clothes, cleaned up behind him, did all the things that caregivers are supposed to do in those delicate and awful situations. Seth was a dying old man, hit with a debilitating and deadly cancer that left him weak and feeble."

Jake turned and looked at Wade Lanier and the gang of lawyers at the other table. "They will imply a lot, ladies and gentlemen, but they can prove nothing. There were no physical relations between Seth Hubbard and Lettie Lang. Only hints, and suggestions, and implications, but no proof because it never happened."

Jake tossed his legal pad on his table and wrapped it up. "This will be a short trial with a lot of witnesses. As in every trial, the issues at times might become confusing. This is often done on purpose by the lawyers, but don't be led astray. Remember, ladies and gentlemen, it's not your job to distribute Seth Hubbard's money. It's your job to determine if he knew what he was doing when he wrote his last will. Nothing more, nothing less. Thank you."

At Judge Atlee's heavy-handed direction, the contestants had agreed to streamline their opening and closing remarks by allowing Wade Lanier to handle them. He strode to the podium in a wrinkled blazer, a tie too short, and a shirttail barely tucked in. The few patches of hair around his ears shot out in all directions. He gave the impression of a scatterbrained plodder who might forget to show up tomorrow. It was all an act to disarm the jury. Jake knew better.

He began with "Thank you, Mr. Brigance. I've been trying lawsuits for thirty years, and I've yet to meet a young lawyer with as much talent as Jake Brigance. You folks here in Ford County are lucky to have such a fine young lawyer among you. It's an honor to be here doing battle with him, and also to be in this grand old courtroom." He paused to look at his notes as Jake stewed over all the fake praise. When he wasn't in front of a jury, Lanier was smooth and articulate. Now, though, onstage, he was folksy, down-to-earth, and immensely likable.

"Now, this is just an opening statement and nothing I say or nothing Mr. Brigance just said is evidence. The evidence comes from only one place, and that's this witness chair right here. Lawyers sometimes get carried away and say things they cannot later prove at trial, and they also tend to leave out important facts the jury should know about. For example, Mr. Brigance did not mention the fact that when Seth Hubbard wrote his last will, the only person in the building with him was Lettie Lang. It was a Saturday morning, and she never worked on Saturdays. She went to his house, and from there she drove him in his nice new Cadillac over to his office. He unlocked it. They went in. She says she was there to clean his office, but she had never done this before. They were alone. For some two hours they were alone in the offices of the Berring Lumber Company, Seth Hubbard's main headquarters. When they arrived there on that Saturday morning, Seth Hubbard had a last will and testament prepared a year earlier by a fine firm of lawyers in Tupelo, lawyers he had trusted for years, and that will gave almost everything to his two adult children and four grandchildren. A typical will. A standard will. A sensible will. The kind of will virtually every American signs at one time or another. Ninety percent of all property that passes through wills passes to the family of the deceased. That's the way it should be."

Lanier was now pacing too, his stocky body lumbering back and forth, bowed somewhat at the waist. "But after spending two hours in his office that morning, alone with no one but Lettie Lang, when he left he had another will, one he'd written himself, one *cutting* out his children and *cutting* out his grandchildren and leaving 90 percent of his fortune to his housekeeper. Does that sound reasonable, folks? Let's put things in perspective. Seth Hubbard had been battling cancer for a year—a terrible struggle, a fight he was losing and he knew it. The closest person in the world to Seth Hubbard during his last days on this earth was Lettie Lang. On good days she cooked and cleaned and took care of his house and things, and on bad days she fed him, bathed him, dressed him, cleaned up after him. She knew he was dying—it was no secret. She also knew he was rich, and she also knew his relationship with his adult children was somewhat strained."

Lanier paused near the witness chair, spread his arms wide in mock disbelief, and asked loudly, "Are we to believe she was not thinking about money? Come on, let's get realistic here! Ms. Lang will tell you herself that she'd spent her career as a housekeeper, that her husband, Mr. Simeon Lang, who's now in jail, had a spotty work record and could not be depended on for a paycheck, and that she'd raised five kids under difficult financial circumstances. Life was tough! There had never been a spare dime anywhere. Like a lot of folks, Lettie Lang was broke. She'd always been broke. And as she watched her boss inch closer and closer to death, you know she was thinking about money. It's human nature. It's not her fault. I'm not suggesting she was evil or greedy. Who among us would not have been thinking about the money?

"And on that Saturday morning last October, Lettie drove her boss to his office where they were alone for two hours. And while they were alone, one of the greatest fortunes in the history of this state changed hands. Twenty-four million dollars was transferred from the Hubbard family to a housekeeper Seth Hubbard had known for only three years."

Brilliantly, Lanier paused as his last sentence rattled around the courtroom. Damn he's good, Jake thought, glancing at the jury as if all was well. Frank Doley was glaring at him with a look that said, "I despise you."

Lanier lowered his voice and continued: "We will attempt to prove Seth Hubbard was unduly influenced by Ms. Lang. The key to this case is the issue of undue influence, and there are several ways to prove it. One sign of undue influence is the making of a gift that is unusual or unreasonable. The gift Seth Hubbard made to Ms. Lang is grossly, unbelievably unusual and unreasonable. Forgive me. I can't think of the right adjectives to describe it. Ninety percent of twenty-four million? And nothing for his family? That's pretty unusual, folks. In my book, that's pretty unreasonable. That screams of undue influence. If he wanted to do something nice for his housekeeper, he could've given her a million bucks. That's a pretty generous gift. Two million? How about five? Actually, in my humble opinion, anything over a million dollars would be considered unusual and unreasonable, given the brief nature of their relationship."

Lanier stepped back to the podium and glanced at his notes, then he looked at his watch. Eight minutes, and he was in no hurry. "We will attempt to prove undue influence by discussing a prior will made by Seth Hubbard. This will was prepared by a leading law firm in Tupelo a year before Seth died, and it left about 95 percent of his estate to his family. It's a complicated will with a lot of legal mumbo-jumbo that only tax lawyers understand. I don't understand it and we'll try not to bore you with it. The purpose of discussing this earlier will is to illustrate the point that Seth was not thinking clearly. The earlier will, because it was prepared by tax lawyers who knew their stuff and not by a man on the verge of hanging himself, takes full advantage of the IRS code. In doing so, it saves over $3 million in taxes. Under Mr. Hubbard's handwritten will, the IRS gets 51 percent, over $12 million. Under the earlier will, the IRS gets $9 million. Now, Mr. Brigance likes to say that Seth Hubbard knew exactly what he was doing. I doubt it. Think about it, folks. A man shrewd enough and clever enough to amass such a fortune in ten years does not throw together a handwritten document that will cost his estate $3 million. That's absurd! That's unusual and unreasonable!"

With his elbows he leaned on the podium and tapped his fingers together. He looked into the eyes of the jurors as they waited. He finally said, "Let me wrap things up here, and I must say you're pretty lucky because neither Jake Brigance nor I believe in long speeches. Nor does Judge Atlee for that matter." There were some smiles. It was almost funny. "I'd like to leave you with my opening thought, my first visual for this trial. Think of Seth Hubbard on October 1 of last year, facing certain death and already determined to speed it up, racked with pain and heavily medicated with painkillers, sad, lonely, single, estranged from his children and grandchildren, a dying, bitter old man who'd given up, and the only person near enough to hear him and console him was Lettie Lang. We'll never know how close they really were. We'll never know what went on between them. But we do know the outcome. Ladies and gentlemen, this is a clear case of a man making a terrible mistake while under the influence of someone after his money."

When Lanier sat down, Judge Atlee said, "Call your first witness, Mr. Brigance."

"The proponents call Sheriff Ozzie Walls." From the second row, Ozzie hurried to the witness chair and was sworn in. Quince Lundy was seated at the table to Jake's right, and though he had practiced law for almost forty years he had aggressively avoided courtrooms. Jake instructed him to glance at the jurors occasionally and make observations. As Ozzie was getting situated, Lundy slid over a note that read, "You were very good. So was Lanier. The jury is split. We're screwed."

Thanks, Jake thought. Portia shoved forward a legal pad. On it, her note read, "Frank Doley is pure evil."

What a team, Jake thought. All he needed was Lucien whispering bad advice and irritating everyone else in the courtroom.

With Jake asking the questions, Ozzie laid out the scene of the suicide. He used four large color photographs of Seth

Hubbard swinging from the rope. These were passed through the jury box for shock value. Jake had objected to the photos because of their gruesomeness. Lanier had objected to the photos because they might evoke sympathy for Seth. In the end, Judge Atlee said the jury needed to see them. Once they were gathered up and admitted into evidence, Ozzie produced the suicide note Seth left behind on his kitchen table for Calvin Boggs. The note was magnified on a large screen set up across from the jury, and each juror was given a copy. It read, "To Calvin. Please inform the authorities I've taken my own life, with no help from anyone. On the attached sheet of paper I have left specific instructions for my funeral and burial. No autopsy! S.H. Dated, October 2, 1988."

Jake produced the originals of the funeral and burial instructions, got them admitted without objection, and displayed them on the big screen. Each juror was handed a copy. They read:

Funeral Instructions:

I want a simple service at the Irish Road Christian Church on Tuesday, October 4, at 4 p.m. with Rev. Don McElwain presiding. I'd like for Mrs. Nora Baines to sing The Old Rugged Cross. I do not want anyone to attempt a eulogy. Can't imagine anyone wanting to. Other than that, Rev. McElwain can say whatever he wants. Thirty minutes max.

If any black people wish to attend my funeral, then they are to be admitted. If they are not admitted, then forget the whole service and put me in the ground.

My pallbearers are: Harvey Moss, Duane Thomas, Steve Holland, Billy Bowles, Mike Mills, and Walter Robinson.

Burial Instructions:

I just bought a plot in the Irish Road Cemetery behind the church. I've spoken with Mr. Magargel at the funeral home and he's been paid for the casket. No vault. Immediately after the church service, I want a quick interment—five minutes max— then lower the casket.

So long. See you on the other side.
Seth Hubbard

Jake addressed the witness and said, "And Sheriff Walls, this suicide note and these instructions were found by you and your deputies in the home of Seth Hubbard shortly after you found his body, correct?"

"That's right."

"What did you do with them?"

"We took them into our possession, made copies, then the following day gave them to Mr. Hubbard's family at his home."

"I have no further questions, Your Honor."

"Any cross-examination, Mr. Lanier?"

"None."

"You are excused, Sheriff Walls. Thank you. Mr. Brigance?"

"Yes, Your Honor, at this time I would like for the jury to be instructed that it has been stipulated by all parties that the documents just admitted into evidence were indeed written by Mr. Seth Hubbard."

"Mr. Lanier?"

"So stipulated, Your Honor."

"Very well, there is no dispute as to the authorship of these documents. Proceed, Mr. Brigance."

Jake said, "The proponents call Mr. Calvin Boggs." They waited until Calvin was summoned from a witness room. He was a large country boy who'd never owned a necktie, and it was obvious he had not even considered buying one for the occasion. He wore a frayed plaid shirt with patches on the elbows, dirty khakis, dirty boots, and looked as though he just wandered into the courtroom from a pulpwood-cutting expedition. He was thoroughly intimidated and overwhelmed by the surroundings, and within seconds began to choke up as he described his horror at finding his boss hanging from a sycamore tree.

"What time did he call you that Sunday morning?" Jake asked.

"Around nine, said to meet him at the bridge at two."

"And you arrived at two on the dot, right?"

"Yes sir, I did."

Jake's plan was to use Boggs to illustrate how Seth took care of the details. He would later argue to the jury that Seth left the note on the table, packed up his rope and ladder, drove to the site, and made sure he was good and dead when Calvin arrived at 2:00 p.m. He wanted to be found not long after he died. Otherwise, it could have been days.

Lanier had nothing to ask. The witness was dismissed.

"Call your next witness, Mr. Brigance," Judge Atlee said.

Jake said, "The proponents call the county coroner, Finn Plunkett."

Finn Plunkett was a rural mail carrier when he was first elected county coroner thirteen years earlier. At the time, he had no experience in medicine; none was required in Mississippi. He had never visited a crime scene. The fact that the state still elected its county coroners was odd enough; it was one of the last states to do so. Indeed, it was one of the few to ever initiate the ritual to begin with. For the past thirteen years, Finn had been called at all hours of the day and night to such locations as nursing homes, hospitals, accident scenes, honky-tonks, rivers and lakes, and homes wrecked by violence. His typical routine was to hover over a corpse and solemnly pronounce, "Yep, he's dead." Then he would speculate on the cause of death and sign a certificate.

He had been present when Seth was lowered to the ground. He'd said, "Yep, he's dead." Death by hanging, a suicide. Asphyxiation and a broken neck. With Jake leading him through his testimony, he quickly explained to the jury what was already painfully obvious. Wade Lanier had no cross-examination.

Jake called to the stand his ex-secretary, Roxy Brisco, who, since she'd left the office with bad blood, had initially refused to testify. So Jake issued a subpoena and explained she might go to jail if she ignored it. She quickly came around, and took the stand dressed fashionably for the moment. Tag-teaming, they walked through the events of the morning of October 3, when she arrived at the office with the mail. She identified the

envelope, letter, and two-page will from Seth Hubbard, and
Judge Atlee admitted them into evidence as exhibits for the
proponents. There was no objection from the other side.
Following a script that had been suggested by His Honor, Jake
projected on the screen an enlarged version of the letter to him
from Seth. He also handed a copy to each juror. Judge Atlee
said, "Now, ladies and gentlemen, we're going to pause for a
moment while each of you carefully reads this letter."

The courtroom was instantly silent as the jurors read their
copies and the spectators studied the screen.

*... herein you will find my last will and testament, every word
written by me and signed and dated by me. I've checked the law
of Mississippi and am satisfied that it is a proper holographic
will, thus entitled to full enforcement under the law. No one
witnessed me signing this will because, as you know, witnesses
are not required for holographic wills. A year ago I signed a
thicker version in the offices of the Rush law firm in Tupelo, but I
have renounced that document.*

*This one is likely to start some trouble and that's why I want
you as the attorney for my estate. I want this will defended at
all costs and I know you can do it. I specifically cut out my
two adult children, their children, and my two ex-wives. These
are not nice people and they will fight, so get ready. My estate
is substantial—they have no idea of its size—and when this is
made known they will attack. Fight them, Mr. Brigance, to the
bitter end. We must prevail.*

*With my suicide note I left instructions for my funeral and
burial. Do not mention my last will and testament until after the
funeral. I want my family to be forced to go through all the rituals of mourning before they realize they get nothing. Watch them
fake it—they're very good at it. They have no love for me.*

*I thank you in advance for your zealous representation. It
will not be easy. I am comforted in knowing I will not be there to
suffer through such an agonizing ordeal.*

Sincerely, Seth Hubbard   *October 1, 1988*

Slowly, as each juror finished, they could not help but glance into the audience and take a look at Herschel Hubbard and Ramona Dafoe. She wanted to cry, but at that moment she correctly assumed anyone looking would think she was only faking it. So she stared at the floor, along with her brother and husband, and waited for this awkward and awful time to pass.

Finally, after an eternity, Judge Atlee said, "Let's take a fifteen-minute recess."

In spite of Seth's warnings about the hazards of smoking, at least half of the jurors needed a cigarette. The nonsmokers stayed in the jury room and had coffee while the rest followed a bailiff to a small patio overlooking the north side of the courthouse lawn. They quickly fired up and began puffing away. Nevin Dark was trying to quit and had whittled his habit down to half a pack a day, but at the moment he was craving nicotine. Jim Whitehurst eased beside him, took a puff, and said, "What do you think, Mr. Foreman?"

Judge Atlee had been explicit in his warnings: Do not discuss this case. But jurors in every trial couldn't wait to discuss what they had just seen and heard. Almost under his breath, Nevin said, "Looks like the old boy knew exactly what he was doing. You?"

"No doubt about it," whispered Jim.

Just above them, in the county law library, Jake gathered with Portia, Lettie, Quince Lundy, and Harry Rex, and there was no shortage of observations and opinions. Portia was unnerved because Frank Doley, Number Twelve, kept staring at her, frowning with his lips moving as if he were cursing. Lettie thought Debbie Lacker, Number Ten, had fallen asleep, while Harry Rex was certain Number Two, Tracy McMillen, had already developed a crush on Jake. Quince Lundy still maintained the jury was already split, but Harry Rex said they'd be lucky to get four votes. Jake politely asked him to shut up and reminded him of his dire predictions during the trial of Carl Lee Hailey.

After ten minutes of mindless chatter, Jake vowed to eat lunch alone.

Back in the courtroom, he called Quince Lundy to the stand and led him through a series of bland but necessary questions about his involvement in the estate, his appointment as the administrator, and his substitution for Russell Amburgh, who wanted out. Lundy dryly explained the duties of the administrator and did a superb job of making it sound as dull as it really was. Jake handed him the original handwritten will and asked him to identify it.

Lundy said, "This is the holographic will that was admitted to probate on October 4 of last year. Signed by Mr. Seth Hubbard on the first day of October."

"Let's have a look," Jake said, and once again projected the document onto the screen as he passed out copies to the jurors.

Judge Atlee said, "Again, ladies and gentlemen, take your time and read it carefully. You will be allowed to take all documents and exhibits back to the jury room when you begin your deliberations."

Jake stood by the podium, held a copy of the will, and pretended to read it as he carefully watched the jurors. Most seemed to frown at one point or another, and he assumed the "perish in pain" phrase made them cringe. He had read the will a hundred times and still had the same two reactions. One, it was mean-spirited, harsh, cruel, and unreasonable. Two, it made him wonder what Lettie was doing to make the old boy so fond of her. But, as always, another reading convinced him Seth knew precisely what he was doing. If a person has testamentary capacity, then that person can make all the wild and unreasonable bequests he or she wants.

When the last juror finished and laid down her copy, Jake turned off the overhead projector. He and Quince Lundy then spent half an hour hitting the highlights of Seth Hubbard's amazing ten-year journey from the ruins of his second divorce to wealth that no one in Ford County had ever seen.

At 12:30, Judge Atlee recessed until 2:00 p.m.

42

The detective was leaving the hospital as Lucien was entering it. They spoke briefly in the main lobby, just a few
words about Lonny Clark, still up there on the third floor and
not doing well. He'd had a rough night and his doctors said no
visitors. Lucien got lost in the hospital and surfaced on the third
floor an hour later. There was no cop by the door, no nurses tending to Lonny. Lucien sneaked into the room, gently shook Ancil's
arm, and said, "Ancil. Ancil, are you there?"

But Ancil wasn't there.

Within the tiny Brigance firm, there was a general agreement
that the morning could not have gone better. The presentation
of the suicide note, funeral and burial instructions, handwritten
will, and the letter to Jake made it perfectly clear that Seth
Hubbard planned everything and was in control until the very
end. Jake's opening statement had been persuasive. Lanier's,
though, was just as masterful. All in all, a good beginning.

Jake began the afternoon session by calling to the stand the
Reverend Don McElwain, pastor of Irish Road Christian
Church. The preacher told the jury he had spoken briefly to
Seth after the worship hour on October 2, a few hours before he
hung himself. He knew Seth was gravely ill, though he did not
know the doctors had given him only weeks to live. On that
morning, Seth seemed to be in good spirits, alert, even smiling,
and told McElwain how much he enjoyed the sermon. Though
he was sick and frail, he did not appear to be drugged or under
the influence. He had been a member of the church for twenty
years and usually showed up about once a month. Three weeks

before he died, Seth had purchased for $350 a plot in the ceme-
tery, the same plot he now occupied.

The church's treasurer was next. Mr. Willis Stubbs testified
that Seth dropped into the offering plate a check in the amount
of $500, dated October 2. For the year, Seth contributed
$2,600.

Mr. Everett Walker took the stand and shared a private
moment in what was likely Seth's last conversation. As the two
walked to the parking lot after church, Mr. Walker asked how
business was going. Seth made a crack about a slow hurricane
season. More hurricanes meant more property damage and
demand for lumber. Seth claimed to love hurricanes. According
to Mr. Walker, his friend was sharp, witty, and did not seem to
be in pain. Of course he was frail. When Mr. Walker later heard
that Seth was dead, and that he'd killed himself not long after
their conversation, he was stunned. The man seemed so at ease
and relaxed, even content. He'd known Seth for many years and
he was not the slightest bit gregarious. Rather, Seth was a quiet
man who kept to himself and said little. He remembered Seth
smiling as he drove away that Sunday, and remarked to his wife
that it was rare to see him smile.

Mrs. Gilda Chatham told the jury she and her husband sat
behind Seth during his final sermon, spoke to him briefly when
the service was over, and picked up no clue whatsoever that he
was on the verge of such a startling act. Mrs. Nettie Vinson testified that she said hello to Seth as they were leaving the church
and that he seemed uncharacteristically friendly.

After a short recess, Seth's oncologist, a Dr. Talbert from the
regional medical center in Tupelo, was sworn in and quickly
managed to bore the courtroom with a long and dry narrative
about his patient's lung cancer. He had treated Seth for almost a
year, and, referring to his notes, went on and on about the
surgery, then the chemotherapy and radiation and medications.
There had been little hope initially, but Seth had fought hard.
When the cancer metastasized to his spine and ribs, they knew
the end was near. Dr. Talbert had seen Seth two weeks before he

died, and was surprised at how determined he was to keep going. But the pain was intense. He increased the oral dosage of Demerol to a hundred milligrams every three to four hours. Seth preferred not to take the Demerol because the drug often made him drowsy; in fact, he said more than once that he tried to survive each day without pain meds. Dr. Talbert did not know how many tablets Seth actually took. In the past two months, he had prescribed two hundred.

Jake's purpose in putting the doctor on the stand was twofold. First, he wanted to establish the fact that Seth was almost dead from lung cancer. Therefore, hopefully, the act of suicide might not seem so drastic and unreasonable. Jake planned to argue later that Seth was indeed thinking clearly in his last days, regardless of how he chose to die. The pain was unbearable, the end was near, he simply sped things along. Second, Jake wanted to confront head-on the issue of the side effects of Demerol. Lanier had some heavyweight testimony lined up, an expert who would say the powerful narcotic, taken in the quantities prescribed, seriously impaired Seth's judgment.

An odd fact in the case was that the last prescription was never found. Seth had purchased it at a pharmacy in Tupelo six days before he died, then he apparently disposed of it; thus, there was no proof of how much or how little he'd actually consumed. At his specific instructions, he was buried without an autopsy. Months earlier, Wade Lanier had suggested, off the record, that the body be exhumed for toxicity tests. Judge Atlee said no; again, off the record. The level of opiates in Seth's blood on Sunday when he died was not automatically relevant to the level the day before when he wrote his will. Judge Atlee seemed to be particularly offended by the notion of digging up a person after he had been properly laid to rest.

Jake was pleased with his direct examination of Dr. Talbert. They clearly established that Seth tried to avoid taking Demerol, and that there was simply no way to prove how much was in his system when he made his last will.

Wade Lanier managed to get the doctor to admit that a patient taking up to six to eight doses a day of Demerol, at a hundred milligrams each, should not consider making important decisions, especially ones dealing with large sums of money. Such a patient should be somewhere resting comfortably and quietly—no driving, no physical activity, no crucial decision making.

After the doctor was excused, Jake called Arlene Trotter, Seth's longtime secretary and office manager. She would be his last witness before Lettie, and since they were approaching 5:00 p.m., Jake made the decision to save Lettie for early Wednesday morning. He had spoken to Arlene many times since Seth's death and was nervous about putting her on the stand. He really had no choice. If he didn't call her, Wade Lanier certainly would. She had been deposed in early February and had been evasive, in Jake's opinion. After four hours, he strongly believed she had been coached by Lanier or someone working for him. Nonetheless, she spent more time with Seth the last week of his life than anyone else, and her testimony was crucial.

She appeared terrified as she swore to tell the truth and settled into the seat. She glanced at the jurors, who were watching closely. Jake asked the preliminary questions, the ones with easy and obvious answers, and she seemed to settle down. He established that from Monday through Friday of the week before he died, Seth arrived at his office each morning around nine, which was later than usual. He was generally upbeat and in good spirits until noon, when he took a long nap on the sofa in his office. He wasn't eating, though Arlene kept offering snacks and sandwiches. He kept smoking—he was never able to stop. As always, he kept his door closed, so Arlene wasn't exactly sure what he was doing. However, he stayed busy that week trying to sell three tracts of timberland in South Carolina. He was on the phone a lot, which was not unusual. At least once an hour, he left the building and went for a stroll around the premises. He stopped and talked to some of his employees. He flirted with Kamila, the girl at the front desk. Arlene knew he was in great pain because at times he couldn't hide it, though he never, ever admitted this. He let it slip once that he was taking Demerol, though she never saw the bottle of pills.

No, he was not glassy-eyed. He did not slur his speech. At times he was fatigued, and he napped often. Usually, he left around three or four.

Jake was able to paint the picture of a man still in charge, the boss at work as if all was well. For five consecutive days before he wrote a new will, Seth Hubbard was at the office, on the phone, tending to his business.

Wade Lanier began his cross-examination with "Let's talk about this timberland in South Carolina, Ms. Trotter. Did Seth Hubbard sell these three tracts of land?"

"Yes sir, he did."

"And when?"

"On that Friday morning."

"The Friday morning before he wrote his will on Saturday, correct?"

"Correct."

"Did he sign any sort of contract?"

"He did. It was faxed to my desk and I took it to him. He signed it, and I faxed it back to the attorneys in Spartanburg."

Lanier picked up a document and said, "Your Honor, I have here Exhibit C-5, which has already been stipulated to and admitted."

Judge Atlee said, "Proceed."

Lanier handed the document to Arlene and said, "Could you please identify that?"

"Yes sir. It's the contract Seth signed on Friday morning, selling the three tracts of land in South Carolina."

"And how much was Seth to receive?"

"A total of $810,000."

"Eight ten. Now, Ms. Trotter, how much did Seth pay for this timberland?"

She paused for a moment, glanced nervously at the jurors, and said, "You have the paperwork, Mr. Lanier."

"Of course." Lanier produced three more exhibits, all of which had been marked and admitted beforehand. There were no surprises here; Jake and Lanier had haggled over the exhibits and documents for weeks. Judge Atlee had long since ruled them admissible.

Arlene slowly reviewed the exhibits as the courtroom waited. Finally, she said, "Mr. Hubbard purchased this land in 1985 and paid a total of one point one million."

Lanier scribbled this down as if it were new. Peering over his reading glasses, with his eyebrows arched in disbelief, he said, "A loss of $300,000!"

"Apparently so."

"And this was only twenty-four hours before he made his handwritten will?"

Jake was on his feet. "Objection, Your Honor. Calls for speculation on the part of the witness. Counsel can save it for his closing argument."

"Sustained."

Lanier ignored the commotion and zeroed in on the witness. "Any idea, Ms. Trotter, why Seth would do such a bad deal?"

Jake rose again. "Objection, Your Honor. More speculation."

"Sustained."

"Was he thinking clearly, Ms. Trotter?"

"Objection."

"Sustained."

Lanier paused and flipped a page of notes. "Now, Ms. Trotter, who was in charge of cleaning the office building where you and Seth worked?"

"A man named Monk."

"Okay, tell us about Monk."

"He's a longtime employee at the lumber yard, sort of a general helper who does all sorts of odd jobs, mainly cleaning. He also paints, fixes everything, even washed Mr. Hubbard's vehicles."

"How often does Monk clean the offices?"

"Every Monday and Thursday morning, from nine until eleven, without fail, for many years now."

"Did he clean the offices on Thursday, September 29, of last year?"

"He did."

"Has Lettie Lang ever cleaned the offices?"

"Not to my knowledge. There was no need for her to do so. Monk was in charge of that. I've never seen Ms. Lang until today."

Throughout the day, Myron Pankey moved around the courtroom. His job was to watch the jury constantly, but to do so without being obvious required a number of tricks. Different seats, different vantage points, a change in sports coats, shielding his face behind a larger person sitting in front of him, the use of various eyeglasses. He spent his career in courtrooms, listening to witnesses and watching jurors react to them. In his learned opinion, Jake had done a steady job of laying out his case. Nothing fancy, nothing memorable, but no blunders either. The majority of the jurors liked him and believed that he was searching for the truth. Three apparently did not. Frank Doley, Number Twelve, was firmly in their corner and would never vote to give all that money to a black housekeeper. Pankey did not know the tragic story of Doley's niece, but he could tell from the opening statements the man distrusted Jake and did not like Lettie. Number Ten, Debbie Lacker, a fifty-year-old white woman, and quite rural, had shot several hard looks at Lettie throughout the day, little messages that Myron never missed. Number Four, Fay Pollan, another fifty-year-old white woman, had actually nodded in agreement when Dr. Talbert testified that a person on Demerol should not make important decisions.

As the first day of testimony came to a close, Pankey called it a draw. Two fine lawyers had performed well and the jurors had not missed a word.

With Ancil unable to talk, Lucien spent the day in a rented car touring glaciers and fjords in the mountains around Juneau. He was tempted to leave, to hustle back to Clanton for the trial, but he was also quite taken with the beauty of Alaska, and the cool air and near-perfect climate. It was already heating up in Mississippi, with longer days and stickier air. As he ate lunch at a hillside café, the Gastineau Channel stretched magnificently below him, he made the decision to leave tomorrow, Wednesday.

At some point, and soon, Jake would inform Judge Atlee that Ancil Hubbard had been located, and verified, though the verification was shaky because the subject might change his mind at any moment and adopt another alias. Lucien doubted this, though, because Ancil was thinking about the money. Such a revelation would not affect the trial. Wade Lanier was right: Ancil had nothing to say about his brother's will or testamentary capacity. So Lucien would leave him to his own problems. He suspected Ancil might serve a few months in prison. If he got lucky and found a good lawyer, he might walk entirely. Lucien was convinced the search and seizure of the cocaine was a clear violation of the Fourth Amendment. Suppress the search, eliminate the cocaine, and Ancil would be free again. If Jake won the trial, Ancil might one day make his long-deferred return to Ford County and claim his share of the estate.

If Jake lost, Ancil would disappear into the night, never to be found again.

After dark, Lucien went to the hotel bar and said good evening to Bo Buck, the bartender, who was now a close friend. Bo Buck had once been a judge in Nevada before things conspired to wreck his life, and he and Lucien enjoyed swapping stories. They talked for a moment as Lucien waited on his first Jack and Coke. He took it to a table and sat down, alone and loving the solitude. Just a man and his sour mash. A minute later, Ancil Hubbard materialized from nowhere and sat across the table.

"Evening Lucien," he said casually.

Startled, Lucien stared at him for a few seconds to make sure. He was wearing a baseball cap, a sweatshirt, and jeans. That morning he'd been unconscious in a hospital bed with tubes running everywhere.

"Didn't expect to see you here," Lucien said.

"I got tired of the hospital, so I walked out. I guess I'm a fugitive, but that's nothing new. I kinda like being on the run."

"What about your head, and the infection?"

"My head's sore, though not nearly as sore as they thought. Remember, Lucien, I was scheduled to go from the hospital to the jail, a transfer I preferred not to make. Let's just say I wasn't nearly as unconscious as they thought. The infection is under control." He pulled out a bottle of pills. "When I left I took my antibiotics. I'll be all right."

"How'd you leave?"

"Walked out. They rolled me downstairs for a scan. I went to the restroom. They thought I couldn't walk, so I ran down some steps, found the basement, found a locker room, changed clothes. Came out through the service ramp. Cops were swarming last time I checked. I was drinking coffee across the street."

"This is a small town, Ancil. You can't hide for long."

"What do you know about hiding? I have some friends."

"You want something to drink?"

"No, but I'd love a burger and fries."

Harry Rex scowled at the witness and demanded, "Did you touch his penis?"

Lettie looked away, embarrassed, then managed a tepid "Yes, yes I did."

"Of course you did, Lettie," Jake said. "He was unable to bathe himself, so you had to do it, and you did it more than once. A bath means bathing the entire body. He couldn't do it; you had to. There was nothing intimate or even remotely sexual about it. You were simply doing your job."

"I can't do this," Lettie said, looking helplessly at Portia. "He won't ask me these questions, will he?"

"He damned sure will," Harry Rex growled. "He'll ask you these and many more and you'd better be ready with the answers."

"Let's take a break," Jake said.

"I need a beer," Harry Rex said, climbing to his feet. He stomped out of the room as if he were sick of them all. They had been rehearsing for two hours and it was almost 10:00 p.m. Jake asked the easy questions on direct examination, and Harry Rex grilled her relentlessly on cross. At times he was too rough, or rougher than Atlee would allow Lanier to be, but better to be ready for the worst. Portia sympathized with her mother, but she was also frustrated by her fragility. Lettie could be tough, then she would fall apart. There was no confidence that her testimony would go smoothly.

Remember the rules, Lettie, Jake kept saying. Smile, but nothing phony. Speak clearly and slowly. It's okay to cry if you feel real emotion. If you're not sure, don't speak. The jurors are watching intently, and they miss nothing. Look at them occasionally, but with confidence. Don't let Wade Lanier rattle you. I'll always be there to protect you.

Harry Rex wanted to scream another piece of advice: "We're talking about twenty-four million bucks here, so put on the performance of a lifetime!" But he controlled himself. When he returned with a beer, Portia said, "We've had enough, Jake. We'll go home and sit on the porch and talk some more, and we'll be here early in the morning."

"Okay. I think we're all tired."

After they left, Jake and Harry Rex went upstairs and sat on Jake's balcony. The night was warm but clear, a perfect spring night that was difficult to appreciate. Jake sipped a beer and relaxed for the first time in many hours.

"Any word from Lucien?" Harry Rex asked.

"No, but I forgot to check the phone messages."

"We're lucky, you know. Lucky he's in Alaska and not sitting right here carping about everything that went wrong today."

"That's your job, right?"

"Right, but I got no complaints, so far. You had a good day, Jake. You made a good opening statement, one the jury heard and appreciated, then you called twelve witnesses, and not a one got burned. The evidence leans strongly in your favor, at least at this point. You couldn't have asked for a better day."

"And the jury?"

"They like you, but it's too early to speculate on how much they like or dislike Lettie. Tomorrow will be revealing."

"Tomorrow is crucial, buddy. Lettie can win the case, or she can lose it."

43

The lawyers met with Judge Atlee in his chambers at 8:45 Wednesday morning and agreed there were no pending motions or issues to iron out before the trial proceeded. For the third day in a row, His Honor was spry, almost hyper, as if the excitement of a big trial had rejuvenated him. The lawyers had been up all night, either working or worrying, and looked as frayed as they felt. The old judge, though, was ready to go.

In the courtroom he welcomed everyone, thanked the spectators for their keen interest in our judicial system, and told the bailiff to bring in the jurors. When they were seated, he greeted them warmly and asked if there were any problems. Any unauthorized contact? Anything suspicious? Everyone feeling okay? Very well, Mr. Brigance, proceed.

Jake stood and said, "Your Honor, the proponents call Ms. Lettie Lang."

Portia had told her not to wear anything fitting or tight or even remotely sexy. Early that morning, long before breakfast, they had argued about the dress. Portia won. It was a navy-blue cotton dress with a loose belt, a nice enough dress but one that a housekeeper might wear to work, nothing Lettie would wear to church. The shoes were low-heeled sandals. No jewelry. No watch. Nothing to indicate she had a spare dime or might be contemplating a haul of cash. In the past month she had stopped tinting her gray hair. It was natural now, and she looked all of her forty-seven years.

She was practically stuttering by the time she swore to tell the truth. She looked at Portia sitting behind Jake's chair. Her daughter gave her a smile—a signal that she should smile too.

The packed courtroom was silent as Jake approached the podium. He asked her name, address, place of employment—softballs that she handled well. Names of children and grandchildren. Yes, Marvis, her oldest, was in prison. Her husband was Simeon Lang, now in jail, awaiting prosecution. She had filed for divorce a month earlier and expected it to become final in a few weeks. Some background—education, church, prior jobs. It was all scripted and at times her answers sounded stiff and rote, even memorized, which they were. She glanced at the jurors, but was rattled when she realized they were staring right back. As her handlers had discussed, when she felt nervous she was to look directly at Portia. At times, she couldn't take her eyes off her daughter.

Jake eventually made it to the subject of Mr. Seth Hubbard. Or simply Mr. Hubbard, as she was to always call him in court. Never Seth. Never Mr. Seth. Mr. Hubbard hired her as a part-time housekeeper three years earlier. How did she hear about the job opening? She did not. He called her and said a friend knew she was out of work. He happened to be looking for a part-time maid. She went through her history with Mr. Hubbard, his rules, habits, routines, and, later, his preferences in food and cooking. Three days a week became four. He gave her a raise, then another. He traveled a lot and she was often in the house with little to do. Not once in three years did he entertain or have another person over for a meal. She met Herschel and Ramona, but rarely saw them. Ramona visited once a year, and for only a few hours, and Herschel's drop-ins were not much more frequent. She had never met any of Mr. Hubbard's four grandchildren.

"But I didn't work on the weekends so I don't know who came and went then," she said. "Mr. Hubbard could've had all sorts of company." She was trying to appear fair, but only to a point.

"But you worked every Monday, correct?" Jake asked from the script.

"I did."

"And did you ever see evidence of weekend guests in the home?"

"No sir, never."

Being nice to Herschel and Ramona was not part of the plan at this point. They had no plans to be nice to Lettie; indeed, based on their depositions, it was safe to expect them to lie considerably.

After an hour on the stand, Lettie felt more comfortable. Her answers were clearer, more spontaneous, and she occasionally smiled at the jurors. Jake eventually got around to Mr. Hubbard's lung cancer. She described how her boss went through a string of unimpressive home-health-care nurses, and finally asked Lettie if she would work five days a week. She described the low points, when the chemo knocked him flat and almost killed him, when he couldn't walk to the bathroom or feed himself.

Do not show emotion, Portia had lectured. Do not show any feelings whatsoever for Mr. Hubbard. The jurors cannot get the impression there was an emotional bond between the two of you. Of course there had been, the same as any dying person and his caregiver, but do not acknowledge it on the witness stand.

Jake hit the high points but did not spend much time on Mr. Hubbard's cancer. Wade Lanier would certainly do so. Jake asked Lettie if she had ever signed a will. No, she had not.

"Have you ever seen a will?"

"No sir."

"Did Mr. Hubbard ever discuss his will with you?"

She managed a chuckle, and sold it perfectly. She said, "Mr. Hubbard was extremely private. He never discussed business or anything like that with me. He never discussed his family or kids or anything. He just wasn't like that."

The truth was that Seth had twice promised Lettie he would leave something behind for her, but he had never mentioned his will. She and Portia had discussed it, and it was Portia's opinion that Wade Lanier and the lawyers on the other side would blow this out of proportion if she admitted it. They would twist it, exaggerate it, and turn it into something lethal. "So you did discuss his last will with him!" Lanier would yell in front of the jury.

Some things are better left unsaid. No one would ever know. Seth was dead and Lettie wasn't talking.

"Did he ever discuss his illness and the fact that he was dying?" Jake asked.

She took a deep breath and pondered the question. "Sure. There were times when he was in so much pain he said he wanted to die. I suppose that's natural. In his last days, Mr. Hubbard knew the end was near. He asked me to pray with him."

"You prayed with him?"

"I did. Mr. Hubbard had a deep faith in God. He wanted to make things right before he died."

Jake paused for a little drama so the jurors could fully absorb the visual of Lettie and her boss praying, instead of doing what most folks thought they had been doing. Then he moved on to the morning of October 1 of last year, and Lettie told her story. They left his house around 9:00, with Lettie behind the wheel of his late-model Cadillac. She had never driven him before; he had never asked her to. It was the first and only time the two had been together in an automobile. When they were leaving the house, she had made some silly comment about never having driven a Cadillac, so he insisted. She was nervous and drove slowly. He sipped on coffee from a paper cup. He seemed to be relaxed and pain-free, and he seemed to enjoy the fact that Lettie was so uptight driving down a highway with virtually no other traffic.

Jake asked her what they talked about during the ten-minute drive. She thought for a moment, glanced at the jurors, who still had not missed a word, and said, "We talked about cars. He said a lot of white people don't like Cadillacs anymore because nowadays so many black people drive them. He asked me why a Cadillac was so important to a black person, and I said don't ask me. I never wanted one. I'll never have one. My Pontiac's twelve years old. But then I said it's because it's the nicest car and it's a way of showin' other folk that you've made it. You got a job, got a little money in your pocket, got some success in life. Something's workin' okay. That's all. He said he's always liked a Cadillac too, said he lost his first one in his first divorce, lost his second one in his second divorce, but since he gave up on marriage nobody's bothered him or his Cadillacs. He was kinda funny about it."

"So he was in a good mood, sort of joking?" Jake asked.

"A very good mood that mornin', yes sir. He even laughed at me and my drivin'."

"And his mind was clear?"

"Clear as a bell. He said I was drivin' his seventh Cadillac and he remembered all of them. Said he trades every other year."

"Do you know if he was taking medication for pain that morning?"

"No sir, I don't know. He was funny about his pills. He didn't like to take them and he kept them in his briefcase, away from me. The only time I saw them was when he was flat on his back, deathly sick, and he asked me to get them. But no, he didn't appear to be on any pain medication that mornin'."

Under Jake's guidance, she continued her narrative. They arrived at Berring Lumber Company, the first and only time she'd ever been there, and while he spent the time in his office with the door locked, she cleaned. She vacuumed, dusted, scrubbed most of the windows, arranged magazines, even washed the dishes in the small kitchen. No, she did not empty the wastebaskets. From the moment they entered the offices until they left, she did not speak to nor see Mr. Hubbard. She had no idea what he was doing in his office; she never thought about asking. He walked in with a briefcase, and walked out holding the same one. She drove back to his house, then she returned home, around noon. Late Sunday night, Calvin Boggs called with the news that Mr. Hubbard had hung himself.

At 11:00 a.m., after almost two hours on the stand, Jake tendered the witness for cross-examination. During a quick recess, he told Lettie she did a fabulous job. Portia was thrilled and very proud; her mother had kept her composure and been convincing. Harry Rex, who'd been watching from the back row, said her testimony could not have been better.

By noon, their case was in shambles.

He was certain harboring a fugitive was against the law in every state, including Alaska, so jail time was a possibility, though Lucien wasn't worried about that at the moment. He woke up at sunrise, stiff from sleeping off and on in a chair. Ancil had the bed, all of it. He had volunteered to sleep on the floor or in a chair, but Lucien was concerned about his head injuries and insisted he take the bed. A painkiller knocked him out, and for a long time Lucien sat in the dark, nursing his last Jack and Coke, listening to the old boy snore.

He dressed quietly and left the room. The lobby of the hotel was deserted. There were no cops poking around, searching for Ancil. Down the street he bought coffee and muffins and hauled them back to the room, where Ancil was awake now and watching the local news. "Not a word," he reported.

"No surprise," Lucien said. "I doubt if they've brought in the bloodhounds."

They ate, took turns showering and dressing, and at 8:00 a.m. left the room. Ancil was wearing Lucien's black suit, white shirt, paisley tie, and the same cap pulled low to hide his face. They hurriedly walked three blocks to the law office of Jared Wolkowicz, a lawyer referred by Bo Buck at the Glacier Inn bar. Lucien had visited Mr. Wolkowicz late the day before, retained him, and organized the deposition. A court reporter and a videographer were waiting in the conference room. At one end of the table, Mr. Wolkowicz stood, raised his right hand, repeated after the court reporter, and swore to tell the truth, then sat facing the camera. He said, "Good morning. My name is Jared Wolkowicz and I'm an attorney, duly licensed by the State of Alaska. Today is Wednesday, April 5, 1989, and I'm sitting here in my law office on Franklin Street in downtown Juneau, Alaska. Here with me is Lucien Wilbanks, of Clanton, Mississippi, and also a man by the name of Ancil F. Hubbard, who currently resides in Juneau. The purpose of the deposition is to record the testimony of Mr. Hubbard. I know nothing about the case that brings us here. My role is to simply vouch for the fact that this will be an accurate recording of what takes place here. If any of the lawyers or judges involved in this matter would like to speak to me, feel free to call."

Wolkowicz left the chair and Lucien stepped forward. He was sworn by the court reporter, then likewise sat facing the camera. He said, "My name is Lucien Wilbanks and I'm well known to Judge Atlee and the lawyers involved in the contest over the last will and testament of Seth Hubbard. Working with Jake Brigance and others, I have been able to locate Ancil Hubbard. I have spent several hours with Ancil and there is no doubt in my mind that he is in fact the surviving brother of Seth Hubbard. He was born in Ford County in 1922. His father was Cleon Hubbard. His mother was Sarah Belle Hubbard. In 1928, his father, Cleon, hired my grandfather Robert E. Lee Wilbanks to represent him in a land dispute. That dispute is relevant today. Here is Ancil Hubbard."

Lucien vacated the chair and Ancil took it. He raised his right hand and swore to tell the truth.

Wade Lanier began his toxic cross-examination by asking about Simeon. Why was he in jail? Had he been indicted? How often had she visited him? Was he contesting the divorce? It was a harsh but effective way to remind the jurors that the father of Lettie's five children was a drunk who'd killed the Roston boys. After five minutes, Lettie was wiping tears, and Lanier looked like a prick. He didn't care. With her emotions in play, and her judgment temporarily impaired, he quickly switched gears and laid his trap.

"Now, Ms. Lang, prior to being employed by Mr. Hubbard, where did you work?"

Lettie wiped a cheek with the back of a hand and tried to collect her thoughts. "Uh, that was Mr. and Mrs. Tingley, here in Clanton."

"What type of work?"

"Housekeeper."

"How long did you work for them?"

"I don't know exactly, but about three years."

"And why did you leave their employment?"

"They died. Both of them."

"Did they leave you any money in their wills?"

"If they did, nobody ever told me." This got a few smiles from the jurors.

Wade Lanier missed the humor. He continued, "And before the Tingleys, where did you work?"

"Uh, before that, I worked as a cook in the school in Karaway."

"For how long?"

"Maybe two years."

"And why did you leave there?"

"I got the job with the Tingleys and I'd rather work as a housekeeper than a cook."

"Okay. Before the job at the school, where did you work?"

She was silent as she tried to remember. Finally, she said, "Before the school, I worked for Mrs. Gillenwater, here in Clanton, as a housekeeper."

"And for how long?"

"About a year, then she moved away."

"Before Mrs. Gillenwater, where did you work?"

"Ummm, that would be the Glovers, in Karaway."

"And for how long?"

"Again, I can't remember exactly, but it was three or four years."

"Okay, I'm not trying to nail down specifics, Ms. Lang. Just remember things as best you can, all right?"

"Yes sir."

"And before the Glovers, where did you work?"

"That was Miss Karsten, here in town. I worked for her six years. She was my favorite. I never wanted to leave her but she died suddenly."

"Thank you." Lanier scribbled on his legal pad as if he was

learning something new. "Now, just to summarize, Ms. Lang, you worked for Mr. Hubbard for three years, the Tingleys three, the school two, Mrs. Gillenwater one, the Glovers three or four, and six years for Miss Karsten. According to my math, that's approximately twenty years. Does that sound about right?"

"It does, give or take a year here, a year there," Lettie said, confidently.

"And you've had no other employers in the past twenty or so years?"

She shook her head. No.

Lanier was going somewhere, but Jake couldn't stop him. The inflections of his voice, the slight hints of suspicion, the arched eyebrows, the matter-of-factness of his sentences. He was trying to disguise all these, but to Jake's trained ears and eyes they meant trouble.

"That's six employers in twenty years, Ms. Lang. How many times were you fired?"

"None. I mean I was terminated after Mr. Hubbard died, and Miss Karsten got sick, and Mr. and Mrs. Tingley passed, but that was just because the job sorta played out, you know?"

"You've never been fired for doing a bad job, or for doing something wrong?"

"No sir. Never."

Lanier abruptly backed away from the podium, looked up at Judge Atlee, and said, "That's all, Judge. I reserve the right to recall this witness later in the trial." He walked smugly to his table, and, at the last second, Jake saw him wink at Lester Chilcott.

Lettie had just lied, and Lanier was about to expose her. Jake, though, had no idea what was coming; thus, he had no way to prevent it. His instincts were to get her off the witness stand. He stood and said, "Your Honor, the proponents rest."

Judge Atlee said, "Do you have some witnesses, Mr. Lanier?"

"Oh yes."

"Then call the first one."

"The contestants call Mr. Fritz Pickering."

"Who?" Jake blurted.

"Fritz Pickering," Lanier repeated loudly and sarcastically, as if Jake were hard of hearing.

"Never heard of him. He's not on your witness list."

"He's out in the rotunda," Lanier said to a bailiff. "Waiting."

Jake was shaking his head at Judge Atlee and said, "He can't testify if he's not listed as a witness, Judge."

"I'm calling him anyway," Lanier said.

Fritz Pickering entered the courtroom and followed a bailiff to the witness stand.

"I object, Your Honor," Jake said.

Judge Atlee removed his reading glasses, glared at Wade Lanier, and said, "All right, let's take a fifteen-minute recess. I'll see the lawyers in chambers. Lawyers only. No paralegals or staff."

The jury was hurried out of the courtroom as the lawyers followed the judge into the rear hallway and into his cramped chambers. He did not remove his robe, but sat down and looked as confused as Jake. "Start talking," he said to Lanier.

"Your Honor, this witness is not an evidentiary witness; thus he does not have to be made known to the other side. His purpose is to impeach the credibility of another witness, not to give evidence. I was not required to put him on the list or in any way divulge his name because I was never certain he would be called. Now, based on the testimony of Lettie Lang, and her inability to tell the truth, this witness is suddenly crucial to our case."

Judge Atlee exhaled as every lawyer in the room racked his brain for bits and pieces of the rules of evidence and the rules of civil procedure. At the moment, there was little doubt Lanier had full command of the rules regarding witness impeachment. This was his ambush, one he and Lester Chilcott had planned perfectly. Jake wanted to gush forth in some cogent and sensible argument, but brilliance failed him miserably at the moment.

"What will the witness say?" Judge Atlee asked.

"Lettie Lang once worked for his mother, Mrs. Irene Pickering. Fritz and his sister fired Lettie when his sister found a handwritten will leaving fifty thousand in cash to Lettie. She just told at least three lies. Number one, she said she had worked for only those people I mentioned, over the past twenty or so years. Mrs. Pickering hired her in 1978, and they fired her in 1980. Number two, she has in fact been fired as a housekeeper. Number three, she said she has never seen a will. Fritz and his sister showed her the handwritten will the day they fired her. There may be another one or two, I can't think of them all right now."

Jake's shoulders fell as his gut clenched, his vision blurred, and the color drained from his face. It was imperative that he say something intelligent, but everything was blank. Then lightning struck and he asked, "When did you find Fritz Pickering?"

"I didn't meet him until today," Lanier said smugly.

"That's not what I asked. When did you find out about the Pickerings?"

"During discovery. Again, Jake, it's another example of us outworking you. We found more witnesses. We've been out there beating the bushes, working our asses off. I don't know what you've been doing."

"And the rules require you to submit the names of your witnesses. Two weeks ago you dumped the names of forty-five new ones on the table. You're not playing by the rules here, Wade. Judge, this is a clear violation of the rules."

Judge Atlee raised a hand and said, "Enough. Allow me to think a moment." He stood, walked to his desk, took one of a dozen pipes from a rack, stuffed it with Sir Walter Raleigh, lit up, blew a thick cloud of smoke toward the ceiling, and drifted away. On one side of the table, Wade Lanier, Lester Chilcott, Zack Zeitler, and Joe Bradley Hunt sat smugly, silently, waiting for a decision that would send the trial either north or south, with no return. On the other side, Jake sat alone, scribbling notes that not even he could decipher. He felt ill and couldn't make his hands stop shaking.

Wade Lanier had pulled a masterful dirty trick, and it was infuriating. At the same time, Jake wanted to grab Lettie and lash out at her. Why had she not mentioned the Pickering matter? They had spent countless hours together since October.

His Honor blew more smoke and said, "This is too crucial to keep out. I'll allow Mr. Pickering to testify, but within limits."

Angrily, Jake said, "Trial by ambush. This will be automatically reversible. We'll be back in two years to do this all over again."

Angrily, Judge Atlee barked, "Don't lecture, Jake. I've never been reversed by the Supreme Court. Never."

Jake took a deep breath and said, "Sorry."

Ancil's narrative ran for fifty-eight minutes. When he finished, he wiped moisture from his eyes, said he was exhausted and couldn't continue, and left the room. Lucien thanked Jared Wolkowicz for his accommodations. He had not told the lawyer that Ancil was a man on the run.

Walking back to the hotel, they saw several policemen loitering around a street corner and decided to duck into a coffee shop. They hid in a booth and tried to maintain small talk. Lucien was still rattled by the stories Ancil told, but neither was in the mood to pursue them.

Lucien said, "I've paid for two more nights at the hotel; it's all yours. I'm leaving now. You can have the clothes, toothpaste, everything. There's a pair of old khakis hanging in the closet with three hundred bucks in the front pocket. It's yours."

"Thanks, Lucien."

"What are your plans?"

"I don't know. I really don't want to go to prison, so I'll probably skip town, as usual. Just disappear. These clowns can't catch me. This is pretty routine for me."

"Where will you go?"

"Well, I might mosey on down to Mississippi since my dear old brother thought so highly of me. When might I see some of his estate?"

"Who knows? They're fighting over it as we speak. Could be

a month. Could be five years. You have my phone number. Call me in a few weeks and we'll catch up."

"I'll do that."

Lucien paid for the coffee and they left through a side door. In an alley, they said good-bye. Lucien was headed for the airport; Ancil, the hotel. When he got there, the detective was waiting.

In a crowded courtroom that was silent, even stunned, Fritz Pickering told his story, every devastating detail. Lettie absorbed it in total defeat, her head bowed, her eyes on the floor, then her eyes closed in agony. She shook her head from time to time as if she disagreed, but no one in the courtroom believed her.

Lies, lies, lies.

Fritz produced a copy of his mother's handwritten will. Jake objected to its admission into evidence on the grounds that there was no way to prove Irene Pickering's handwriting, but Judge Atlee barely heard him. It became evidence. Wade Lanier asked his witness to read the fourth paragraph, the one giving $50,000 to Lettie Lang. He read it slowly and loudly. A couple of the jurors shook their heads in disbelief.

Wade Lanier hammered away. "So, Mr. Pickering, you and your sister sat Lettie Lang down at the kitchen table and showed her the will handwritten by your mother, correct?"

"Correct."

"And if she testified earlier that she had never seen a will, then she was lying, correct?"

"I suppose."

"Objection," Jake said.

"Overruled," His Honor snarled from the bench.

It was apparent, at least to Jake, that Judge Atlee was now the enemy. He viewed Lettie as a liar, and in his world there was no greater sin. Over the years he had jailed several litigants when they were caught red-handed telling lies, but always in divorce cases. A night in jail worked wonders in the search for veracity.

Lettie was in no danger of going to jail; that would be far more preferable. At that dreadful moment, with the jurors squirming nervously and glancing around, she was in danger of losing about $20 million, give or take, before taxes of course.

When a witness is telling the truth, and the truth hurts, a trial lawyer has no alternative but to attack the witness's credibility. Jake sat stone-faced as if he expected Fritz to say what he was saying, but just under the skin he was desperately searching for a soft spot. What did Fritz have to gain by testifying? Why would he waste his time?

"Mr. Brigance," Judge Atlee said when Lanier tendered the witness.

Jake stood quickly and faked as much confidence as possible. The first rule every trial lawyer learns is to never ask a question if you don't know the answer. But when you're staring at certain defeat, toss the rules. Shooting wildly from the hip, Jake said, "Mr. Pickering, how much are you being paid to testify here today?"

The bullet landed between his eyes. He actually flinched as his jaw dropped, and he shot a desperate look at Wade Lanier. Lanier shrugged and nodded. Go ahead, it's no big deal.

Fritz said, "Seventy-five hundred dollars."

"And who's paying you?" Jake demanded.

"The check came from Mr. Lanier's office."

"And what's the date on the check?"

"I don't remember exactly, but I got it about a month ago."

"So about a month ago you guys closed the deal. You agreed to come here and testify, and Mr. Lanier sent you the money, right?"

"That's right."

"Didn't you in fact demand more than seventy-five hundred?" Jake asked, still shooting wildly with no idea what the facts were. But he had a hunch.

"Well, yes, I did ask for more."

"You wanted at least ten thousand, didn't you?"

"Something like that," Fritz admitted and looked at Lanier again. Jake was reading his mind.

"And you told Mr. Lanier that you would not testify unless you got paid, right?"

"At the time, I wasn't talking to Mr. Lanier. It was one of his investigators. I didn't meet Mr. Lanier until earlier this morning."

"Regardless, you were not going to testify for free, right?"

"That's right."

"When did you drive over from Shreveport?"

"Late yesterday afternoon."

"And when are you leaving Clanton?"

"Just as soon as I can."

"So, a quick trip, say twenty-four hours?"

"Something like that."

"Seventy-five hundred bucks for twenty-four hours. You're an expensive witness."

"Is that a question?"

Jake was getting lucky but he knew it couldn't last. He looked at his notes, chicken scratch he could not read, and changed course. "Mr. Pickering, didn't Lettie Lang explain to you that she had nothing to do with the preparation of your mother's will?"

Jake had no idea what Lettie had done; he had yet to discuss the incident with her. That would be an ugly conversation, probably during lunch.

"That's what she said," Fritz replied.

"And didn't she try to explain that your mother never said a word to her about the will?"

"That's what she said."

"Where did you get this copy of the will?"

"I kept it." Actually, it had arrived anonymously in the mail, but who would ever know the difference?

"Nothing further," Jake said as he sat down.

Judge Atlee announced, "We'll be in recess until one thirty."

44

J ake and Harry Rex fled town. With Jake driving, they raced
deep into the countryside, putting distance between themselves and the nightmare in the courtroom. They wouldn't risk
bumping into Lettie or Portia, or the other lawyers, or anyone,
for that matter, who had just witnessed the bloodletting.

Harry Rex was the eternal contrarian. When a day in trial
went smoothly, he could always be counted on to see nothing
but negatives. A bad day, and he could be unbelievably optimistic about tomorrow. As Jake drove and seethed, he kept waiting
for his foxhole buddy to pass along an observation that might
lift his spirits, if only for a moment. What he got was: "You'd
better come off your high horse and settle this son of a bitch."

A mile passed before Jake responded. "What makes you think
Wade Lanier would talk settlement now? He just won the case.
That jury wouldn't give Lettie Lang fifty bucks for a sack of
groceries. You saw their faces."

"You know the bad part, Jake?"

"It's all bad. It's worse than bad."

"The bad part is that it makes you question everything about
Lettie. I've never thought for a minute that she manipulated
Seth Hubbard into redoing his will. She's not that slick and he
wasn't that stupid. But now, all of a sudden, when you realize
she's done it before, you say, 'Okay, could this be a pattern.'
'Could this old gal know more about will and estate law than we
give her credit for?' I don't know, it just rattles you."

"And why would she cover it up? Hell, I'll bet she's never told
Portia, never told anyone about getting caught at the Pickerings'.
I guess I should've been smart enough to ask her six months

ago—say, Lettie, have you talked anyone else into changing their wills and adding a nice provision for you?"

"Why didn't you think of that?"

"Stupid I guess. I feel pretty stupid right now."

Another mile passed, then another. Jake said, "You're right. It makes you question everything. And if we feel this way, think about the jurors."

"The jurors are gone, Jake, and you'll never get 'em back. You've called your best witnesses, put on a near-perfect case, saved your star to go last, and she did a fine job, and then, in a matter of minutes, the case was totally destroyed by a surprise witness. You can forget this jury."

Another mile passed. Jake said, "A surprise witness. Surely that's grounds for a reversal."

"Don't bet on it. You can't let it get that far, Jake. You gotta settle this case before it goes to the jury."

"I'll have to resign as the attorney."

"Then so be it. You've made some money, now get out of the way. Think about Lettie for a moment."

"I'd rather not."

"I understand, but what if she walks out of that courtroom without a penny?"

"Maybe that's what she deserves."

They slid to a stop in the gravel parking lot of Bates Grocery. The red Saab was the only foreign car there; every other vehicle was a pickup truck, and not a one less than ten years old. They waited in line as Mrs. Bates patiently filled their plates with her vegetables and Mr. Bates collected $3.50 from each customer, sweet iced tea and corn bread included. The crowd was almost shoulder to shoulder and there were no empty chairs. "Over there," Mr. Bates said, nodding, and Jake and Harry Rex sat at a small counter not too far from the massive gas stove that was covered with pots. They could talk, but carefully.

Not that it mattered. Not a single person having lunch knew a trial was under way in town, and they certainly didn't know how badly the trial had turned against Jake. Perched on a stool and hunched over his plate, he sat forlornly and looked through the crowd.

"Hey, you gotta eat," Harry Rex said.

"No appetite," Jake said.

"Can I have your plate?"

"Maybe. I envy these people. They don't have to go back into that courtroom."

"Neither do I. You're on your own, buddy. You've screwed up the case so bad it can never be rescued. I'm outta there."

Jake pinched off a bite of corn bread and stuck it in his mouth. "Didn't you go to school with Lester Chilcott?"

"I did. Biggest prick in law school. Nice enough guy when we started, but then he got a job with a big Jackson firm and, bam, just like that, he became a flaming asshole. I guess it happens. He's not the first. Why?"

"Grab him this afternoon and whisper to him. See if they'll talk settlement."

"Okay. What kind of settlement?"

"I don't know, but if they'll come to the table, we'll cut a deal. If I resign, I think Judge Atlee will take charge of the negotiations and make sure everyone gets something."

"Now you're talking. It's worth a shot."

Jake managed a bit of fried okra. Harry Rex was half-finished and eyeing Jake's plate. He said, "Look, Jake, you played football, right?"

"I tried."

"No, I remember when you were the quarterback for scrawny little Karaway, never had a winning season, as I recall. What was the worst ass-whipping you ever took on the field?"

"Ripley beat us fifty to nothing my junior year."

"How bad was it at halftime?"

"Thirty-six to nothing."

"And did you quit?"

"No, I was the quarterback."

"Okay, you knew at halftime that you were not going to win, but you led the team back onto the field for the second half, and you kept playing. You didn't quit then and you can't quit now. A win looks pretty doubtful at this point, but you gotta drag your ass back onto the field. Right now you look thoroughly defeated, and the jury is watching every move you make. Eat your vegetables like a good boy, and let's go."

The jurors scattered for lunch and reconvened in the jury room at 1:15. In little pockets of whispered conversations, they talked about the case. They were surprised and confused. Surprised that the trial had turned so abruptly against Lettie Lang. Before Fritz Pickering showed up, the evidence was mounting and it was becoming clear that Seth Hubbard was a man who did whatever he wanted, and knew exactly what he was doing. That changed suddenly, and Lettie was now viewed with great suspicion. Even the two black jurors, Michele Still and Barb Gaston, appeared to be jumping ship. The confusion was about what was next. Who would Jake put on the stand to undo the damage? Could it be undone? And if they, the jurors, rejected the handwritten will, what would happen to all that money? There were many unanswered questions.

There was so much chatter about the case that the foreman, Nevin Dark, felt compelled to remind them that His Honor frowned on what they were doing. "Let's talk about something else," he said politely, not wanting to offend. He was not, after all, their boss.

At 1:30, the bailiff entered the room, counted heads, and said, "Let's go." They followed him into the courtroom. When they were seated, all twelve looked at Lettie Lang, who was not looking up from her note-taking. Nor did her lawyer glance over at the jury box for one of his cute little smiles. Instead, he sat low in his chair, chewing on a pencil, trying to appear relaxed.

Judge Atlee said, "Mr. Lanier, you may call your next witness."

"Yes sir. The contestants call Mr. Herschel Hubbard." He took the stand, smiled goofily at the jury, swore to tell the truth, then began answering a lot of mundane questions. Wade Lanier had groomed him well. Back and forth they went, covering all aspects of Herschel's uneventful life. As always, the spin was in and Herschel recalled with great fondness his childhood, his parents, his sister, and the grand times they'd all had together. Yes, the divorce was quite painful, but the family struggled through it and persevered. He and his old man were very close: talked all the time, saw each other whenever they could, but, hey, both were living busy lives. Both were big fans of the Atlanta Braves. They followed the team religiously and talked about the games all the time.

Lettie stared at him, dumbfounded. She had never heard Seth Hubbard say one word about the Atlanta Braves, and she had never known him to watch a baseball game on television.

They tried to make it to Atlanta at least once each season to catch some games. Say what? This was news to Jake and everyone else who'd read Herschel's depositions. He had never mentioned such a road trip with his father. But there was little Jake could do. It would take two days of hard digging to prove the trips to Atlanta never took place. If Herschel wanted to invent tales about him and his old man, Jake couldn't stop him at this point. And Jake had to be careful. If he had any credibility left with the jury, he could seriously damage it by attacking Herschel. The man had lost his father, then he'd been cut out of his will in a very cruel and humiliating manner. It would be easy and only natural for the jurors to feel sympathy.

And how do you argue with a son who wasn't close to his father, but now swears that he was? You don't, and Jake knew it was an argument he could not win. He took notes, listened to the fiction, and tried to keep a poker face as if everything was going great. He could not bring himself to look at the jurors. There was a wall between him and them, something he'd never before experienced.

When they finally got around to Seth's cancer, Herschel became somber and even choked back tears. It was just awful, he said, watching this active and vigorous man dry up and shrivel with the disease. He had tried to quit smoking so many times; father and son had engaged in long, heartfelt conversations about the smoking. Herschel quit when he was thirty, and he begged his father to quit also. In his final months, Herschel visited him as often as possible. And, yes, they talked about his estate. Seth was clear about his intentions. He might not have been too generous with Herschel and Ramona when they were younger, but he wanted them to have it all when he died. He assured them that he had prepared a proper will, one that would insulate them from financial worries and also secure the future for their children, Seth's beloved grandchildren.

Seth was not himself toward the end. They talked all the time by phone, and at first Herschel noticed his father's memory was fading. He couldn't remember the score of last night's baseball game. He repeated himself constantly. He would ramble on about the World Series, though the Braves were not in the Series last year. But to Seth they were. The old guy was slipping away. It was so heartbreaking.

Not surprisingly, Herschel was wary of Lettie Lang. She did a fine job cleaning the house, and cooking and caring for his father, but the longer she worked there, and the sicker Seth became, the more she seemed to protect him. She acted as though she didn't want Herschel and Ramona in the house. Several times Herschel called his father, but she said he wasn't feeling well and couldn't come to the phone. She tried to keep him away from his family.

Lettie glared at the witness, slowly shaking her head.

It was quite a performance, and by the time it was over Jake was almost too stunned to think or move. Through skillful and no doubt exhaustive preparation, Wade Lanier had pieced together a fictional narrative that any father and son would envy.

Jake walked to the podium and asked, "Mr. Hubbard, on these trips to watch the Braves play, what hotel did you and your father usually stay in?"

Herschel squinted and his mouth opened but nothing came out. Hotels have records that can be checked. Finally, he recovered and said, "Uh, well, we stayed in different hotels."

"Did you go to Atlanta last year?"

"No, Dad was too sick."

"The year before?"

"I think so, yes."

"Okay, so you went in eighty-seven. Which hotel?"

"I can't remember."

"All right. Who did the Braves play?"

Games and schedules are records that can be checked. "Well, gee, I'm not sure, you know. Maybe it was the Cubs."

Jake said, "We can check on that. What was the date?"

"Oh, I'm terrible with dates."

"Okay, in eighty-six. Did ya'll make it to Atlanta for a game or two?"

"I think so, yes."

"Which hotel?"

"Maybe the Hilton. Not sure."

"Who'd the Braves play?"

"Well, let's see. I can't be sure, but I know we saw them play the Phillies one year."

"In eighty-six, who played third base for the Phillies?"

Herschel swallowed hard and looked straight ahead, as if staring at headlights. His elbows were twitching and he kept glancing at the jurors. His lying had caught up with him. Lanier's fictional masterpiece had holes in it.

Finally, "Don't know."

"You don't recall Mike Schmidt, the greatest third baseman in the game. He's still there and on his way to the Hall of Fame."

"Sorry, no."

"Who played center field for the Braves?"

Another painful pause. It was obvious Herschel didn't have a clue.

"Ever hear of Dale Murphy?"

"Sure, that's him. Dale Murphy."

For the moment, Herschel gave every indication of being a liar, or at least a great embellisher. Jake could poke and prod around the rest of his testimony, but there was no guarantee he could score again. Instinctively, he decided to sit down.

Ramona was next, and she was crying not long after she was sworn in. She still couldn't believe her beloved "daddy" had been so lost and distraught that he took his own life. With time, though, Lanier settled her down and they plowed through their scripted testimony. She had always been Daddy's girl and she just couldn't get enough of the old guy. He adored her and her children and came to visit them often down in Jackson.

Once again, Jake grudgingly admired Wade Lanier. He had prepared Ramona well for her deposition back in December and taught her the art of sandbagging. He knew that at trial there was no way Jake could rebut her testimony, so offer a few crumbs during the deposition, just enough to vaguely answer the questions, then load up the fiction for the jury.

Her testimony was a dramatic blend of emotion, bad acting, lying, and exaggerating. Jake began stealing glances at the jury to see if anyone was suspicious. As she bawled again, Tracy McMillen, number two, met Jake's look and frowned as if to say, "Can you believe this?"

At least that was Jake's reading. He could be wrong. His instincts had been rattled and he didn't fully trust them. Tracy was his favorite juror. Their eyes had been meeting for two days now, and things had been elevated almost to the point of flirting. It wasn't the first time Jake had used his good looks to win over a juror, nor would it be the last. Another glance over and he caught Frank Doley shooting one of his patented "I can't wait to burn you" looks.

Wade Lanier wasn't perfect. He kept her on direct far too long and began to lose people. Her voice was grating and her crying was a tired old act. Those watching suffered along with her, and when Lanier finally said, "I tender the witness," Judge Atlee quickly tapped the gavel and said, "Let's recess for fifteen minutes."

The jurors left and the courtroom cleared out. Jake stayed at his table, as did Lettie. It was time to acknowledge each other. Portia moved her chair closer so the three of them could speak softly in a small huddle. Lettie began with "Jake, I'm so sorry. What have I done?" Her eyes were instantly wet.

"Why didn't you tell me, Lettie? If I had known about the Pickerings, I could have been prepared."

"It didn't happen that way at all, Jake. I swear I never discussed no will with Miss Irene. Never. Not before she wrote it, not after. I didn't even know about it until I came to work that mornin' and all hell broke loose. I swear, Jake. You gotta let me explain this to the jury. I can do it. I can make them believe me."

"It's not that simple. We'll talk about it later."

"We need to talk, Jake. Herschel and Ramona are lyin' through their teeth. Can't you make 'em stop?"

"I don't think the jury is buying much of this."

Portia said, "They don't like Ramona."

"I can understand that. I need to run to the restroom. Any word from Lucien?"

"No, I checked the phone messages during lunch. Some lawyers, some reporters, and one death threat."

"A what?"

"Some dude said they gonna burn your house again if you win all that money for them niggers."

"How nice. I sort of like it. It brings back fond memories of the Hailey trial."

"I saved it. You want me to tell Ozzie?"

"Sure."

Harry Rex caught Jake outside the restroom and said, "Spoke with Chilcott. No deal. No interest in talking settlement. In fact, he almost laughed in my face, said they have another surprise or two."

"What?" Jake asked in a panic.

"Well, of course he wouldn't tell me. That would ruin the ambush, right?"

"I can't take another ambush, Harry Rex."

"Just keep your cool. You're doing fine. I don't think Herschel and Ramona impressed too many jurors."

"Should I go after her?"

"No. Take it easy. If you pin her down, she'll just start crying again. The jury's sick of her."

Five minutes later, Jake walked to the podium and said, "Now, Mrs. Dafoe, your father died on October 2 of last year, correct?"

"Yes."

"Before he died, when was the last time you saw him?"

"I didn't keep notes, Mr. Brigance. He was my daddy."

"Isn't it true that you last saw him in late July, over two months before he died?"

"No, that's not true at all. I saw him all the time."

"The last time, Mrs. Dafoe. When was the last time?"

"Again, I didn't keep up with the dates. Probably a couple of weeks before he died."

"Are you sure about that?"

"Well, no, I'm not positive. Do you make a note every time you visit your parents?"

"I'm not the witness, Mrs. Dafoe. I'm the lawyer who's asking the questions. Are you sure you saw your father a couple of weeks before he died?"

"Well, uh, I can't be positive."

"Thank you. Now, what about the children, Will and Leigh Ann? When was the last time they saw their grandfather before he died?"

"Oh, heavens, Mr. Brigance. I have no idea."

"But you testified they saw him all the time, right?"

"Of course, yes. They loved their granddaddy."

"Did he love them?"

"He adored them."

Jake smiled and walked to the small table where the exhibits were kept. He picked up two sheets of paper and looked at Ramona. "This is the will your father wrote the day before he died. It's in evidence and the jury has already seen it. In paragraph six, your father writes, and I quote: 'I have two children—Herschel Hubbard and Ramona Hubbard Dafoe— and they have children, though I don't know how many because I haven't seen them in some time.' End quote."

Jake placed the will back on the table and asked, "By the way, how old is Will?"

"Fourteen."

"And how old is Leigh Ann?"

"Twelve."

"So it's been twelve years since you had a child?"

"Yes, that's very true."

"And your own father didn't know if you'd had any more kids?"

"You can't believe that will, Mr. Brigance. My daddy wasn't in his right mind when he wrote that."

"I guess that's up to the jury. No further questions." Jake sat down and got a note from Quince Lundy that read, "Brilliant. You killed her." At that moment in the trial, in his career, in his life for that matter, Jake needed a boost. He leaned over and whispered, "Thank you."

Wade Lanier stood and said, "Your Honor, the contestants call Mr. Ian Dafoe, husband of Ramona Hubbard." Ian slinked to the stand, no doubt primed and ready to fabricate another trip down memory lane. Halfway through his testimony, Quince Lundy slipped over another note. It read, "These people are trying way too hard to convince the jury. Don't think it's working."

Jake nodded as he looked for an opening, a stray word that he might seize and turn against the witness. In the wake of his wife's over-the-top drama, Ian came across as harmlessly dull. He gave many of the same answers, but without the emotion.

Through sources and back channels, Jake, Harry Rex, and Lucien had picked up some dirt on Ian. His marriage had been on the rocks for some time. He preferred to stay away from home and blamed his absences on business. He ran the women hard. His wife drank too much. And, some of his deals were in trouble.

On cross, Jake's first question was, "You say you're a commercial real estate developer, right?"

"That's correct."

"Do you own all or part of a company called KLD Biloxi Group?"

"I do."

"And is that company attempting to renovate the Gulf Coast Mall in Biloxi, Mississippi?"

"It is."

"Would you say that company is financially sound?"

"Depends on how you define 'financially sound.'"

"Okay, let's define it like this: Two months ago, was your company, KLD Biloxi Group, sued by the First Gulf Bank for the nonpayment of a $2 million line of credit?" Jake was holding and waving some papers clipped together. He had the proof.

"Yes, but there's a lot more to the story."

"I didn't ask for more. Was your company also sued last month by a New Orleans bank known as Picayune Trust for $2.6 million?"

Ian took a deep breath and finally said, "Yes, but these cases are still pending, and we countersued."

"Thank you. Nothing further."

Ian stepped down at 4:45, and for a moment Judge Atlee considered recessing until Thursday morning. Wade Lanier offered to help by saying, "Judge, we can put on a witness that won't take long."

If Jake had an inkling of what was coming, he would have stalled some more with Ian, burned some clock, and dodged another ambush, at least until the next day. As it turned out, however, the jury left for the night with an even lower opinion of Seth Hubbard and his proclivities.

Lanier said, "We call Julina Kidd."

Jake immediately recognized the name as one of the forty-five Lanier had dumped on his desk two weeks earlier. Jake had tried twice to phone her, but got nowhere. She was fetched from a witness room and led to the stand by a bailiff. Per Wade Lanier's rather clear and firm instructions, she wore a cheap, blue dress that was similar to what Lettie had on. Nothing tight, nothing sexy, nothing to show off a figure that usually commanded a second look. No jewelry, nothing fancy. She tried her best to look plain, though that would have been impossible.

The message was subtle: if Seth would chase this attractive black woman, then he would also chase Lettie.

She took the stand and smiled nervously at the jury. Lanier walked her through some preliminaries, then got right to the point. He handed her some paperwork and asked, "Can you please identify this?"

She took a quick look and said, "Yes, this is a claim for sexual harassment I filed against Seth Hubbard about five years ago."

Jake was on his feet, practically yelling, "Objection, Your Honor. Unless counsel can explain to us why this is relevant, it should not be admitted." Lanier was standing too, ready to rumble. "Oh, it's very relevant, Your Honor," he said loudly.

Judge Atlee raised both hands and said, "Silence." He glanced at his watch, looked at the jurors, paused for a second, and said, "Let's keep everyone right here and take a five-minute break. Counsel, meet me in chambers." They hurriedly marched back into his chambers. Jake was bitter enough to throw a punch and Lanier seemed willing to mix it up. When Lester Chilcott closed the door, Judge Atlee said, "What's her testimony?"

Lanier said, "She worked for one of Seth Hubbard's companies in south Georgia. They met there, he came on strong, forced her to have sex, then fired her when she decided she didn't want any more. They reached an out-of-court settlement on the harassment suit."

"And this was five years ago?" Jake asked.

"It was."

"How is it relevant to our issues today?" Judge Atlee asked.

"Oh, it's very relevant, Your Honor," Lanier said casually and with the benefit of months of preparation. Jake was thoroughly blindsided and almost too angry to think. Lanier continued, "It goes to the issue of undue influence. Ms. Kidd was an employee, as was Ms. Lang. Seth had a propensity to seduce women who worked for him, regardless of color. This weakness led him to make decisions that were not financially sound."

"Jake?"

"Bullshit. First, Judge, she should not be allowed to testify because she was not listed as a witness until two weeks ago, in clear violation of the rules. Second, what Seth did five years ago has nothing to do with his testamentary capacity last October. And, obviously, there is not one shred of proof that he was intimate with Lettie Lang. I don't care how many women, black or white, he was screwing five years ago."

Lanier said, "We think it's probative."

Jake said, "Bullshit, everything's probative."

"Your language, Jake," Judge Atlee warned.

"Sorry."

Judge Atlee held up a hand and all was quiet. He lit a pipe, exhaled mightily, paced to the window and back, then said, "I like your point, Wade. Both women were his employees. I'll allow the testimony."

Jake said, "Who needs a rule book?"

"See me after court today, Jake," Judge Atlee said sternly, then blew some more smoke. He laid down his pipe and said, "Let's carry on."

The lawyers reassembled in the courtroom. Portia leaned forward and whispered to Jake, "What happened?"

"The judge has lost his mind, that's all."

Julina told her story to a breathless crowd. Her sudden promotion, the new passport, the trip to Mexico City with the boss, the luxury hotel with adjoining rooms, then the sex and the guilt. Back home, he fired her immediately and had her escorted out of the building. She sued, and Seth quickly settled out of court.

The testimony was not relevant to the will contest. It was scandalous and certainly memorable, but as Jake listened to it he became convinced Judge Atlee had blundered badly. The trial was lost, but the appeal was looking stronger by the hour. Jake would have a grand time exposing Wade Lanier's trickery to the Supreme Court of Mississippi. He would take great satisfaction in finally getting Reuben V. Atlee reversed.

Jake admitted to himself that it was a lost cause if he was already thinking about the appeal. He quizzed Julina Kidd for a few minutes, just long enough to extract the admission that she was being paid to testify. She would not say how much—Lanier had obviously talked to her in time.

"So you swapped sex for money, and now it's testimony for money, right, Ms. Kidd?" he asked. It was a harsh question, and as soon as he uttered it he wished he could take it back. She was only telling the truth.

She shrugged but didn't respond, perhaps the classiest answer of the day.

At 5:30, Judge Atlee adjourned until Thursday morning. Jake stayed in the courtroom until long after everyone had left. He chatted quietly with Portia and Lettie, and tried in vain to assure them things were not as bad as they really were. It was a hopeless exercise.

He finally left as Mr. Pate was turning off the lights.

He did not stop by Judge Atlee's office, as directed. Instead he went home. He needed some quiet time with the two people he loved the most, the two who would always think of him as the greatest lawyer in the world.

45

The flight to Seattle was overbooked. Lucien got the last seat on one to San Francisco, where he would have twenty minutes to catch a nonstop to Chicago. If all went well, he would land in Memphis just after midnight. Nothing went well. He missed the connection in San Francisco, and while berating a ticket agent almost got himself handcuffed by a security guard. To get him out of the airport, they put him on a shuttle to L.A. with the promise he'd get a better connection to Dallas. En route to L.A., he drank three double bourbons on ice, and had the flight attendants glancing at each other. Upon landing, he went straight to a bar and continued drinking. He called Jake's office four times but got only the recording. He called Harry Rex's three times, but was told the lawyer was in court. When the nonstop to Dallas was canceled at 7:30, he cursed another ticket agent and threatened to sue American Airlines. To get him out of the airport, they put him on a four-hour flight to Atlanta, first class with free drinks.

Tully Still drove a forklift for a freight company in the industrial park north of town. He was working the night shift and easy to find. At 8:30 Wednesday night, Ozzie Walls gave him the nod and they walked outside into the darkness. Still lit a cigarette. The two were not related, but their mothers had been best friends since elementary school. Tully's wife, Michele, was Juror Number Three. Front row, dead center, Jake's prize.

"How bad is it?" Ozzie asked.

"Pretty bad. What happened? Things were rockin' along fine, then the case blows up."

"Couple of witnesses came outta nowhere. What are they sayin' in there?"

"Ozzie, even Michele's got doubts about Lettie Lang. The woman looks bad, man, sneakin' round, gettin' old white folks to change their wills. Michele and the Gaston woman'll stick with her, don't worry, but that means they got two votes. And the whites on the jury ain't bad people, maybe a couple, but most were goin' with Lettie until this mornin'. It's not all black against white in there."

"So there's a lot of talk?"

"Didn't say that. I think there's a lot of whisperin'. Ain't that pretty normal? You can't expect folk to not say a word until the end."

"I suppose."

"What's Jake gonna do?"

"I'm not sure he can do anything. He says he's called his best witnesses."

"Looks like he got blindsided, like those Jackson lawyers got the best of him."

"We'll see. Maybe it's not over."

"Looks bad."

"Keep a lid on it."

"Don't worry."

They were not celebrating with champagne at the Sullivan firm, though fine wine was being poured. Walter Sullivan, the retired partner who founded the firm forty-five years earlier, was a connoisseur who had recently discovered fine Italian Barolos. After a light working dinner in the conference room, he pulled some corks, brought in some fine crystal goblets, and a tasting came to life.

The mood was nothing short of triumphant. Myron Pankey had watched a thousand juries and had never seen one flip so quickly and so thoroughly. "You own them, Wade," he said. Lanier was being revered as a courtroom magician, able to pull rabbits out of hats in spite of the rules of evidence. "Give the judge the credit," he said modestly, and more than once. "He just wants a fair trial."

"Trials are not about fairness, Wade," Mr. Sullivan chided. "Trials are about winning."

Lanier and Chilcott could almost smell the money. Eighty percent of the gross estate for their clients, less taxes and so forth, and their little ten-man litigation firm would net a fee in excess of $2 million. It could arrive quickly. After the hand-written will was declared void, they would move on to the prior will. The bulk of the money was in cash. A lengthy probate might be avoided.

Herschel was in Memphis, commuting to the trial with his two children. The Dafoe family was staying in the guesthouse of a friend near the country club. All were in fine spirits and eager to get the money and get on with their lives. After he finished his wine, Wade would call them and receive their accolades.

An hour after he spoke to Tully Still, Ozzie was leaning on the hood of his patrol car in front of Jake's house, smoking a cigar with his favorite lawyer. Ozzie was saying, "Tully says it's ten to two."

Jake puffed and said, "No real surprise there."

"Well, it looks like it's time to fold up your chair and go home, Jake. This little party's over. Get somethin' for Lettie and get the hell out. She don't need much. Settle this damned thing before it goes to the jury."

"We're trying, Ozzie, okay? Harry Rex approached Lanier's guys twice this afternoon. They laughed at him. You can't settle a case when the other side is laughing at you. I'd take a million bucks right now."

"A million! How many black folk around here got a million bucks, Jake? You're thinkin' too much like a white man. Get half a million, get a quarter, hell, get somethin'."

"We'll try again tomorrow. I'll see how the morning goes, then approach Wade Lanier during lunch. He knows the score and he obviously knows how to play the game. He's been in my shoes before. I think I can talk to him."

"Talk fast, Jake, and get out of this damned trial. You want no part of this jury. This ain't nothin' like Hailey."

"No, it's not."

Jake thanked him and went inside. Carla was already in bed, reading and worrying about her husband. "What was that all about?" she asked as he undressed.

"Just Ozzie. He's concerned about the trial."

"Why is Ozzie out roaming around at this hour?"

"You know Ozzie. He never sleeps." Jake fell across the end of the bed and rubbed her legs under the sheets.

"Neither do you. Can I ask you something? Here you are in the middle of another big trial. You haven't slept four hours in the past week, and when you are asleep you fidget and have nightmares. You're not eating well. You're losing weight. You're preoccupied, off in la-la land half the time. You're stressed-out, jumpy, testy, sometimes even nauseous. You'll wake up in the morning with a knot in your stomach."

"The question?"

"Why in the world do you want to be a trial lawyer?"

"This might not be the best time to ask that question."

"No, it's the perfect time. How many jury trials have you had in the last ten years?"

"Thirty-one."

"And you've lost sleep and weight during each one, right?"

"I don't think so. Most are not quite this significant, Carla. This is exceptional."

"My point is that trial work is so stressful. Why do you want to do it?"

"Because I love it. It's what being a lawyer is all about. Being in the courtroom, in front of a jury, is like being in the arena, or on the field. The competition is fierce. The stakes are high. The gamesmanship is intense. There will be a winner and a loser. There is a rush of adrenaline each time the jury is led in and seated."

"A lot of ego."

"A ton. You'll never meet a successful trial lawyer without an ego. It's a requirement. You gotta have the ego to want the work."

"You should do well, then."

"Okay, I admit I have the ego, but it might get crushed this week. It might need soothing."

"Now or later?"

"Now. It's been eight days."

"Lock the door."

Lucien blacked out somewhere over Mississippi at thirty-five thousand feet. When the plane landed in Atlanta, the flight attendants helped him off. Two guards put him in a wheelchair and rolled him to the gate for the flight to Memphis. They passed several airport lounges, all of which he noticed. When the guards parked him he thanked them, then got up and staggered to the nearest bar and ordered a beer. He was cutting back, being responsible. He slept from Atlanta to Memphis, landing there at 7:10 a.m. They dragged him off the plane, called security, and security called the police.

Portia took the call at the office. Jake was upstairs frantically reviewing witness statements when she buzzed through with "Jake, it's a collect call from Lucien."

"Where is he?"

"Don't know but he sounds awful."

"Take the call and put him through."

Seconds later, Jake picked up the receiver and said, "Lucien, where are you?"

With great effort, he was able to convey the message that he was in the Memphis City Jail and needed Jake to come get him. He was thick-tongued, erratic, obviously bombed. Sadly, Jake had heard it all before. He was suddenly angry and unsympathetic.

"They won't let me talk," Lucien mumbled, barely intelligible. Then he seemed to be growling at someone in the background. Jake could visualize it perfectly. He said, "Lucien, we're leaving in five minutes for the courtroom. I'm sorry." But he wasn't sorry at all. Let him rot in jail.

"I gotta get there, Jake, it's important," he said, his words slurred so badly that he repeated himself three times.

"What's important?"

"I got deposition. Ancil's. Ancil Hubbard. Deposition. It's important Jake."

Jake and Portia hurried across the street and entered the courthouse through the rear doors. Ozzie was in the hallway on the first floor talking to a janitor. "Got a minute?" Jake asked with a look that was dead serious. Ten minutes later, Ozzie and Marshall Prather left town in a sprint to Memphis.

"Missed you yesterday," Judge Atlee said when Jake entered his chambers. The lawyers were gathering for the morning's pregame briefing.

"Sorry Judge, but I got tied up with trial details," Jake replied.

"I'm sure you did. Gentlemen, any preliminary matters this morning?"

The lawyers for the contestants smiled grimly and shook their heads. No. Jake said, "Well, yes, Your Honor, there is one matter. We have located Ancil Hubbard in Juneau, Alaska. He is alive and well and unable to rush down here for the trial. He is an interested party to these proceedings and should be included. Therefore, I move for a mistrial and suggest we start over when Ancil can be here."

"Motion denied," Judge Atlee said without hesitation. "He would be of no assistance in determining the validity of this will. How did you find him?"

"It's quite a long story, Your Honor."

"Save it for later. Anything else?"

"Not from me."

"Are your next witnesses ready, Mr. Lanier?"

"They are."

"Then let's proceed."

With the jurors so deeply in his pocket, the last thing Wade Lanier wanted to do was to bore them. He had made the decision to streamline his case and get to the jury as soon as possible. He and Lester Chilcott had mapped out the rest of the trial.

They would spend Thursday calling their remaining witnesses. If Jake had anything left, he would then be permitted to call rebuttal witnesses. Both lawyers would deliver their closing arguments mid-morning on Friday, and the jurors would get the case just after lunch. With the weekend looming, and with their minds already made up, they should finish and deliver a verdict long before the courthouse closed at five. Wade and Lester would be in Jackson in time for a late dinner with their wives.

As seasoned lawyers, they should have known better than to plan the rest of the trial.

Their first witness Thursday morning was a retired oncologist from Jackson, a Dr. Swaney. For decades he had worked as a practicing physician while teaching at the medical school. His résumé was impeccable, as were his manners, and he spoke with a deep backcountry drawl that carried no pretensions. He was thoroughly credible and believable. Using as few medical terms as possible, Dr. Swaney explained to the jury the type of cancer that was killing Seth Hubbard, with emphasis on the tumors that metastasized to his spinal cord and ribs. He described the intense pain involved with such tumors. He had treated hundreds of patients with a similar condition, and it created some of the worst pain imaginable. Demerol was certainly one of the most effective drugs available. An oral dosage of a hundred milligrams every three to four hours was not uncommon and would alleviate some of the pain. It usually rendered the patient drowsy, sluggish, dizzy, often nauseous, and unable to carry out many routine functions. Driving was certainly out of the question. And, obviously, important decisions should never be made while under the influence of that much Demerol.

As a younger lawyer, Jake had learned the futility of arguing with a true expert. A bogus expert often provided the opportunity for some real carnage before the jury, but not so with witnesses like Dr. Swaney. On cross, Jake made it clear that Seth Hubbard's own treating physician, Dr. Talbert, was not certain how much Demerol Seth was taking in the days before his death. The witness agreed it was all speculation, but politely reminded

Jake that patients rarely buy more of an expensive drug if they're not using it.

The next expert was another medical doctor, a Dr. Niehoff, from the medical school at UCLA. Small-town juries are easily impressed with experts who travel great distances to spend time with them, and no one knew this better than Wade Lanier. An expert from Tupelo would have their attention, while one from Memphis would be even more believable. But bring in the same guy from California and the jury would hang on every word.

For $10,000 of Wade Lanier's money, plus expenses, Dr. Niehoff explained to the jury that he had spent the last twenty-five years researching and treating pain in cancer victims. He was well acquainted with the tumors under discussion and did a thorough job of describing their effects on the body. He had seen patients cry and scream for prolonged periods of time, turn deathly pale, vomit uncontrollably, beg for medications, pass out, and even beg for death. Thoughts of suicide were quite common. Actual suicide was not rare. Demerol was one of the more popular and effective treatments. Here, Dr. Niehoff ventured off script when he lapsed into a bit of technical jargon, as happened so often when experts couldn't resist the temptation to impress their listeners. He referred to the drug as meperidine hydrochloride, said it was a narcotic analgesic, an opiate pain reliever.

Lanier stopped him and brought his vocabulary back in line. Dr. Niehoff told the jury that Demerol was a powerful pain reliever and highly addictive. He had worked with the drug for his entire career and had written numerous articles about it. Doctors prefer to dispense it in the hospital or in their clinics; however, in a case like Seth Hubbard's, it was not unusual to allow the patient to take it orally at home. The drug was easy to abuse, especially for a person in severe pain like Seth.

Jake rose and said, "Objection, Your Honor. There is not a shred of evidence that Seth Hubbard abused this drug."

"Sustained. Stick with the facts, Doctor."

Jake sat down, relieved to have finally received a favorable ruling on something.

Dr. Niehoff was an excellent witness. His descriptions of the tumors, the pain, and the Demerol were detailed, and after forty-five minutes on the stand it was easy to believe Seth was suffering greatly and his pain was relieved only by massive doses of Demerol, a drug that practically knocked him out. In his expert opinion, Seth Hubbard's judgment was so adversely affected by the daily dosages and cumulative effects of the drug that he could not have been thinking clearly in his final days.

On cross, Jake lost even more ground. When he tried to make the point that Dr. Niehoff had no idea how much of the drug Seth was taking, the expert "guaranteed" Jake that anyone suffering like Seth would be desperate for Demerol.

"If he had access to a prescription, then he was taking the pills, Mr. Brigance."

After a few more pointless questions, Jake sat down. The two doctors had accomplished precisely what Wade Lanier had intended. At that moment, in the minds of the jurors, and practically everyone else in the courtroom, Seth had been disoriented, dizzy, drowsy, light-headed, and unable to drive so he asked Lettie to do it.

In summary, he lacked testamentary capacity.

After a ten-minute recess, Lanier continued when he called Lewis McGwyre as a witness. Because the Rush firm had made such an ungraceful exit from the case, and was thus cut out of the fees, McGwyre at first refused to testify. So Wade Lanier did the unthinkable: he subpoenaed another lawyer. In short order, Lanier established that McGwyre had prepared a thick will for Seth in September 1987. That will was admitted into evidence, and McGwyre stepped down. As much as he wanted to hang around and watch the trial, his pride wouldn't allow it. He and Stillman Rush hurried from the courtroom.

Duff McClennan took the stand, took the oath, and proceeded to explain to the jury that he was a tax lawyer with a three-hundred-man firm in Atlanta. For the past thirty years he had specialized in estate planning. He drafted wills, thick ones, for wealthy people who wanted to avoid as much of the death taxes as possible. He had reviewed the inventory of assets filed by Quince Lundy, and he had reviewed the handwritten will signed by Seth Hubbard. Lanier then flashed onto a large screen a series of calculations, and McClennan launched into a windy explanation of how federal and state death taxes gobbled up the unprotected estate. He apologized for the intricacies, the contradictions, the mind-numbing banalities of "our dear tax code," and apologized for its complexities. Twice he said, "I didn't write this. Congress did." Lanier knew perfectly well that the jury would be bored if not repulsed by this testimony, so he labored diligently to skip along, hitting the high points and leaving much of the code in the dust.

Jake was not about to object and prolong this agony. The jurors were already antsy.

When McClennan mercifully got to the bottom line, he said, "In my opinion, the total tax bill, state and federal, will be 51 percent." On the screen, in bold letters, Lanier wrote, "$12,240,000 in taxes."

But the fun was just starting. McClennan had analyzed the will prepared by Lewis McGwyre. It was primarily a collection of related and complicated trusts that gave $1 million outright to Herschel and Ramona each, then tied up the remainder for many years while doling it out to the family. He and Lanier had no choice but to discuss it in detail. Jake watched the jurors as they began to nod off. Even McClennan's light version of what the will was intended to do was dense and, at times, comically impenetrable. Lanier, though, was on a mission. He plowed ahead and began running the numbers on the big screen. The bottom line was that the tax bill under the 1987 will would be, in McClennan's expert opinion, only "$9,100,000, state and federal, give or take a few bucks."

The difference of $3,140,000 was printed in bold numbers on the screen.

The point was well made. Seth's hastily written holographic will cost his estate a lot of money; more proof he was not thinking clearly.

Jake had learned to avoid the IRS code in law school, and for the past ten years had readily stiff-armed any potential client looking for tax advice. He had none to offer because he knew so little about that area of the law. When Lanier tendered the witness, Jake passed. He knew the jurors were bored and ready for lunch.

"We'll be in recess until one thirty," Judge Atlee said. "Mr. Brigance." Jake planned to grab Wade Lanier and ask if he had five minutes to chat, but his plans were suddenly changed. He met Judge Atlee in his office down the hall. After His Honor removed his robe and lit his pipe, he sat down, stared at Jake, and calmly said, "You're not pleased with my rulings."

Jake snorted and said, "No, I am not. You've allowed Wade Lanier to hijack this trial with a couple of dirty tricks, a couple of surprise witnesses that I had no chance to prepare for."

"But your client lied."

"She's not my client. The estate is my client. But, yes, Lettie was not truthful. She was caught off guard, Judge, ambushed. In her deposition she clearly stated she could not remember all the white families she'd worked for. The Pickering episode was so unpleasant I'm sure she tried to forget it. And the most important aspect of that little story is that Lettie never knew about the handwritten will. I could have prepared her, Judge. That's my point. I could have softened the impact. You, though, allowed an ambush, and the trial flipped in a matter of seconds."

Jake glared at the old man as he spoke, though he was well aware that Reuben V. Atlee was not one to be reprimanded. But this time the judge was wrong, and Jake was angry at the injustice. He had nothing to lose at this point, so why not lay it all on the table?

The judge puffed and seemed to eat the smoke, then it drifted out. "I disagree. Regardless, though, I expect you to maintain your dignity. Lawyers do not curse in my chambers."

"My apologies. I sometimes curse in the heat of the battle, doubt if I'm the only one."

"I'm not sure the jury has flipped, as you say."

Jake hesitated. He almost reminded the judge that he knew almost nothing about juries. He so rarely saw them, which was part of the problem. In Chancery Court, he ruled supreme as judge and jury and had the luxury of admitting all evidence. He could sift through it, separate the good from the bad, and issue a ruling he deemed fair.

Jake was not about to argue. Instead, he said, "Judge, I have a lot of work to do."

Judge Atlee waved at the door, and Jake left. Harry Rex caught him as he was leaving the courthouse and said, "Ozzie called the office, said they're still at the jail in Memphis and trying to get him out. Right now they can't get a bond set."

Jake frowned and said, "A bond, for what?"

"He's charged with public drunkenness and resisting arrest. It's Memphis. They throw in the resisting charge every time they haul someone in."

"I thought Ozzie had contacts there."

"I guess he's lookin' for them. I told you it was a mistake to send that drunk to Alaska."

"Is this really helpful right now?"

"No. What are you doin' for lunch?"

"I'm not hungry."

"Let's get a beer."

"No, Harry Rex. Some juries get offended when the lawyer reeks of alcohol."

"You're not still worried about this jury, are you?"

"Knock it off, would you?"

"I gotta go to court in Smithfield this afternoon. Good luck. I'll check in later."

"Thanks." As Jake crossed the street to his office, he realized that Harry Rex had not missed a word in the courtroom since Monday morning.

Dewayne Squire was the vice president of Berring Lumber Company. On the Thursday before the suicide, he and Seth had engaged in a disagreement over a large shipment of heart pine to a flooring company in Texas. Squire had negotiated the deal, and was surprised to learn that his boss then called the company and negotiated another deal at a lower price. Back and forth they went throughout that Thursday morning. Both men were upset, both convinced they were right, but at some point Squire realized that Seth was not himself. Arlene Trotter was out of the office and missed the conflict. At one point, Squire entered Seth's office and found him with his head in his hands, claiming to be dizzy and nauseous. They spoke later and Seth had forgotten the details of the contract. He claimed Squire had negotiated a price that was too low, and they argued again. By the time Seth left around 3:00 p.m. the deal was done and Berring would eventually lose about $10,000. To Squire's recollection, it was the largest loss on any customer contract Seth was ever involved in.

He described his boss as being disoriented and erratic. The following morning he sold the timberland in South Carolina for a substantial loss.

Jake was well aware that Wade Lanier was pushing hard now and trying to get the case to the jury before the weekend. Jake needed to stall, so on cross-examination he pulled out the Berring financials and walked Squire through them. Nineteen eighty-eight was the most profitable year of the last five, though revenues dipped in the last quarter, after Seth's death. As the jurors faded away, Jake and Squire talked about the company's performance, its contracts, strategies, costs, labor problems, plant depreciation. Twice His Honor said, "Move along, Mr. Brigance," but he didn't push too hard. Mr. Brigance was already unhappy with him.

After Dewayne Squire, Lanier called to the stand a Mr. Dewberry, a land broker who specialized in farms and hunting clubs. He told the story of dealing with Seth in the days before he died. Seth had been interested in buying five hundred acres in Tyler County for a hunting club. He and Dewberry had been looking at land for the past five years, but Seth would never pull the trigger. He finally paid for a one-year option on the five hundred acres, then got sick and lost interest. As the option was about to expire, he called Dewberry several times. Dewberry did not know Seth was dying, nor did he have any idea he was on painkillers. One day Seth wanted to exercise the option; the next day he did not. Several times he could not remember the price per acre, and on one occasion forgot who he was talking to on the phone. His behavior became more and more erratic.

On cross, Jake managed to stall even more. By late Thursday afternoon, the trial had ground to a near halt, and Judge Atlee adjourned early.

46

After butting heads with the Memphis bureaucracy, Ozzie was about to quit when he remembered something he should have thought of sooner. He phoned Booker Sistrunk, whose office was four blocks from the city jail. After a rough beginning, the two had kept in touch, and over the months had visited on two occasions when Ozzie was in Memphis. Booker had not been back to Clanton and wasn't keen to return. Both realized that two black men, living sixty minutes apart and with some measure of power in a white world, should find common ground. They should be friends. Of particular interest to Booker was the fact that he still had $55,000 on loan to the Langs, and he wanted to protect his money.

The Memphis police loathed Booker Sistrunk, but they were also afraid of him. Fifteen minutes after he arrived in his black Rolls, paperwork was hopping from one desk to another with Lucien Wilbanks a high priority. He walked out thirty minutes after Booker walked in. "We need to go to the airport," Lucien said.

Ozzie thanked Booker and promised to catch up later.

As the story unfolded, Lucien had left his briefcase on the airplane. He thought it was under the seat, but it could have been in the overhead compartment. Regardless, the flight attendants were idiots for not finding it. They were much too concerned with dragging him off the airplane. Ozzie and Prather listened and fumed as they raced to the airport. Lucien looked and smelled like a skid row bum they'd picked up for vagrancy.

American's lost and found had no record of a briefcase being turned in on the flight from Atlanta. Reluctantly, the lone clerk began the task of trying to find it. Lucien found an airport lounge and ordered a pint of ale. Ozzie and Prather had a bad buffet lunch on a busy concourse, not far from the lounge. They were trying to keep an eye on their passenger. They called Jake's office but there was no answer. It was almost 3:00 p.m., and he was obviously tied up in court.

The briefcase was located in Minneapolis. Because Ozzie and Prather were law enforcement officers, American was by then treating the briefcase as if it were valuable evidence and crucial to an important investigation, when in reality it was a battered old leather bag with a few notepads, some magazines, some cheap soap and matches taken from the Glacier Inn in Juneau, and one videocassette tape. After a lot of uncertainty and haggling, a plan was put into place to route it back to Memphis as soon as possible. If all went well, it would arrive around midnight.

Ozzie thanked the clerk and went to find Lucien. As they were leaving the airport, Lucien came to life and said, "Say, my car is here. I'll just meet you guys in Clanton."

Ozzie said, "No, Lucien, you're drunk. You cannot drive."

Lucien angrily replied, "Ozzie, we're in Memphis and you got no jurisdiction here. Kiss my ass! I'll do any damn thing I want to do."

Ozzie threw up his hands and walked away with Prather. They tried to follow Lucien as they left Memphis at rush hour, but couldn't keep up with the dirty little Porsche as he weaved dangerously through heavy traffic. They drove on to Clanton, to Jake's office, and arrived there just before seven. Jake was waiting for the debriefing.

The only slightly good news in an otherwise dreadful and frustrating day was Lucien's arrest for public drunkenness and resisting arrest. It would kill any talk of a possible reinstatement to the practice of law, but at the moment that was small satisfaction, something Jake could not even mention. Other than that, things were as grim as they could possibly be.

Two hours later, Jake drove to Lucien's house. As he pulled in to the driveway, he noticed the Porsche wasn't there. He spoke briefly to Sallie on the front porch and she promised to call as soon as he came home.

Miraculously, Lucien's briefcase arrived in Memphis at midnight. Deputy Willie Hastings picked it up and drove to Clanton.

At 7:30 Friday morning, Jake, Harry Rex, and Ozzie gathered in the conference room downstairs and locked the door. Jake inserted the cassette into his video recorder and turned down the lights. The words **Juneau, Alaska . . . April 5, 1989** appeared on the television screen, then disappeared after a few seconds. Jared Wolkowicz introduced himself and explained what they were doing. Lucien introduced himself and said that this was a deposition and he would be asking the questions. He looked clear-eyed, sober. He introduced Ancil F. Hubbard, who was sworn in by the court reporter.

Small, frail, his head as slick as a white onion, he was wearing Lucien's black suit and white shirt, both several sizes too big. There was a bandage on the back of his head, and a strip of the adhesive tape holding it was barely visible above his right ear. He swallowed hard, looked at the camera as if in terror, then said, "My name is Ancil F. Hubbard. I live in Juneau, Alaska, but I was born in Ford County, Mississippi, on August first, 1922. My father was Cleon Hubbard, my mother Sarah Belle, my brother Seth. Seth was five years older than me. I was born on the family farm, near Palmyra. I left home when I was sixteen and never went back. Never. Never wanted to. Here's my story."

When the screen went blank fifty-eight minutes later, the three men sat for a while and stared at it. It was not something they ever wanted to see or hear again, but that would not be the case. Finally, slowly, Jake rose and pushed the eject button. "We'd better go see the judge."

"Can you get it admitted?" Ozzie asked.

"No way in hell," Harry Rex said. "I can think of ten different ways to keep it out, and not a single way to get it in."

"All we can do is try," Jake said. He raced across the street, his heart pounding, his mind spinning. The other lawyers were milling around the courtroom, happy it was Friday and eager to get home with a major win under their belts. Jake spoke briefly to Judge Atlee and said it was urgent the lawyers meet in his office down the hall where there was a television and a VCR. When they were assembled there, around the table, and when His Honor had filled and lit his pipe, Jake explained what he was doing. "The deposition was given two days ago. Lucien was there and asked some questions."

"Didn't know he was a lawyer again," Wade Lanier said.

"Hang on," Jake said dismissively. "Let's watch the tape, then we can fight."

"How long is it?" asked the judge.

"About an hour."

Lanier said, "This is a waste of time, Judge. You can't admit this deposition if I wasn't there and didn't have the chance to examine the witness. This is absurd."

Jake said, "We have time, Your Honor. What's the rush?"

Judge Atlee puffed away. He looked at Jake, and, with a twinkle in his eye, said, "Play it."

For Jake, the second time through the video was just as gut grinding as the first. Things he wasn't sure he heard right the first time were confirmed. He glanced repeatedly at Wade Lanier, whose indignation wore off as the story overwhelmed him. By the end, he seemed deflated. All of the lawyers for the contestants had been transformed. Their cockiness had vanished.

When Jake removed the tape, Judge Atlee kept staring at the blank screen. He relit his pipe and exhaled a gust of smoke. "Mr. Lanier?"

"Well, Judge, it's patently inadmissible. I wasn't there. I didn't have the chance to examine or cross-examine the witness. Not really fair, you know?"

Jake blurted, "So it's in keeping with the spirit of this trial. A surprise witness here, an ambush there. I thought you understood these tricks, Wade."

"I'll ignore that. It's not a proper deposition, Judge."

Jake said, "But what could you ask him? He's describing events that happened before you were born, and he's the only surviving witness. It would be impossible for you to cross-examine him. You know nothing about what happened."

Lanier said, "It's not properly certified by the court reporter. That lawyer in Alaska is not licensed to practice in Mississippi. I could go on and on."

"Fine. I'll withdraw it as a deposition and offer it as an affidavit. A statement given by a witness sworn before a notary public. The court reporter was also a notary public."

Lanier said, "It has nothing to do with Seth Hubbard's testamentary capacity on October 1 of last year."

Jake countered, "Oh, I think it explains everything, Wade. It proves without a doubt that Seth Hubbard knew exactly what he was doing. Come on, Judge, you're letting everything else in for the jury to hear."

"That's enough," Judge Atlee said sternly. He closed his eyes and seemed to meditate for a moment. He breathed deeply as his pipe went out. When he opened his eyes he said, "Gentlemen, I think the jury should meet Ancil Hubbard."

Ten minutes later, court was called to order. The jury was brought in and the large screen was set up again. Judge Atlee apologized to the jurors for the delay, then explained what was happening. He looked at the contestants' table and said, "Mr. Lanier, do you have any more witnesses."

Lanier rose as if crippled by arthritis and said, "No. We rest."

"Mr. Brigance?"

"Your Honor, I would like to recall Ms. Lettie Lang for limited purposes. It will just take a moment."

"Very well. Ms. Lang, please remember that you have already been sworn and are still under oath."

Portia leaned forward and whispered, "Jake, what are you doing?"

"Not now," he whispered. "You'll see."

With her last visit to the witness stand still a horrible memory, Lettie settled herself in and tried to appear calm. She refused to look at the jurors. There had been no time to prepare her; she had no idea what was coming.

Jake began, "Lettie, who was your mother, your biological mother?"

Lettie smiled, nodded, understood, and said, "Her name was Lois Rinds."

"And who were her parents?"

"Sylvester and Esther Rinds."

"What do you know about Sylvester Rinds?"

"He died in 1930 so I never met him. He lived on some land that the Hubbards now own. After he died, Esther signed the land over to Seth Hubbard's father. Sylvester's father was a man named Solomon Rinds, who also owned the land before him."

"No further questions, Your Honor."

"Mr. Lanier?"

Wade walked to the podium without notes. "Ms. Lang, have you ever had a birth certificate?"

"No sir."

"And your mother died when you were three years old, correct?"

"Correct."

"When we took your deposition in December, the week before Christmas, you were not so sure about your ancestry. What makes you so sure now?"

"I've met some of my kinfolk. A lot of questions have been answered."

"And you're certain now?"

"I know who I am, Mr. Lanier. I'm certain of that."

He sat down, and Judge Atlee addressed the courtroom. "At this time we will watch the videotaped deposition of Ancil Hubbard. Let's dim the lights. I want the doors locked and no traffic. This will take about an hour and there will be no interruptions."

The jurors, who had been so relentlessly bored the entire day before, were wide-awake and eager to witness this unexpected twist in the case. Many of the spectators shifted to the far-right side of the courtroom for a better look at the screen. The lights went low, the movements stopped, everyone seemed to take a deep breath, and then the tape began to roll. After Jared Wolkowicz and Lucien gave their introductions, Ancil appeared.

He said, *"This is my story. But I really don't know where to start. I'm living here in Juneau but it's not really my home. I have no home. The world is my home and I've seen most of it. I've been in some trouble over the years but I've also had a lot of fun. Lots of good times. I joined the Navy when I was seventeen, lied about my age, anything to get away from home, and for fifteen years I was stationed all over the place. I fought in the Pacific on the USS* Iowa. *After the Navy I lived in Japan, Sri Lanka, Trinidad, so many places I can't recall them all right now. I worked for shipping companies and lived on the oceans. When I wanted a break I settled down somewhere, always in a different place."*

Off camera, Lucien said, *"Tell us about Seth."*

"Seth was five years older, and it was just the two of us. He was my big brother and he always took care of me, as best he could. We had a tough life because of our father, Cleon Hubbard, a man we hated from the day we were born. He beat us, beat our mother, seemed like he was always fighting with someone. We lived way out in the country, near Palmyra, on the old family farm, in an old country house that my grandfather built. His name was Jonas Hubbard, and his father was Robert Hall Hubbard. Most of our other relatives had moved to Arkansas, so we didn't have a lot of cousins and kinfolks around. Seth and I worked like dogs around the farm, milking cows, chopping cotton, working in the garden, picking cotton. We were expected to work like grown men. It was a tough life, what with the Depression and all, but like they always said, the Depression didn't bother us in the South because we'd already been in one since the war."

"How much land?" Lucien asked.

"We had eighty acres; it had been in the family for a long time. Most of it was in timber but there was some farmland my grandfather had cleared. Cotton and beans."

"And the Rinds family had the adjacent property?"

"That's right. Sylvester Rinds. And there were some other Rindses there too. In fact, Seth and I played with a bunch of the Rinds kids from time to time, but always when Cleon wasn't looking. Cleon hated Sylvester, hated all the Rindses. It was a feud that had been boiling for a long time. You see, Sylvester owned eighty acres too, right next to our land, to the west of it, and the Hubbards always felt as though that land belonged to them. According to Cleon, a man named Jeremiah Rinds took title to the property in 1870 during Reconstruction. Jeremiah had been a slave, then a freed slave, and somehow purchased the land. I was just a kid and never really understood what happened back then, but the Hubbards always felt like it was their rightful land. I think they even went to court over it, but at any rate, it remained in the Rinds family. This infuriated Cleon because he had only eighty acres, but yet these black folks had the same. I remember hearing many times that the Rindses were the only blacks in the county who owned their own land, and that they had somehow taken it from the Hubbards. Seth and I knew we were supposed to dislike the Rinds kids, but we usually had no one else to play with. We'd sneak off and go fishing and swimming with them. Toby Rinds was my age and he was my buddy. Cleon caught Seth and me swimming once with the Rindses and beat us until we couldn't walk. He was a violent man, Cleon. Vengeful, mean, filled with hatred and with a quick temper. We were terrified of him."

Because it was his third viewing that morning, Jake didn't focus as hard. Instead, he watched the jurors. They were frozen, mesmerized, absorbing every word, as if in disbelief. Even Frank Doley, Jake's worst juror, was leaning forward with an index finger tapping his lips, thoroughly captivated.

"What happened to Sylvester?" Lucien asked.

"Oh yes. That's what you want to hear. The feud got worse when some trees got cut near the property line. Cleon thought they were

his trees. Sylvester was sure they were his. Because the boundary line had been disputed for so long, everybody knew exactly where it was. Cleon was ready to blow a gasket. I remember him saying he'd put up with their crap for far too long, that it was time to do something. One night some men came over and drank whiskey behind the barn. Seth and I sneaked out and tried to listen. They were planning something against the Rinds bunch. We couldn't tell exactly what it was, but it was obvious a plot was being hatched. Then one Saturday afternoon, we went to town. It was hot, August I think, 1930, and everybody went to town on Saturday afternoon, blacks and whites. Everybody had to shop and stock up for the week. Palmyra in those days was nothing but a farming village, but on Saturdays it was packed, the stores and sidewalks were crowded. Seth and I didn't see anything, but later that night we heard some kids talking about a black man who had said something smart to a white woman, and this had everybody upset. Then we heard that the black man was Sylvester Rinds. We rode home in the back of the truck with my parents in the front, and we knew something was about to happen. You could just tell. When we got home, Cleon ordered us to go to our rooms and not to come out until he said so. Then we heard him arguing with our mother, a bad argument. I think he hit her. We heard him drive away in his truck. We pretended to be asleep, but we were outside in a flash. We saw the taillights of his truck headed west, toward Sycamore Row."

"Where was Sycamore Row?"

"It's not there anymore, but in 1930 it was a small settlement on the Rinds land, near a creek. Just a few old houses scattered around, leftover slave stuff. That's where Sylvester lived. Anyway, Seth and I put a bridle on Daisy, our pony, and took off bareback. Seth had the reins, I was holding on for dear life, but we rode bareback all the time and we knew what we were doing. When we got close to Sycamore Row, we saw the lights from some trucks. We got off and led Daisy through the woods, then we tied her to a tree and left her. We went on, closer and closer, until we heard voices. We were on the side of a hill, and looking down we could see three or four white men beating a black man with sticks. His shirt was off and his pants were torn. It *was Sylvester Rinds. His wife, Esther, was in front of their house, fifty yards or so away, and she was yelling and crying. She tried to get close, but one of the white men knocked her down. Seth and I got closer and closer until we were at the edge of the trees. We stopped there and watched and listened. Some more men showed up in another truck. They had a rope, and when Sylvester saw the rope, he went crazy. It took three or four of the white men to hold him down until they could bind his hands and legs. They dragged him over and shoved him up into the back of one of the trucks."*

"Where was your father?" Lucien asked.

Ancil paused, took a deep breath, then rubbed his eyes. He continued: *"He was there, sort of off to the side, watching, holding a shotgun. He was definitely part of the gang, but he didn't want to get his hands dirty. There were four trucks, and they drove slowly away from the settlement, not far, to a row of sycamore trees. Seth and I knew the place well because we had fished in the creek. There were five or six tall sycamore trees in a perfect row; thus the name. There was an old story about an Indian tribe planting the trees as part of their pagan rituals, but who knows? The trucks stopped at the first tree and made a semicircle so there would be enough light. Seth and I had crept along in the woods. I didn't want to watch, and at one point I said, 'Seth, let's get out of here.' But I didn't move and neither did he. It was too awful to walk away from. They strung the rope over a thick branch and wrestled the noose around Sylvester's neck. He was twisting, yelling, begging, 'I ain't said nothin', Mista Burt, I ain't said nothin'. Please, Mista Burt, you know I ain't said nothin'.' A couple of them yanked the other end of the rope and almost pulled his head off."*

Lucien asked, "Who was Mr. Burt?"

Ancil took another deep breath and stared at the camera in a long, awkward pause. Finally, he said, *"You know, that was almost fifty-nine years ago and I'm sure all of these men have been dead for a long time. I'm sure they're rotting in hell, where they belong. But they have families, and nothing good can come from naming their names. Seth recognized three of them: Mista Burt, who was the leader of the lynch mob. Our dear father, of course. And one other, but I'm just not going to give names."*

"Do you remember the names?"

"Oh yes. I'll never forget them, as long as I live."

"Fair enough. What happened next?"

Another long pause as Ancil fought to compose himself.

Jake looked at the jurors. Number three, Michele Still, was touching her cheeks with a tissue. The other black juror, Barb Gaston, number eight, was wiping her eyes. To her right, Jim Whitehurst, number seven, handed her his handkerchief.

"Sylvester was practically strung up but his toes were still touching the bed of the truck. The rope was so tight around his neck he couldn't talk or scream, but he tried to. He made this awful sound that I'll never forget, sort of a high-pitched growl. They let him suffer there for a minute or two, all of the men standing close and admiring their work. He danced on his tiptoes, tried to free his hands, and tried to scream. It was so pathetic, so awful."

Ancil wiped his eyes with the back of his sleeve. Someone off camera handed him some tissues. He was breathing heavily.

"God, I've never told this story. Seth and I talked about it afterward for days and months, and then we agreed to try and forget about it. I've never told anyone else. It was so awful. We were just kids, we couldn't have stopped it."

After a pause, Lucien asked, *"So what happened, Ancil?"*

"Well, the obvious. Mista Burt yelled 'Go' and the guy driving the truck lurched forward. Sylvester swung kinda wild at first. The two men on the other end of the rope pulled some more and he shot up another five or six feet, I guess. His feet were about ten feet off the ground. It wasn't long before he became still. They watched him for a while, no one wanted to leave, then they tied the rope off and left him there. They drifted back toward the settlement, which was probably a tenth of a mile away from the tree, some of the men were walking, some in trucks."

"How many total?"

"I was just a kid, I don't know. Probably ten."

"Continue."

"*Seth and I were creeping along in the trees, in the shadows, listening as they laughed and patted themselves on the back. We heard one of them say, 'Let's burn his house.' And the mob gathered close to Sylvester's place. Esther was on the front steps, holding a child.*"

"*A child? A boy or a girl?*"

"*A girl, not a toddler, but a little girl.*"

"*Did you know this child?*"

"*No, not then. Seth and I found out about her later. Sylvester had only one child, the girl, and her name was Lois.*"

Lettie gasped so loud that she startled most of the jurors. Quince Lundy handed her a tissue. Jake glanced over his shoulder at Portia. She was shaking her head, as stunned as everyone else.

Lucien said, "*Did they burn the house?*"

"*No, a strange thing happened. Cleon stepped forward with his shotgun and stood between the men and Esther and Lois. He said no one was burning the house, and the men got in their trucks and left. Seth and I took off. The last thing I saw was Cleon talking to Esther on the front steps of their little shack. We hopped on our pony and sprinted home. When we sneaked through the window to our room, our mother was waiting. She was angry and wanted to know where we had been. Seth was the better liar and he said we'd been out chasing fireflies. She seemed to believe us. We begged her not to tell Cleon, and I don't think she ever did. We were in bed when we heard his truck approach and park. He came into the house and went to bed. We couldn't sleep. We whispered all night. I couldn't help but cry and Seth said it was okay to cry, as long as no one else saw me. He swore he wouldn't tell anyone that I was crying. Then I caught him crying too. It was so hot and these were the days before air-conditioning. Long before daybreak, we sneaked out the window again and sat on the back porch where it was cooler. We talked about going back to Sycamore Row and checking on Sylvester, but we really weren't serious. We speculated about what would happen to his body. And we were certain the sheriff would come out and arrest Cleon and the other men. The sheriff would need witnesses, and that's why we could*" *never breathe a word of what we'd seen. Never. We did not go to sleep that night. When we heard our mother in the kitchen, we sneaked back to bed, just in time for Cleon to walk in and yell at us to get to the barn and milk the cows. We did that every morning at dawn. Every morning. It was a tough life. I hated the farm, and from that day on I hated my father like no child has ever hated a parent. I wanted the sheriff to come get him and take him away forever."*

Off camera, Lucien seemed to need a break himself. He paused for a long time before continuing with *"What happened to the Rinds families?"*

Ancil dropped his head and shook it in an exaggerated way. *"Awful, just awful. The story gets worse. A day or two later, Cleon went to see Esther. He gave her a few bucks and made her sign a deed to the eighty acres. He promised her she could stay there, and she did for about forty-eight hours. The sheriff showed up all right. He and a deputy and Cleon went out to the settlement and told Esther and the other Rinds folks that they were being evicted. Immediately. Pack up your stuff right now and get off his land. There was a small clapboard chapel, a church where they had worshipped for decades, and to prove he owned everything, Cleon torched it. Burned it to the ground to show what a big man he was. The sheriff and the deputy helped him. They threatened to torch the shacks too."*

"And you saw this?"

"Sure. Seth and I missed nothing. We were supposed to be chopping cotton, but when we saw the sheriff pull up in front of our house, we knew something was up. We were hoping he would arrest Cleon, but that's not the way things worked in Mississippi back then. Not at all. The sheriff was there to help Cleon clean up his land and get rid of the blacks."

"What happened to the blacks?"

"Well, they left. They grabbed whatever they could and ran into the woods."

"How many?"

"Again, I was a kid. I wasn't counting. But there were several families of Rindses living on the land, not all around the settlement, but they were fairly close to each other." Ancil took a deep breath and mumbled, *"I'm really tired all of a sudden."*

Lucien said, *"We're almost finished. Please continue."*

"Okay, okay. So, they were running away, into the woods, and as soon as a family vacated their shack, Cleon and the sheriff would set it on fire. They burned everything. I vividly remember some of the blacks standing at the edge of the woods, holding their kids and whatever possessions they could grab, and looking back at the fires and the thick gray smoke and crying and wailing. It was just awful."

"What happened to them?"

"They scattered. For a while, a bunch of them were camping beside Tutwiler Creek, deep in the woods near the Big Brown River. Seth and I were looking for Toby and we found him there with his family. They were starving and terrified. We loaded up the horses one Sunday afternoon, sneaked away, and took as much food as we could steal without getting caught. That was the day I saw Esther and her little girl, Lois. The kid was about five years old and completely naked. She had no clothes. It was just awful. Toby came to our house a couple of times and hid behind the barn. Seth and I gave him as much food as we could. He hauled it back to the campsite, which was several miles away. One Saturday, some men showed up with rifles and shotguns. We couldn't get close enough to hear anything, but our mother told us later they went to the campsite and ran off all the Rindses. A couple of years after that another black kid told Seth that Toby and his sister had drowned in the creek, and that some folks had been shot. I think by then I'd heard enough. Could I have some water?"

A hand slid a glass of water to Ancil, who sipped it slowly. He continued: *"When I was thirteen my parents split. It was a happy day for me. I left with my mother and went to Corinth, Mississippi. Seth didn't want to change schools so he stayed with Cleon, though they rarely spoke to each other. I really missed my brother, but after a while we naturally grew apart. Then my mother remarried a jackass who was not much better than Cleon. I ran away when I was sixteen and joined the Navy when I was seventeen. Sometimes I think I've been running ever since. Once I left, I never had any contact with my family. My head is killing me. That's all. That's the end of a really bad story."*

47

The jurors filed silently out of their room and followed the bailiff down a back stairway to a side door of the courthouse, the same route they had taken every day since Tuesday. Once outside they scattered without a word. Nevin Dark decided to drive home for lunch. He did not want to be around his colleagues at that moment. He needed time to digest the story he had just heard. He wanted to breathe, to think, to remember. Alone in his truck with the windows down, he almost felt dirty; maybe a shower would help.

Mista Burt. Mista Burt. Somewhere on the shadier side of his wife's family tree, there had been a great-uncle or a distant cousin named Burt. Many years ago he lived near Palmyra, and there had always been whispers about Burt's involvement with the Klan.

It couldn't be the same man.

In his fifty-three years in Ford County, Nevin had heard of only one other lynching, but he had almost forgotten the story. It supposedly happened around the turn of the century. All witnesses were dead, and the details had been forgotten. Nevin had never heard a description of such a killing by a real witness. Poor Ancil. He looked so pitiful with his little round head and oversized suit, and wiping tears with a sleeve.

Disoriented by Demerol or not, there was no doubt Seth knew what he was doing.

Michele Still and Barb Gaston had no plans for lunch, and they were too emotional to think clearly. They jumped into Michele's car and fled Clanton, taking the first road out with no destination in mind. The distance helped, and after five miles on an empty county road they were able to relax. They stopped at a country store and bought soft drinks and crackers, then sat in the shade with the windows down and listened to a soul station out of Memphis.

"We got nine votes?" Michele asked.

"Girl, we may have twelve."

"Naw, we'll never get Doley."

"One day, I'm gonna slap his ass. Might be today, might be next year, but I'll do it."

Michele managed to laugh and their moods were lifted considerably.

Jim Whitehurst also drove home for lunch. His wife was waiting with a stew and they ate on the patio. He had told her everything else about the trial, but he did not want to replay what he had just heard. But she insisted, and they hardly touched their lunch.

Tracy McMillen and Fay Pollan drove together to a strip mall east of town where a new sub shop was doing a booming business. Their "Juror" buttons got a few looks but no inquiries. They got a booth so they could talk and within minutes were in complete agreement. Seth Hubbard might have been fading in his final days, but there was no doubt he planned things perfectly. They had not been too impressed with Herschel and Ramona anyway. And, they didn't like the fact that a black housekeeper would get all the money, but, as Jake had said, it was not for the jurors to decide. It wasn't their money.

For the Hubbard family, a morning that had begun with such promise had turned into a humiliating nightmare. The truth was out about their grandfather, a man they'd hardly known, and now their family name would be permanently stained. They could learn to handle the stain, but losing the money would be a catastrophe. They suddenly wanted to hide. They sprinted to the home of their host, out by the country club, and ignored lunch while debating whether they should return to the courtroom.

★   ★   ★

Lettie and Portia returned to the Sappington place during the break, but there were no thoughts of lunch. Instead, they went to Lettie's bedroom, kicked off their shoes, and lay side by side, holding hands, and began to cry.

Ancil's story had closed so many circles.

With so many thoughts swirling around there were almost no words. Emotions were too high. Lettie thought of her grandmother Esther and the horror of the story. And her mother, a little girl with no clothes, no food, no shelter.

"How'd he know, Mom?" Portia asked.

"Who? Which one? Which story?"

"Seth. How'd he know it was you? How did Seth Hubbard ever find out you were the daughter of Lois Rinds?"

Lettie stared at the spinning ceiling fan and couldn't begin to answer. Finally, she said, "He was a very smart man, but I doubt if we'll ever know."

Willie Traynor stopped by Jake's office with a platter of sandwiches and invited himself to lunch. Jake and Harry Rex were upstairs, on the balcony, having a drink. Coffee for Jake, beer for Harry Rex. They appreciated the sandwiches and helped themselves. Willie chose a beer. He said, "You know, when I had the paper, somewhere around 1975, some guy published a book about lynchings. He did his homework, had lots of gory photographs and such, and it was a good read. According to him, and he was from up north and eager to make us look bad, between 1882 and 1968 thirty-five hundred blacks were lynched in the United States. There were also thirteen hundred whites, but most were horse thieves out west. From 1900 on, almost all lynchings were of blacks, including some women and children."

"Is this really appropriate during lunch?" Harry Rex asked.

"I didn't know you had such a delicate stomach, big boy," Willie shot back. "Anyway, guess which state leads the nation in lynchings."

"I'm afraid to ask," Jake said.

"You got it. We're number one, at almost six hundred, and all but forty were black. Georgia is a close second, Texas a close third. So I remember reading this book and thinking, Six hundred is a lot. How many were in Ford County? I went back a hundred years and read every copy of the *Times*. I found only three, all black, and there was no record of Sylvester Rinds."

"Who compiled these numbers?" Jake asked.

"There have been studies, but you have to question their validity."

"If they knew of six hundred," Harry Rex said, "you can bet there were a lot more."

Willie took a swig of beer and said, "And guess how many people were charged with murder for taking part in a lynch mob."

"Zero."

"You got it. Not a single person. It was the law of the land, and black folks were fair game."

"Kinda makes me sick," Jake said.

"Well, old buddy, your jury's sick too," Willie said, "and they're on your side."

At 1:30, the jurors reassembled in the deliberation room, and there was not a single word uttered about the trial. A bailiff led them into the courtroom. The large screen was gone. There were no more witnesses. Judge Atlee looked down and said, "Mr. Brigance, your closing argument."

Jake walked to the podium without a legal pad; he had no notes. He began by saying, "This will be the shortest closing argument in the history of this courtroom, because nothing I can say could ever be as persuasive as the testimony of Ancil Hubbard. The longer I talk, the more distance I put between him and your deliberations, so I'll be brief. I want you to remember everything he said, not that anyone who heard it is likely to forget. Trials often take unexpected turns. When we started this one on Monday, none of us could have predicted that a lynching would explain the mystery of why Seth Hubbard left his fortune to Lettie Lang. His father lynched her grandfather in 1930. And after he killed him, he took his land and scattered his family, and Ancil told that story far better than I'll ever be able to. For six months, many of us have wondered why Seth did what he did. Now we know. Now it's clear.

"Personally, I have a new admiration for Seth, a man I never met. In spite of his flaws, and we all have our own, he was a brilliant man. Who else do you know who could put together such a fortune in ten years? But beyond that, he somehow managed to keep track of Esther and Lois, and then Lettie. Some fifty years later, he called Lettie and offered her the job; she did not call him. He planned it all, folks. He was brilliant. I admire Seth because of his courage. He knew he was dying, yet he refused to do what would have been expected. He chose a far more controversial route. He knew his reputation would be tarnished, that his family would curse his name, but he didn't care. He did what he thought was right."

Jake stepped over and picked up the handwritten will. "And lastly, I admire Seth because of his sense of justice. With this handwritten will, he is trying to fix a wrong inflicted upon the Rinds family by his father decades ago. It falls upon you, ladies and gentlemen of the jury, to help Seth correct that injustice. Thank you."

Jake slowly returned to his seat, and, as he did, glanced at the spectators. Sitting on the back row, smiling and nodding, was Lucien Wilbanks.

Three minutes and twenty seconds, Harry Rex said to himself as he punched the timer on his watch.

Judge Atlee said, "Mr. Lanier."

Wade was limping worse than usual as he made his way to the podium. He and his clients were watching helplessly as the money slipped away yet again. They had had it in the bag. As recently as eight o'clock that morning, they had been mentally spending it.

Wade had little to say at this urgent moment. History had suddenly and unexpectedly reared up and crushed him.

However, he was a veteran who'd been in tough spots before. He began, "One of the most important tools a lawyer has in the courtroom is the chance to cross-examine opposing witnesses. The lawyer almost always gets the opportunity to do this, but occasionally, like now, that opportunity is not available. And it's very frustrating. I feel handcuffed. I'd love to have Ancil here, to ask him some questions. For example, I'd say, 'Now, Ancil, isn't it true that you are now in the custody of the Juneau police?' And, 'Now, Ancil, isn't it true you're under arrest for cocaine distribution and escape from custody?' And, 'Now, Ancil, isn't it true that you're wanted by the authorities in at least four states for such things as obtaining goods under false pretenses, grand larceny, and nonpayment of child support?' And, 'Tell the jury, Ancil, why you haven't filed a tax return in the past twenty years.' And, the big one: 'Isn't it true, Ancil, that you're all set to collect a million bucks if Seth's handwritten will is declared valid?'

"But I can't do that, ladies and gentlemen, because he is not here. All I can do is caution you. I caution you that everything you've just seen and heard from Ancil might not be all that it purports to be.

"For a moment, let's take Ancil out of the picture. I want you jurors to go back to last night. Remember what you were thinking last night? You left here after hearing some powerful testimony. First, by doctors with unimpeachable credentials, experts who've worked with cancer patients and understand the extent to which powerful pain medications disrupt one's ability to think clearly." Lanier then went through summaries of the testimonies of Drs. Swaney and Niehoff. It was a closing argument and much leeway was given for the art of persuasion, but Lanier slanted things so perversely that Jake was compelled to stand and say, "Your Honor, I object. I don't believe that's what Dr. Niehoff said."

"Sustained," Judge Atlee said rudely. "Mr. Lanier, I'll ask you to stick to the facts."

Stung, Lanier rambled on about what these fine doctors had said. They had taken the stand only yesterday. It was not necessary to replay such recent testimony. Wade Lanier was stumbling now, and off his game. For the first time since the opening bell, Jake thought he looked lost. When he couldn't think of anything, he said, repeatedly, "Seth Hubbard lacked testamentary capacity."

He brought up the 1987 will, and much to Jake's delight, and much to the jurors' dismay, he fleshed it out once more. "Three point one million dollars wasted, just like that," he said, snapping his fingers. He described a tax ploy known as the generation-skipping trust, and just when Juror Number Ten, Debbie Lacker, was about to nod off, he said again, "Three point one million dollars wasted, just like that," and snapped his fingers loudly.

It was a cardinal sin to bore jurors who were pinned down and required to listen, but Wade Lanier was pouring it on. Wisely, though, he did not attack Lettie Lang. Those listening had just learned the truth about her family; it would not be wise to belittle or condemn her.

As Lanier took a painful pause to assess his notes, Judge Atlee said, "You might want to wrap this up, Mr. Lanier. You're over the time limit."

"Sorry, Your Honor." Flustered, he offered a sappy thanks to the jury for their "wonderful service" and concluded with a plea for faithful considerations, free from emotion and guilt.

"Rebuttal, Mr. Brigance?" Judge Atlee asked. Jake was entitled to ten minutes to counter anything Lanier had said. As the lawyer for the proponent, he got the last word, but he wisely declined. "No, Your Honor, I think the jury has heard enough."

"Very well. Now, ladies and gentlemen, I need to spend a few minutes and instruct you as to what the law is and how it applies in this case, so listen carefully. When I'm finished, you will retire to the jury room and begin your deliberations. Any questions?"

The waiting was always the worst part. A great load was lifted after the jury retired. All the work was finished; all the witnesses had testified; all the worrying about opening statements and closing arguments was over. Now the waiting began. There was no way to predict how long it would take.

Jake invited Wade Lanier and Lester Chilcott to his office for a drink. It was, after all, Friday afternoon and the week was over. They opened beers on the balcony upstairs and watched the courthouse. Jake pointed to a large window in the distance. "That's the jury room," he said. "That's where they are right now."

Lucien showed up, ready as always for a drink. He and Jake would have words later, but at the moment the mood demanded alcohol. With a laugh, Wade said, "Come on, Lucien, you gotta tell what happened in Juneau."

Lucien gulped down half a beer, and started talking.

After everyone had either coffee, a soft drink, or water, Nevin Dark called their little meeting to order and said, "I suggest we start with this verdict worksheet that the judge has given us. Any objections to that?"

There were none. There were no guidelines on jury deliberations. Judge Atlee said they could figure things out themselves.

Nevin said, "Okay, here is the first question: Was the document signed by Seth Hubbard a proper holographic will, in that it was (1) written entirely by Seth Hubbard, (2) signed by Seth Hubbard, and (3) dated by Seth Hubbard? Any discussion?"

"Ain't no doubt about that," Michele Still said.

The others agreed. The contestants had not argued otherwise.

Nevin continued: "Next, and the big one, testamentary capacity, or sound and disposing mind. The question is, Did Seth Hubbard understand and appreciate the nature and effect of his holographic will? Since this is what the case is all about, I suggest we each take a turn and say what's on our minds. Who wants to go first?"

Fay Pollan said, "You go first, Nevin. You're Juror Number One."

"Okay, here's what I think. I think it's wrong to cut out the family and give all the money to another person, especially someone who Seth knew for only three years. But, as Jake said at the beginning, our job is not to decide who should get the money. It's not our money. Also, I think Seth was slipping in his last days and was pretty doped up, but after seeing Ancil, I have no doubt he knew what he was doing. He'd been planning it for a long time. I'm voting in favor of the will. Tracy?"

Tracy McMillen said quickly, "I agree. So much about this case troubles me, but so much of it I'm not supposed to worry about. We're suddenly dealing with decades of history, and I don't think any one of us should tamper with that. Seth did what he did for some very good reasons."

"Michele?"

"Ya'll know how I feel. I just wish we weren't here. I wish Seth had given Lettie some money if he wanted to, then taken care of his family, even if he didn't like them. Can't say as I blame him. But I don't care how bad they are, they don't deserve nothing."

"Fay?"

Fay Pollan evoked less sympathy than anyone else in the room, maybe with the exception of Frank Doley. She said, "I'm not too concerned about his family. They've probably got more money than most of us, and they're young and educated. They'll be fine. They didn't help Seth make his money, why should they expect all of it? He cut 'em out for a reason, reasons we'll never know. And his son didn't even know who played center field for the Braves. My God. We've been fans of Dale Murphy for years now. I think he was just lying. Anyway, I'm sure Seth was not a nice person, but, like Jake said, it's not our business who he gives his money to. He was sick but he wasn't crazy."

It was a two-beer deliberation. After the second, a clerk called and said there was a verdict. All laughter ceased immediately as the lawyers shoved gum in their mouths and straightened their ties. They walked into the courtroom together and took their places. Jake turned to the spectators and saw Carla and Hanna seated on the front row behind him. They smiled and Carla mouthed, "Good luck."

"Are you okay?" Jake whispered as he leaned over to Lettie.

"I'm at peace," she said. "Are you okay?"

"I'm a wreck," he said and smiled.

Judge Atlee took the bench and the jurors were brought in. It is impossible for a trial lawyer not to look at the jurors as they return with a verdict, though every trial lawyer vows to ignore them. Jake looked straight at Michele Still, who sat down first, then gave him a quick little grin. Nevin Dark handed the verdict to the clerk who handed it to Judge Atlee. He reviewed it forever, then leaned an inch or two closer to his mike. Enjoying the drama, he said, "The verdict appears to be in order. The jury was to answer five questions. Number one: Did Seth Hubbard execute a valid holographic will on October 1, 1988? By a vote of 12 to 0, the answer is yes. Number two: Did Seth Hubbard understand and appreciate the nature and effect of what he was doing when he executed his holographic will? By a vote of 12 to 0, the answer is yes. Number three: Did Seth Hubbard understand and appreciate who the beneficiaries are to whom he had given gifts in his holographic will? By a vote of 12 to 0, the answer is yes. Number four: Did Seth Hubbard understand and appreciate the nature and amount of his property and how he wanted to dispose of it? By a vote of 12 to 0, the answer is yes. And, number five: Was Seth Hubbard unduly influenced by Lettie Lang or anyone else when he executed his holographic will on October 1, 1988? By a vote of 12 to 0, the answer is no."

Ramona gasped and began crying. Herschel, who had moved himself to the second row, rose immediately and stormed out of the courtroom. Their children had left the trial the day before.

Judge Atlee thanked the jurors and dismissed them. He adjourned court and disappeared. There were hugs among the victors and long faces among the losers. Wade Lanier was gracious in defeat and congratulated Jake on such a fine job. He spoke kindly to Lettie and wished her the best.

If she was on the verge of being the richest black woman in the state, she did not look it. She just wanted to go home. She ignored a couple of reporters and brushed aside some well-wishers. She was tired of being pawed at and fawned over.

Harry Rex organized a party on the spot, hot dogs on the grill in his backyard and beer in the cooler. Portia said she would be there after she took care of Lettie. Willie Traynor was always ready for a party. Lucien said he would come early, and he might bring Sallie, a rare occurrence. Before they left the courthouse, Lucien was already taking credit for the win.

Jake wanted to choke him.

48

The sermon was the annual call to stewardship, the usual chiding to tithe a bit more, the challenge to step up and give the Lord his 10 percent, and to do so happily. Jake had heard it a hundred times and, as always, found it difficult to maintain prolonged eye contact with the reverend while his mind dwelled on matters far more important. He admired the reverend and labored diligently each Sunday to appear entranced by his homilies, but often it was impossible.

Judge Atlee sat three rows up, at the end by the aisle, the same revered seat he had claimed for at least the last ten years. Jake stared at the back of his head and thought about the trial, and now the appeal. With the verdict so fresh, the case would hit a brick wall. The process would take forever. Ninety days for the court reporter to transcribe hundreds of pages of courtroom proceedings; ninety plus because they seldom delivered on time. Meanwhile, post-trial motions and maneuverings would take months. Once the final record was indeed final, the losers would have ninety days to file their appeal, and more time if necessary. When the Supreme Court, and Jake, received the appeal, he would have his own ninety days to respond. After the deadlines were met and the paperwork was on file with the court, the real waiting began. Typically, there were backlogs, delays, and continuances. The lawyers had learned not to ask what was taking so long. The court was doing the best it could.

The average appeal in a civil case in Mississippi consumed two years. In preparation for the Hubbard trial, Jake had run across a similar case in Georgia that had dragged on for thirteen

years. It had been fought before three different juries, went up
and down to the Supreme Court like a yo-yo, and was eventually settled when most of the contestants died off and the lawyers
had taken all the money. The issue of the attorney's fees did not
bother Jake, but he did worry about Lettie.

Portia had told him her mother had stopped going to church.
There were too many sermons about tithing.

If the collective wisdom of Harry Rex and Lucien could be
trusted, Jake's verdict was in trouble. The admission of Ancil's
video was a reversible error. The Fritz Pickering surprise was not
as clear-cut, but would probably upset the Supreme Court. The
"witness dump" pulled by Wade Lanier would attract a harsh
rebuke, but standing alone it would not get the case reversed.
Nick Norton agreed. He had watched the trial on Friday and was
surprised to see the video. He was deeply moved by its content
but bothered by its admissibility. The four lawyers, along with
Willie Traynor and other experts, had debated and celebrated
over hot dogs and beer until late Friday night while the ladies
sipped wine by Harry Rex's pool and chatted with Portia.

Though the Hubbard case had saved Jake financially, he was
ready to move on. He didn't like the prospect of clipping the
estate for a monthly fee for years to come. At some point, he
would begin to feel like a leech. He had just won a big trial and
was looking for another one.

Not a single person at the First Presbyterian Church
mentioned the trial that morning, and Jake was grateful.
Afterward, as they mingled under two giant oaks and exchanged
pleasantries while inching toward the parking lot, Judge Atlee
said hello to Carla and Hanna and commented on such a beautiful spring day. He walked down the sidewalk with Jake, and
when no one could hear them, he said, "Could you stop by this
afternoon, say around five? There is a matter I'd like to discuss."

"Sure, Judge," Jake said.

"And could you bring Portia with you? I'd like her insights."

"I think so."

*   *   *

They sat at the dining room table, under a creaking fan that did nothing to cut the heat and stickiness. It was much cooler outside—the porch would have been nice—but for some reason the judge preferred the dining room. He had a pot of coffee and a platter of cheap pastries, store-bought. Jake took one sip of the weak and dreadful coffee, then ignored it.

Portia declined it all. She was nervous and could not control her curiosity. This was not her part of town. Her mother might have seen some nice homes because she cleaned them, but never as a guest.

Judge Atlee sat at the head of the table with Jake to his right and Portia to his left. After a few awkward preliminaries, he announced, as if on the bench and looking down at a pack of anxious lawyers, "I want this case settled. For the next two years, the money will be tied up while the appeal runs its course. Hundreds of hours will be spent. The contestants will make a strong argument that the verdict should be reversed, and I see their point. I admitted the video of Ancil Hubbard because it was the fair thing to do at that moment. The jury, and I suppose all of us, needed to understand the history. It gave meaning to Seth's motives. It will be argued forcefully that I was wrong procedurally. From a selfish point of view, I prefer not to be reversed, but my feelings are not important."

Like hell they're not, Jake thought as he glanced at Portia. She was staring at the table, frozen.

"Let's suppose for a moment that the case comes back for a retrial. The next time around you will not get blindsided by the Pickering matter. You will be ready for Julina Kidd. And, most important, you will have Ancil here as an interested party and a live witness. Or, if he's in jail, you will certainly have time to conduct a proper deposition. At any rate, your case is much stronger the next time, Jake. Do you agree?"

"Yes, of course."

"You'll win the case because you should win the case. That's exactly the reason I allowed Ancil's video. It was the right and fair thing to do. Do you follow me, Portia?"

"Oh, yes sir."

"So, how do we settle this matter, stop the appeal, and get on with life?" Jake knew he had the answer and really didn't want much input.

"I've thought of nothing else since Friday afternoon," the judge continued. "Seth's will was a desperate, last-minute attempt to correct a horrible injustice. By leaving so much to your mother, he was in reality trying to make amends to your great-grandfather and to all the Rinds families. Do you agree?"

Agree, damn it, Portia, agree. Jake had been here a hundred times. When he asks, "Do you agree?" he's already assuming that you agree enthusiastically.

"Yes sir," she said.

He took a sip of coffee, and Jake wondered if he drank the same wretched brew every morning. Judge Atlee said, "I'm wondering, Portia, at this point, what does your mother really want? It would be helpful to know that. I'm sure she's told you. Can you share this with us?"

"Sure, Judge. My mother doesn't want a lot, and she has reservations about getting all that money. For lack of a better term, it's white folks' money. It doesn't really belong to us. My mom would like to have the land, the eighty acres, and she'd like to build a house on it, a nice house but not a mansion. She's seen some nice houses but she's always known she'd never have one. Now, for the first time in her life, she can dream of having a beautiful home, one she can clean for herself. She wants plenty of room for her kids and grandkids. She'll never marry again, although there are a few buzzards circling. She wants to get away and to live way out there in the country where it's peaceful and nobody will bother her. She didn't go to church this morning, Judge, she hasn't been in a month. Everybody's got their hand out. My mother just wants to be left alone."

"Surely she wants more than a house and eighty acres," Jake said.

"Well, who doesn't want some money in the bank? She's tired of cleaning houses."

"How much money?" Judge Atlee asked.

"We didn't get that far. In the past six months, she's never sat around and thought, 'Okay, I'll take five million and I'll give each kid one million and so on.' That's not my mother, okay? She doesn't think in those terms. It's just so far beyond her." She paused for a second, then asked, "How would you divide the money, Judge?"

"I'm glad you asked. Here's my plan. The bulk of the money should go into a fund for the benefit of your blood relatives, not a cash giveaway that would turn into a feeding frenzy, but a foundation of sorts that would be used solely for education. Who knows how many Rindses are out there, though I'm sure we would quickly find out. The foundation would be tightly controlled by a trustee who would report to me. The money would be invested wisely and spread over, say, twenty years, and during that time it would be used to help as many students as possible. It must be limited to a sole purpose, and education is the most likely. If it's not limited, then there would be a thousand requests for everything from health care to groceries to housing to new cars. The money is not guaranteed, but must be earned. A blood relative who studies hard and gets admitted to college will qualify for funding."

"How would you split the money?" Jake asked. Portia was smiling.

"In broad strokes, I suggest this: Let's work with the figure of twelve million. We know that's a moving target but it'll be close. Fund the bequests to Ancil and the church at half a million each. Down to eleven. Take five million of that and place it in the trust fund I just described. That's a lot of tuition, but then we can anticipate a lot of kinfolks, both old and new."

"They're still arriving by the carload," Portia said.

Judge Atlee continued, "That leaves six million. Split it equally among Lettie, Herschel, and Ramona. Of course, Lettie gets the eighty acres that was once owned by her grandfather."

Jake took a deep breath as the numbers rattled around. He looked across the table and said, "Lettie's the key, Portia."

Portia, still smiling, said, "She'll take it. She gets a nice house and a nice cushion, yet she won't be hassled by a fortune every-body wants a piece of. She told me last night the money belonged to all of Sylvester's people, not just her. She wants to be happy and she wants to be left alone. This will make her very happy."

"How do you sell it to the rest of them?" Jake asked.

"I assume Herschel and Ramona will be thrilled. Who knows about Ancil and the church. Keep in mind, Jake, that I still control the estate, and I will for as long as I so choose. Not a dime can ever be distributed without my approval, and there is no deadline to close an estate. I'm sure no one has ever called me a jackass behind my back, but if I want to be one I can sit on Seth's money for the next ten years. As long as the assets are protected, I can keep them bottled up as tightly as I wish."

He had slipped into his Chancellor's tone, one that left little doubt Judge Reuben V. Atlee was about to get his way. He contin-ued, "Indeed, it may be necessary to keep the estate open indefinitely to administer the education trust we're talking about."

"Who will run the trust?" Jake asked.

"I was thinking about you."

Jake flinched, then almost fled at the thought of dealing with dozens, maybe hundreds of eager students clamoring for money.

"That's a great idea, Judge," Portia said. "My family would feel better if Jake stayed involved and kept an eye on the money."

"Whatever, we can work it out later," Jake said, on his heels.

"Do we have a deal?" the judge asked.

"I'm not a party," Jake said. "Don't look at me."

"I'm sure Lettie will approve, but I need to talk to her," Portia said.

"Very well. You do that and get back with me tomorrow. I'll prepare a memo and float it to all the lawyers. Jake, I suggest you go see Ancil this week and get some answers. I'll schedule a meet-ing with all parties in about ten days. We'll lock the door and hammer out a settlement. I want this to happen, understand?"

They clearly understood.

★ ★ ★

A month after the verdict, Ancil Hubbard sat low in the passenger's seat of Lucien's old Porsche and gazed through the window at the rolling hills of Ford County. Of the land, he remembered nothing. The first thirteen years of his life had been spent in those parts, but he had worked hard for the past fifty to forget them. Nothing looked familiar.

He had been released on a bond arranged by Jake and others, and he had been cajoled south by his pal Lucien. Just one last visit. You might be surprised. Thin gray hair was sprouting again and partially covered the ugly scar across the back of his head. He wore jeans and sandals, same as Lucien.

They turned onto a county road and approached Seth's home. There was a "For Sale" sign in the front yard. Lucien said, "That's where Seth lived. You want to stop?"

"No."

They turned again onto a gravel road and drove deeper into the woods.

"Recognize any of this?" Lucien asked.

"Not really."

The woods thinned and they came to a clearing. Ahead were cars parked haphazardly and people milling about, including some children. Smoke rose from a charcoal grill.

Farther on, they approached overgrown rubble and ruins, all choked with kudzu. Ancil raised a hand and said, "Stop. Here." They got out. Some of the others were nearby and walking over to say hello, but Ancil did not see them. He was looking away, far in the distance. He began walking toward the sycamore tree where they had found his brother. The others followed quietly; some were left behind. With Lucien trailing closely, Ancil walked a hundred yards or so to the tree, then stopped and looked around. He pointed to a small hill covered with oaks and elms and said, "We were up there, Seth and me, hiding in the woods. It seemed farther away back then. They brought him here, under this tree. There were more trees back then. A whole row of five or six, in a perfect line, along the creek here. Now there's only one."

"There was a tornado here in sixty-eight," Lucien said from behind him.

"This is where we found Seth," Ozzie said. He was standing next to Lucien.

"Is it the same tree?" Jake asked. He was standing next to Ozzie.

Ancil heard their voices and looked at their faces, but he did not see them. He was in a daze, in another time and place. He said, "I can't say for sure, but I think so. All the trees were the same, a perfect row. We fished right over there," he said, pointing again. "Seth and me. Right over there." He exhaled heavily and seemed to grimace, then he closed his eyes and shook his head. When he opened them, he said, "It was so awful."

Lucien said, "Ancil, Sylvester's granddaughter is here. Would you like to meet her?"

He took a deep breath and snapped out of his dream. He turned abruptly and said, "I'd be delighted."

Lettie walked over and offered a hand, a hand Ancil ignored. Instead, he gently took her shoulders and squeezed tightly. "I'm so sorry," he said. "I'm so sorry."

After a few seconds, she unwrapped herself and said, "Enough of that, Ancil. The past is the past. Let's say it's over. I want you to meet my kids and grandkids."

"I'd be delighted." He was then introduced to Portia, Carla, Ozzie, Harry Rex, and to the rest of Lettie's family. Then he met Herschel Hubbard, his nephew, for the first time. They all talked at once as they left the tree and headed for the picnic.